FAMOUS LAST WORDS
NEW YORK THUNDER SERIES
BOOK 1

SHANN MCPHERSON

Famous Last Words is a work of fiction, created without use of AI technology. Any names, characters, businesses, places, and events are products of the author's imagination, and used in a fictitious manner. Any resemblance to actual events, places or persons, living or dead, is entirely coincidental or fictional.

Copyright © 2024 by Shann McPherson.

All rights reserved.

No part of this publication may be reproduced, distributed, or transmitted in any form or by any means, including information storage and retrieval systems, photocopying, recording, or other electronic or mechanical methods, without prior written permission of the publisher, except as permitted by U.S. copyright law. For permission requests, contract Shann McPherson.

Cover by: Sonia Garrigoux

Edited by: Tina Otero

Proofread by: Tina Otero

PLAYLIST

Welcome to New York - Taylor Swift
Pony - Ginuwine
Thunderstruck - AC/DC
Ain't No Mountain High Enough - Marvin Gaye
Late Night Talking - Harry Styles
Baby, I Love Your Way - Big Mountain
I Wanna Be Your Slave - Måneskin
Maroon - Taylor Swift
Love Of My Life - Harry Styles
abcdefu (angrier) - Gayle
Fkin' Problems - A$AP Rocky
You're So Vain - Carly Simon
The Alchemy - Taylor Swift
Or Nah - Ty Dollar $ign
Don't Stop Believin' - Journey
Down Bad - Taylor Swift
Be My Baby - The Ronettes

A NOTE FROM SHANN

Hi bestie!

Thanks so much for giving *Famous Last Words* a chance. But before you begin, please take a moment to practice some self-care by reviewing the potentially distressing content that is mentioned within the book.

First and foremost, *Famous Last Words* is a romance, and it's a funny romance with a guaranteed happy ever after. However, this book does contain content that may be triggering to some readers: off-page cheating (not between the main characters), off-page substance abuse, on-page drug references, off-page suicidal thoughts, chronic illness, a parent with cancer (end of life), mention of childhood trauma caused by a parent, on page explicit sexual references, on-page explicit language, on-page kinks including consensual degradation, spit play, and breath play.

I want you to make an informed decision as to whether *Famous Last Words* is right for you and your mental well-being. Because at the end of the day, that's what matters most!

Reading is meant to be enjoyable, and from the bottom of my heart, I truly hope you love reading Fran and Robbie's love story.

Love always,

Shann xoxo

For Auston Matthews' mustache.

CHAPTER 1

ROBBIE

A fight in ice hockey isn't uncommon. Hell, it's why so many people love the game. But as I sit here, in a dimly lit boardroom in the NHL headquarters, forced to watch myself projected up on the screen as I throw my stick and shuck my gloves before launching myself at Ben Harris, I can't help but wince because, unfortunately, I know what happens next.

Thankfully, before I land the first blow that will effectively cause Ben's jaw to be wired shut for the next six-to-eight weeks, the playback is paused, and an unnerving silence settles heavily around the room.

I shift in my seat, feeling the weight of all eleven sets of eyes laser-focused on me.

To my right is my agent-slash-unofficial-manager-slash-only real friend left in the world.

To my left is the general manager of the only team in the league willing to give me another shot.

In front of me are the aforementioned eleven officials dressed in impeccable suits, with the collective power to take everything away.

Andy, my agent, rises from his chair, and begins addressing the disciplinary board with the conviction of a defense attorney in the middle of a murder trial. Did I kill anyone? No. But you'd be forgiven for thinking that I had with the way this is playing out like an episode of *Law and Order*.

"Gentlemen, I'll be the first to admit that the footage is more than disturbing. But, my client," Andy points at me, "has used this time since the… *incident*… to reflect on his actions and think about what he can do moving forward to better manage his emotions and improve himself, to prevent anything like this from happening again."

I watch Andy as he walks around the room, and I must admit, even I'm impressed. I suppose this is why I pay him the big bucks.

"Robbie has committed to regular counseling sessions to help him manage his *anger*." His eyes cut to me with a knowing look, right as my hands ball into fists beneath the table at the mention of anger management, because this is some straight-up bullshit; I'm the least angry person I know. Cocky and self-assured? Without a doubt. But angry? No way. Unfortunately for me, the paused image of the crazed lunatic about to land a left hook to his own teammate's jaw up on the screen begs to differ.

"He's donated close to a quarter of a million dollars to various organizations that help educate at-risk youths of the importance of drug and alcohol abstinence."

At the mention of drugs, my jaw clenches so hard my teeth hurt.

"He's even written a formal apology to Benjamin Harris."

Vitriol burns the back of my throat because, you know what? Fuck Ben Harris. My written apology was fake as fuck. If I had my time again, I'd have broken his damn nose too.

"My client is understandably upset over the actions that led to that night; however, now is the time to move forward." Andy continues, pointing to the man sitting stoically to my left. "New York has written a very strict yet fair offer for my client, with terms I've never seen in my twelve-year career, but terms my client is willing to adhere to if it means he can continue doing what he is most passionate about, what he has done for almost six years without incident. Play professional hockey." Andy glances at me, the contrite look in his eyes Oscar-worthy. "Please, I implore you, do not let one moment of recklessness in an otherwise untainted and remarkable career take away Robbie Mason's livelihood."

Andy moves back to his chair, sitting down next to me with another cursory glance in my direction. And normally I can tell what he's thinking, but it's that impassive look in his eyes that only increases my anxiety. My left knee bounces uncontrollably as I look out at the men surrounding the table. I wish I could say I was confident, but I'm not. This is literally make or break.

"Mr. Mason."

I turn my head, spearing the man sitting at the end of the table, the one who holds my future in the palm of his hand—David Ferris, retired player and now Head of the Department of Player Safety.

He doesn't even acknowledge me, choosing instead to stare down at whatever is on the papers in front of him. "Your actions leading up to the incident that occurred on the evening of Thursday, September twenty-third, single handedly brought the game of ice hockey into disrepute."

David lifts his steely gaze, eyes full of disdain as they meet mine. I make sure to keep my chin held high, ready to take whatever it is he has to throw at me if it means I might be able to play again.

He continues. "Never in my career have I witnessed anything as sickening as what I witnessed from the footage of that night."

Andy suddenly pipes up, spluttering, "Oh, come on, David, that's ridic—"

David holds his hand up, silencing my agent. "Mr. Hoffman, you've had your chance to speak."

Andy huffs, muttering something under his breath, and all I can do is swallow around the painful lump at the back of my throat because, holy shit, this is it. Suddenly, a future without the one thing I've ever been any good at flashes through my mind, and my stomach rolls at the realization of just how close I am to losing everything that's ever mattered to me.

"In my years playing hockey, and in the time spent since, here in Player Safety, I've seen men do much less and be expelled from the league, their careers over like *that*." He snaps his fingers for effect.

I nod once.

David sighs. "The only reason we're here today, having this conversation, is because not only are you the best defensive player this game has seen in decades, but thanks to your loyal... *fan base*... you're also the league's most profitable player."

Andy flashes me a smug smirk which I ignore, because no, *Andy*, that doesn't make me feel any better. In fact, it makes me feel worse. Basically, what David Ferris is saying right now is that the only reason I haven't been shown the door is because of the money they make off the millions of women who've dedicated their lives to posting thirst trap videos of me on the internet. It all started a couple years back when footage of me innocently warming up on the ice, stretching my hip flexors, set to the soundtrack of Ginuwine's "Pony," went viral. I mean, sure, I helped bring the game to a new demographic, but at what cost?

David Ferris shifts in his chair. "Mr. Mason, on behalf of the National Hockey League, and the Department of Player Safety, I am hereby approving your New York Thunder contract."

"Hell yeah, baby!" Andy explodes with an inappropriate cheer, punching his fist in the air like he's at a goddamn baseball game.

FAMOUS LAST WORDS   5

I release the breath I've been holding, somehow keeping my cool despite the fact that I could actually cry right now.

"*However*—" David offers my agent a warning glance, "—we have made an adjustment to the contract."

"What?" Andy sits up straighter, clearing his throat. "It's not *your* contract. You can't do that."

"As the governing body, I can assure you we can, Mr. Hoffman," David says, his tone assertive. "We're imposing a twelve-week probationary period. If within that time you do *anything* that goes against the terms of your contract, we will deem it null and void, and you'll be released not only from New York but from the league altogether."

Andy scoffs, looking around me to Chris Garret, the Thunder's GM.

Chris offers nothing but a resigned shrug in response.

"We've also included a clause that requires mandatory weekly drug and alcohol testing to be completed here, on site, by a third party every Tuesday, with the exception of away games, in which case Mr. Mason will report to a testing site as nominated by us, in whatever city he is in at the time."

Andy takes a breath, and I can tell he's on the verge of an objection, but before he can say anything, I place a hand on his shoulder, stopping him.

"I'll do it," I say.

Andy's eyes are wide as he leans in, whispering, "Robbie, at least let me speak to legal first."

I shake my head, keeping my gaze set firm on David Ferris, as I stand and clear my throat. "I've got nothing to hide," I begin. "I know I've done some shitty things the last few months, but I maintain my innocence when it comes to drugs. I've never touched them, and I never will. And I'll do whatever I need to do to prove that, because hockey's literally all I've got. It's all I've ever been good at. It's all I know, and I *cannot* lose it. You have my word that I will not do anything to risk my future or risk further tarnishing the reputation of the league."

With a hard exhale, David Ferris shuffles the papers sitting in front of him, avoiding my eyes. "Well, I hope so, Mr. Mason. For your sake." He glances around at his colleagues. "Thank you, gentlemen."

Andy stands and reluctantly shakes the hands of a few of the men as they begin filing out of the meeting room, but all I can do is sink back into my chair, elbows on my knees, head in my hands, collecting myself as best as I can because, man, that was a close one.

———

As we wait for Andy's car, I stand with my arms folded across my chest, sunglasses on despite the gray, gloomy day, baseball cap pulled low in an attempt to conceal my identity from the hordes of people walking up and down the busy sidewalk.

"Great job, Hoffman." Chris Garret shakes Andy's hand before looking at me. He slaps me on my shoulder, nodding once. "We'll see you on the ice for your first practice tomorrow."

"Yes, sir." I nod, standing a little taller and shaking his hand. "And thank you. For everything."

He offers me a pointed look, leaning in a little closer to be heard over the Midtown traffic. "You just scored yourself a second chance, kid. Now's your time to prove to everyone who trashed you over the last few months that you're not that bad guy you've been made out to be. Don't fuck it up."

Chris slaps my shoulder again before turning and walking to the car that idles at the curb to collect him, and I silently thank whatever God may or may not exist because he's right. Second chances don't come by often. I can't fuck this up.

"This is Hoff." Andy answers his cell phone like a cranky bastard, and while I wait, I take my phone from the pocket of my jeans, texting Ma.

> Me: Hey Ma, just got out of the meeting. The board approved my contract. Barely. But I'm officially part of the New York Thunder.

Her reply comes through almost instantly, and I know that's because she'd have been sitting around waiting with bated breath.

> Ma: Oh, hon. I knew they would. I'm so happy. Something tells me this is going to be the best thing that's ever happened to you.

I can't help but smile. Going from the top team for the last three years in a row to the team that's come dead last for the last two regular seasons is less than ideal, but I know she's just trying to make me feel better. It's what she does.

"I need to check... hold on."

Andy nudges me, and I look up from my messages to find him pressing his phone against his chest, leaning in closer. "That apartment you liked. The one in Chelsea with the parking spot?"

My brows knit together. "What about it?"

"It's the listing agent." He indicates his phone. "We can go look at it today."

I offer a noncommittal shrug.

Andy lifts the phone back to his ear. "Can you do three o'clock?"

At that very moment, over the din of the city going about its business around us, I hear my name being called. *Fuck*. Thankfully, Andy's car pulls up to the curb, and I make a run for it, quickly hopping into the shiny SUV right as a photographer comes into view across the street.

Through the tinted window, a few flashes go off, but I shield my face with my hand as Andy ends his call and directs the driver where to go. Heaving a relieved sigh, I allow my head to fall back as we pull away from the curb.

"How about a celebratory lunch?"

Eyes closed, I nod because I'm suddenly starving. I've barely been able to eat these last few days, racked with stress over what the Player Safety Board decision was going to be today.

Andy punches my arm. "Good. You're buying."

I can't fight the grin that tugs at my lips because the man next to me, the one who's been on my side ever since I was nineteen with nothing but an unbelievable ability to play hockey, saved my ass today, and I owe him a lot more than a fucking lunch, that's for sure.

CHAPTER 2

FRAN

Being called to your boss's office as an adult is the equivalent of being sent to the principal's office as a kid.

As I stand outside Tony Carlton's office, panic courses through me. I stare at the door, at his name etched into the glass in bold platinum letters, my heart thundering. A fortifying breath does little to placate the anxiety churning in my belly because I know why I'm here. It'd be stupid to pretend like I don't. But that doesn't make me feel any more prepared for what I know I'm about to face. So, with a deep breath, I lift a trembling hand and knock, because there really is no avoiding the inevitable.

"Come in," Tony's booming voice calls from behind the door.

I plaster on a smile I know doesn't reach my eyes as I open the door and step inside. But the moment I do, I'm rendered frozen at the sight of *him* sitting there, smirking at me in that way that tells me almost everything I need to know. I might as well turn around and walk back out.

"Fran, take a seat." Tony motions to the vacant chair, the one next to *him*.

I hurry in, smoothing down the front of my skirt before taking a seat, ignoring the asshole beside me despite the obviousness of his gaze as it bores into me. He's trying for a reaction, but I refuse to give him one. *Not today, dick bag.* Instead, I lift my chin in a show of confidence I sure as shit don't feel on the inside, smiling at Tony when he finally graces me with eye contact.

Tony Carlton is an attractive man. A quintessential silver fox: tall, broad shouldered, tan skin, and veneers so white they're almost blinding. Actually, maybe it's just the power that makes him sexy. Sexy or intimidating, possibly both—I'm not entirely sure.

"You wanted to see me?" I play dumb and so sickeningly sweet that I momentarily hate myself. But acting like a clueless twit with a man like Tony Carlton is really the only way to succeed in this business. It's either that or offer to give him a blow job under his desk. Or so I've heard.

Beside me, Tadd snickers under his breath, concealing his laughter with a cough, and again, I do everything in my waning power to ignore him.

"Let's talk about Allora," Tony begins with a disappointed sigh.

I nod once, swallowing hard around the ball of nerves that's wedged itself into the back of my throat.

"What happened?" Tony removes his designer glasses and rubs his eyes like I'm one of his teenage daughters who's given him a headache.

I clear my throat, searching for words he's not immediately going to call bullshit over. "Um, I… had a lot of interest initially. An up-and-coming tech guy really loved the apartment. But when I asked if he was ready to put an offer in, he said he was still deciding between here and San Francisco. He ultimately chose a three-acre ranch in Saratoga because… he wants to buy a race horse." I can't help but shrink at my own words because I know exactly how ridiculous they sound.

Sitting up a little straighter, I'm reluctant to continue, but I do because Tony's intense gaze is unwavering and I have a tendency to ramble when I'm nervous. "There was a social media influencer who liked the building, but she said the altitude made her hair… *frizzy*." I can't even conceal my own wince as I say it out loud. "She said she'd be interested in something on a lower floor if it ever came up."

I nervously wring my hands together. "Um, I do have an email that came through late last night from a potential buyer… I was just about to phone him to gauge interest and maybe set something up."

Tony's shrewd gaze narrows, and I take that as my cue to shut the hell up.

"You were given an exclusive ninety-day contract. It's been seventy-eight days," he says, looking down at the papers in his hand. "We've done two broker opens, multiple caravans, spent far more than we should have on marketing."

I catch Tadd's shit-eating grin from my periphery at the same time as Tony says, "Tadd is going to take over the listing."

My resolve slips and my mouth falls open on a gasp. With Tadd practically gloating beside me, and Tony barely able to look at me, I can't remember a time I've ever felt so insignificant. I take a breath, ready to object, but Tony continues before I can get a single syllable out.

"Tadd has *kindly* offered for you to shadow him." He juts his chin in Tadd's direction, but I refuse to acknowledge him. I'm afraid if I do, I'll see that smug smirk on his face, and I won't be able to stop myself from reaching across and grabbing the fancy gold pen off Tony's desk and using it to stab Tadd in his eye.

"I know there's history between the two of you," Tony says, shifting awkwardly in his chair.

History? I almost laugh out loud. Tadd Jennings straight up took advantage of me. He used his power and status as the best sales agent in the company to manipulate me. Sure, I was the idiot who fell for his bullshit, and yeah, I put up with it for far too long, but I was a naive twenty-two-year-old, fresh out of college and new to the city, seduced by an almost thirty-year-old man. I didn't know any better.

"Tony, please don't take my listing. I worked so hard for it." Great. Now I've resorted to begging. I've officially lost every last ounce of self-respect, and in front of Tadd no less. I'm never going to live this one down. But, dammit, I can't lose this. "Please, just give me one last chance. I have such a great relationship with the seller. Marie *trusts* me." I don't add that I'm almost certain Marie would take one look at Tadd and slam the door in his face. "I know I can do this. I'll make some calls as soon as I get back to my desk. I'll set up private showings. I- I-I'll door knock if I have to. I can do this, Tony. I'm so close. *Please.*"

With a heavy exhale, Tony relaxes back in his leather chair, staring at me for a slightly too long moment, chin resting on steepled fingers. His expression is void of any and all emotion, and it's intimidating to say the least. I'm sure he can hear my heart hammering in my chest, see the sweat beading my forehead. But I'm desperate, and frankly, I don't care if he can smell my fear. I need this.

"Fine," Tony practically grunts. "One more chance."

I hear Tadd scoff beside me, but I don't chance even a sideways glance in his direction, instead watching Tony with bated breath, awaiting his terms.

"If I don't have a deal sheet on my desk by the end of the week, then Tadd gets the listing," he says, ultimately dismissing me as he turns his attention to my ex, offering Tadd the sort of smile I've never been on the receiving end of because I don't have a penis in my panties.

Choosing not to risk waiting around a second longer in case he changes his mind, I jump up like my ass is on fire and make a beeline out of the office to the tune of Tony's low rumbling voice

FAMOUS LAST WORDS   13

saying something indecipherable, accompanied by Tadd's grating laugh.

It takes everything I have not to break into a full-blown sprint as I make my way down the stairs that connect the executive level to the bustling sales floor. I weave my way through the maze of cubicles, past the glass offices occupied by the high-profile agents, the ones with their own teams, like stupid Tadd, finally making it to my desk.

Hunching over my laptop, I massage my temples, racking my brain with what the hell I'm going to do now despite knowing there really isn't a lot I *can* do. I have one lead. One. And, let's face it, an *is-this-still-available* email from an unknown contact isn't exactly a *lead*.

Carlton Myers is one of the top five real estate agencies in all of Manhattan. If I lose Allora, I can kiss this job *and* real estate goodbye; no other agency will risk touching me.

I've always been ambitious—sometimes to a fault—but despite my drive and determination, growing up I never knew what I wanted to do with my life. All I wanted was to get the hell out of Dodge and find my passion.

It was never my dream to be a real estate agent, but it was never my dream to go home after college and work in my parents' drugstore, either. Despite graduating magna cum laude, I had no prospects, no idea what I was going to do. Then I found out how much money real estate agents can make, especially in New York City, and I figured why the hell not?

In the three years since I started, I studied for my real estate license and worked my way up the ranks from leasing desk to Tadd's assistant to junior sales agent. But it seems I've reached some sort of an impasse because the problem is, I can't sell, which is kind of a prerequisite in this industry. I've come close a few times. But I just can't seem to close. I don't have that *kill-or-be-killed* instinct agents like Tadd have.

But now, it's literally make or break.

Clicking open my inbox, I scroll to the email I received last night from a Mr. Andy Hoffman asking if the Allora apartment is still available. Instead of replying to the email, I grab my phone and dial the cell number that's listed in the signature at the bottom.

I pick at my fingernails, my heart climbing higher into my throat with every ring as I wait for him to answer. Just as I'm anticipating having to leave a message and overthinking what I'm going to say without sounding like an idiot, a male voice comes through, barking an abrupt, "This is Hoff."

I sit up a little straighter, my gaze furtively looking about my cubicle for what, I have no idea.

"Oh, um. Hi. Is this Mr. Andy Hoffman?"

"Yeah." He sounds pissed. Great. Love that for me.

I clear my throat, putting on my most professional voice. "Hi, Mr. Hoffman. This is Fran Keller—"

"Frank *who*?" His voice is drowned out by the sound of a siren wailing in the background of wherever he is.

I quickly jump up from my chair, ducking out through the emergency exit and into the concrete stairwell so I can at least raise my voice without the risk of nosey colleagues listening in.

"*Fran* Keller." I emphasize my name. "I'm a sales agent with Carlton Myers. You sent an email regarding a property I have listed in Chelsea."

"Oh, yeah. West Twenty-Ninth?"

"Yes." I smile, relieved when he doesn't immediately hang up on me.

"Not really Chelsea, is it?" Andy says, his tone flat.

I swallow hard. A local. Fabulous.

"I mean, it's on the border, yes. But the price reflects that," I continue before he can tell me he's no longer interested. "What the price *doesn't* reflect is that it's a brand-new state-of-the-art building, right on the High Line. Around-the-clock security. Twenty-fifth floor, one-hundred-and-eighty-degree views of the city *and* the Hudson. Not to mention a designated parking spot in the underground garage which, in Manhattan, can go for a million on its own." My heart is racing, and I know I need to lock this down before I talk too much and effectively lose him. "I've had a last-minute cancellation this afternoon, and I can meet you at the property for a private showing at a time that suits you." *Be assertive, direct, and don't take no for an answer.* Yeah, right. Easier said than done.

Mr. Hoffman hesitates before saying, "I need to check…"

I fully expect him to tell me he'll call me back only to never call me back because people suck.

"Hold on."

I gasp. Hold on? He isn't hanging up on me.

Muffling comes through the line, and I can hear the murmured sound of a voice, maybe two. And a few seconds later, Mr. Hoffman returns to the call. "Can you do three o'clock?"

I swallow the lump of emotion that threatens to ruin my already depleted composure, but honestly, I could cry right now.

With a deep breath, I try to sound casual in my reply, "Three o'clock works. I'll send you the details."

With a curt yet professional goodbye, I end the call before he can change his mind. Staring down at the screen on my phone, my mind is working a mile a minute, my excitement making way for self-doubt and anxiety as they rear their disheveled heads.

I tamp down the doubt with a deep breaths "You've got this. You've got this. You've got this." The sheer notion that I do, in fact, *got this* is laughable, but this is my last chance.

———

Standing by the wall of glass that looks out over Manhattan, I release a sigh, taking in the dizzying vista of sky-scraping buildings, trying not to check my watch for the millionth time in the last five minutes.

16 SHANN MCPHERSON

For the record, Andy Hoffman is forty-two minutes late. I know Midtown traffic can be a fickle bitch at the best of times, so I'm really trying not to get in my head too much, despite my subconscious trying to convince me that he's a no-show. Thankfully, I know better. This is nothing more than a power play. The oldest trick in the book. Andy Hoffman is trying to show me who's in charge. But he doesn't know how desperate I am. I can wait.

Suddenly, the silence is inundated by the shrill buzz of the intercom, and I release the breath I've been holding as I practically bolt for the security panel, pressing the button.

"Miss Keller, I have Mr. Hoffman and his client in the lobby."

"Thank you. Please send him up." Honestly, I almost tell the man I love him.

Wait. Did he just say Mr. Hoffman and his *client*?

My stomach dips. Is Andy Hoffman a buyer's agent?

Oh, God, please, no. That is literally the last thing I need right now. I am in no way prepared to be dealing with a fast-talking buyer's agent who thinks he knows more than I do.

I unlock my phone and start scrolling to Andy's email from last night, re-reading his signature.

Andy Hoffman
Managing Director, HMC Management Inc.

The name of the company doesn't ring any bells. But just as I'm opening Google, I'm interrupted by a knock on the door.

Shit.

Fumbling, I lock my phone, gripping it like it's my lifeline as I slip my feet back into my turquoise pumps and tread carefully across the shiny floor to the foyer, all while attempting my most no bullshit game face.

When I pull open the door, I'm met with a handsome man who looks to be in his late thirties, dressed down for a buyer's agent in a pair of chinos and an untucked button down. Slightly bloodshot eyes meet mine and a kind, if not slanted, smile greets me.

"Mr. Hoffman?" I hold a hand out, willing it not to tremble and give away just how nervous I am.

"Ms. Keller," he says with a curt nod, shaking my proffered hand before inviting himself inside. As he passes, I'm almost certain I catch a whiff of whiskey in his wake, and I'm forced to tamper down the annoyance that bubbles inside of me when I realize that's likely the reason he's late. Don't get me wrong, I love a sneaky mid-week wine like the rest, but not at the risk of being late to an appointment.

A man—the *client*, I presume—hangs back in the hallway and I study him while I stand awkwardly in the doorway, wondering if he's coming in or not.

He's tall, at least six-foot-something, broad shouldered, dressed casually in sneakers, faded jeans and a sweatshirt, head down, focused intently on the phone in his tattooed hands, dark hair sticking out underneath a Red Sox ball cap that shields most of his face.

"Hi, I'm Fran Kel—" I'm stopped mid-sentence the moment he lifts his chin, and I swear, it's as if everything around me comes to a violently crashing stop.

It seems he's just as stilted, stumbling over his own feet as recognition flares in his dark gaze. A deep crease burrows between his eyebrows as he looks me up and down in a combination of shock and thinly veiled disdain.

My shoulders sag on a resigned sigh, eyes narrowing, and I know I have a duty to remain professional, and this is hardly the time or the place, but unfortunately the words are out of my mouth before I can stop myself. "You have got to be *fucking* kidding me."

CHAPTER 3

ROBBIE

Fuck all the way off.

Fran *fucking* Keller?

After a day like today, this has got to be some sort of sick joke.

I look over the head of my old high school nemesis, spearing Andy who's suddenly far too busy tapping away on his phone to notice my predicament.

Stepping around Keller, I storm into the apartment which, by the way, is pretty fucking sick—but that's not important right now. I grab my agent by his shoulder, pushing him to the other side of the room, as far away from *her* as we can get. Naturally he looks up at me like I've lost my mind.

"Is this a joke?" I hiss, my voice deathly quiet.

Andy blinks at me.

From my periphery, I see Keller still standing in the foyer. Arms folded over her chest, hip popped, high-heeled foot tapping obnoxiously on the shiny floor. I seethe. How one person's existence can be so fucking annoying, I have no idea.

"What the hell are we doing here?"

FAMOUS LAST WORDS   **19**

Andy's brows knit together at my question. "You—I… this is the apartment you wanted to look at," he says as if I've forgotten.

I glance over at Keller to find her inspecting her nails, clearly trying hard not to give away the fact that she's totally eavesdropping. I lean in closer to Andy. "I can't be here with… *her*."

He looks from me, over his shoulder to Fran, and back again, one of his brows arching slightly higher. "You know her?"

A derisive snort comes from the foyer. See? Eavesdropping. *Snake.*

"From prep school," I mutter under my breath. "Remember how I told you I *literally* shit myself during my first game at Belmont?"

Andy just stares at me, evidently confused.

I fold my arms across my chest, my jaw clenching painfully tight at the memory. "Yeah, well—" I jut my chin in her direction only to find her watching. "It was all *her* fault." I narrow my eyes in a glare, and she's suddenly storming toward us, heels clacking on the tile with every determined step.

"Ex-*cuse* me?" She stops right beside me, hands on her hips, looking up at me like *I'm* the delusional one. "Are you forgetting about the shampoo incident?" She glares at me. "I looked like a deranged Smurf in my yearbook photo thanks to *you*!"

I look down my nose at her. "You *laced* my Gatorade with *laxatives*!"

"In retaliation!" She's shrill and pitchy, pointing a finger at me. "You're the one who started it."

I step closer, effectively closing the distances between us, using my height advantage to stare her down. "Well, if you hadn't ratted on me about the party in the boat shed, I wouldn't have even known you existed. Should've kept your preppy mouth shut."

She rolls her eyes in response, another huff added for good measure as she looks away.

Shaking my head, I turn to Andy because he's on my side. At

least, I think he is… right now it looks as if it's taking all he has not to laugh.

"There was shit all over the ice," I say incredulously. "Men in HAZMAT suits came. Closed the arena for *three* days."

"Okay," Andy finally interjects, holding his hands up like a parent placating a toddler. "So, you two *do* know each other."

"What are you even doing here?" Fran interrupts, ignoring Andy completely. "I thought you were in Michigan."

"Minnesota," I bite back, correcting her dumb ass.

"*Minnesota*," she mutters some immature imitation of me.

I'm about to let her have it, when Andy chooses that moment to take control of the situation. And with the money I pay him, it's about damn time.

"Ms. Keller," he says in that business-like way he's perfected over the years of being one of the top sports agents in the country. "My client has recently signed with the New York Thunder."

Keller just blinks at him as if she has no idea what he's talking about. And it doesn't shock me. I'm the biggest name in the NHL right now, but her head's always been too far up her own ass to care about anything that doesn't involve her.

"New York is unfamiliar to my client, so we're looking for a centrally located apartment that's close to his gym, the team's training center, Madison Square Garden, and—" he casts me a furtive glance before tentatively continuing, "—and close to NHL headquarters on Ninth Avenue."

I spear him with a warning look because I swear to God, if he so much as hints to her the reason I need to be close to league headquarters, I will drop his ass faster than a cocky rookie who thinks he's on the verge of a breakaway.

Keller turns from Andy to me, the icy look in her eyes thawing some.

She studies me, lips pursed, arms folded across her chest, and I've never been able to stand her rich-bitch holier-than-thou attitude. She was like this at school, and it's safe to say not much has changed. It doesn't matter to her that I'm no longer the hood-rat kid from Dorchester, picked up by her fancy prep school and given a scholarship just because I was good on the ice. It doesn't matter that I'm now a professional hockey player with three championships, multi-million-dollar contracts, and major sponsorship deals. She's still looking at me like I'm beneath her. So you know what? Fuck her.

"Look, forget it." I snap, throwing my hands in the air. "This place fucking sucks anyway." That last part's a flat out lie but, again, fuck her.

I spin around, heading directly for the door.

Andy hurries behind me, lowering his voice as he says, "Will you stop and think of the terms to your contract."

And, yeah, I need to have secured a permanent place of residence before game one, but I'd rather do a deal with the Devil himself than Fran fucking Keller.

"Wait!"

I stop. Not because she told me to. It's the tone in her voice that causes me to pause mid-step. A little less self-assured than usual.

Intrigue sufficiently piqued, I turn slowly, clocking her where she stands with one hand gripping her phone, the other toying nervously with the thin gold chain that sits around her neck. Her throat bobs with a swallow and she takes a moment, as if the words are hard for her to say, before finally speaking.

"At least let me show you around first?" she says hopefully, posing it as a question, and it's that uncharacteristic vulnerability that doesn't make me immediately flip her off and storm out.

I feel Andy glance in my direction, and I really wish I had a choice. But frankly, he's right. The terms of my Thunder contract are strict, to say the least. If I fuck this up, I can wave goodbye to the NHL, because no matter how good a hockey player I am, no other team will touch me.

I'm about to relent, but before I do, Keller speaks again.

"Ninth Avenue is literally right down there," she says,

pointing out one of the glass walls. When she turns back to me, her face is suddenly fraught with panic.

Wait a second. Is she desperate?

Call me an asshole, but I decide to play hard to get, setting my jaw even tighter, staring at her long and hard because she's about to break. I can almost see the telltale cracks in her otherwise gleaming armor.

Worrying her bottom lip between her teeth, Keller glances down at her phone, staring at it as if it holds all the answers, her mind obviously working overtime. And suddenly, I realize the tapping of her shiny blue stiletto isn't her being obnoxious, it's nerves. I'm forced to bite back my shit-eating grin because oh, how the mighty have fallen.

"Come on, Andy," I say pointedly. "Let's go see that condo in Brooklyn."

Andy looks at me again like I've lost my mind. For the record there is no Brooklyn condo. I'm bluffing, but it seems to be working when Keller's head snaps up, eyes comically wide and full of dread.

"Please don't go!"

Both Andy and I gape at her outburst; I try not to laugh while Andy looks between Keller and me, like he's wondering what the hell is going on.

Keller seems to consider her words, looking down at her phone once more, shoulders falling a little. I'd almost feel sorry for her if I didn't know first-hand what an A plus asshole she is.

"Look," she begins tentatively, avoiding my eyes. "I really need to sell this place."

And there it is. What do you know, she is desperate. And I can't say I hate it.

She releases a breath, and I don't miss the way it tremors. "I have until Friday. If I don't get a signed deal, my boss is going to give this listing to my... *asshole* ex-boyfriend, and I'm effectively going to lose my job because there is no way in the nine circles of hell that I am working with him again." She snaps her mouth shut as if she's said too much, and I catch an unexpected fragility in her gaze as her eyes flit from me to Andy and back again before dropping to the floor.

And I'm a lot of things, but a heartless prick isn't one of them. So, after a brief pause, I huff, rolling my eyes like I've never been more inconvenienced in my life. "Okay, fine. Show us around," I say with a bored sigh.

Her eyebrows climb high, the dark cloud above her lifting just a little. "Really?"

I nod, remaining stoic so as to not give myself away.

She spins around on her heel and immediately transforms back into a self-assured woman who clearly knows what she's doing, taking us from room to room, pointing out useless shit like what kind of plaster is on the walls, and where the marble in the bathroom is from. And I must admit, I don't really care about all that stuff, but I'm quietly impressed by her knowledge, although I'd never admit it out loud.

By the end of the tour, I'm sold. This place is perfect for me. A secure building to stop the unhinged puck bunnies from breaking in, which unfortunately happened more than a few times back in St. Paul. Two bedrooms, so my mom has her own space if she ever comes to stay. Kick-ass views of the city. A patio. A parking spot. And close to everything I need to be close to, as stipulated in my contract.

Keller stops at the sprawling island counter, looking across at Andy and me with her chin held high in a show of confidence that doesn't fool me one bit. "So, what do you think?"

"They're asking six even?" Andy speaks first.

She nods. "Yes, but my client is willing to negotiate if presented with the right terms."

Andy looks down at something on his phone, probably texting my finance manager.

"Okay, we'll be in touch," I say.

I feel Andy shoot me a look which I ignore, holding Keller's gaze. And frankly, I don't even know if that's something people say in these types of situations, but the way I see it, Keller deserves to sweat a little given the trauma she put me through back in high school. I know I'm not entirely innocent, but she didn't shit herself in front of the entire school, half the town, and a whole squad of college scouts.

She glances at me, lips twitching like she wants to say more, but she doesn't. Instead, her shoulders sag, and she tries to conceal the look of defeat in her big blue eyes with a tight smile. And I realize then that she's clearly not much of a sales person. No wonder she's desperate; I can see why she's on the verge of losing her job.

CHAPTER 4

FRAN

Thanks to a day full of shitty men, I'm late to work my shift at The Exchange, a bar in the lobby of a Wall Street building where I serve *pretentious* drinks to *pretentious* assholes who think it's okay to playfully smack my ass and make lewd comments just because they tip so generously.

Dressed in my uniform, which is ultimately nothing more than a little black dress so short it should be illegal, I scurry through the dimly lit bar toward the back room, muttering an apology to anyone who'll listen.

I place my tote bag into one of the lockers and grab a tablet and an apron, pausing to reapply a sweeping of red lipstick and make sure my bun is still as together as it was when I left my apartment.

I've been working at The Exchange ever since I was promoted to junior sales agent because, although it was considered a promotion, it came with a significant drop in salary. Working in sales includes the added benefit of earning a commission—something I've yet to experience—therefore my retainer at Carlton Myers barely covers my rent, so I needed to find something that would pay enough and that I could do in the evenings. A few people told me how much servers can make working in the right bars, and they weren't wrong. On a good month, my tips from working at The Exchange cover most of my expenses. Apart from the occasional sexual harassment, it's not a bad gig.

"You're *late*," Vera, one of the other servers, teases as she brushes past me, leaving a cloud of sweet perfume in her wake. "You missed knock-off. I made three hundred bucks in tips!" She pulls a wad of cash from the pocket of her apron, theatrically fanning herself with the money.

Damn. Knock-off is always the best time for tips. It's mostly men on a high after a successful day trading stocks or whatever it is they do down here, probably high on cocaine, spending cash like it's going out of style, tipping big as a show of who has the bigger penis. It's laughable, but as a server reliant on tips, I can't complain.

I groan, throwing my head back. I swear, if I don't make some decent money tonight, that puck slinging pain in the ass is going to pay for wasting my damn time at Allora. I'll personally troll his social media accounts and tell all his adoring fans that he has a festering case of chlamydia and a weird goat fetish.

"Sorry I'm late," I say to Vera. "Work was… *work*."

She winces. "Ugh. Not Tadd drama again?"

"Don't ask." I wave a dismissive hand.

"Well, I have a casting call on Monday that might run late, so maybe you can cover for me?"

Vera and I have become close since working together. She's from a small town in West Virginia. A model-slash-actress-slash-server. Her boyfriend is a DJ who has his own residency in a SoHo nightclub.

I never had a lot of friends growing up, so having Vera come into my life now, and the two of us complimenting one another like we do, was exactly what I needed after moving to a city where I didn't know a single soul.

I smile. "Of course I can cover for you. I hope you get the gig."

"Thanks." Vera hands me a rolled up fifty from her wad of cash.

"No, I can't, I—"

"Take it!" She stops my objection, tucking the money into my ample cleavage. "We're a team, remember?"

She's right. We are a team. Working in a place like this, you have to be.

Grudgingly, I accept the cash, removing it from between my breasts and placing it into the pocket of my apron with a contrite smile. "Thanks, V."

She flashes me a wink and continues back out to the bar. And, with a deep breath and a quick mental pep talk, I plaster on a smile and follow her out there, ready or not for round number two.

Two hours into my shift, my phone vibrates against my hip for the fifth time. I'm not sure what is so damn important, but a group of businessmen from Texas walked into the bar half an hour ago, and they're tipping like crazy with every round we deliver to their table. Vera and I are tag-teaming, and I really don't want her to have to cover for me again, but it might be Andy Hoffman. What if Robbie Mason actually wants to put in an offer?

Sneaking into the break room, I pull my phone from my apron and glance down at the screen to see five new text messages, all from an unknown number. *Weird.* I take a seat on one of the plastic chairs, gasping at the first message that displays on the screen.

Unknown: Hey, it's Robbie.

What the ever-loving fuck is Robbie Mason doing texting me? I thought that's what he had Andy for; I didn't know I'd be forced to associate with the cretin.

28   SHANN MCPHERSON

> Unknown: Mason.

I roll my eyes. No shit, genius.

> Unknown: You're seriously ignoring me?

God, even in text format he's an arrogant jerk.

> Unknown: K, well I guess you don't wanna sell an apartment then…

Oh God! No. I almost hit the call button, but then I read the next message, and I pause.

> Unknown: I have a proposition for you.

A what?

Sufficiently confused, and definitely not wanting to miss out on the opportunity to prove myself to Tony all while sticking it to stupid Tadd, I hit the call button, my pulse thrumming in my ear so loud it almost drowns out the sound of the ringing tone.

"Well, well, well, look who's come crawling back…"

I swear, it takes everything I have not to hang up on his ass. But I'm reminded of my predicament; I need to sell this apartment, and the ass-face on the other end of the line really is my only option.

"Sorry," I murmur.

"Okay, so here's the thing," he starts. "I'll give you a full-ask offer, all cash, no contingencies, quick close."

I squeal. I actually *squeal*. In fact, I'm so loud, I hear someone on the other side of the door drop a glass. I slap a hand over my mouth.

"Jesus Christ!" Robbie barks. "Are you *done*?"

"Sorry," I mutter, my mouth full of my own palm.

With an exasperated huff he continues. "I'll sign the offer and you'll have it in your inbox first thing in the morning… *but—*"

My skin pricks at the warning tone in his voice, and I sit up a little straighter, my stomach suddenly in knots. I don't like the sound of that "but." Buts are only ever bad. Buts suck. I swallow hard, waiting for the blow.

"I have one condition."

"You want the furniture? Another parking spot? What?" I rack my mind, wondering what strings I might be able to pull to give him whatever the hell it is he wants. But Marie's already come down a quarter of a million dollars. It's unlikely she's going to want to move much more.

Robbie chuckles. *Chuckles.* I'm barely breathing, and he has the audacity to laugh. He is such an asshole. My teeth clench in an attempt to contain the vitriol threatening to spew out of me.

"On the condition that you—" he pauses suddenly, and I hear him clear his throat. "That you… pretend to be my… my *girlfriend.*"

I blink once, twice, three times, slowly processing exactly what he's just said.

Shaking my head in an attempt to snap myself out of the daze I'm in, I snort. "Sorry, I think I just blacked out for a second. Did you just say you want me to *pretend* to be your *girlfriend*?"

"Yes."

"In exchange for *buying* an *apartment* from me?"

"Yes."

I'm not sure what I'm pissed about most—the blatant solicitation or the fact that he's so goddamn blasé about it. I shake my head again. "Um. Okay. Give me a second—" I pause, pinching the bridge of my nose, eyes squeezed shut. "First, are you serious?"

"Yes."

"STOP SAYING YES!" I scream, my voice indignantly shrill.

I'm met with another low chuckle, and I almost throw my phone against the cement floor. In an attempt to collect myself, however, I take a deep breath in through my nose and out through my lips, but it doesn't help one bit.

"Okay, second, have you lost your goddamn mind?" I can feel the blood rushing through my veins, pumping hard and fast, rising up my chest, my neck, my face heating with pure, unbridled rage. "I don't know who the hell you think you are, but I am not some... some *hooker* you can just—"

"Okay, calm down," Robbie interjects.

My jaw drops. "I know you did not just tell me to *calm down*."

"First of all, I'm not expecting you to have *sex*," he says as if the sheer notion of sex with me is disgusting. Frankly I'm still too shocked by his proposition to take offense.

"Second of all—" He pauses, and it's the unexpected hint of dejection in his tone that somehow pacifies me enough to at least hear him out. "The thing is, today when Andy told you I recently signed with New York, it wasn't the whole truth."

I wait for him to continue.

With a hard exhale, he does. "The truth is, I was released from my old team because I... well, because I got into a bit of *trouble*."

Trouble? I quirk a brow, suddenly more than a little curious.

"New York is the only team willing to pick me up. Probably because they've sucked ass the last few years, and I can only assume they're desperate," he mutters. "But no other team will touch me. To everyone that matters, I'm a liability."

I continue listening, silenced by the unexpected fragility in his words.

"The terms of my new contract are totally unfair, but I can't lose hockey. It's the only thing in my life I've ever been any good at. I didn't finish college. I don't have a degree. I'm useless at pretty much everything. Without hockey, I honestly don't know what I'd do."

"So, what does me pretending to be your girlfriend have to do with any of that?"

FAMOUS LAST WORDS 31

He hesitates for so long I'm forced to check the screen to make sure I haven't been cut off, but then he talks. "My reputation is at an all time low. Half the officials in the league fucking hate me. They say I brought the game of ice hockey into disrepute."

My eyes widen.

He sighs. "Anyway, my new GM told me that now is the time for me to prove that I'm not the *bad boy* of hockey that everyone thinks I am. And so… I don't know… maybe if it looks like I've settled down, maybe they'll stop giving me such a hard time."

The tension in my shoulders eases a little in the wake of his confession. Frankly, I didn't know Robbie Mason had a vulnerable bone in his body.

He continues. "And, I don't know, I guess I just thought because you need to sell that place to keep your job, and I need a place to live… maybe we could help each other out, y'know?"

The more he talks, the more I'm listening. I mean, of course, it's completely absurd, and the sheer thought of being in any way romantically linked to Robbie Mason, fake or not, is giving me a serious case of the ick. But the thing is, in a weird way, it kind of makes sense. Maybe with a fake boyfriend, Tadd might finally accept that I want nothing to do with him.

Before I can respond with anything, the door opens and Vera sticks her head inside, eyes frantically wide as they land on me. She motions back out to the bar, whispering loudly, "I'm drowning out here."

I wave a hand, indicating to her that I'll be right out.

"Hey, Robbie. I have to get back to work."

"Work?"

"Yeah, I work nights at a bar downtown."

"You have *two* jobs?" He's clearly confused.

"Yeah." I snort. "Have you seen what they charge for rent in this city?"

"But—but you're rich."

I actually laugh out loud at that. "Um, what?"

"You're rich," he says again as if it's a fact.

"Uh, no, I'm not."

"But you went to Belmont."

"Yeah, because I was on an academic scholarship. Why do you think I was so high strung?"

A contemplative silence fills the line.

"Look, let me think about this, and I'll get back to you." I love how casual I sound, as if I'm not currently considering being the fake girlfriend of my sworn enemy in exchange for a signed deal sheet on a six-million-dollar apartment. It's sordid and seedy and surely a breach of my fiduciary responsibility.

"Okay, well—" Robbie clears his throat. "I'll be waiting for your answer, *baby*." The way he says baby, all low and rasped, would almost be hot if I didn't know firsthand what a disgusting bag of dicks he is.

"Gross," I murmur.

His low chuckle is the last thing I hear before he ends the call and the line falls dead.

CHAPTER 5

FRAN

When I first moved to New York, there was no way I could afford to live on my own, but I was terrified of moving in with a stranger. What if they left toenail clippings in the sink or, worse, never emptied the dishwasher? Thankfully, I lucked out, finding a studio apartment in the Lower East Side.

My apartment is on the third floor of an old five story red brick building with a rusted external fire escape, faded graffiti covering most of the ground floor façade, and an elevator that's out of order more than it's not because the building super will happily accept our rent but refuse to fix anything in a timely manner.

By the time I trudge up the three flights of stairs and into my tiny shoebox apartment, it's close to midnight, and I can't decide if I'm tired or hungry. Aside from the handful of olives I snacked on at the bar, I haven't eaten anything since the cream cheese bagel I practically inhaled after my morning meeting. But before anything, I'm in dire need of a shower, not only because I've been working all day and night, but Robbie Mason's indecent proposal is lingering like a bad smell.

After a long shower, I change into an old college t-shirt and some sweats, and I settle on my bed with my laptop and a steaming cup of ramen, which is precisely when the MacBook chimes, startling me. My stomach knots when I see a new message pop-up from UNKNOWN. I quickly update the contact so that I can at least screen his calls if I need to.

Asshat: Time's ticking...

I glare at his taunting threat, but then curiosity gets the better of me.

Clicking on a new webpage, I enter *Robbie Mason* into the search engine, my brows immediately knitting together at the page that appears, full of links to news articles with unflattering headlines. Placing my noodles on the nightstand, I decide to get comfortable. When Robbie mentioned his reputation was in trouble, I just assumed he was being a drama queen; I certainly didn't think it was *this* serious.

Most Valuable Player to Most Despised Man in the League

At just twenty-five, Robbie Mason already has two Hart Trophies, three Stanley Cup wins, and sponsorship deals with some of the biggest brands in the world. Yet, in the wake of the news that St. Paul has released their star defenseman only two games into the pre-season, the hockey world has been left in shock, wondering where it all went wrong for the game's most valuable player?

Fans first began to express their concern for Mason following the Lions' Stanley Cup win in June when, during the break, he was often spotted looking disheveled, stumbling out of nightclubs in Las Vegas, Los Angeles, and Miami, photographed partying with Hollywood celebrities amidst his rumored relationship with controversial influencer, Lola Grey.

When photos appeared of Mason asleep on a couch, shirtless, with a suspicious looking bag of white powder sitting in his lap, concern increased for the athlete.

When asked about the photo at a press conference, Mason declined to respond before unplugging and abruptly exiting the media room.

Following the Lions' pre-season opener loss against the Bears, it appeared that the once unbeatable team had lost momentum on the ice. A few days later, as the Lions faced off against the Miners at home, fans were forced to watch on as their beloved team fell apart right in front of them. Fights aren't uncommon in the sport of ice hockey, but this was the first time in NHL history that a brutal, bloody, mid-game brawl had broken out between players on the same team, and it sent shockwaves throughout the sporting community.

The question that remains on everyone's lips is what on earth could possibly have caused Robbie Mason to drop mitts and launch at his own teammate, Ben Harris? There's been no mention of the incident, no explanation, no apology from the club, the league, or the man himself, and fans are understandably reeling.

The New York Thunder are rumored to have been in contact with the now free agent, but Mason's future lies in the hands of David Ferris and the league's Player Safety Board, who will ultimately decide whether he is cleared to continue playing, or whether his professional hockey career has come to a sudden and unexpected end. More to come on this breaking story.

I puff air from my cheeks, shocked by what I've just read. I'm the first to admit I know nothing about sports, but even I can tell this is big. In fact, the whole thing screams messy. Robbie's gone from being the best player on the number one team in the league, to a team that has come last two years in a row. I'm no expert, but I imagine that's not something anyone would willingly volunteer to do during the height of his career.

I pinch my bottom lip between my thumb and forefinger, staring at the screen, at the photograph accompanying the story: a shot of Robbie walking out of the Newark arrivals terminal, chin dipped low, a hoodie pulled over a ball cap, and sunglasses at dusk. He looks broken. Granted, I don't really know the man in the photo. Hell, I barely even knew him in high school. He was just *that* guy. The guy who chose to, for some reason, make my life a living hell. And no, it wasn't some secret harbored crush he was trying to hide; Robbie Mason despised me. And, in return, I despised him right back. But after graduation we went our separate ways, mutually happy to see the back of one another. But now he's here, and it looks like a lot has happened in the time that's passed, and I don't know if it's something I'm ready to be dealing with right now.

Sure, I need to sell Allora, and in two days no less, but is it worth making a deal with the man these articles are written about?

On the flip side, if I don't sell the apartment, then Tadd wins.

I click on my messages, staring at Robbie's last text.

> Asshat: Time's ticking...

With a deep breath, I type a response.

> Me: What exactly does "pretending to be your girlfriend" actually entail?

Sending my reply, I stare at the screen, chewing on my thumbnail. I cannot for the life of me believe I'm actually considering this. Maybe I've finally lost my mind. My great aunt had a mental breakdown; maybe it's hereditary.

> Asshat: Coming to my games, wearing my jersey, waiting for me outside the locker room at the end of the night. Looking at me like you can't get enough of me. That sort of thing. I just need my coaches and the higher-ups in the league to see that I have a serious girlfriend. That I've changed.

I cringe at the thought. Having to spend my free time with the likes of Robbie Mason is punishment enough, but then to have to act like I don't want to slap him in his stupid smug face is the stuff of nightmares.

A follow-up appears in the message window before I can even reply.

FAMOUS LAST WORDS   **37**

Asshat: We can practice on Friday. See what works best.

Me: Friday? As in two days from now?

Asshat: No, Friday, March 16. Next year.

I roll my eyes.

Me: What's happening Friday?

Asshat: Oh, no big deal or anything. Just my first official game with the Thunder.

Me: And what if I already have plans?

Asshat: Not my problem.

I balk. The nerve of this guy.

Me: And if I say yes to this farce, what's the deal with PDA.

Asshat: You really want me that bad huh, Keller?

Me: Dream on, loser. I swear, if you so much as even touch me, I will claw your face off.

Asshat: I need to see some return on my investment.

Me: You're getting a whole ass Chelsea apartment!

Asshat: You're gonna have to at least hold my hand. Maybe even kiss me on my cheek.

> Me: I think I just threw up in my mouth.

> Asshat: Ok, so imagine I'm walking out of the locker room after the game on Friday, and you're hanging around in the tunnel, waiting for me. What are you gonna do when I come out to meet you? High five me?

I heave a sigh. This is all too much. Maybe losing Allora, and my job, and not being able to afford to stay in New York, and having to go home to live the rest of my life working as assistant manager at Keller's Drug Store won't be so bad after all. I can live in the loft above my parents' garage, rent-free. At least I wouldn't have to see stupid Tadd every day.

But with the thought of Tadd taking my listing, the one I worked my ass off to secure, and the image of his stupid face filling my mind, I'm almost on autopilot as I send my response.

> Me: Okay. Whatever. I'll do it.

CHAPTER 6

ROBBIE

'm forced to hide my smirk as I watch Andy pace the length of his office, spluttering a slew of incomprehensible words, hands flailing in the air. He's understandably pissed, trying to make sense of what I've just told him, and it's almost funny. I'd laugh if I knew it wouldn't piss him off even more.

"So, let me get this straight." He stops pacing, looking at me as he grips the back of his chair. "You asked her to *pretend* to be your *girlfriend*, in *exchange* for *purchasing* a six-million-dollar apartment off her?"

I nod.

He pinches the bridge of his nose. "And there are text messages pertaining to this?"

I nod again.

He gawks at me. "Have you lost your goddamn mind?"

"That's exactly what she said!" I laugh, but he doesn't seem to see the funny side.

"Robbie…" He lowers his voice. "That's blackmail."

My brows knit together. "Blackmail?"

Andy throws his head back. "Yes, Robbie. Congratulations. You've officially committed a felony."

Fuck. Suddenly I'm scrambling, pulling my phone from the pocket of my jeans, more than a little panicked as I scroll through to Fran's number. I call her on speaker, and thankfully, she picks up after the first ring.

"Please don't tell me you've changed your mind," she says instead of the customary hello.

"Hey—" My gaze flits to Andy's as he watches on with bated breath, "You're not gonna, like, tell anyone about this, are you?"

"Actually, I was just about to post it on Facebook for all my friends and family to see." She laughs hollowly. "You think I'm actually proud of this?"

Fuck me, she's a snarky bitch.

Andy starts frantically gesticulating, and all I can do is stare at him because I have no idea what he's fucking doing.

"NDA!" he whisper-yells.

"Okay, well, I'm gonna need you to sign an NDA," I say casually, squeezing my eyes closed in preparation for her rebuttal.

"An NDA? Are you serious?" She doesn't disappoint, her voice shrill and incredulous. "Who do you think you are? Harry Styles?"

Honestly, I'm kind of offended, but I keep my cool as best as I can, shifting in my chair. "Look, it's not that I don't trust you—"

"Actually, Robbie, that's entirely the basis of a Non-Disclosure Agreement. You don't *trust* that I won't say something, and you want it in writing so I legally *can't* say something."

"Okay, well, if I'm being honest, then, no. I don't trust you. Do you blame me?" I scoff. "You literally doped me with laxatives and made me shit myself."

"Ugh, get over it," she mutters.

I guffaw, but before I can respond, my phone is ripped out of my hand.

FAMOUS LAST WORDS   41

"Hey, Fran, it's Andy," he says, turning the phone off speaker. "Yeah, I know. Sorry about him."

With a muttered curse, I drop my head back, staring up at the ceiling as I listen to one side of the conversation.

"You're totally right. He's not in his right mind."

I snort, but I say nothing, instead just shaking my head as my agent badmouths me to the bane of my existence. Talk about winning at life.

"An NDA is standard practice, but it's not just to protect Robbie. It's in your best interest too." He pauses. "Yes… I know… Uh-huh."

I look up as Andy sits at his desk, taking a pen and jotting something down on a Post-it.

"Okay… Yep… Uh-huh… Sure… I can do that." He meets my eyes. "Yes. Of course… I'll let him know."

He hands the phone back to me, still writing shit down.

I make sure the call is dead before asking, "What the hell was that about?"

"She said she'll sign," he says, still focused on his notes. "She wants a detailed itinerary of the schedule of events she's expected to attend with you."

I roll my eyes. A million girls would kill to be in her position, and she's over here making demands? Straight up audacity.

"She wants it in writing that she will *hold your hand* and *hug you*, but you are explicitly not allowed to *kiss* her."

I scoff. "Pfft, yeah, right. She fucking wishes."

Andy looks up at me then, his gaze almost bored. "She also wanted me to inform you that you are—" He pauses to glance down at whatever he's just finished writing on the Post-it. "A disgusting dick bag and if you so much as even look at her the wrong way, she will cut off your balls with your hockey skates and feed them to the squirrels in Central Park." He meets my eyes once more, lips pressed together in a firm line.

"Sounds like true love to me," I grin.

Again, Andy doesn't appear to see the funny side of all this, heaving a frustrated sigh instead. "I don't like this, Robbie. This is risky. NDA or not, if you get found out, I…" He trails off, shaking his head. "I won't be able to protect you this time."

"Andy, buddy, pal, you really need to stop stressing so much. You're gonna give yourself a goddamn heart attack." I offer him a cocky smirk, but all he does is roll his eyes at me, picking up his desk phone and asking his assistant to patch him straight through to legal.

CHAPTER 7

FRAN

"So, I heard you're officially in escrow."

Startled, I look up from my laptop to see Tadd peering over my cubicle wall.

With an obvious sigh, I sit up a little straighter, squaring my shoulders all while trying to act like he doesn't make my skin crawl. The thing about Tadd Jennings is when he knows he's affecting you, good or bad, he takes it as a win. Textbook narcissistic behavior.

"You heard right." I lift my chin.

He lowers a brow, his icy gray gaze dubious. "Who's the buyer?"

Thankfully, Robbie's finance manager outlined an LLC on the sales contract, so the famous—or, infamous—hockey star won't appear in the public record as the buyer. It was my main concern with the whole fake-girlfriend thing, knowing that it would raise alarm bells for anyone bright enough to put two and two together. Seeing me, the woman who was on the precipice of losing her job if she didn't sell a six-million-dollar apartment, suddenly hanging off the buyer's arm would be sure to raise some eyebrows. Hopefully by the time someone does manage to figure it out, my faux romance with Robbie will be long forgotten.

"I'm not sure," I lie with a nonchalant shrug. "I only met the manager."

Tadd narrows one eye. "How long is escrow?"

"Ten days," I answer without missing a beat.

"Ten days, full ask, no contingencies?"

I nod.

He stares at me long and hard, his eyebrows climbing slightly higher in a way that almost looks like he's impressed. "Good girl."

My nose scrunches up of its own accord. The way he says it, low and rasped. Gross. I am absolutely *not* his good girl, and I will *never* be his good girl again. The man is a goddamn predator.

When I catch the flash of a devious smirk tug at his lips as if he can tell what I'm thinking, I quickly turn back to my laptop in an attempt to put an end to whatever this whole interaction is. But, of course, Tadd struts around the divider of my cubicle, inviting himself in and perching his ass right there on the side of my desk. He's far too close. I'm inundated by his Gucci aftershave, and it's sickeningly overwhelming.

I make a show of rolling away on my chair as far as the limited space will allow, but he just sniggers, like I'm playing with him. I eye the stapler next to my coffee mug, ready to use it if I have to.

"What do you want, Tadd?"

"What?" He laughs, holding his hands up in surrender. "I can't be proud of my best girl?"

I steady him with a no-bullshit look. "I am not your best *anything*."

He bites down on his bottom lip, concealing his smirk, eyes darkening as they trail down my body and back up again. "We used to have some fun, you and me."

I balk. "Yeah, I used to love being used and cheated on, having everyone else in this office laughing behind my back because I was stupid enough to fall for your bullshit."

He doesn't deny it. How can he when I caught him red-handed? He does, however, have the audacity to cock his head to the side, looking at me like I've wounded him.

"Look, Tadd," I begin through gritted teeth, "I'm really busy, so if you don't mind—" I glance pointedly at the exit.

"I have a potential listing. Columbus Circle. A penthouse overlooking the park," he says instead of leaving like he knows I want him to.

"Congratulations," I say flatly.

Tadd chuckles under his breath, folding his arms across his chest. "Well, I was going to see if you might want to come along to the pitch with me. If it goes the way I expect it to, then maybe we can figure something out."

He presses his tongue against the inside of his cheek, and I swear everything he does is suggestive and disgusting, but it's his tone that irks me more than anything. By "figure something out" he's referring to something crude and inappropriate, and all I do is blink at him because, frankly, I'd rather stick a cardboard fork in my eye.

"I have an appointment with the seller on Tuesday," he says after a moment, pushing off my desk and standing to his full height. "Think about it and let me know." And with that, he offers me one last lingering look before turning and sauntering out.

I release the breath I've been holding, my shoulders relaxing some, but then he pauses and casts me one last glance over his shoulder, that same arrogant smirk ghosting his lips. "Good job with Allora, sweetheart."

I glare at his back as he walks away, strutting through the sales floor like he's God's gift. He's something alright. A painful reminder of just how naïve I'd been not so long ago.

Rolling my eyes, I go back to my emails, which is when my

cell starts to ring. I glance at the device, grimacing as ASSHAT flashes on the screen. I signed the NDA, so what more does he want?

With an annoyed sigh, I answer. "Yes?"

"Well, hello to you too, *baby*..."

Seriously. I must really need to get laid, because the way he says *baby* does things to me I do not want to explore. I cringe at the thought. "What do you want?"

He laughs, and I close my eyes on an exhale. I'm already regretting this.

"Get my schedule?"

Snapping into gear, I click open the unread email I have sitting in my inbox from Andy Hoffman, my eyes bulging as the document loads. "*Two* pages?" I hiss, keeping my voice low.

"I'm in demand. What can I say?"

I scrunch up my nose as I scour the long list. "Three games a week?"

"Sometimes four."

"You have got to be kidding me."

"You literally know nothing about hockey, huh?"

"You say that like it's a bad thing," I sass.

"You don't need to come to *every* game," he relents. "Just a home game every now and again."

"And what if I have a shift at the bar?" I close my eyes again, massaging the hollow of my cheek. The stress is wreaking havoc on my jaw from all the clenching.

"You're gonna need to quit."

My painful jaw drops at his blatant audacity. "Um, I beg your pardon?"

"I have a lot of evening commitments that I'm going to need you to attend with me," he says with the conviction of Richard Gere in *Pretty Woman*. "And, besides, why would the girlfriend of the highest paid NHL player need to work nights in a bar?"

"Gee, I don't know. Maybe because not all women are unemployed freeloaders."

"You're not unemployed, Fran," Robbie says smugly, and I can almost hear the cocky grin curling his lips. "You're a successful real estate agent thanks to *me*."

I hate him. I actually *hate* him.

"I have to go. I have a headache."

"Maybe you should go rub one out," he says casually. "It always helps me."

"Ugh, you're *disgusting*." I end the call to the tune of his grating chuckle, tossing my phone off to the side of my cluttered desk.

With a huff, I sag in my chair, pushing my hair back from my face and closing my eyes.

Robbie Mason is a twelve-year-old boy in a man's body. Arrogant and insolent and everything in between. I cannot believe I actually agreed to do this. I mean sure, the commission check will look pretty once it's cleared in my bank account, and even if I never sell another property, it'll at least afford me some extra time in the city to find another job. And Tony did personally congratulate me in this morning's sales meeting, which was a nice boost to my ego. But is all that really worth having to associate with the likes of Robbie Mason? So far, I'm unconvinced.

CHAPTER 8

ROBBIE

Exhausted, I sit shirtless on the bench in front of my cubby, hunched over, elbows on my knees, head in my hands, feeling every bone in my body ache. I'm twenty-five years old, but right now, I feel like I'm eighty. And I can't help but wonder if my new coaches are purposely punishing me or if it's just a coincidence.

As far as I'm aware, of the twenty-one players out on that ice, I'm the only one with three consecutive Stanley Cup wins under my belt, and yet I'm the one being targeted, forced to repeat the same basic drills over and over again like I'm a goddamn call-up from the minors trying to prove himself. Shit's fucked.

I drag a hand over my face as the door swings open, and I look up to see Dallas Shaw, Thunder's starting goalie, walking in on his skates. He stops at his cubby and begins the arduous task of shedding his gear, glancing at me as he does. "You okay, my man?"

"Yeah," I mutter, looking down at the floor.

Of all the guys I've met so far on the team, Dallas is the only one who hasn't immediately treated me like I'm public enemy number one. I think it's because Dallas is one of Andy's clients too, so it's kind of like an unspoken truce we have. I've heard stories about the notorious Dallas Shaw—he's a cocky asshole on the ice, and a total playboy off the ice—but so far, he's the only one not giving me the stink eye.

"Hey, don't take it to heart," Dallas says. "Coach has a hard-on for asserting himself with the newbies."

I look up at him again, meeting his eyes.

"I mean—no offense," he says quickly. "I know you're not a newbie, per se. But, given the circumstances, Coach is just trying to show you who's boss." He slumps down on the bench beside me with an almighty harrumph. "The guy's a fucking asshole. Daughter's a total smoke show, though." He winks at me.

I chuckle lightly, relaxing some. It's at least nice to know it's not just me who thinks the head coach, Lance Draper, is a dick.

"Hey, some of us are gonna meet up for a few beers later tonight." Dallas slaps my arm. "You in?"

I consider his question. And while it's nice to be invited, since I've only been in the city for a few days and I know practically nobody, I'm reminded of the terms of my contract. Unless it's an approved team event, I'm not allowed out past nine. I cannot believe this is my life right now.

I rub at the tension that knots in the back of my neck. "No can do, man." With a sidelong glance, I mutter, "Curfew."

"Oh, shit, yeah, the probation." Dallas offers a remorseful look. "What's the deal with that, anyway?"

Legally, I'm not allowed to divulge the terms of my contract, although the media managed to catch wind of a few of the more ridiculous call outs, such as my curfew. But there are so many stipulations, my measly nine-million, three-year deal is more like a fucking prison sentence.

"It is what it is," is all I say with a noncommittal shrug, heaving myself up and heading for the showers.

"Mason?"

I'm stopped on my way out of the training center, turning to see my defense coach, Coach Bromley, leaning over the railing from the upper mezzanine of the lobby.

"Coach?"

"Draper's office," is all he says before turning and disappearing out of sight.

My shoulders sag in resignation because what the fuck now? Gripping my bag strap, I make my way up the stairs and follow the corridor lined with glass meeting rooms to the very end, where Coach Draper's office is situated.

I pause at the door, taking a few breaths before knocking.

"Come in," the deep voice barks from the other side.

Tentatively, I open the door and continue inside, a little taken aback to see not only Coach Draper, but Bromley too, and one of the assistant coaches I haven't yet had anything to do with.

"Sit." Coach Draper points to the chair directly opposite him, and like a fucking dog, I do as I'm told.

I like to think I'm a pretty confident guy, but right now, I have no idea what's going on. Are they done with me already? Fuck. I go over the last few hours in my head, thinking what it was I might've done to fuck up bad enough to be shown the door after my first on-ice practice.

Coach looks up at me from his phone, tugging his wireframe glasses off, steely blue eyes intense when they meet mine. "Do you know what I did when Chris Garret told me he wanted to sign you?"

I'm not sure if this is a rhetorical question, so I say nothing.

"I laughed in his goddamn face." He slaps his big paw on the desk so unexpectedly, I can't help but flinch. "Because sure as shit he had to be pulling my damn leg."

I cast a furtive glance in Coach Bromley's direction, but he gives nothing away.

"Why the hell would we want to risk signing the biggest liability in the NHL?"

I swallow hard, forced to bite my tongue.

Coach looks down at the papers in front of him. "Drinking. Partying. *Drugs.*"

"I've never touched a drug in my life, Coach," I interject, because fuck it. I'll cop a lot on my chin, but not that. "I don't even take Tylenol."

Coach says nothing, but the smirk ghosting his lips tells me he doesn't believe a word I say. I suppose I can't blame him. The media royally screwed me over.

"Fighting with your own teammates," Coach scoffs as he reads the paper in front of him. He glances up at me with one quirked brow. "They're saying Ben Harris might miss the whole season because of you."

Fuck Ben Harris. He's a pussy ass bitch, milking it for all he can.

When I remain silent, Coach continues, "Promiscuity with your little internet… *fangirls.*"

I almost laugh at that because Lola Grey sure as hell ain't no "fangirl," and if she knew this old man was referring to her as one, with condescending air quotes and all, she would lose her ever-loving shit.

"Lola was a mistake in judgment, Coach." I don't add that she was nothing but a rebound. One I wish I'd stayed the hell away from. And that, frankly, it was all Ben fucking Harris's fault. Instead, I clear my throat, sitting up a little straighter. "I've settled down. I've got a girlfriend now, Coach. A real nice girl I've known since high school." Honestly, it takes all I have not to gag at my own words.

Coach studies me for a few silent moments. "Well, I hope for your sake you have settled down. Because we spent more money signing you than any other player on our roster."

Probably the reason you've sucked ass the last two years, I don't say.

"Half the fans have turned on us because of the decision Chris made offering you a contract," Coach adds.

Frustrated, I pull on the back of my neck, because there's only so many proverbial kicks a guy can take when he's already down.

"So, what I wanna know is where the fuck is Robbie Mason, three time Stanley Cup champion and MVP last two years in a row, because I sure as shit didn't see him out on that ice today." Coach sags back in his chair, folding his arms across his chest, watching me, waiting.

He's right. But I'm at a loss, and all I can do is shake my head because honestly, I don't know what's wrong with me. When I skated out onto the ice today, it was like coming home. But there was something off, and I don't even know what it is so that I can make sure it doesn't happen again.

"I'll be better, Coach." I look him straight in his eyes. "I promise you; I will be the best damn decision Chris Garret's ever made for this team."

Coach stares at me long and hard, his face a blank mask, void of any and all emotion. He's quietly terrifying, if I'm honest. And I find my mind wandering back to what Dallas said earlier in the locker room. I know it's not the time or the place, but all I keep thinking is how the hell does *this* guy have a hot daughter?

"You better not let me down, son." Coach looks down at his phone again and starts tapping something into it.

I stand, lingering a moment or two before I realize I've been dismissed. Grabbing my bag off the floor I turn, and I'm out of there so damn fast.

"Mason!"

I stop halfway down the corridor, turning to see Coach Bromley standing there, hands tucked in his pockets, the hint of a grin curling his lips. And it's not lost on me that this is the first sign of a smile I've received from any of the coaching staff since I've arrived.

"Let's you and me grab some time on the ice tomorrow, before everyone gets here," he says. "I wanna do a review of your edgework. You're one of the best skaters in the league, but you were looking a little sloppy out there today."

I nod. Because I do agree with him that I'm one of the best skaters in the league—possibly the best. His mention of my edgework, however, almost has me laughing out loud, because is he serious?

"Be here at ten."

"Sure thing, Coach."

Bromley nods but doesn't say anything more before turning and disappearing back into Draper's office. Probably to talk more about how shit I am.

I turn, hurrying back along the corridor, down the stairs and through the lobby of the training center. And as I walk out into the afternoon, the city chaos hitting me like brutal slap to the face, I realize something; I seriously need to get my shit together before I fuck this whole thing up.

CHAPTER 9

FRAN

Clutching the *officially in escrow* bottle of champagne Tony Carlton presented me in our morning meeting, I try so hard to play it cool, like it's no big deal as I walk through the sales floor. But it's hard not to smile. This is my first escrow. Sure, the way it came about might be a little shady, but no one knows that; to everyone that matters, I sold a six-million-dollar apartment.

"Good job, Fran," someone says from the other side of the floor.

Smile beaming, I continue on the way to my desk only to be stopped by my name coming from behind me. Turning, my eyes bulge at the sight of Giselle, Carlton Myers' receptionist, advancing on me, carrying a box of red roses almost as big as she is.

"Fran!" Giselle calls out again, grinning at me with a slight skip in her step.

"Hey," I say, dubiously eyeing the flowers.

"These just came for you." Giselle hands me the box and the small gift bag she'd had hanging off her arm.

Confused, I look at her, my eyebrows knitting together because it's definitely *not* my birthday.

"Someone has an admirer," Giselle says with a conspiratorial wink before spinning on her heels and practically prancing off.

I peer into the bunch of expensive looking roses for a card, but there's nothing. I turn and head to my desk, ready to do some serious digging.

"Nice flowers."

Loaded down with the flowers, the gift bag, and my bottle of champagne, I almost stumble, gawking up as Tadd steps out of his office and directly into my path. Craning my neck to look up at him, I don't miss the way his smile totally contradicts the darkness in his gaze.

I force a smile.

"Who's sending *you* roses?"

"None of *your* business," I sass, stepping around him and hurrying all the way back to my desk, thankful for the semblance of privacy my cubicle walls provide.

I huff a breath, gathering my wits, looking from the gaudy display of roses to the white gift bag secured by a black ribbon. Tucking my hair behind my ears, I slowly tug on the ribbon, opening the bag, gasping when I find MASON glaring back at me in big bold letters.

"Oh my God," I groan as realization settles low in my belly.

Pulling the sorry excuse for a *gift* out of its bag, the white and black jersey unfurls in my hands. I hold it up, studying it with serious disdain. I hope he doesn't actually expect me to wear this thing.

Shoving the Thunder paraphernalia back inside the bag, I'm tempted to pop the bottle of Veuve right here at my desk; it's five o'clock somewhere, right? Instead, I take my phone out and scroll to my messages.

> Me: For future reference, I'm more of a chocolates girl.

Asshat: I'll have you know those roses cost me 400 big ones!

Me: Sucker. A box of chocolates would've set you back no more than ten bucks.

Asshat: I take it you got the gift, too?

I snap a photo of the jersey crumpled up in the bag and insert it into my message.

Me: Yeah, thanks. So thoughtful.

Asshat: Wear it tonight.

Me: Can't I just wear a team scarf or something.

Asshat: You need to have my name on your back.

Me: Branding a woman with your name on her back. How 1950s.

Asshat: It's basic dating-a-hockey-player 101.

Me: I must've missed that class in college.

Asshat: Lucky you got me as your tutor then, huh?

I roll my eyes.

Me: I've never been to a game before. Where do I even go?

Asshat: Madison Square Garden.

I scoff at his response.

Me: No shit.

Asshat: When you get there, Andy will meet you and take you where you need to go. Then after the game you'll come down to the locker room and I'll meet you there so you can swoon all over me.

Me: In case you can't tell via text, I'm literally bursting at the seams with excitement.

Asshat: You need to put your socials on private.

Me: Huh?

Asshat: I followed you on Insta today.

Me: Ok?

Asshat: My fans are on another level. Well, they're not really my fans because most of them don't know shit about me or hockey. But they seem to notice who I follow on social media.

Me: Weird.

Asshat: Yeah. Don't accept any DMs.

Interest sufficiently piqued, I scroll to *TikTok*, shocked to find the account I've never even used other than to look at cute dog content tagged in a whole bunch of videos. When I click on the first, I can't help but gasp when I see photos of me that have clearly been taken from my own personal *Instagram*, attacking me.

58 SHANN MCPHERSON

@HockeyGal89: I refuse to believe it until I see them together.

@MasonStan92: He went from Lola Grey to THAT???

@ThunderLover: A solid 4 with the lights on LOL

"They're so mean," I mutter under my breath.
A message notification pops up on the screen.

> Asshat: You're looking at TikTok aren't you?

> Me: Who are these people?

> Asshat: Mostly losers with nothing better to do.

I'm on the verge of a panic attack, quickly doing as he said and switching every social media profile I have from public to private.

When I agreed to be Robbie Mason's fake girlfriend, I knew I'd need to work on my patience in order to deal with someone as intolerable as he is. I certainly didn't think I'd need to deal with online bullying. The comments on the video are horrible, and they go on and on, based on nothing more than pure speculation because he *followed* me on *Instagram*? Man, I'm going to get eaten alive when we're actually spotted in public together.

Raking my teeth over my bottom lip, I briefly consider myself before tapping out a new message, sending it before I can stop myself.

> Me: So, why me, anyway?

> Asshat: What do you mean?

FAMOUS LAST WORDS   59

> Me: Why did you ask me to be your fake girlfriend? From what I can see on social media, you could have your pick of literally anyone. I'm certainly no Lola Grey, that's for sure.

> Asshat: Okay, first of all, don't ever mention her name to me again. Got that?

I bristle at the tone of his message. But before I can try to analyze it, he sends a follow up.

> Asshat: Second of all, who better to fake a relationship with than someone you can't fucking stand?

I scoff. But then I find myself looking at the mean comments again before forcing myself to close out of the stupid app.

> Me: I'm going to be the most hated woman in New York City.

> Asshat: The price of dating a superstar, baby.

> Me: Question: is your hockey helmet custom made?

> Asshat: Random, but no. Standard Bauer. Why?

> Me: Your ego's so inflated, I just assumed you'd need a custom size to fit your humongous head.

> Asshat: Nah. My cup's custom tho 🥒

> Me: Ew.

———

I spent most of my afternoon at work frantically searching the internet for ideas on what the hell one is supposed to wear to a hockey game, met with links to *Reddit* and *Pinterest*, and *Instagram* feeds full of beautiful women dressed in cute wintry outfits. *Puck bunny chic,* apparently. Who knew there were entire blogs dedicated to this exact topic? Not me, that's for sure.

But now, after leaving the office early so I could rush home to get ready, it seems my research has been in vain, because the longer I stand here, staring at myself in the reflection of the mirror, I can't help but come to the conclusion that instead of an adorable little *puck bunny,* dressed in a pair of jeans and Robbie's stupid jersey, I look more like Adam Sandler.

I've always been a little thicker. A size twelve for most of my adult life, at only five-foot-four, sometimes I can't help but feel like an actual meatball. Sure, I'm pretty. I'm not denying that. Big blue eyes, blonde hair that's probably my best asset. But my hips have always been wide, I've never had a thigh gap, I've often wished my D cup would miraculously shrink to a B cup overnight, and as a long-time sufferer of PCOS, I'm conscious of the extra weight I carry around my middle depending on what time of the month it is. Sometimes, being a woman really blows.

Realizing this is as good as it's going to get, I throw my head back with a groan.

Slipping on my checkerboard Vans, I shrug on my leather bomber jacket, and that's it. I'm done. I mean, let's face it, I'm definitely not winning any *puck bunny* awards any time soon, but maybe I'll get lucky and take home runner-up in some Adam Sandler lookalike competition.

With a quick mental pep talk, I shove my things into my purse and make my way to Madison Square Garden to watch my fake boyfriend chase a stupid puck around a stupid ice rink. Because what else would a single girl rather do on a Friday night in New York City?

God, I can't believe I got myself into this mess.

CHAPTER 10

FRAN

've only ever been to Madison Square Garden once, to see One Direction when I was fourteen. And that was understandably chaotic because, I mean, *hello*, it was One Direction.

You expect mayhem with a bunch of hysterical teenagers swooning over the biggest boy band in the world, but I certainly wasn't expecting the same scene to be occurring outside the Garden for some silly little hockey game.

It's legitimate chaos. I'm pushed and shoved by eager fans, shouted at by a group of frat-looking guys trying to get me to join in in some sort of war cry. It's almost too much. I'm only thankful that once I pass through the overzealous throng crowding the main gates and show my pass to an official looking man that I spot Andy.

"Hey, you made it." Andy tucks his phone in his pocket, his gaze doing a sweep of me.

"Hey." With a reluctant smile, I remove my jacket, suddenly feeling very self-conscious with MASON splayed across my back like a damn billboard.

Obviously picking up on my trepidation, Andy places his hand at the small of my back and leads me through a cordoned off doorway, and together we follow a long corridor before coming to the end where a woman wearing a pant suit greets us with a no-bullshit smile. She nods at Andy before scanning the barcode on my pass, directing us through another door.

"This way." Andy points, and we continue down a hallway until we come to a set of doors that barely contains the commotion coming from the other side.

Andy pulls open one side of the double doors, and I'm immediately taken aback as the expanse of the MSG arena comes into view. The sounds, the smells, the dizzying view of what looks like a million people. I don't know what I was expecting, but it definitely wasn't this.

"We're just down this way." Andy points down the steps before leading me about half way down the aisle, just a few rows behind the bench where I assume the players will sit.

"Hoffman!" A voice booms.

"Hi, Bob." Andy shakes an older man's hand. "How's the wife?"

"Still alive." The man smirks, surprising me with his words.

Andy laughs hollowly, and I can only assume—and hope— the man was joking.

The older man glances at me then, arching a bushy white brow. "And who do we have here?"

Andy places his hand on my shoulder. "Bob, this is Fran. Robbie Mason's… girlfriend."

Thankfully, I'm the only one who seems to notice the pause.

The man, *Bob*, stands then, holding a hand out for me. "Well, welcome to the New York Thunder, Fran. I'm Bob Oakley."

I shake the man's proffered hand, smiling up at him.

"We're real excited for your boy to join us," Bob says with a smirk. "You just make sure you keep him in line for us, won't ya?"

I smile tightly.

FAMOUS LAST WORDS   **63**

"First time at a game, Fran?"

I nod, my eyes scanning the overwhelming sight. "Yes."

"It's a sell out." Bob chuckles, indicating the crowd. "People love a comeback story."

I don't know if I like this man or not, but I assume he's someone important, so I maintain the saccharine smile that makes my cheeks ache.

"Bob." Andy nods, taking my elbow and leading me further along the row to our designated seats.

"That was Bob Oakley," Andy murmurs as we take our seats. "He owns the franchise."

I glance back at the older man who, on closer inspection, is sitting rather close to a woman at least half his age, her pert breasts pressed inappropriately against his arm as he leans in, whispering something in her ear that causes her to throw her head back and laugh.

"Let me guess, that's his *granddaughter*?" I say drolly.

Andy chuckles, biting back his smirk. And as he goes back to his phone, I look around, taking it all in. It's an eye-opener, that's for sure. People decked out in fan gear, excited children cheering and holding signs with what I presume to be the names of their idols written on them. The refreshing chill in the air, the slightly nauseating scent of hot dogs and popcorn, the distant sound of music being lost to the consistent roar of the crowd. It's like nothing I've ever experienced before. The energy is electric; I can feel it vibrating up through the cement floor and all the way through to my bones and, for the first time in a long time, I actually feel like I'm living in the moment instead of just existing in it.

Suddenly, I feel my phone vibrate from my purse. Pulling it out, I'm confused by the name glaring back at me from the screen.

Tadd: I want to see you.

I roll my eyes. He must be drunk.

Me: No.

Tadd: We're good together.

I almost laugh.

Me: No, we aren't.

Tadd: I miss you.

Despite the fact that Tadd and I haven't been a thing for more than six months, these sorts of messages aren't uncommon. But they usually come much later in the evening. When he's drunk and more than likely lucked out with the ladies in whatever bar or nightclub he's in.

Me: What do you want, Tadd?

Tadd: Meet me for dinner.

Okay, now he's just annoying me.

Me: I'm busy.

Tadd: Doing what?

Me: Absolutely none of your business.

Tadd: Where are you?

Oh my God, he cannot be serious.

Tadd: Who are you with?

> Tadd: Are you with whoever sent you the
> roses?

Suddenly the lights go dim and I snap my head up, startled by an obvious shift in the energy that sweeps through the arena, an ear-splitting roar causing me to flinch. I tuck my phone back into my purse without bothering to respond to Tadd. He's drunk. And clearly delusional.

"What's going on?" I ask Andy, my gaze flitting about, searching for the source of the excitement.

"Game time." Andy flashes me an excited grin, jutting his chin in the direction of the rink.

I follow his gaze as bright lights and lasers start to dart about the crowd, the ice illuminating, glowing like a beacon as the opening chords of AC/DC's "Thunderstruck" start cranking throughout, bringing the crowd to their feet.

Andy stands, and I look around to see that I'm currently one of the only able-bodied people still seated. Reluctantly, I make my way to my feet, almost jumping out of my skin the moment every person in the place starts punching the air and chanting in unison to the song. "Thunder!"

It's a little terrifying, if I'm honest. Like some sort of deranged cult. But I'd be lying if I said it doesn't get my heart racing.

Andy nudges me, and I glance at him to find him laughing, probably at me because no doubt I look entirely out of place standing like a stick in the mud with my arms folded across my chest. He nudges me again, and I roll my eyes, relenting and jabbing my fist into the air with everyone else, finding myself smiling as I do, which is when the arena erupts, cheering as a succession of hulking ice hockey players start skating out onto the ice, eliciting pure mayhem from the crowd.

It's an entire production. The lasers. The song. The hysteria. And I now realize I was wrong; a One Direction concert has nothing on an NHL game.

My gaze lands on the last player to hit the ice—number nine —the player who causes the crowd to lose their ever-loving shit.

Robbie breaks away from his teammates and does a slow yet determined lap of the rink, seemingly in the zone. If it weren't for his last name emblazoned across his back, I wouldn't even know it's him. He looks taller than normal thanks to the added inches of the skates, imposing with all that extra padding and more than a little intimidating.

As he continues his lap, chewing on his mouthguard, he waves up into the crowd, but then he comes to such a sudden stop on his skates it causes shards of ice to spray up into the air, only adding to the theatrics. And it's then I realize exactly what he's doing.

My stomach drops, eyes widening when they meet his. *No.*

As if he can read my thoughts, Robbie grins around his mouthguard, flashing that trademark cocky smile, dimples and all. *Yes.*

Tipping his chin in my direction, he lifts his stick, points it at his chest—his goddamn heart—before aiming it directly at me with a wink.

When I see my face suddenly projected on the Jumbotron, a part of me dies. Sinking into my chair, my cheeks flame with embarrassment as the excitement of the crowd ricochets around the arena.

I glare down at Robbie, shaking my head when he offers me a devious smirk, chuckling to himself as he skates off to join the rest of his teammates in preparation for the national anthem. *Asshole.*

CHAPTER 11

ROBBIE

I can't remember the last time I ever worked my ass off as much as I have in this game. I've fucking near killed myself, and for what? For the Wolves to come in and tear us apart in the third. We were actually winning, 3-1. Now we're tied in overtime because Rusty Morris can't control a puck to save his goddamn life. Dude should've retired fucking years ago.

With twelve seconds left on the clock, I take a heavy hit, smashed up against the boards and pinned there by two of the Wolves' third line goons. As their left winger breaks away and rounds the crease, I manage to shake off my opponents, spinning around just in time to see Dallas save a slapshot, every player scrambling to secure the puck.

It's knocked out of the scrum and secured by the Wolves' center who must not see me approach because he stupidly passes it to their right winger, giving me a chance to intercept.

There's a moment of clarity, as the deafening roar of the crowd fades into nothingness, my thudding heartbeat and ragged breaths all I can hear. It's now or never. With three seconds remaining, I secure the puck between my skates and my stick, cradling it as I break through two Wolves' players launching at me.

Taking off down the ice, I skate with everything I have toward the net, and then, from the top of the circles, I send the puck sailing the rest of the way with a trademark Robbie Mason danger shot, holding my breath as the Wolves' goalie throws himself in front of it, a fraction of a second too early, the lamp lighting up nanoseconds before the final siren sounds.

Done.

Satisfied, I turn to skate back to our bench, when I'm inundated by my teammates swarming in, jumping on me until I'm taken to the ice and piled upon in the kind of celebration you'd expect from a championship win. And it's in this very moment, seeing the unshed tears in the eyes of my teammates, catching a glimpse of the crowd on their feet cheering, the emotion in the air palpable, that I realize something; so far in my career, I've scored the winning goal in countless games, so often that it somehow became expected of me. And without realizing it, it was that expectation that took the joy away. Just another goal, just another win, and onto the next. But here, tonight, scoring the winning goal in my first game with a team that hasn't won a round one game in three seasons, I finally understand what I lost over the last year, what I've been missing—passion for the game that I love. And man, it feels fucking good to be back.

———

Shrugging on my button down, I stifle a groan, my body objecting to the movement. I look down, running my fingers over the angry purple welt bruising the skin below my ribs.

I spent more time against the boards tonight than any game I've ever played. Charged at, cross checked from behind, high-sticked. It wasn't until I was blatantly speared in my gut that the

FAMOUS LAST WORDS   69

ref finally called a penalty, and only because the footage was being shown on the Jumbotron at the time.

"Mason!"

Jumping, I pull my shirt closed, covering my injuries before turning to find Coach looking at me with that same scowl of disdain he wears so well.

"Yes, Coach?"

He says nothing, just looks at me long and hard, brow furrowed with an angry crease, lips downturned in a perma-frown.

With my jaw set tight, I don't back down, keeping my chin held high. I mean, I won the fucking game. What can he possibly have to bitch me out about now?

"Good game," Coach mutters, nodding once before turning and disappearing into the adjoining office.

I stare at the space he just occupied as I button my shirt, wondering for a moment if I just imagined that whole interaction. Was that a compliment? I'm pretty sure it was, despite it looking as if he wanted to punch me in the dick.

"Unfortunately, that's as good as it gets, my guy."

I turn, finding Josef, our second line winger grinning at me from his locker as he towel dries his long blond hair.

"Huh?" I tip my chin at him, confused by the cryptic comment hidden within his thick Icelandic accent.

"Draper." He laughs. "He's a hard ass. But him telling you good game? It's basically the equivalent of him telling you he loves you."

"Oh, yeah..." I manage a light laugh, grabbing my suit jacket. But I'm stopped by what sounds like an argument starting in the showers, my ears pricking at Dallas's Texan accent uncharacter-istically raised.

"Don't tell me how to do my fucking job when you can't even do your own, bro!"

A humorless laugh follows, and I'm pretty sure it's Rusty. Great.

"My six-year-old daughter could've stopped that goal!"

Tossing my jacket back into my locker, I hurry through to the showers to make sure everything's copacetic, but when I see Dallas and Rusty standing toe to toe, surrounded by the rest of the guys, my brows knit together. What the fuck is going on? And I know this is the shower room, but why the fuck is Dallas just standing there, butt-ass naked?

"Maybe learn how to control a fucking puck."

Someone laughs and Dallas grins, casually drying his dick with a towel.

Rusty scoffs, glancing back at the crowd they've garnered, his eyes spearing me through the steam, and narrowing in a way I've become accustomed to. Here we fucking go.

"Yeah, well, maybe if our new *star* D-man could pry himself off the boards once in a while, Koslov wouldn't have even made it over the blue line."

I snort because yeah, whatever bud. You try having three men target you for the best part of an hour and a half and see how you do. I say nothing though, because I'm in no position to be starting shit with my new captain, considering my recent history.

Dallas throws his thumb in my direction. "You're talking about the D-man who scored two of our four goals tonight?"

Rusty says nothing.

Dallas scoffs. "The fact that half their team was too busy cornering Mason should've meant that you could get through their line easier. Instead, you kept fucking up, turning over the puck, and now you're doing what you do best—" Grin still in place, Dallas leans closer, his face less than a few inches from Rusty's as he continues, "Blaming everybody else."

Rusty pushes Dallas in his chest. His naked chest. And frankly, there's so much skin on display, it's starting to get weird up in here. And since no one else seems to be stepping in, I decide to take the lead, shouldering my way through the barricade of onlookers.

"Come on, you guys." I stand next to Dallas, offering his dick an unimpressed glance and quirking a brow at him which he thankfully takes as a hint, wrapping his towel around his waist.

I throw my hands in the air. "We won. Quit your bitching, and let's focus on Monday's game against the Bucks." I spear Rusty with a pointed look because he's the goddamn team captain and should know better than to be fighting with his naked goalie.

"Whatever," Rusty mutters, turning to step into one of the shower stalls.

Dallas looks to me, eyes incredulously wide as he shakes his head. I turn, leading the way back out to the locker room and he follows.

"A guy can't even enjoy a post-game shower without assholes trying to blame him for their own fuck ups!" Dallas says behind me, and I can tell by the tone of his voice he's saying it loud enough to get a rise out of Rusty. I roll my eyes.

"You coming for a beer?"

I stop at my locker, shrugging on my suit jacket, trying not to wince at the pain in my side. "Nah. Can't. Curfew," I remind him.

"Dude!" Dallas guffaws, slapping my arm. "It's our first game one win in like… *forever*. I'm sure they'll let you off just for one night, considering we wouldn't have won without you."

I shake my head although he's probably right. But the truth is—the truth I haven't told anyone yet, not even Andy—I'm sober. I have been for more than a month. Not that I ever had an issue with alcohol. Although the media chose to tell a different story. Drugs. Alcohol. Women. You name it, they wrote it. I am the prodigal bad boy of hockey, after all. But what they don't know, what no one knows, is that I stopped drinking after everything went down because there was one night, when I was drunk and alone, that I found myself standing on the Wabasha Street bridge, staring down at the Mississippi, contemplating shit I never want to think about again in my life. I can't risk getting to that state of intoxication again; my mom needs me.

"No can do." I shrug, hitching my bag onto my shoulder, ready or not for the big reveal. "Actually, um, my girl's here. Gonna have a quiet night in, if you know what I mean." I wink suggestively, trying so hard to keep a straight face when the actual idea of doing anything even remotely *suggestive* with Fran fucking Keller is both nauseating and laughable. Although, I must admit, seeing her tonight on her feet, cheering for me, was kind of cool. And her face up on the Jumbotron when I pointed my stick at her? Fucking priceless.

"Your *girl*?" Dallas spins around, eyes comically wide, gawking at me in a combination of shock and disappointment. "Wait! You have a *girlfriend*?"

I can't help but laugh at the tone in his voice when he says *girlfriend* like it's a dirty word, as if the sheer notion is absurd and disgusting.

Hitching my bag higher on my shoulder, I nod.

Dallas's lips twist to the side momentarily before he asks, "She got any hot friends?"

I snort, shaking my head at him. Dude is such a man whore.

"Good game tonight, bro," Dallas says, clasping his hand with mine and pulling me into a side hug.

I'm fully aware that he's still only wearing a towel, but I allow it. It almost feels like I'm making a friend. And if I'm being honest, it's been a long time between friends. *Real* friends, at least.

The second I step out of the locker room and into the tunnel, I'm inundated by kids. Kids fucking everywhere.

"Robbie? Can I get a photo?"

I'm temporarily blinded by the flash of a camera.

"Robbie, will you sign my jersey?"

Sharpies galore are thrust in my face.

"Robbie!"

"Robbie!"

"Robbie!"

My heart rate increases, and it's suddenly stifling. It's not that I don't like kids. I love them. Their excitement is genuine. Hell, I used to be these kids. But sometimes it's hard to feel like nothing more than an object.

I go through the motions, signing what I can, smiling whenever I see a phone shoved in my face, but I'm not really present, and I hate that. These kids wait around all night to see me, and most of them probably live out of the city. I owe it to the kids; they're the reason I'm here.

Just as I'm getting done with the last of the adorable little hockey wannabes, I'm mid-autograph on an oversized Thunder foam finger when I glance up, doing a double-take when my eyes land on Keller. She's oblivious to me, talking animatedly to a hot brunette I've never seen before, and something unfamiliar stirs in my chest. Strangely, it's got nothing to do with the hot brunette and everything to do with Fran Keller. What the hell?

As one of the kids says something to me, I'm not even listening; my attention is wholeheartedly captivated by the bane of my existence, standing there wearing *my* jersey. I know I told her to wear it. But seeing her now is doing something to me that I do not fucking like.

I don't know. Maybe I took more blows to the head tonight than I remember because, fuck me, with those tight jeans hugging her thick thighs and curvy ass, her blonde hair cascading down over her shoulders, and my name adorned across her back... call me fucking crazy but does she look... hot?

At that moment, as if she can hear my thoughts, Fran turns her head, her big blue eyes meeting mine. And the genuine smile I saw on her face seconds ago immediately falls. And thank God, too, because it's like a refreshing slap to the face; she's still the same old stick-up-her-ass Keller, the girl who made me shit myself during my first game with Belmont Prep when I was seventeen.

I release the breath I've been holding and hand the Sharpie back to one of the kids' parents, smiling down at my fan club of fourteen-year-olds before stepping around them and closing the distance between me and my fake fucking girlfriend.

CHAPTER 12

FRAN

I stand back against the wall, watching Robbie start toward me. And holy shit. The man can wear a suit like nobody's business. I find myself unable to look away. Dressed in a navy two piece that fits him like a glove, there's a serious swagger to his strides, and it's almost as if he's in slow motion.

Pushing his damp hair out of his eyes, Robbie lifts his chin at me, offering that cocky smirk as he comes closer. And come on. I'm not a complete ignoramus; I know the man is attractive. In that conceited way that's obnoxious and a complete turnoff. Absolutely *not* my type, but I can see how he has his fangirls in a chokehold.

"Hey, *baby*," Robbie murmurs, his voice low and raspy, doing that thing to me again. The thing I refuse to acknowledge because if I pretend it's not happening, then it is *not* happening.

He wraps an arm around me, pulling me close, and my body goes rigid at his touch. I hold a hand against his unsurprisingly rock-hard chest in a way that I hope comes across as a tender, loving touch when, in actual fact, it's me holding him at bay because if he gets any closer, I might very well punch him in the dick and risk blowing our cover.

"Who's your friend?" Robbie lifts his chin at Hannah, and I don't miss the spark of interest flare in his dark eyes. Men are so obvious, it's embarrassing.

Before I can respond, Robbie extends his hand to Hannah. "Robbie Mason. Hero of the night."

I almost laugh out loud when Hannah glances at me, one of her eyebrows arching slightly higher. I can tell she's biting back a guffaw as she shakes his proffered hand. "Hannah Draper. Daughter of your coach."

My gaze flits to Robbie just in time to see his face paling, Adam's apple bobbing with a hard swallow. "Um, oh. H-hey—" He squares his shoulders. "N-nice to meet you."

I'm forced to contain my smirk, pressing my lips together, because Robbie Mason bumbling all over himself is hilarious.

"You played a good game," Hannah says.

Before Robbie can collect himself enough to respond, we're interrupted by a tall drink of water who looks as if he stepped straight off the cover of the latest *GQ*, dressed in a Gucci monogram suit that hugs him in all the right places and on anyone else would look utterly ridiculous, fashionable scruff shadowing his jaw, golden brown hair damp and tousled to perfection. Is being unfairly attractive an ice hockey prerequisite or what?

"Yo, Han, how's your bod, baby?" the man says by way of greeting, an obvious southern accent laced through his words.

Hannah looks at me and scoffs, rolling her eyes before craning her neck to spear the man with a bored glance. "Dallas, don't you have a bevy of desperate bunnies to go chase?"

The man, *Dallas*, snickers, and like a walking, talking cliché proceeds to place a worn Stetson on his head. And I can't stop staring at him. Who knew I had a cowboy kink? When his green eyes land on me, I actually feel my knees weaken.

"And who do we have here?" Without waiting for an introduction, Dallas steps forward, holding his hand out. "Dallas Shaw, voted hottest goalie in the league, two years in a row."

Hannah shakes her head, muttering something under her breath. And I can't help but smile. I really like her. It was by sheer chance I ran into her outside the bathroom during the second period. We immediately hit it off, and thank God, too, because she helped make tonight a little more tolerable.

Pointing his finger between us, Robbie finally speaks. "Dallas Shaw, Fran Keller." His eyes meet mine as he continues, "My girlfriend."

With a nervous smile, I accept Dallas's hand, but instead of shaking it like a normal person, he bows his head and presses a kiss to the back of my fingers, lips lingering far longer than socially acceptable.

"It's a pleasure to meet you. Robbie's told me absolutely *nothing* about you, and I can see why." His gaze is almost lewd as it sweeps over me from head to toe, but in a weird way it's not creepy like it probably should be. I can tell this guy is nothing more than a harmless flirt, and it's kind of endearing.

"How'd you enjoy the game, Fran?" Dallas asks.

"It was good…" I trail off, glancing at Robbie. "Is it normal for you to be pinned against the boards that much, though?"

Robbie's face becomes serious.

Hannah hides a smile behind her hand.

Dallas laughs so loud he attracts the attention of everyone around us. Smacking Robbie's shoulder, his laughter subsides long enough to say, "Shots fired, son."

"Yeah, yeah," Robbie mutters, rolling his eyes, although there's a smile hinting at his lips, and I have no idea what's so funny, but whatever.

"Robbie, man, you sure you don't wanna come for a drink with the guys? I'm sure Hannah can convince dear ol' daddy to let you off the hook for one night." Dallas nudges Hannah who, in return, glares up at him in disgust.

"Girlfriends are welcome too, Franny," Dallas adds, winking at me, and I swear I almost giggle.

Robbie snakes his arm around me again, pulling me impossibly close. "Nah, man. Like I said—" he glances down at me, lifting one of his eyebrows conspiratorially, "—romantic night in with my girl."

I swear to God, I almost laugh. In fact, I have to turn away because, between the look in his eyes and the pathetic smile on his lips, it's too much. Who's even buying this?

"Aw, you two are so adorable together," Hannah whispers, nudging me with her elbow.

All I can do is smile despite my gritted teeth, inwardly groaning at the feel of Robbie's hand resting far too low on my hip and squeezing me, as if he knows just how much it's pissing me off.

———

The second we get into Andy's Porsche SUV, I slap Robbie around the back of his head. Not hard, just hard enough.

"What the hell was that for?" He rubs the back of his head, glaring at me over his shoulder.

I spear him with a dagger glare. "For touching my ass, you perv!"

"Robbie!" Andy chides.

"I was just trying to make it look believable." Robbie shrugs, laughing under his breath as Andy clears the parking garage boom gate, pulling out into the Midtown traffic. Thankfully, the windows are tinted enough so that the Thunder fans lining the sidewalk outside the Garden probably can't see in, but I still shield my face as best as I can, just in case.

The plan was to leave together, and Andy will drop Robbie off at the hotel he's staying at until escrow closes on his apartment, then drop me at my apartment before continuing to his home in Park Slope. And as Andy and Robbie are busy discussing the game, all I can do is doom scroll social media, finding countless pictures of me from tonight, wearing Robbie Mason's jersey. I've gone viral and for all the wrong reasons. I feel sick to my stomach.

"Are you fucking kidding me?"

Startled by Robbie's outburst, I look up just as Andy is slowing down to a stop at the curb outside the hotel on West 44th, where a throng of people appear to be crowding the entrance.

"What's going on?" I ask, watching as the people in the crowd turn to take in the car, many of whom are men holding cameras with huge lenses. Suddenly, I'm blinded by a barrage of flashes, and all I can do is cover my face with my hand.

"It must be the no press clause," Andy mutters cryptically, tapping something into his phone.

I look at Robbie for answers.

"I'm not allowed to talk to the press," he explains with a sigh, staring out the window as the flashes continue. "Which is ridiculous. Of course, they wanna talk to me... I won the fucking game," he scoffs.

My heart races as I chew on the inside of my cheek. "So, what do we do now?"

Andy heaves a sigh. "Fran, would you mind going up?"

My brows knit together because surely I heard him wrong. "What?"

"I know I said I'd drop you off after Robbie, but it's going to look like some sort of PR stunt if he goes in and you come with me—" he shrugs a shoulder, offering me an apologetic look. "I'll have a car here the second the coast is clear."

My jaw drops as I glance out at the sea of photographers and journalists waiting impatiently on the sidewalk. There're even some eager fans in the mix. "What if they *don't* leave?"

Robbie turns around in his seat then, a devilish smirk tugging on his lips. "Slumber party, baby."

"I'd rather jump off the roof," I snap back.

"Just head on up," Andy interjects. "I'll sort it out."

My shoulders sag on an exhale. I do believe Andy when he says he'll sort it out, but going up to Robbie's hotel room with him was so not part of the deal.

With a muttered curse, I grab my bag and my jacket, unfastening my seatbelt right as the passenger door is yanked open with gusto, the silence in the car inundated by too many people trying to talk at once.

"Robbie, over here!"

"Robbie, what did Lance Draper say to you after the game?"

"Robbie, how does it feel to score the winning goal?"

Robbie stands with his back to the reporters, waiting for me with an annoyed look on his face like I'm taking too long. Fuck him. My gaze dips to his hand held out for me, and reluctantly I take it, holding on to it tightly.

I'm careful as I step out of the SUV, ignoring the cameras and their bright flashes as best as I can, keeping my face void of emotion despite wanting to cower beneath the weight of the unwanted attention, the stares, the raised voices. It's all too much. I choose to focus on the ground, allowing Robbie to lead me through the throng. And I can tell he's done this before, ignoring the camera lenses and microphones that are being thrust in his face like a seasoned pro, all the while holding my hand firmly behind him, keeping me close.

By the time we make it inside the safety of the lobby, ushered in by hotel staff, I allow myself to finally breathe.

Sweat pricks the back of my neck. My face is hot, heart hammering against my ribs, knees trembling. I'm on autopilot, staring blankly at Robbie's back as we continue through the sleek lobby and into a waiting elevator. It isn't until the doors glide closed that I realize I'm still holding his hand. But as I look down to where our fingers are intertwined, I notice Robbie's holding mine just as tight. As if he's noticed too, he quickly pulls away.

"Ew," I mutter, folding my arms across my chest with a huff.

FAMOUS LAST WORDS 81

"You have dead people hands," he murmurs, pulling his phone from his pocket and proceeding to ignore me by focusing intently on the screen.

When I catch a glimpse of what he's looking at on his phone —highlights of the game he literally *just* played—I can't help but wonder if he could be more obsessed with himself.

I roll my eyes, staring up at the counter as it ticks slowly with every level we pass on our incline, considering whether or not I should press the button to get off at the next floor. Walking down fifty-two flights of stairs sounds a lot less excruciating than being stuck in a hotel room with an asshat.

CHAPTER 13

FRAN

When the elevator chimes our arrival on the fifty-eighth floor, Robbie is out before the doors even finish opening, as if he can't get away from me fast enough.

I make sure to keep a few feet of distance as I trail him along the corridor until he comes to a stop at a door at the very end. He pulls a card from his pocket, swiping it against the scanner, the lock releasing with a soft beep. When he proceeds inside, I'm surprised when he actually holds the door open for me; I half-expected him to let it slam in my face.

Stepping over the threshold, the room illuminates automatically, and I take it all in. A giant bed, a separate living area, floor-to-ceiling windows that look out over New York City lit up against the darkness of the night sky. This hotel room is fancy, and at least three times the size of my studio apartment.

Caught in a daze, I walk directly across the room and stop at the window, taking in the spectacular view.

"You hungry?"

"No," I reply bluntly.

"You sure?" he asks. "They could be out there all night."

At that, I spin around, gawping at him when he looks up from the room service menu.

"I am *not* staying here all night with you!"

He rolls his eyes. "What do you want me to do? Tie all the bedsheets together and kick out one of the windows so you can scale down the building?"

He actually has the audacity to grin. *Ugh.* He's so infuriating.

Stomping my way around the sofa, I flop down onto the cushion with a dramatic huff. And yes, I'm fully aware I'm acting like a child, but this is such bullshit.

"This is such bullshit," I mutter my thoughts out loud, folding my arms across my chest.

Robbie goes to speak, but I cut him off. "Coming back to your hotel was *never* part of the deal."

He snorts. "Yeah, like I'm totally jazzed about—"

"Spending my Friday night watching a bunch of moronic jocks chase a stupid puck around an ice rink is bad enough. Now to be stuck *here* with *you*…" I trail off, narrowing my eyes as I look him up and down.

He blinks at me and, after a moment, holds the room service menu up in the air. "Yeah, so, anyway, do you want food or not, because I'm fucking starving."

"No, I don't want *food*. I *want* to go *home*," I snap, bitchier than intended, but I mean, can you blame me? I'm basically being held hostage in a hotel room with the man who made my life a living hell in high school, and all he's worried about is food.

With another huff, I cross one leg over the other and twist my body away from him.

"Suit yourself," Robbie mutters, picking up the hotel phone.

After he finishes speaking with room service, the television suddenly comes to life, startling me. I look up to see a replay of tonight's Thunder versus Wolves game playing on the screen, and I can't help but roll my eyes. I spear him with an incredulous look, but I'm rendered shocked when I notice he's causally unbuttoning his shirt, shrugging it off, as if he's somehow forgotten that I'm sitting right here.

"Um, what the hell do you think you're doing?"

Robbie looks at me as tosses his shirt over the back of the armchair. His brows knit together, staring at me like I've lost my mind. "What?"

I wave a hand in the air, indicating his suddenly naked upper body.

He glances down at himself, and I find myself following his gaze. Damn. He's ripped. Broad shoulders, defined muscles, intricate tattoos covering his arms and much of his chest. It's then I notice Robbie's gleaming gaze on me, a knowing smirk curling his lips.

"Get a good look?"

I narrow my eyes. "You're practically naked and I'm literally sitting right here."

"You realize you're the first woman I've ever heard say that like it's a bad thing?"

I snort, pushing up from the couch. "You're *disgusting*."

He chuckles as I push past him, storming into the bathroom. Slamming the door shut, I lock it for good measure, leaning back against it to collect a breath. I don't even need to use the restroom, but like hell I'm just going to sit out there while he disrobes.

Scanning the bathroom, I'm hardly surprised to see that it's a mess. Calvin Klein boxer briefs are lying on the floor, and I doubt they're clean. A wet towel hangs over the glass shower screen. And there, in the sink, possibly my biggest ick of all: dried toothpaste spittle. So gross.

I rest my hands on the countertop, looking at my reflection for a long moment. I'm a mess. My eyes are red-rimmed and tired, cheeks flushed with frustration, hair a wild nest.

Splashing my face with cool water, I towel it dry, securing my hair into a messy pile on top of my head, staring at myself for another few minutes. But when I realize I can't hide out in the bathroom all night, I heave another sigh and walk back out into the suite, but the moment I do, I'm stopped dead in my tracks because you have got to be fucking kidding me.

No, Robbie's not butt naked. In fact, it's almost worse. He's lying on the bed wearing nothing but a pair of gray fucking sweatpants. *Gray.*

I remain frozen in place, forcing my gaze anywhere but in his general direction because if I'm not mistaken there's an obvious dick outline in those pants, and, like a solar eclipse, I don't trust myself not to stare directly at it.

"You good?" Robbie asks after a beat.

I meet his eyes—*only* his eyes—finding something taunting in his dark gaze as he stares at me from the bed. One brow arched slightly higher, almost cunning, his intense gaze trails me from head to toe, making me shift my weight awkwardly from foot to foot.

It's like he knows. I mean, of course he knows. He's hot, and he knows it, that much is a given. But there's something else in his eyes, something I can't quite figure out, and I find myself suddenly nervous.

"Uh, yeah," I mutter when I remember he asked me a question. Tucking a loose strand of hair behind my ear, I scurry around the bed and directly to the sofa, as far from Robbie as the room will allow.

"Your phone was going off."

Sitting down, I reach for my purse, pulling out my phone to find six missed calls and seven new messages. My brows knit together as I open the call log, but the minute I see Tadd's name listed multiple times, my face falls.

I open his latest text, gasping at the screenshot of the picture taken of Robbie and me when we were walking out of the arena together, hand-in-hand.

Oh my God.

> Tadd: What the fuck is this??

And, because I'm a sucker for punishment, I listen to his most recent voice message, immediately regretting my decision the moment I hear his slurred words.

"I guess now I know why you've been ignoring my calls..."

I almost laugh because no, Tadd, I'd have ignored your call if I was in jail and you were my one shot at making bail.

"What the hell is going on, Fran? I tell you I miss you, that I think we should try again, and then I see on social media that you're... what? That you're dating some hockey player!" He scoffs. *"I know you miss me too. Don't think I haven't seen the way you look at me when you walk past my office. Don't think I haven't noticed the low-cut tops you wear around me. You want me. Remember how good we were together, how hard I made you come when I —"*

I quickly end the message, refusing to listen to his nonsense. I delete the voice message and the *five* others, shaking my head. Tadd talks a big game, but the truth is, I faked it every time.

I tuck my phone back into my purse and toss it onto the armchair by my jacket.

"Everything okay?"

I glance over my shoulder, finding Robbie's gaze on me instead of the television.

"Yeah," I say with a nonchalant shrug, staring up at the hockey game playing on the screen. It's switched to a different game, and when I notice the score in the corner, my interest piques.

"Your old team?"

"Yep."

Robbie's terse with his response, so I decide not to pry, instead watching the game. I don't know much about hockey, but I know it's probably not great when the score is 5-0, six minutes into the third period.

FAMOUS LAST WORDS   **87**

"I thought the Lions won last year…" I muse out loud.

A humorless chuckle comes from the bed, and I look back at him.

"They did," he says. "But then they released me, and their only other half-decent player is injured."

"Ben Harris?"

When I'm met with no response, I turn again, finding Robbie looking contemplatively at me, brow furrowed. "How'd you know that?"

I snort. "As if I wasn't going to Google you!"

He rolls his eyes, mutters something under his breath.

"What happened?" I press. "I mean, why'd you hit him?"

Robbie stares at the television, his face void of all emotion, save for the slightest crease etched between his brows. He's silent for so long, I'm convinced he's going to ignore my question. But then he lifts one of his broad shoulders in a shrug, drags a hand through his dark hair and meets my gaze. "He deserved it."

There's more. I can tell. I wonder if it has anything to do with Lola Grey, but I'm not willing to ask, because he warned me never to say her name again, and if we're going to be stuck in this hotel room together, I should probably not poke the bear. But then again, I've always been a nosy asshole.

"Is it to do with a certain… social media influencer?" I ask, blanching at the warning look in Robbie's eyes.

"I didn't say her name," I sass.

He tears his fingers through his hair again, huffing another hard exhale. "No, it doesn't have anything to do with *her*."

We're interrupted by a knock on the door.

"Who's that?" I gasp, worried it's some lunatic fan who might've snuck into the hotel.

"That'll be the food," Robbie says, stifling a groan as he forces himself up off the bed.

I manage to relax some, watching him pad toward the door, barefoot, gray sweats pulling criminally tight around his firm butt. *Ew.* Forcing myself to turn away, I watch as the St. Paul Lions get their firm butts handed to them instead.

Suddenly I'm hit with a smell that makes my stomach growl and I realize just how hungry I am. I haven't eaten since this morning.

From the corner of my eye, I watch Robbie wheel a cart into the room, removing shiny silver tops from plates and revealing a burger and fries, a cobb salad, an entire pizza, and a bowl of hot wings.

"Well, Keller, this food isn't gonna eat itself."

"I told you I don't want anything." My stomach objects, but I'm far too stubborn.

Robbie cocks his head to the side offering me a disbelieving look. "I heard your stomach rumble in the elevator on the way up here. Sounded like a goddamn Yeti."

I roll my eyes, ignoring him.

"Fine, whatever," he murmurs.

Moments later, Robbie's flopping down onto the sofa next to me, his big frame so close he's pressed right up against my side. A plate rests precariously on his knee, and he ignores me, staring at the television as he picks up the burger and takes a huge bite, groaning obnoxiously as he savors the taste.

My eyes narrow when he looks at me.

"What?" he asks with his mouth full of food.

"You have ketchup on your chin."

"Be a doll and lick it off for me."

I glare at him, but he simply grins, sticking his tongue out to try reach it before giving up and wiping at it with the back of his hand. Then licking it off his hand.

"You're so gross."

He chuckles. "You really hate me, huh?"

"Yes."

"Answer faster next time, seriously," he says drolly.

I shrug.

His gleaming eyes fall from my face and drag down, openly

lingering on my chest for a moment too long. And just as I'm about to tell him to stop staring at my tits, his gaze meets mine again, and that cocky smirk is back.

"What?" I sigh, although I'm not entirely sure I want to know.

He shrugs, popping a fry into his mouth. "You look surprisingly good in my jersey."

My traitorous cheeks flush of their own accord because, apparently, I'm pathetic.

"You sure did grow up, Keller," he adds, smirk lingering as he takes another big bite of his burger.

My heart stammers at his words, and I momentarily hate myself.

Thankfully, before any more can be said, we're saved by the shudder of vibration coming from behind us. We both jump, and I realize the sound is coming from the nightstand where Robbie's phone sits charging.

"It might be Andy," I say hopefully.

Robbie places his food onto the coffee table before showing off his agility with an oddly impressive commando roll over the back of the sofa. Hurrying to grab the device, he takes a seat on the side of the bed, reading whatever is on the screen, and I spring up, grabbing my jacket and purse, ready to flee.

"Is it Andy?" I ask, shrugging on my jacket.

Robbie nods, still looking at his phone.

"Is he sending a car?" I press impatiently.

"They're still down there," he says after a silent pause.

"No," I whisper as my hope dwindles.

"Andy says it's probably best to just wait it out for the night."

My jaw drops. "Are you serious?"

Robbie nods, a deep crease etched between his brows as he types something into his phone.

"Fucking *great*," I mutter, taking off my jacket again and tossing it and my purse back onto the armchair.

I kick off my Vans and move to the cabinetry lining the far

wall. Opening the door to the fridge, I find the stash of hotel goodies kept inside, helping myself to an expensive looking bottle of wine because if I have to stay here all night in a hotel room with Robbie Mason, you bet your ass I'm not doing it sober.

CHAPTER 14

ROBBIE

Tugging on my bottom lip, I stare at my phone, wondering what the hell I'm even doing.

Andy: I just called the night manager. He said everyone's gone. I'll order Fran a car.

Me: She's asleep.

Andy: Huh?

Me: She fell asleep.

Andy: So... wake her up.

Me: Nah, it's okay. She can just leave in the morning.

Andy: You're not fucking are you?

Me: Gross.

Maybe I've finally lost my mind. It was bound to happen eventually. I just never imagined I'd lose it over a girl I can't even stand.

Call me crazy, but I don't want Fran to leave. I've spent so much of my adult life alone in hotel rooms that it's nice to have someone here with me. Even if that person is Fran fucking Keller.

If I'm honest, I think something might've happened to me in the elevator on the way up here. Because I haven't been the same since. Being so close to her, just the two of us, confined to a tiny six-by-eight steel box, her sweet scent accosted every one of my senses. And don't even get me started on that fucking jersey. Why I didn't just grab her one from the merch closet I have no idea, but the fact that she's wearing *my* jersey—specifically made for me—that's some serious relationship shit. I'm a fucking idiot.

"Robbie?"

I startle, looking up from my phone finding Fran holding a wine bottle.

Oh, yeah. I think she asked me a question.

"Um, no." I shake my head. "None for me."

I switch my phone to sleep mode and place it face down on the nightstand, standing and wiping my suddenly clammy hands on the back of my sweats.

Fran shrugs, grabbing one of the glasses. "All the more for me."

I stop by the room service cart, looking down at all the food I ordered. "You gonna eat something now that you're stuck here, or what?"

Fran finishes filling her glass to the very brim, eyes scanning the food as she sips her wine.

"I can order something else if you want," I say, pointing to the card by the hotel phone. "Room service is open all night."

She takes a tentative step closer to the cart, eyeing the pizza.

"The pizza's pretty good," I add. "Truffle."

"Truffle pizza?" She arches a brow, glancing at me. "This place *is* fancy."

She takes a slice of the pizza and a napkin and carries it and her wine back to the sofa.

I remain standing on the spot, arms folded over my chest like an awkward weirdo wondering yet again what the hell I'm doing. Now that I know she's here all night, I'm at a loss. I clearly didn't think this through. I have to be up early for PT. Then we're flying out for a week-long road trip.

"So, what are we supposed to do now?"

I snap myself out of my thoughts, finding Fran looking at me as she takes a bite of her pizza. She closes her eyes a moment as if it's the best thing she's ever tasted, and my heart does an unfamiliar jump in my chest. What the ever-loving fuck was that? I rub at my sternum.

"Because I am not sitting here all night watching fucking hockey highlights," she adds.

Ah, there's that bossy asshole I know and hate. With a relieved sigh, I walk around the sofa and flop down next to her, grabbing the remote. I start surfing the channels, but there's not a lot on at this time of night.

"Don't you have Netflix or something?"

I shake my head, flashing her a grin. "Just ESPN."

She looks at me like I've sprouted another head. "What is wrong with you?"

I shrug. "I don't get a lot of time to watch TV. And when I do, it's usually game tape."

Again, she stares at me like I'm crazy. Then she reaches across and grabs her purse, pulling out her phone, and I watch her unlock the device, my eyes bulging when I see her screen. Fifteen missed calls and eleven new text messages.

"Someone's popular," I tease.

"Yeah," she scoffs, shaking her head dismissively. But then just as she ignores the notifications and scrolls to her Netflix app, the device starts ringing with a new call.

I catch a glimpse of the name flashing on the screen. "Who's Tadd?"

Fran presses the phone against her chest, shielding it from me. She spears me with a pointed look. "Has anyone ever told you it's rude to snoop?"

"Yeah." I shrug. "Hasn't deterred me though."

She rolls her eyes, holding her phone out, staring at it as *Tadd* continues calling. And I notice the way her shoulders fall with a heavy exhale.

"Tadd's my ex." She says it like she's ashamed.

"The same ex who was going to steal your listing?"

"Yep." With a resigned sigh, she continues. "He's one of the top agents at work. A real dick. Not long after I started, Tadd took me on as his assistant, and I stupidly fell for his bullshit."

I don't know why, but her tone is off, and I don't like it.

"We broke up six months ago when I found he was sleeping with an agent at another brokerage." She shakes her head as if she's suddenly remembering something horrible, trying to rid it from her mind, and I feel an incessant gnawing at the back of my neck.

"He mostly leaves me alone at work. But every now and again he'll call me late at night when he's drunk, asking to see me." She grimaces, holding up her phone right as it starts ringing again. "Case in point."

"Does he want you back?"

She laughs out loud, but it's a bitter sound, void of humor. "No. Tadd wants—" She pauses as if to consider her words. "Tadd wants someone gullible enough to put up with his shit. He doesn't realize that I'm no longer that person."

"Did he ever hurt you? Put his hands on you?" The question is out of my mouth before I can stop myself.

She scoffs. "Hands? No. Words? Yes."

I study her as she stares down at her wine. "What did he say?"

She shakes her head. "Your ass is too big. You shouldn't wear

FAMOUS LAST WORDS **95**

dresses that tight. If you lost a little weight, you'd be so much prettier. I only went out with you because I felt sorry for you. Who's going to want you now? You know, the usual."

I don't even know this guy, but I hate him with every fiber of my being. Who the fuck actually says those kinds of mean things to someone?

"Does he know about me?" When she looks at me again, I offer her my cockiest smirk despite the rage searing my insides.

I'm not sure if I'm imagining it, but I'm almost certain I catch a flush tinge her cheeks as she looks back down at her glass. "He saw that I got a box of roses delivered at work." She looks pointedly at me. "And he saw photos of us on the internet tonight."

"There're photos of us already?"

The screen on her phone lights up with yet another fucking call from this guy, and I can't help but smile because talk about timing. I snatch the device from Keller and hit answer.

"Robbie!" she hisses, covering her gaping mouth with her hand.

With the phone against my ear, I listen for a moment, not saying a word.

"It's about time you came to your senses, *sweetheart*," a low voice says, smacking with smugness.

"I ain't your fuckin' sweetheart, *bud*."

"I—" I imagine him glancing at the phone, checking he's dialed the right contact. He clears his throat, suddenly sounding very authoritarian as he demands, "Who is this?"

Frankly, I don't like his tone. "Who the fuck is *this*?"

Keller's eyes are wide as she stares at me, cheeks paling.

"Oh, you must be the hockey goon," he says with a derisive scoff.

Goon? I swear to God, I clench my jaw so tight I'm sure I feel a molar crack. "And you must be the irrelevant ex who can't seem to take no for a fuckin' answer."

"Put Fran on the phone," he responds with a bored tone, but

I can tell the irrelevant ex comment really irked him by the way his words are spoken through seemingly gritted teeth.

I glance at Keller to find her watching me with wide eyes. I flash her a reassuring grin, waving a hand placatingly. "No can do, bud. She's fast asleep. On my chest."

"Put her on the goddamn phone."

"No, I won't," I say slowly. "But I'll tell you what I will do." He goes to speak, but I cut him off. "If you don't stop calling, or texting, or harassing *my girl*—" My gaze flits to Keller to find her hanging onto every one of my words, and I wink at her. "Me and my hockey stick'll stop by for a visit, and I'll show you just how much of a fuckin' goon I can be. I'm from Dorchester, mother-fucker. We don't play nice, so don't fuckin' test me."

He's silent.

"You got that, *Chad*?"

"It's Tadd." He's positively seething.

I scoff. "Nah, bud. It's whatever the fuck I tell you it is." And before he can say anything more, I end the call, smirking down at the black screen as I imagine the fucker's face.

"Oh my God…" Keller whispers, her face fraught with panic when I meet her eyes.

I simply grin, handing her back the phone.

"He's going to go ballistic!" She tosses back her entire glass of wine in a few big gulps.

I relax into the sofa, kicking my feet up on the coffee table. "Can't wait to meet him."

"I need another drink." She hops up and makes a beeline for the fridge.

And as I track her movements, watching her, I don't miss the protective instinct that comes over me at the thought of that fuck face doing something to hurt her. And it's only then that I realize I actually give a shit. About Fran *fucking* Keller.

CHAPTER 15

FRAN

I groan as bright light burns through my eyelids, blinding me before I even wake up. My head throbs so bad, I'm sure it's about to implode.

"Kill me now," I croak.

Self-inflicted death is the only way to describe this level of hangover. In fact, I think I might still be drunk. I know they say the more expensive the wine, the less harsh the hangover, but FYI that's some straight-up bullshit. An entire bottle of wine—regardless if it's a six-dollar screw top from the corner liquor store, or a three-thousand-dollar vintage imported direct from the south of fucking France—is a guaranteed morning after regret.

My insides roil as I roll over, but then something hits me. Call it intuition mixed with a somewhat familiar scent that is both delicious and nauseating at the same time. My eyes fly open when I remember exactly where I am. *Oh shit.*

Against my better judgment, I sit up, immediately regretting my decision as I do, groaning as the sprawling hotel room starts to spin.

With one eye squeezed shut, I search the space around me, looking for what, I don't even know.

"Hello?" My voice is broken and hoarse, throat like sandpaper.

"Robbie?" My stomach lurches and I choke back the acid on my tongue as his name leaves my lips.

But when I'm met with nothing but the gentle whir of the recycled air coming through the ducts, panic slowly starts to settle over me.

I notice an unopened bottle of water sitting on the nightstand. Perched against it is a note written on the hotel stationery. My brows knit together, and with another unattractive groan, I reach for the note with a trembling hand.

Had to leave.
I have a week of away games.
Let yourself out.

Robbie

I'm not saying that after last night Robbie and I should be besties, but I'm kind of confused by the abruptness of his note. I heave a sigh, tossing it onto the bed beside me. Grabbing the water, I gulp back more than half of it without coming up for air.

I'm still dressed in my jeans and Robbie's jersey, and as far as I can tell, I slept alone if the makeshift bed of pillows and blankets lying on the sofa is anything to go by. *How the hell did his six-foot-three frame even fit on that thing?*

Dragging a hand over my face, I think back to last night, to what I remember.

I vaguely remember the phone call with Tadd. Oh God, those ramifications are going to be fun to deal with in the office on Monday.

I remember Netflix. I put on my latest obsession—one of those reality dating shows where they try to prove that looks aren't a main factor when it comes to falling in love. Which is total bullshit, by the way; we all know looks matter, and I don't care what anyone says. When Robbie wouldn't stop talking, I finally gave up and switched on *The Mighty Ducks* for shits and gigs. But as Emilio Estevez's stretch limousine slowly rolled onto the frozen lake, we lost interest in the film and actually started to get to know one another.

———

"Please tell me you did not try to dress like a puck bunny?" Robbie shook his head, covering his eyes with a hand while obviously trying not to laugh.

"Yeah." I shrugged. "That's what the Reddit posts were suggesting."

Throwing his head back with laughter, he clutched his stomach as if this was the funniest thing he'd ever heard.

"What is so damn funny?"

Grin still lingering, he steadied me with a serious look. "Keller, a puck bunny is—" he shook his head again, concealing another laughter bubble with a cough before clearing his throat "—a puck bunny is a chick who goes around trying to fuck hockey players."

I took a moment to consider what he was telling me. And, I mean, I'm not one to yuck anyone's yum, and if that's how "puck bunnies" like to spend their free time, then good for them, but that is absolutely not me. The sheer thought of looking like I was trying to find a hockey player to rail made my cheeks flame, heat reaching all the way to the tips of my ears. I'd rather look like Adam Sandler.

"Oh, God. Please tell me I didn't look like a puck bunny!" I gawked at Robbie, mortified.

Robbie chuckled. "Nah. You looked cute."

I snapped my head up at that, cheeks still burning. Cute? Me?

Surely I misheard him. Lowering one of my brows, I bit back a smug grin. "Did you just say I looked... cute?"

"You're drunk, Keller," Robbie deadpanned, rolling his eyes at me before turning to focus on The Mighty Ducks.

Maybe I was a little tipsy, but I wasn't a complete idiot. Robbie Mason called me cute. And sure, he's gross and I hate him and all that, but I'm not denying that it did something to me, something I'd never felt before, deep down in the depths of my chest. And I had no idea how to process that reaction.

———

"Robbie Mason called me cute..." I whisper against the silence, brows pinched together as I try to make sense of last night's grainy memories.

But then, another blurry flashback hits me like a Mack truck and I gasp, slapping a hand over my mouth to stop myself from screaming or throwing up because holy shit.

Lips. Kissing lips.

I blink hard, squeezing my eyes closed.

Oh my God. Oh my God. Oh my God.

Bile rises up the back of my throat.

I'm in full blown panic mode now as I try to comprehend exactly what happened. It's fuzzy and pixelated at best, and there are some blackout moments for sure, so I can't be entirely certain because, again, fucking wine. But I'm pretty sure I—*oh God*—I think I tried to kiss Robbie Mason last night.

And even worse than that—I think Robbie Mason turned me down.

I glance at the note. *Fuck.*

Suddenly the icy tone of his note, and the fact that he snuck out while I was passed out, makes complete sense. And I want to die.

I stare out the windows, at the sunlight peaking between the sky-scraping buildings of Midtown, and for a moment, I seriously consider taking a running jump and crashing through the glass. Because I am never going to live this down. I might as well jump. Plummeting fifty-eight stories to my death seems way less painful than dealing with the aftermath of whatever happened last night.

With another groan, I fall back against the mountain of pillows, throwing an arm over my eyes. But then that menacing bile gets the better of me, and I jump up and run to the bathroom, barely making it to the toilet before emptying the entire contents of my stomach.

CHAPTER 16

ROBBIE

Someone send help. It appears I've fallen down the Fran Keller *Instagram* feed rabbit hole, and now I'm eighteen months deep, looking at a photo of her and some smug, frat-looking douche-bag tagged as *RadTadd93*, the two of them huddled together in Central Park in the middle of winter. I don't know how I got here, but it officially sucks, and I want out.

"Fuck me," I mutter, tossing my phone onto the nightstand.

Suddenly, the bathroom door flies open and Dallas steps out, followed by a swirl of steam and slightly too much cologne. Freshly showered, dressed in jeans and a button down, trademark cowboy hat perched on his head, he stops so fast in his tracks he almost topples over, staring at me where I lie on my bed, hands propped behind my head.

"Dude, what the fuck are you doing?" His eyes are wide like he can't believe what he's seeing.

I quirk a brow.

"You're not coming?"

"No…" I shake my head. "I never said I was."

FAMOUS LAST WORDS **103**

He scoffs. "You're seriously not coming."

I shake my head again, slowly this time, because he seems to have a hard time following.

"Dude." Dallas tilts his head to the side. "Draper gave you his personal blessing to come out and get shitfaced with us, and you're in bed—" his gaze dips to the room service menu lying on my stomach, "—about to order cold pizza and questionable chicken tendies?"

I blink at him.

"We're three for three."

I blink again.

His eyes move to my phone on the bed next to me, eyebrows raising. "Oh, I get it. You're gonna stay in and have hot, kinky phone sex with your girl, huh?" He smirks knowingly. "You dirty dog."

I ignore him, focusing instead on the highlights of the Detroit-Boston game playing on the muted television.

"You're so fucking lame," he teases. "There's an unopened box of Kleenex in the bathroom cabinet."

A few seconds later, the door slams shut and he's gone, and I release a heavy sigh, staring up at the ceiling because the truth is, I'm not really watching the game on TV at all. My mind is too fucking racked over a certain *fake* girlfriend who's taken up permanent rent-free residency in my brain. Man, I'm so fucked.

It's been four days, and I thought the distance would help me get over the moment we shared in my hotel room, but instead, the distance has only gone and made everything worse. Because not only have I *not* been able to stop thinking about our almost kiss, but my dick has had a mind of its own, and on more than a few occasions I've been forced to jerk off as visions of Fran *fucking* Keller play in my mind.

I'm blaming the fact that it's been a while since the big guy's had any action, but I guess that doesn't explain the downright perverted scenarios of her that play through my mind at the most inconvenient times. I'm desperate; that's all I can put it down to. Desperate, and Fran Keller's my only option at this point in time.

Sure, technically, I could go out with the guys tonight and pick up some bunny, bring her back here and fuck her senseless, but I can't, because I'm in a stupid *fake fucking relationship* with the woman I'm trying not to think about while I jerk off in the shower like a fucking loser.

I keep replaying that moment in my mind over and over again. The almost kiss.

Fran had been a smart ass and put *The Mighty Ducks* on the TV. We watched for a while, and I pointed out the inaccuracies which made her throw a pillow at me. As we quickly lost interest in the film, it continued to play in the background while we started talking.

But the more wine Fran consumed, the sassier she became. And the sassier she became, the more her confidence grew. And it was something else. Who knew Fran Keller, the girl who used to walk around Belmont Prep like she had a stick permanently wedged up her ass, the girl who used to look down on everyone, the girl who tried to start a neighborhood watch program in the dorms that unsurprisingly never took off... who knew *that* girl could be so damn freaky?

———

"Favorite color?"

I rolled my eyes. Yes, we were really playing twenty questions.

When Fran asked if I wanted to play, I specifically said no. But it's like she has this creepy ability to make you do things you don't want to do because, suddenly, without even realizing, I was already up to question fucking five.

"You know, if I'm going to be forced against my will to play this stupid ass game, can we at least make it interesting?" I arched a brow.

"What do you propose?" Fran asked, taking a sip from her wine.

FAMOUS LAST WORDS   105

I shrugged. *"I don't know. Something a little more thrilling than favorite colors."*

She seemed to ponder that for a moment, tapping her nails against the glass in her hand, and then she took me by complete surprise. "Okay then. Favorite sexual position?"

Stunned. That was the only way to describe what I felt in the wake of her question. Fucking stunned. My mouth opening and closing like a goddamn fish. Did she actually just ask me that?

"I'll go first," Fran said after a moment, since I was clearly too shocked to speak. She took another sip of her wine before blurting it out like nobody's business. "I like it from behind. Like, the whole works. Pull my hair, spank me, wrap your hand around my throat and fucking choke me..." She trailed off, eyes closed, the hint of a wistful smile playing on her lips.

Again, I just stared at her, mouth hanging open because... who the fuck was this woman sitting in front of me and what the hell did she do with Fran Keller?

I swallowed hard, shifting awkwardly when I felt my dick twitch. "Um, is that what you, um, did with, um, Tadd?"

She laughed out loud, actually snorted. "God, no. Tadd's... conservative. I don't even think he likes sex. He's a missionary kind of guy at best. I remember one time, I begged him to call me his dirty little slut because it gets me off," she said, shrugging like it was no big deal, "and he looked at me like I was certifiable."

I silently threatened my dick if it wouldn't stop reacting, but goddamn.

"What about you?" Fran asked all casual like, as if she wasn't sitting right there, telling me she liked to be fucking choked.

I cleared my suddenly dry throat, searching for my voice. "I, um—"

"I bet you're a selfish asshole in bed," she interrupted me, narrowing one of her eyes. "The quintessential hockey star who doesn't have to work for it because the puck bunnies throw themselves at your feet. A wham, bam, fuck you ma'am, kinda guy."

For the record, she couldn't be more wrong, but again, I was at a loss for words. In fact, I couldn't even find my voice to respond. I was literally rendered frozen, barely even breathing. The only sign that I hadn't dropped dead from the shock of it all was that my dick was rising to attention. Fuck me.

"Or maybe girl on top," Fran mused, tapping her chin with her finger.

Now we were getting somewhere, and I couldn't help but grin. Girl on top, riding my cock, tits bouncing in my face. Yes fucking please.

"Oh my God!" Fran's face suddenly went stark, eyes bulging as she slapped a hand over her gaping mouth. "I can't believe I'm saying this," she muttered into her own palm.

I chuckled, my throat still thick and dry. "Well." I shrugged. "It sure is a lot more interesting than colors."

With a sheepish grin she giggled, and I was momentarily stilted by the sound. Fran Keller giggling was definitely not on my BINGO card for things that might turn me on. But her giggle, mixed with the fact that I now knew she had a fucking degradation kink, was enough to make me shake my head in the hope it might snap me out of whatever this whole Keller-induced intoxication thing was that was happening to me. She was drunk. I was stone-cold sober. A disaster waiting to happen.

She looked at her empty glass then, still smiling to herself, when her big blue eyes lifted to meet mine. And as my gaze dipped down to her full lips, I realized her mouth was literally right there, inches from mine, and something unexpected came over me.

I found myself leaning in, as if my body was moving of its own accord. I leaned in so close I could feel her soft breath fan against my skin. So close I could smell the sweetness of the wine that lingered on her lips. So close I was almost certain I could hear the erratic thud of her pulse in her throat. Or maybe it was mine.

I'm not sure if it was just me, but it felt like everything in that one moment changed, as if the world around us came to a sudden standstill, and it was just me and Fran, the air between us fizzing with electricity.

But then just as I lifted a hand, ready to cup her cheek and make possibly the most unexpected move of my life, the invisible hold she had on me snapped like a worn rubber band, and before I could do anything, she jumped up so quickly, I almost fell head-first into the couch cushion.

"You're not going to judge me if I finish the last of the wine, are you?" She paused on her way to the fridge, offering me a hopeful smile. Casual, like whatever the hell that *was that had just happened didn't actually happen at all and was all in my mind.*

"Um, yeah—I mean no." I cleared my throat. "I mean, sure. Go ahead." Cool. Apparently, I'd lost the ability to form a sentence. I managed a tight smile as the skin at the back of my neck burned.

What the fuck was wrong with me?

I'm pretty sure I almost kissed Fran Keller. My lips were definitely within kissing range. And now I can't even function like a normal human. I'd never been like this before. I was normally so calm and collected, aloof and indifferent. But I was suddenly bumbling all over myself like a goddamn dumbass.

While Fran busied herself, filling her glass, I jumped up and made a beeline for the bathroom, disappearing inside and closing the door behind me, resting back against it for a moment to try and steel myself as best as I could under the circumstances.

Scrubbing my face with my hands, I tore my fingers through my hair, taking a few deep breaths. I blamed the fact that she was wearing my jersey. And her scent. And the perfect shape of her lips, the way they curled up into a smile, causing that adorable dimple to burrow into the apple of her cheek.

"Aw, man I'm so fucked," I muttered under my breath.

I took longer than I should have in the bathroom—Fran probably thought I was taking a shit—but I needed to tamper the raging erection that'd been tenting the front of my sweats and give myself a mental pep talk. But by the time I walked back out into the suite, The Mighty Ducks *had finished and Fran was curled up on the sofa, her fourth and final glass of wine barely touched and balancing precariously in her hand while she snored like a damn lumberjack.*

I paused, rubbing at the tension in the back of my neck, staring at the girl who, not so long ago, I despised with everything I had. Suddenly, over the course of one night, things had changed to the point where I almost kissed Fran fucking Keller. But that wasn't even the worst part. The most fucked up thing about tonight wasn't that I'd almost kissed her, it was that I'd absolutely try to kiss her again if I knew she'd kiss me back.

———

My phone vibrates, pulling me from the thoughts that have plagued me for the last four excruciating days. I grab the device and glance at the screen, half expecting it to be Dallas or one of the guys, telling me to get my ass down to the bar to celebrate our winning streak.

But it isn't Dallas or any of my teammates. *Fuuuuuuuck.*

I consider not answering, allowing it to go to my messages, but I know I can't do that. I need to stop being a pussy. She's my girlfriend, for all intents and purposes.

"Hey…" I answer.

"Hey," Fran's voice is tight and tentative, and an annoying sliver of worry shoots through me like I give a shit about her.

"You okay?" I ask before I can stop myself. *My God, did I mention I'm fucked?* I roll my eyes.

"Yeah, so, I've been going over this for the last few days," she says quickly, as if the words are a Band-Aid she's ripping off a freshly healed wound.

My stomach drops into the pit of my ass at the prospect of talking about kiss-gate. I close my eyes and pinch the bridge of my nose. *Please don't. Please don't.*

"I've been debating over whether I should call because I really *really* don't want to talk about it."

Then don't. Don't talk about it. Shut your stupid adorable mouth, and never speak of it again, Keller.

"But I know we need to," she continues.

I fling my arm over my eyes. *Fuck me.*

"Can we please just go back to how things were when we hated each other—"

FAMOUS LAST WORDS   **109**

"I never hated—"

She interjects, "—before I made a drunken fool of myself and tried to kiss you?"

Wait. What? I sit bolt upright.

"I didn't realize I was *that* drunk. And I have no idea what I was even thinking." She huffs dramatically. "I'm so embarrassed, Robbie."

She thinks *she* tried to kiss *me*? She doesn't remember. I'm the fool who tried to kiss her. A stupid decision I regret more than anything because, well, firstly, she was drunk, and I've never been the kind of guy to take advantage of any woman under the influence. But also, because she's Fran fucking Keller, the girl from high school who made me shit myself. The woman who now likes having her ass spanked and her hair pulled. *Chrissake.*

"Robbie?" Fran's voice breaks through my thoughts, more than a little panicked. "Are you still there?"

"Uh, yeah." I look around the hotel room for what, I have no idea. "Um, yeah. Whatever."

"Whatever?" Fran scoffs through the phone. "That's it?"

I scratch at a persistent itch at the back of my neck, but no matter what, it won't subside. A phantom itch. Probably guilt. "Um, I mean, what, what do you *want* me to say?" I offer a forced laugh. "I'm Robbie Mason. You think you're the first drunk chick to try and kiss me?" Another forced laugh.

For the record, I'm going to hell.

"Well, okay then," Fran finally says. "I just wanted to make sure things wouldn't be awkward between us, but it's clear to see you're back to your d-bag self, so good." Before I can say anything, she continues, "Bye."

And with that, she's gone.

My shoulders sag under the weight of resignation... or regret, I'm not quite sure. And as I stare at the screen, tongue pressed against the inside of my cheek, I can't help but wonder what the hell just happened.

Fran thinks she tried to kiss me. She thinks I turned her down. This is a good thing.

Heaving a sigh, I fall back against my pillows still staring at my phone.

Who the fuck am I trying to kid? If this is a good thing, then why do I feel so shitty?

CHAPTER 17

FRAN

I haven't heard from Robbie since our awkward phone call. Not even one arrogant or bossy message. It's almost like we've bypassed the hating each other and gone straight back to forgetting the other existed. And, I'm not saying this isn't what I was hoping for—anything is better than having to spend every minute of my day dwelling over that almost-kiss—but I'd be lying if I said there wasn't a tiny and very confused part of me that didn't wonder what he might be up to… every single waking moment of my day.

So while I've spent my days *not* thinking about Robbie Mason (yeah, right), I have been forced to deal with the aftermath of the phone call between Robbie and Tadd.

My laptop chimes with a new Teams notification, and I click on the flashing icon, my skin crawling immediately. Speak of the devil.

TADD: IS IT SERIOUS?

I throw my head back, stifling a groan. It's been like this non-stop. I've successfully managed to ignore his calls and text messages, but at work, he's a lot harder to avoid. I'm forced to pass his office every time I come and go, and he's now resorted to using Teams because he knows I don't have the access level to block him.

> ME: I'VE ALREADY TOLD YOU, IT'S NONE OF YOUR BUSINESS.
>
> TADD: HOW LONG HAS IT BEEN GOING ON?
>
> ME: AGAIN, IT HAS NOTHING TO DO WITH YOU.
>
> TADD: YOU KNOW HE'S A DRUG ADDICT, RIGHT?
>
> ME: DO I NEED TO REPORT YOU TO HR... AGAIN?
>
> TADD: GO AHEAD. THEY DIDN'T DO ANYTHING ABOUT IT LAST TIME.

Ugh, he's such a smug asshole.

> TADD: YOU CAN DO SO MUCH BETTER THAN SOME WASHED-UP HOCKEY PLAYER.

I almost laugh out loud. Washed-up? From what I've seen on social media, Robbie Mason has single-handedly pushed the New York Thunder to the top of the Eastern conference leaderboard with four straight wins. In their game against Detroit last night, he scored two goals and three assists. The media is having a field day, calling him the comeback kid. Hardly washed-up, but go off, Tadd.

> TADD: IT'S NOT A GOOD LOOK FOR YOU, SWEETIE.

Okay, that's enough fuckery for one morning.

I shake my head and switch my Teams status to **Do Not Disturb** because I just don't have it in me to deal with his shit any more today; it's been non-stop all week and I've officially reached my dickhead tolerance.

As if my computer can hear me, a meeting request suddenly pops up and I click the invitation, my heart jumping into the back of my throat at the sight of Tony Carlton's name. *Fuck.*

FAMOUS LAST WORDS   113

He's called a meeting with me in his office in five minutes. *Double fuck.*

My eyes narrow when I see who else is invited. Tadd Jennings. *Are you fucking serious?*

Slamming my laptop shut, I push up from my seat so fast, the chair goes rolling back and straight into my cubicle wall with a loud thud that causes a few of the other agents to stand, glancing in my direction to see what the commotion is.

I offer my colleagues a tight-lipped smile, smooth down the front of my dress and, with a resigned sigh, I start the trek to Tony's office, mentally preparing myself for whatever this bullshit is all about.

By the time I make it upstairs, Tony's office door is open, and I can see him standing by the wall of glass, looking out over the view, hands tucked into his trouser pockets. I knock, and he turns, his brows rising as he waves me in.

I glance sideways, finding Tadd perched on the sofa by the far wall, long legs spread, arm draped casually over the back of the couch, menacing smirk playing on his lips. Ignoring him, I make my way to one of the chairs across from Tony's desk, but before I can take a seat, Tony stops me.

"Come sit, Fran," he says, waving me with him.

He closes his office door before moving to the armchair and taking a seat, and I'm left with no other choice than to sit on the couch next to Tadd. With a muttered curse, I take a seat on the very end, as far from him as I can possibly get, but his hand resting on the back is so close that I feel his fingertip graze my shoulder. I'll give him one, because I'm hoping for his sake it was an accident. But if he tries it again, I will not hesitate to slap him. I don't care that our boss is sitting less than a few feet away.

Tony smiles from me to Tadd and back again, crossing one of his legs over the other, and I don't like this one bit.

"How are you, Fran?" Tony asks, and it's not lost on me that this is literally the first time he's ever asked me that question.

My brows dips, but I manage somewhat of a smile. "Fine, thanks."

"Escrow going smoothly with Allora?"

I nod, lifting my chin a little higher because if there's one thing that I'm confident of, it's that Allora will close without issue. "Yes."

Tony nods, his gaze flitting to Tadd, and I feel like there's some silent conversation occurring between them that immediately has me on edge. Do they know? Has Tadd done some digging and put two and two together?

"Well, come Monday, you'll have one on the board," Tony finally says. "And this is where you can really gain some momentum." Again, he looks at Tadd.

Beside me, I feel Tadd shift, facing me, and I do all I can to keep a straight face, forcing myself to look at him like I don't want to break his nose.

"Fran, I secured the listing I was telling you about," Tadd begins, all smooth and charming, like he hasn't been harassing me all week about my love life. "Columbus Circle."

I nod but remain silent because I now know exactly what's happening here.

Tadd's gaze flits to Tony before meeting mine again, a self-assured grin claiming his face. "Tony and I have been talking, and we really think it's in your best interest if you come on the listing with me."

I open my mouth to object, but before I can speak, he continues.

"I know this is a high-profile listing, very out of *your* league." He chuckles condescendingly. "But I'll help you. We can work together."

Breathe, Fran.

"This is a tremendous opportunity," Tony adds.

Before I can get a word in, Tadd continues. "We can work out a fair and reasonable commission split, and you can leverage the use of my team."

FAMOUS LAST WORDS   115

I can't help but glare at him. Here he is, acting like he's doing me this selfless favor, when in actuality it's nothing of the sort. This is his way of getting close to me again, controlling me. I have so many responses on the tip of my tongue, although none are appropriate considering Tony is sitting right there.

"Okay, well I think that settles it," Tony says, clapping his hands together. "Put together a marketing plan, and we can start straight away."

Too shocked to move, I remain seated as Tony and Tadd stand, their conversation shifting to a game of golf or some other irrelevant shit. I swallow hard, forcing myself to stand just as Tadd turns to me again, hand held out.

"Welcome aboard, partner." His smile is almost taunting.

I stare at his hand a moment before reluctantly shaking it, making sure my nails dig into his too-soft-for-a-man hands. He tries to conceal his wince, letting go of me quickly before tucking the hand in his pocket and staring down at me, eyes flaring.

And without saying a word, I spin on my heel and hurry out of the office while the two of them continue chatting about fucking golf.

———

After a day like today, I am absolutely not in the mood to be dealing with this shit tonight. But since escrow doesn't close until Monday, and because Carlton Myers' ridiculous policy states that all escrow funds are to be held for twenty-one days after close, unfortunately I'm at the mercy of working for tips. So, with my tablet in hand, I walk out of the back room and into The Exchange, the bar thrumming with a typical Friday night energy, full of Wall Street d-bags.

I'm stopped the second I step out of the back room, Vera all up in my grill, hip popped, hand on her waist, looking down at me with one brow arched high.

"Hey?" I pose my greeting as more of a question, because what is happening?

"So, you know my boyfriend, Tyler?" she starts.

My brows pinch together because no, I don't. We haven't yet met. "I know *of* him."

"Well, aside from being the love of my life, and a really awesome DJ who is going to make it big one of these days," she says this with a flick of her hair, "do you know what else he is?"

I blink at her, totally lost. "Um, a vegan?"

She folds her arms across her chest. "Tyler's a huge hockey fan."

Oh, great.

"And not just any hockey fan, but a Thunder fan, like, since birth."

I purse my lips.

Vera's eyes go comically wide as she leans in even closer. "When were you planning on telling me that you're dating—"

"Shhhh!" I hiss, looking around and noticing just how busy this place is.

Thankfully she lowers her voice as she says, "Robbie Mason!"

I throw my hands up in a shrug. "It's—it's new."

"Well, I would hope so, since you hadn't told *yours truly* yet," she says indignantly, holding a hand against her chest.

I roll my eyes. "We went to high school together. He just moved here, and we crossed paths. And here we are. No big deal." That's our story, and I'm sticking to it. Believable, to the point, and not a complete and utter lie. I make a mental note to relay this back to Robbie so we can at least keep our stories straight.

"Okay, but you do realize Tyler is now harassing me to set up a double date so he can meet and possibly become besties with your guy."

I laugh out loud, unable to stop myself because the thought

of Robbie on a double date is absurd, but I try not to give away my doubt. "I'll see what I can do."

Thankfully, before Vera can question me any further, we're interrupted by Peter, tonight's bartender, impatiently ringing the bell for service, and we both scurry off to earn our tips.

CHAPTER 18

ROBBIE

At the final siren, we're five for five. I scored my second ever hat trick, Dallas scored his first ever shutout, and as we skate off the ice to the roar of the home crowd, the atmosphere throughout the arena is electric.

It really feels like something has clicked. Not just between me and the guys on the team, but with everyone, everything. Coach is being less of a sullen asshole, and even Rusty seems to have pulled his head out of his ass and stepped up as captain.

Removing my helmet, I trail behind as we file into the locker room, and everyone gathers around Dallas, spraying him with water or Gatorade or whatever they can get their hands on, christening him on his very first shutout.

The merriment in the room is palpable; there're slaps on the back, hugs, high fives, all accompanied by the sound of everyone yelling to be heard over each other. Randomly, "Baby I Love Your Way" by Big Mountain starts to play from somewhere, Dallas singing at the top of his lungs completely offkey and somehow already naked from the waist up, cowboy hat secured on his head.

I take a seat in front of my cubby, wiping the sweat from my forehead with a towel before taking off my skates, and as I look around, I can't help but smile, because this is what it used to be like. This is what I loved about hockey. Coming back into the locker room after a win and acting like absolute dorks with the guys you just busted your ass for out on the ice, to celebrate the moment, not to think about tomorrow or the next game. It used to be like this when I first started with the Lions, but somehow along the way, the fun was lost and it became just another grind.

A hush falls over the room as Coach takes center floor, and I'm a little taken aback by the smile on his face. Well, it's almost a smile. Probably as much of a smile as he's willing to give, but a smile nonetheless.

Everyone settles as Coach starts talking about all the things we did right, and the improvements we can work on in preparation for our game on Monday night.

"I wanted to take a moment to call out Robbie Mason." He points a finger at me, and the room erupts in applause. I roll my eyes at the unwanted attention, grunting a chuckle when Dallas wraps his arm around my neck and gives me a fucking noogie.

Coach continues. "Son, you've found your voice out there on the ice, and you're proving to be a true leader. We're glad to have you on the team," he says quickly, as if the words were painful to say.

I bow my head in return, an unspoken truce seemingly shared between the two of us in that one fleeting moment.

"Now." Coach holds the game puck in the air. "Game puck."

The guys all cheer.

"This one goes to the backbone of our team, the one guy who goes out on to that ice every damn night and gives it his all. The *mouth from the South*, voted—" he pauses to roll his eyes, "— *sexiest goalie, two years in a row*."

Beside me, Dallas is already on his feet, theatrically bowing like a dickhead to everyone.

"Celebrating his very first shutout, Dallas Shaw!" Coach closes the distance and pulls Dallas in for an awkward side hug.

Grinning ear-to-ear, Dallas takes the puck, looking at it with the kind of revered awe reserved for a firstborn child, and I can't help but jump up to slap him on his back, which he takes as an open invitation to wrap his arms around me in a half-naked, sweaty hug.

"Couldn't have done it without this fucking boss!" he yells, pointing at me, and again, I roll my eyes, not wanting to steal his moment.

The celebrations continue around the room, the social media team popping in to take a few quick videos of us for the team's social media accounts, but my mind drifts to the one thing that's been nagging at me all night. Keller never showed.

I texted her this morning to tell her Andy wasn't going to be at the game tonight, that she was on her own. Her response had been laced with that smart mouth tone of hers, telling me she's a *big girl* and that she can *take care of herself*. I rolled my eyes, maybe even laughed a little, and my dirty fucking mind might've even wandered to the gutter momentarily, imagining her *taking care* of herself alright. Naked and wet, in a steamy shower. But when we got out onto the ice for warm up, my eyes immediately went to the friends and family section to look for her, to make sure she was on time, maybe even fuck with her by trying to get her on the Jumbotron again, but she wasn't there. And by the time the first period had well and truly kicked off, she still wasn't there.

I'd considered texting her during the break, but there's a strict no phone rule, and I didn't want to piss off Coach. Now, she's a definite no show, and I wish I could say that I'm pissed, but if I'm being honest, I'm more concerned.

I pull out my phone, staring at the last message she sent me as I consider my response; I don't want to come across as a complete asshole.

FAMOUS LAST WORDS **121**

Me: You're not here.

I re-read my message and can't help but scoff because that's literally all I've got.

Staring at the text window, I wait for her reply, but nothing comes. She's usually super quick with responding, but it's crickets. Not even those dots show up to indicate she's replying with something sassy.

I don't miss the way my gut twists. But before I can think of a follow-up message or, I don't know, fucking call her like a grown-ass adult, I'm stopped by Coach Bromley tapping me on my shoulder.

"What's up, Coach?" I tuck my phone into my bag.

Coach points to the corridor that leads to the office. "Office."

Following behind him, I know I can't be in trouble given how stoked everyone is with our fifth win, but as I enter the office to see Coach Draper and Chris Garret, and the team fucking owner, Bob Oakley, all standing around, my heart flies up into the back of my throat. This can't be good.

"Robbie, you know Bob?" Chris Garret says, pointing to the imposing billionaire.

I clear my throat, stepping forward and holding out my hand. "It's an honor to meet you, sir."

Bob grins behind his Fu Manchu mustache, shaking my hand with gusto. "Son, the pleasure is all mine. I'm glad to have you on board."

I smile tightly, eyes flitting about the men in the room, still unsure what I'm doing here.

"Robbie, take a seat," Coach says, pointing to one of the chairs.

I do as I'm told, stiffening a little when Bob takes the chair right next to me.

"Okay, so I know you're probably wondering why you've been called in here, Robbie, and we'll just get straight down to it," Chris begins, glancing at the other men. "We're really impressed with just how well you've fit into the team. You've more than proved that you're here for all the right reasons, and your determination is rubbing off on a lot of the younger guys."

"Yes, sir." I nod, unsure what else to say to that.

Chris grins. "Robbie, I understand Coach Draper gave you permission to go out with the guys after the win on Wednesday, but you didn't." He cocks his head to the side. "Why is that?"

I shrug a shoulder. "I don't like to go out after a game when I'm out of town."

Chris nods, staring at me for an uncomfortably long moment.

"Is there something wrong?" I ask, confused by what the hell is even happening.

"No, nothing at all." Chris shakes his head. "In fact…" He glances at Bob and Coach Draper, "We've discussed your contract and the terms, and we've decided that we're going to relax some of the stipulations made prior to signing, specifically your curfew."

My brows climb higher because I sure as shit wasn't expecting that. "Oh, really?"

Chris nods.

"We understand it's only been a week, son, but you've more than proven that you can be trusted." Coach Draper spears me with a steely look, "But… know that we will be watching you closely, and if we need to revert back, we absolutely will."

"Unfortunately, we have no jurisdiction when it comes to the additional terms set by Player Safety, so we can't do anything about those," Chris adds reluctantly.

"You've been keeping up with your piss tests?" Coach asks, one brow quirked.

"Yes, Coach." I nod.

"Must be that girl of yours." Bob grins at me.

I quirk a brow, confused, and a little uncomfortable by the look in his eyes.

"Met her at game one," he answers my unspoken question.

FAMOUS LAST WORDS **123**

I didn't know Fran met Bob Oakley.

"She must be doing *something* right," Bob chuckles.

"Uh, yeah," I say, shifting awkwardly because old men insinuating shit about my sex life is all kinds of gross.

Thankfully, Chris interjects. "Why don't you go back out there and celebrate with the rest of the guys, Robbie. Maybe go out and have a beer."

I smile tightly, pushing up from my chair. And I mean, sure, I could tell them that I'm currently sober, that I haven't touched a drop of the stuff since August, but what's the point?

"Thank you." I nod at my coaches and Chris. "Mr. Oakley, sir." I turn to the owner of the team and hold my hand out once again.

"Mr. Oakley was my father, son. Call me Bob." The man shakes my proffered hand.

"I'm afraid I can't do that, sir. My ma raised me right." With another tight smile, I wave at the men and turn quickly, hurrying out of the office.

The locker room is still utter chaos, and I try to slip between Dallas and our right winger, Logan, but I'm stopped by an arm wrapping around my neck.

"You're coming out tonight, huh, Mason?" Logan asks.

"I don't know. Maybe," I murmur.

"Franny outside?" Dallas asks.

At the thought of Keller, my smile falters before I can catch myself.

"Uh-oh, trouble in paradise," Dallas teases.

I roll my eyes, shrugging out of his grip. "Na, she never showed," I explain, glancing back at my locker. "She was supposed to."

Dallas straightens, and for the first time since I've known the guy, I witness firsthand his playboy charm make way for seriousness, brows lowering as he leans in a little closer. "Everything okay?"

All I can do is shrug as I make my way back to my locker.

Retrieving my phone, I check my messages. Still nothing. I know we're not really together, but it doesn't mean I'm not worried.

As I sit down on the bench, elbows on my knees, I rack my mind over the possibilities as I stare at my phone. Even if she'd been called urgently into work at the bar, she'd have told me. She wouldn't just not show up.

"All good, man?" Dallas wobbles in front of me as he struggles to take off his bulky pants.

Sitting up a little straighter, I glance up at him. "Uh, yeah. I might pass on drinks tonight."

His gaze flits down to my phone clutched in my hands. "She okay?"

I puff air from my cheeks, raking my fingers through my sweaty hair. I shake my head. "I can't get a hold of her. I need to go check in."

Dallas's eyes flare with concern. "Shit, of course, man. We can go get beers any time." He nudges me in what I assume is an attempt to keep things light. "Plenty more wins to celebrate."

I manage a smile, but it's forced. Because I'm still fully aware that Fran hasn't messaged me back, and I'm more worried than I even care to admit to myself.

CHAPTER 19

ROBBIE

The Uber rolls to a stop in a quiet street somewhere in the Lower East Side, right outside one of those quintessential New York City apartment buildings with the external fire escape, and graffiti tags sprayed around what appears to be a sketchy security door.

Climbing the stoop, I check my phone with the address I got from Andy, scanning the list of apartments on the panel before pressing the button for 3B. But after waiting a moment, there's no response. I press the button again, holding it down a little longer. Still nothing.

I step back and look up at the building to the third floor. It looks as though there's a light on.

Cursing under my breath, steam plumes from my mouth on a hard exhale, and I step up to the intercom again, holding my finger down on 3B for so long it'll probably piss off the neighbors. And sure, Fran might not even be there, but if she's not home, then she should be responding to my text messages, dammit.

"Jesus, fuck. *What?*" A croaky yet somewhat familiar voice crackles through the ancient intercom speaker.

Surprised by the unwelcome greeting, I hold the *talk* button down. "Keller?"

Silence.

"Robbie?"

I roll my eyes. "Yeah."

"You know stalking is illegal in the state of New York."

I can't help but smirk. "Well, there go my weekends."

"What are you doing here?"

"You missed the game," I say slowly. "Are… are you okay?"

After a pause, her broken voice comes back through the speaker. "Oh, shit. I didn't even realize…"

My brows bunch together. Is she drunk? I shake my head again. "Can I come up?"

The buzzer sounds, and the pitiful lock on the door unlatches with a click. I take that as my invitation, pushing through the door and into the tiny foyer that smells like mold and something gross.

With a skeptical glance at the elevator, I decide I'd rather not risk my life tonight, so I opt for the stairs instead. When I reach the third floor, the door to 3B is on my right and I don't hesitate before knocking probably a little too abruptly.

"Hold your damn horses."

I scoff at the faint voice muffled through the wood, glancing up at the ceiling and grimacing at the old cobwebs that hang from the moldings.

The door opens and I take a step back, but then I get a look at her and my eyes widen. Dressed in a pale pink sweatsuit, a chocolate stain smeared down the front her sweatshirt, fluffy socks covering her feet, hair a messy knot on top of her head that bobbles with her movements, her blue eyes are at half-mast, a little bloodshot, and she's keeled over, gripping the door with one hand and her stomach with the other.

"I'm sick," she croaks.

FAMOUS LAST WORDS   127

Instinctively, I take a step back because I can't afford to catch whatever she has, not before our game against Charlotte on Monday night.

"Don't worry." She waves a hand. "You can't catch it."

I quirk a brow, looking her up and down again. "How do you know?"

"Because I'm pretty sure you *don't* have a uterus."

I relax at that, and she turns and shuffles slowly down the short hallway, clutching her stomach. And before I know it, I'm walking inside, closing the door behind me and following her like I have any business being here.

Fran lets out a stifled groan, gripping the wall, and I quickly come up behind her, bracing my hands in case she falls over or something.

"Um, do you need anything?" I ask after a moment.

Glancing at me over her shoulder, a small crease pulls between her eyebrows, and I can't help but wonder if she didn't realize I'd followed her inside.

"What are you doing here?" she grumbles, clearly annoyed by my presence.

"You literally look like you're about to die," I say. "Like hell I'm going to leave you alone like this."

When she eyes me curiously, I realize that probably came across pretty heavy, so with a casual shrug and the hint of a smile, I keep it light by adding, "I can't risk being the last person to see you alive. You end up dead? The media will have a fucking field day."

She rolls her eyes, but then suddenly she stops and crouches over again, a helpless whimper coming from her, and I don't know what the fuck is up with my heart, but I've never felt it clench in my chest the way it just did. *Weird.*

I look around at the apartment. It's small. An all-in-one studio, her bed by the window, a tiny sofa, a kitchenette lining the far wall. I almost feel too big for the space.

Dumping my bag on the scratched wood floor, I move

forward and lift Fran's arm, ducking lower so I can drape it around my neck, helping her whether she wants me to or not.

"Where do you wanna go?" I ask, even though our options are limited.

She points, and I pull her closer as I walk her to the bed which is covered by a mountain of pillows all colors of the rainbow, perched right under the big window that opens up to the fire escape and looking out over the street below.

I help Fran onto the bed, and she lays back, rolling into a ball, and I just stand there taking in the sight of her. She looks so small and defenseless, nothing like her usual ball-busting self. I notice a few pill bottles on the nightstand and I feel something start to gnaw at the inside of my gut, and there goes my fucking heart again.

Pushing off my beanie, I tear my fingers through my hair, releasing a breath and considering my options. She's obviously sick and in pain, and I'm probably the last person she wants hanging around. And sure, I should probably leave her to fend for herself, but I can't go. I know she's not really going to die, but I simply can't leave her like this. It wouldn't be right.

"What can I do?" I ask, looking around for some sign of what, I don't even know. "Do you need anything? Food?" My gaze flits to the pill bottles. "More medicine?"

Fran holds a bright pink object up in the air. "Microwave. Ninety seconds on high."

I take the item, realizing it's a wheat bag, and I take it over to the kitchenette, popping it in the microwave. While I wait the ninety seconds, I snoop around, noticing the small fridge is empty save for a bottle of wine, some old cheese, and a bag of lettuce way past its use by date. The cupboards are just as bare, and frankly, that pisses me off and I don't even know why.

Tugging my phone from my pocket, I see a new text message from Dallas, but I ignore it and scroll to one of the delivery apps, because I don't know about Fran, but I'm fucking starving. I

FAMOUS LAST WORDS   129

make quick work of placing a few different orders, before clicking back to Dallas's text message.

Dallas: Everything okay, my guy?

I rub my chin, considering my response.

Me: Hey, yeah. Sorry, Fran's sick.

Dallas: Aw, you taking care of your girl?

I roll my eyes.

Me: Yeah, she is my girlfriend.

Dallas: Whipped!

Dallas: Jk.

Dallas: Give Franny a big hug from me.

Before I can respond, the microwave beeps loudly, echoing through the silence.

I walk back to the bed to find Fran lying on her back, sweatshirt pulled up, and her pants pulled down low enough to expose a very swollen belly. Eyes closed, face etched with pain, she clutches her stomach, and I hesitate before stepping closer and sitting tentatively on the edge of the bed.

"Here you go." I hold out the steaming wheat bag.

"Thanks," she mutters, taking it and placing it directly onto her stomach.

I almost tell her that it's too hot, that she should put something between the bag and her skin, but I think twice and shut my stupid mouth because clearly this isn't her first rodeo.

Keller releases a ragged sigh, and finally after a long moment of me just sitting here staring at her, she opens her eyes and looks at me.

Her brows pull together. "What are you doing here?"

It's the second time she's asked me this. Confused, I glance at the pills on her nightstand. She's really out of it.

"You... I... You let me in, and I helped you into bed. I just heated up your wheat bag." I reach forward, picking up one of the orange bottles and scanning the label. "Just how fucked up are you?"

She rolls her eyes, snatching the bottle from me. "I mean *why* are you here?"

"You didn't show up to the game. And you weren't replying to my messages." I shrug a shoulder. "I was worried—" I snap my mouth shut again, clearing my throat, hoping like hell she didn't just hear that last part. But if her teasing grin is any indication, she heard me alright.

"Careful there, Mason." She pokes me lightly in my arm. "Almost sounds like you give a shit about me."

Great. Even sick and hopped on meds she's a brat.

"How was the game?" she asks, closing her eyes again, smile still lingering despite that same crease of discomfort burrowing between her eyebrows.

"We won."

"Five for five," she says under her breath.

I can't help the smile that curls my lips. "Someone's been following the games."

"Yeah, I have to. Vera's boyfriend is *obsessed* with hockey, so I figured I should probably at least pretend like I care."

I have no idea who Vera or her boyfriend are, but I can't help but chuckle.

"Get into any fights tonight?"

"Nah, just a couple of tussles up against the boards. Why?" This time it's my turn to tease, gently poking her thigh. "You worried about me, Keller?"

"No," she scoffs. "But it's pretty fucking hot watching you

throw your gloves down and square up," she mumbles almost incoherently, and I wonder if she even knows she just said that out loud.

And I know she's currently high on codeine, but my eyes still widen at that confession. Fran Keller thinks it's hot when I fight. Noted. But before I can do something stupid like ask her what else she thinks is hot about me, a shrill buzz sounds through the apartment, startling me and waking her from her light sleep.

"What the fuck is this? Visiting hour?" she cries, throwing an arm over her eyes.

"I ordered food," I say softly. "I'll go down and grab it."

————

Keller cried because I had the food delivery guy stop in at a bodega and grab a pint of Ben & Jerry's cookie dough ice cream and a giant packet of Skittles. She actually cried. Real tears. And then she proceeded to consume more than half the ice cream and a few heaped handfuls of the candy mixed in with it, while I ate the entire pizza that I ordered.

Now, between her bathroom breaks and my trips to the microwave to warm up her wheat pack, we're watching one of the *Halloween* movies on the small flat screen hanging on the wall opposite her bed. I hadn't intended on staying. I was just going to eat and leave her be. But then she suggested a movie and shuffled over so I could sit next to her on the bed. With her nestled into my underarm nook, the intoxicating scent of vanilla and mango wafting up from her hair, I don't want to leave, although I know I have to.

"Why would you go up the stairs?" Fran mutters to herself. "Everyone knows if a masked psychopath comes into your house, the best thing to do is to run outside."

Truthfully, I haven't been watching the film. Between the conscious thoughts of what Fran feels like pressed into the side of my body, her scent, and the fact that, even though there's no way in hell I'd ever admit it to anyone, horror movies legitimately terrify me, there's no way I could possibly focus on a movie right now.

"Yeah, so dumb," I add, my eyes doing all they can to avoid the screen.

I reach for my phone on the nightstand and check the time. It's past midnight and I really should be heading back to the hotel, but—and this is something else I'll never admit out loud—I don't want to leave.

Stretching, I move my head side to side to crack my neck. This bed sure as hell ain't big enough for the both of us. I've only been laying here for forty-five minutes and already my back is cramping.

Fran cranes her neck, big blue eyes peering up at me. "Are you okay?"

"Yeah," I say through a stifled yawn. "I should probably go."

She checks the time on the alarm clock next to her bed and gasps. "I didn't realize it was so late."

I sit up with a groan, my muscles sore after tonight's game.

"You're probably really tired. Sorry."

I glance back at her, offering her a slow smile. "Fran Keller apologizing?"

"I take it back," she snaps, but then a small whimper falls from her lips as she struggles to sit up, and I turn around, helping her, putting another pillow behind her. And although she looks a little less out of it and a little more herself than she did when I first showed up, she's obviously still in a lot of discomfort.

"You gonna be okay if I go?"

"No. I think my life might actually fall apart without you," she deadpans.

I can't help but laugh because there she is.

Unlocking my phone, I scroll to the Uber app to order a ride which is precisely the moment a bolt of lightning flashes outside, followed immediately by a deafening crack of thunder that causes the entire building to shake. Less than a few seconds later, rain is hammering hard against the windows, and I reach over Fran, pulling aside the mesh curtain, barely able to make out the buildings across the street through the blanketing sheets of rain.

"Ominous," Fran says.

I glance at her, arching a brow.

"Maybe you should stay…" she shrugs.

I eye her, scanning the limited space in the bed, forced to swallow around the lump that's wedged itself in the back of my throat.

"I promise I won't try to kiss you again," she says with a lighthearted laugh, hands held up in surrender and fuck me, now I feel like an asshole again thinking about our almost-kiss and how I've let her believe it was all her.

I drag a hand over my face, exhaling heavily. "You sure it's okay?"

"Yeah. I'll try not to bleed all over you in my sleep." She waggles her eyebrows menacingly.

I huff a laugh, shaking my head at her. "Gross…"

She snorts, pushing me playfully, and I guess that's that settled. I'm staying the night. With Fran Keller. In her bed. And I know I've said it before, but I will continue saying it… I am so fucked.

CHAPTER 20

FRAN

Am I having some sort of codeine-induced hallucination, or is Robbie Mason actually standing beside me at the sink in my bathroom brushing his teeth? I blink hard, glancing up at the hulking hunk of a man who seems almost too big for the tiny room. His eyes smile down at me, one eyebrow cocked as he continues brushing.

I finish first, spitting into the sink before rinsing my mouth out, fully realizing that I've invited Robbie Mason, my once-was nemesis, and the man I almost drunkenly kissed a week ago, to stay the night in my bed. If anyone asks, I'm blaming the pain pills.

When I unexpectedly came down with a flare up today, I did what I always do; I hopped myself up on pain relief and dragged my sorry ass to bed, in the hope of passing out until the agony subsided. I didn't mean to sleep as long as I did. And when Robbie showed up at my door, I was shocked, confused and a little touched, if I'm honest.

I lead the way back to my bed, Robbie following close behind me. His spicy, chocolatey scent wraps around me, and I almost feel like I'm floating. Jesus, I must be high.

"I hope you don't mind that I sleep naked."

"I hope you don't mind waking up with one less testicle."

He chuckles, but as I climb into bed and shuffle up against the wall, I still momentarily when he lifts his hoodie up over his head in one fell swoop, his New York Thunder t-shirt climbing up with it, giving me a glimpse of his defined abs and the V that disappears into his sweatpants. I allow myself to breathe again when he tugs the t-shirt back down, leaving it on. Thankfully, the pants remain firmly in place, too, as he climbs into the bed next to me, pulling the sheets up to just beneath his chin.

This is weird. I'm not going to lie. Robbie Mason is in my bed, under my covers, his firm body pressed up next to mine due to the limited space. I swear, it feels like my heart is about to thump right out of my chest. Even over the sound of the pouring rain, I'm sure he can probably hear it. *Thaddum. Thaddum. Thaddum.*

All I can do is stare up at the ceiling, the only light coming from the occasional flicker of lightning flashing outside.

"Does this happen often?"

I turn, looking at Robbie, barely making out the silhouette of his profile.

"What?" My brows knit together. "The storm?"

He snorts, and I see his head turn to face me. As my eyes adjust to the darkness, I make out the flicker of gold in his irises as they bore into mine.

"The… pain." He clears his throat and then continues, "Period pain, yeah?"

I know we're both adults, but I've honestly never spoken candidly about periods before with a man, especially not in my bed. But he's so casual about it. Not in the slightest bit uncomfortable. And I don't know if it's just my hormones running amok inside of me, but that's kind of hot.

"Um, yeah. Well, not usually *this* bad." I tuck a hand behind my head, looking back up to the ceiling because the weight of Robbie's gaze is almost too much, even in the dark.

"I have PCOS." When he doesn't say anything, I continue. "Polycystic ovarian syndrome. For the most part, I have it under control, but occasionally I'll get a flare up which is kind of like period pain but a million times worse. Like a heavyweight boxer punching me over and over again."

"What causes a flare up?"

Frankly, I'm shocked that he's asking these kinds of questions. I remember I once had a flare up when I was with Tadd, and he didn't want to know about it. In fact, he abandoned me and told me to call him when it was over. After that, I assumed all men were the same when it came to this sort of stuff.

"All different things. Lack of sleep, stress, too much alcohol, trash food…" I add, sheepishly, "I haven't really been taking care of myself lately."

The mattress dips as Robbie rolls onto his side, facing me. "Is there anything I can do to help?"

I'm taken aback by his offer, and I can't stop my own snort. "Okay, who are you and where is Robbie *asshat* Mason?"

Robbie laughs quietly, but then he speaks and his words shock me. "My mom has cancer. Cervical."

I gasp at his unexpected admission, turning to look at him, finding his eyes through the darkness.

"She's… end of life."

"Oh my God, Robbie." This time it's me who rolls onto my side despite my uterus objecting at the sudden movement.

"She was first diagnosed when I was twelve. I used to look after her when the chemo was really tough. So periods and gross stuff are nothing to me," he jokes. "Trust me, I've seen it all."

"What about your dad?" My heart breaks at the thought of a twelve-year-old boy having to take care of his mom in ways no child should have to.

Robbie scoffs. "He was an addict who used to beat on my mom. He took off when I was eight. Haven't heard from him since. Probably dead. He must be, considering he hasn't crawled out of some gutter to ask me for money."

I puff air from my cheeks, but I say nothing.

"Mom went into remission, and she was good for a long time. But then when I was seventeen, she had a recurrence. She didn't tell me because I was away at Belmont at the time, and she knew how important hockey was, so she kept it to herself because she didn't want me to lose focus."

I think back to Robbie Mason when we were at Belmont Prep together. He was such an arrogant jerk. At least that's what I thought at the time. And for many years after. But now, with the added benefit of hindsight, I'm starting to see that Robbie was just a kid who'd been through way too much at his age, was trying to fit in, trying to make it, with the weight of the world secretly resting upon his shoulders.

"Mom beat it again the second time. But then it came back just last year. And it's... everywhere. And it makes me so fucking angry." He exhales heavily. "She spent all her time and all her money on me when I was growing up because *I* wanted to play hockey, and *I* had to have the newest skates and the best gear, even though sometimes at night I'd eat dinner and she wouldn't. She'd tell me it was because she wasn't hungry, or she'd had a big lunch, but I knew the truth. And I chose to ignore it and eat my dinner like a spoiled fucking brat." He scoffs again, only this time it's self-deprecating.

"Robbie, you were just a kid," I interject, trying to reassure him.

"I promised myself that as soon as I made it big, as soon as I got some money, I'd take care of her. But then hockey took over and now it's too late."

"I'm so sorry, Robbie," I say sincerely, my heart breaking for him.

"It all happened so fast this time. Once the chemo stopped working, the doctors basically told us there's not a lot they can do. I looked into trials and programs all over the world, but Ma said she didn't want to do any of that. Said she's been through so much, and now it's just about keeping her comfortable."

Thank God it's dark because the last thing I want is for Robbie to see the tears brimming in my eyes, threatening to spill over. I clear my throat. "Is she, um, still in Boston?"

"Yeah, she's still there. Still in the shitty house I grew up in because she refused to let me buy her a new one. She's always been like that, my ma. She's the most selfless person I know." I can hear the fondness in his tone, and my heart swells. "I've arranged for a nurse to live with her, to keep her safe and comfortable. And I try to get there as much as I can to see her. I'd love for her to come here to New York, stay with me for a while, but travel is hard for her, and I know she's comfortable at home."

An obvious heaviness settles between us, and it's at that moment I realize just how close we are. I can feel Robbie's breath fan against my cheek, feel his warmth, feel his sadness.

"Thanks for coming here tonight to check on me," I say after a moment.

"Are you still in pain?" he asks, his voice dangerously low and right there.

"Yeah," I whisper. "But I'll be okay, I'm—"

"Lie back," he interjects.

"Huh?"

"Roll onto your back."

Confused, I slowly roll over so that I'm facing the ceiling again, but just as I'm about to ask what the heck he's doing, Robbie shifts even closer, one of his muscular thighs coming to rest over mine. His hand trails tentatively down my hoodie from just underneath my breasts, over my stomach before dipping underneath and stopping at my bare skin. When his fingers toy with the waistband of my sweatpants, I can't help but suck in a tremulous breath. *What is happening?*

"It's okay," he whispers so close I'm sure I can feel a brush of his lips against my ear. "I got you."

Again… What. The. Fuck. Is. Happening?

I'm about to remind him that it's really not a great time for him to delve any further south, but he stops, and his palm rests flat against my lower belly before his strong fingers start to move with the perfect amount of pressure, massaging away the painful ache beneath the surface. It's so good, I almost moan, but I manage to keep my sounds in, sighing instead, and allowing my head to sink deeper into my pillows.

"Is this okay?" Robbie asks, his voice barely a whisper.

"Mmm… yeah." I stifle another moan, feeling my body become lax beneath the totally non-sexual ministrations of his fingers.

This is something I've never experienced before, and I can't say I hate it.

"Go to sleep, Keller," he whispers again, those lips and the stubble lining his jaw brushing against my skin.

I make a sound. At least, I think I make a sound. And I'm pretty sure whatever sound it was, was met with a low chuckle. But my eyelids are too heavy, and before I know it, I'm swallowed up by a cloud of bliss.

———

When I wake in the morning, to the sound of the city alive outside, I'm still in pain, but it's a dull pain, misty with the morning-after fog of one of the best night's sleep I've had in as long as I can remember.

I stretch languorously with a loud groan, which is when I notice the bed beside me is empty. Heaving myself to sit up, my hazy gaze scans the apartment for any hint of Robbie, but nothing more than the long-forgotten hint of his spicy scent remains. I pull back the curtains to find it's still raining out and at least mid-morning, and I reach for my phone sitting on the nightstand, my heart doing a ridiculous hop, skip, and jump when I see a text message waiting for me. *Pathetic.*

> Asshat: I had to leave so I could make my PT.
> Didn't want to wake you. I hope you feel a little
> better.

Before I do anything, I change his contact in my phone, because if Robbie did anything last night, he proved that he's no longer the asshat I thought he was.

For a moment, I stare at his words on the screen. *I hope you feel a little better.* Suddenly, all I keep thinking about is the feel of his fingers on my skin, massaging me until I drifted off to sleep.

Biting back my smile, I tap out a reply.

> Me: Hey. I just woke up. I'm feeling much
> better. Thank you for last night. For everything.

I bury my head in my hand when I realize I'm actually giddy. *Giddy.* What the hell is wrong with me? I'm giddy texting Robbie Mason. What the fuck happened between us last night?

My phone vibrates in my hand, interrupting my internal freakout.

> Robbie: Anytime, Keller x

I stare at his words, at the kiss. And… oh God.

Flopping back against my pillows, I release a loud sigh.

I think I might be in trouble.

CHAPTER 21

ROBBIE

> Keller: Can you imagine my surprise when I
> answered the door to a man delivering enough
> groceries to feed a family of five?

As I lie on my stomach while the PT works me over, I'm grinning at my phone like a fucking lunatic.

> Me: So random.

> Keller: Oh, so you have nothing to do with this?
> Despite your cell number literally being on the
> order form?

> Me: So weird.

> Keller: Why did you do this, Robbie?

I roll my eyes.

> **Me:** Can a guy do something nice without being interrogated?

> **Keller:** Chocolates are nice. Jewelry. Wine. Perfume. They're all nice... Groceries?

> **Me:** You said you haven't been taking care of yourself and it might've caused your flare up. You need to eat properly to look after yourself and I couldn't help but notice your cupboards and fridge were completely bare last night. So I ordered you some groceries... no big deal.

She doesn't reply right away, and the longer I stare at my unanswered text message, the more I'm starting to wonder if I might've actually annoyed her. I mean, groceries Robbie... really? What the fuck, man? I groan at my own stupidity.

"Yeah, you're really tight there," Jace, the PT says, paying extra attention to my right glute.

I don't let him know that my groan had nothing to do with my butt cheek and everything to do with a certain blue-eyed girl I bought fucking *groceries* for. But then my phone vibrates in my hand, and I find myself releasing the breath I didn't even realize I'd been holding.

> **Keller:** Ok, now I'm crying.

My skin pricks and I feel something knot my gut.

> **Me:** What's wrong? Why are you crying?

> **Keller:** Robbie! That's literally the nicest thing anyone has ever done for me.

I stare at her words, my brows knitting together. A hundred bucks of groceries is the nicest thing anyone's ever done for her? Is she bullshitting me right now?

Me: Buying you a few groceries is the nicest thing anyone's ever done for you?

Keller: Well, no. I mean... it's more the sentiment behind it. If that makes sense?

Me: No. You're gonna have to spell it out.

Keller: No one's ever worried about me enough to care whether or not I look after myself. Other than my parents, of course.

I drag my teeth over my bottom lip as an unfamiliar feeling tugs in my chest.

Me: Not even Tadd?

Keller: Especially not him!

That pisses me off. I rub my stubbled chin, staring at her response, but before I can reply, another text comes through.

Keller: OMG.

Me: What??

Keller: Are we FRIENDS?

I feel my chest tighten, but I force myself not to overthink anything.

Me: Just say thank you, Keller.

Keller: Thank you, Keller.

I shake my head.

Me: Are you feeling better?

Keller: Yeah, a little better. Thanks.

Me: What are you doing right now?

Keller: I'm having a lazy John Hughes day.

Me: John Hughes day?

Keller: Yeah. I started The Breakfast Club. I'm currently in the middle of Sixteen Candles. And up next is Pretty In Pink.

Me: For the record I have no idea what you're talking about.

Keller: Are you serious?

Me: ...

Keller: Ok, no offense but I'm totally judging you.

Me: ...

Keller: Anyway... what are you doing today?

Me: Right now, I'm getting my ass pounded.

Keller: Casual Sunday morning ass-pounding?

Me: PT. My glutes are tighter than normal. I think it might be from being stuck in one position last night.

FAMOUS LAST WORDS 145

> Keller: I'm sorry. You should have shoved me
> over. I have a habit of hogging the bed.

I don't miss the way my heart shifts at the memory of sharing the bed with Fran last night. She sleeps like a dead person, and I doubt I could've moved her even if I tried. But, at that thought, I'm suddenly taken back to last night.

I'd woken up at about three a.m., thirsty as a motherfucker. It was still pouring rain out, and the lightning flashing through the window was enough to illuminate the tiny apartment for me. I took Fran's wheat pack and popped it in the microwave to reheat it. I pissed. Chugged a glass of water. And I tiptoed back to the bed and carefully made my way under the covers. But just as I was placing the wheat pack gently against Fran's stomach, she rolled over and curled into me, thigh wrapping around my hip, arm draping over my chest, a soft moan slipping from her lips. And I froze. Literally froze, there on my back, balancing precariously on the edge of the bed, scared that if I moved, I'd wake her. I didn't know what to do. And so that's how I stayed for the rest of the night. In the one position with Fran clinging to me like a goddamn koala. And, if I'm being honest, it was one of the best nights I've had in a long while.

I smile at the memory, but then I find myself responding without even considering my words.

> Me: Nah, it was surprisingly nice to share a bed
> with someone.

Keller: It's been a while huh?

I could lie. But what's the point?

> Me: Yeah. Coming up 26 years now.

Keller: Wait. What? You've never shared a bed
with someone?

I chuckle.

> Me: Fran. I'm Robbie Mason. I've shared beds with plenty of people.

Keller: I think I just pulled a muscle from rolling my eyes so hard.

> Me: Last night was the first time I've stayed.

Keller: You've never stayed the night at a girlfriend's house?

> Me: I've never had a girlfriend.

Keller: Shut the fuck up!

> Me: ...

The three dots appear in our text window before disappearing. Then they're back. Gone. Back. Gone. And I think this goes on for about four whole minutes.

> Me: You're Googling me again, aren't you?

Keller: Can you blame me? Like you said. You're Robbie Mason, the hot-shot hockey player. And if there's one thing I've learned really quickly over the last couple of weeks, it's that hockey players are renowned playboys. I find it hard to believe you've never had at least one girlfriend. Unless you're a manwhore like your buddy, Dallas. According to Google, he's slept with over 500 women.

> Me: There was someone. Back in St. Paul. We dated for a while. I was ready to make it official, but then Ma got sick, and I had to go back to Boston for a few weeks.

Keller: What happened?

I stare at my phone, pinching my bottom lip between my fingers. I haven't admitted this to anyone. Not even Andy. It's not a trust issue. More of a pride thing. But, for whatever reason, after last night, I feel like I can open up to Fran in a way I've never felt like I could open up to anyone else.

> Me: Remember when you asked me why I fought Ben Harris?

Keller: You're gay???

I can't help but snort. "Gay?"

Jace pulls his hands abruptly from my ass. "Sorry. Too close?"

I realize I just said that out loud. Really loud. And I glance over my shoulder to find Jace's face fraught with panic. Of course, our head PT just so happens to be a proud gay man. "Oh. No. Sorry, Jace." I manage a light laugh, suddenly more than a little awkward. "Just reading a… a text message."

Jace arches a questioning brow, and I don't miss the curious smirk that ghosts his lips, and awesome. Homeboy probably thinks I'm gay now.

> Me: No, I'm not gay. What??

Keller: Sorry. You lost me.

> Me: Obviously…

Keller: So, you were seeing someone?

Me: Yes. I was seeing someone. FEMALE. I'd never been serious with anyone before. It's hard to get serious with someone when you're a professional hockey player. But we were dating for a while, and I really thought she might've been the one. Hell, I'd even planned on taking her home to meet Ma.

Keller: What happened?

My jaw clenches as anger courses through me at the memory.

Me: She hooked up with Ben while I was in Boston. Turns out she was nothing but a fucking puck bunny in disguise. And I was the stupid ass who'd been too blind to see it.

Keller: And Ben Harris was your friend?

Me: Yeah. We lived together for our first two years at the Lions. He became one of my best friends.

Keller: I'm sorry that happened to you. And at a time when you were going through so much with your mom.

As much as the memory of Ben and Macy's betrayal still stings, it's actually good to get it off my chest for once. Like a weight being lifted.

> Me: I tried to keep it together as long as I could through the playoffs. But then afterwards, without the distraction of hockey, it all became too much. Between all the stuff with my ma, and Ben and Macy, I don't know... I guess I just went a little off the rails.

Keller: The drinking and the drugs?

> Me: Drinking, yes. Drugs, absolutely not. Hell, I've never even smoked a joint.

Keller: But what about the picture of you with the cocaine?

Keller: Sorry. That was rude. I know you probably don't want to talk about it.

I drag a hand over my face with a hard exhale. That fucking photograph. I swear, it's going to haunt me for the rest of my life. I take a deep breath, contemplating myself for a moment.

> Me: Lola Grey took that photo of me.

Keller: Shut up!

I really consider my next move. Telling Fran about Ben and Macy is one thing. Admitting the truth about Lola is something else entirely. But maybe this is what I need. To tell someone the truth once and for all...

> Me: I started hanging out with Lola after we met in LA at a mutual friend's birthday. She seemed fun at first. But I didn't realize until I was in too deep that she had some serious issues. When I found out she was into drugs and shit, I tried to end it with her, but then she threatened to kill herself.

Keller: Oh my God.

Me: Yeah, so I stayed with her that night, slept on the couch, just to make sure she didn't hurt herself. The next day, a photo of me passed out with a bag of fucking coke was splashed all over social media.

Keller: Why would she do that?

Me: She said if I didn't want her, she was going to make me regret it by making my life a living hell. And she succeeded. The media had a fucking field day. I mean, sure, I lost a few million dollar sponsorship deals, but worst of all, it broke Ma's heart. I had to try and convince her I wasn't turning into my father.

Keller: And then you had to go back and play hockey again.

Me: Being forced to line up on the ice with Ben after what he did and try to pretend like everything was fine. I just couldn't do it. It almost felt like it was all his fault. Like if it hadn't been for the shit he pulled with Macy, then maybe none of that shit would have happened, you know?

Keller: That was the catalyst.

Me: Yeah. I mean, don't get me wrong. I know I fucked up, and no one held a gun to my head. But things would've been so different if Ben hadn't been a traitorous fuck, and Macy hadn't been a cheating whore.

Keller: Can I ask you something?

Me: Shoot.

FAMOUS LAST WORDS **151**

> Keller: Why didn't you come out and tell the
> truth about Lola and the drugs.

I stare at her text, mulling over my response for a long moment.

> Me: Lola was already so messed up. I worried if I told the truth, then it would only cause her more pain. And I wouldn't be able to live with myself if she hurt herself because of me.

> Keller: I get it. I'm so sorry that happened to you, Robbie.

> Me: I can't believe I just told you all that. You officially know more than anyone. Even Andy.

I grin as I tap out a follow up.

> Me: Maybe we are friends...

> Keller: Thank you for telling me. I know how hard that must have been, but I want you to know that I won't repeat a word to anyone. I've got your back. I promise.

"Okay, we're all done, Robbie," Jace says, tapping my thigh.

I tear my focus from my phone, pushing up from the bench.

"Thanks, Jace." I offer an apologetic smile, still feeling bad about the gay comment.

He nods, flashing me a conspiratorial wink before turning back to his station.

I hop off the bench and pull my shorts back on and head back through to the locker room to where most of my teammates are getting geared up for a skate.

Stopping at my cubby, I tap a quick reply to Fran.

> Me: Thanks, Fran. I've gotta get on the ice. Talk later?

Her message comes through almost instantly, and it does something to my heart.

> Keller: I'd like that.

CHAPTER 22

FRAN

Freshly showered, dressed in pajamas, with a big mug of the anti-inflammatory protein hot chocolate Robbie included in the grocery order, I snuggle under my covers with Tessa Bailey's latest release, opening it right as my phone shudders from my nightstand.

I can't help but grin because I already know it's Robbie. We've been texting all day. After he confessed what happened to him with his ex-teammate and the girl he'd been dating, and with Lola Grey, my heart ached for him. But after his on-ice practice, he started back up with the text messages, and he's well and truly back to his cocky, unapologetic self.

> Robbie: How was your shower?

I don't know why, but my cheeks flame from his question. Yes, I told him I was going to have a shower, and no, I don't know why. He didn't need to know that. But something has definitely shifted between us. I suddenly feel like I can tell him things like that. Is that weird? Probably. Do I hate it? Absolutely not.

> Me: Wet.

> Robbie: Jesus, Keller. Warn a guy 😳

My eyes widen when I realize exactly what I just sent him.

> Me: OMG I meant like literally wet. It was the first thing that came into my head. Excuse me while I quietly die.

> Robbie: Nah, you're okay. I mean, it's nothing on the shit you were telling me the night in my hotel room.

I stare at his message, reading it at least a few times while trying to rack my brain. But that night is nothing more than a distant blur of *The Mighty Ducks*, truffle pizza, and almost-kiss gate. *Oh God*. What the hell did I tell him?

> Me: What did I say?

> Robbie: You seriously don't remember??

My stomach twists at the thought.

> Me: Clearly not, or I wouldn't be asking!

> Robbie: Trust me, you don't wanna know 😈

> Me: I don't like you very much right now.

> Robbie: Maybe you'd like me more if I pulled your hair. Or spanked you. Or choked you. You dirty little slut...

FAMOUS LAST WORDS   155

I scream. Actually scream, and I throw my blanket over my head and all but cry.

I am *never* drinking again.

> Me: Okay, so I guess I'm moving to another country, changing my name, dying my hair. It was nice knowing you.

>> Robbie: Don't worry, your kinky little secrets are safe with me 😊

> Me: So, anyway... Escrow closes tomorrow. Are you excited to get the keys?

>> Robbie: Smooth transition there, Keller. But yes. I am excited. My first house. Well... apartment.

My brows knit together.

> Me: Your first?

>> Robbie: Yeah.

> Me: You didn't own a place back in St. Paul?

>> Robbie: Nope. Rented. Call me psychic but I had a feeling it wasn't going to work out there.

I'm suddenly in a panic. I feel terrible. I sold Robbie his first home. Suddenly the obligatory bottle of champagne the agency gives to all buyers feels less than adequate.

> Me: I wish I'd known. That's so exciting!

>> Robbie: It's just a place to live. No big deal.

> Me: It's so much more than just a place to live, Robbie. Aside from being 6 million bucks, it's your first home. It's a huge deal!

I rake my teeth over my bottom lip, contemplating whether or not I tell him. But then I realize he already knows so much about me already, what's one more tidbit.

> Me: This is what I love about real estate. It's not about the selling for me, which is probably a good thing since I suck at it. But I love the thought of helping someone buy a first home. The excitement. The emotion. All of it. There's just something about being able to help people start the next chapter of their life. It's why I've stuck at it through all the shit.

> Robbie: Maybe you should look at helping people to buy instead of helping people to sell. That's a thing, right?

> Me: It is. A buyer's agent. But I don't know. They're always so... pushy and impersonal.

> Robbie: Well, maybe that could be your niche. New York's first buyer's agent who actually gives a shit.

I ponder his suggestion.

> Me: Maybe...

> Robbie: Actually, there's a guy on the team, Alex. He's looking for a place in the city. He lives up in Westchester somewhere, but he has a newborn and wants a place to stay after the games instead of driving home late and waking the baby. I'll introduce you if you'd like.

FAMOUS LAST WORDS   157

My heart jumps at the thought. Not only of the possibility of a new client, but that Robbie would even think to do that. For me.

> Me: OMG Robbie! That would be awesome! I'm already thinking of a couple of places we have listed at the moment, although one of the listing agents is Tadd 🙄

> Robbie: How is the royal bag of dicks since I had words with him? Hasn't been giving you any more trouble?

I consider telling Robbie about Tadd. About how he's been harassing me at work, and how he practically cornered me with Tony to co-list with him. But as much as I love seeing someone stand up to Tadd, I don't think I want to risk upsetting him again; I need my job. And unfortunately, Tadd Jennings has the power to make things very uncomfortable for me at work.

> Me: No. Not at all.

> Robbie: Good. You tell me if he does. I'll pay him a visit.

Why is that so hot?

> Me: Nope. All good.

> Robbie: Can I ask you something?

I relax back against my mountain of pillows, grabbing my mug of hot chocolate and taking a sip that warms me through.

> Me: Sure.

158 SHANN MCPHERSON

The three dots appear in the text window for a long time. But then they're gone. Then they're back. Gone again. And then...

> Robbie: Actually, can I call you?

My eyes nearly pop out of their sockets. I feel entirely unprepared for a phone call. And if there's one thing I hate, it's being unprepared.

> Me: Ok...

A few seconds later, the device illuminates in my hand, vibrating with a call from Robbie Mason. I take a deep breath, centering myself as best I can before sliding to answer.

"Hey," I say, like it's no big deal he's calling me at ten p.m.

"Hey." Even through the phone, his baritone is like chocolate, rich and velvety, a slight rasp that does things to me I don't necessarily dislike.

"What's up?" My own voice is a lot less self-assured than it normally is—basically a mortifying squeak—and I close my eyes in the hope that he doesn't notice.

"Okay, so, you can totally say no if you want—"

I wait a few seconds, but he doesn't continue. "O-kay..."

Robbie clears his throat, and although I can't see him, something tells me he's suddenly a lot less cool, calm, and collected than he usually is; he almost sounds nervous. Very un-Robbie Mason.

"We have a game coming up... in Boston." He releases a breath like he'd been holding onto it. "I spoke to my coaches and told them about my ma, and they've given me special consideration to stay up there for a couple extra nights."

I roll my lips between my teeth, confused as to how this has anything to do with me.

"I know it wasn't included on the itinerary I sent you, but I

FAMOUS LAST WORDS **159**

was wondering if you w-would um… if you would wanna maybe come meet her?"

Stunned, shocked, and everything in between, I'm at a loss for words and breath, it seems. The only part of me that's working is my brain, completely overthinking what he's just asked me.

"You still there?"

I clear my throat. At least he knows the call hasn't died. "Umm, I—"

"I'm gonna fly straight to Boston from Toronto. And I thought you could meet me there. And then, I was going to drive my car back to New York the next day."

"You have a car?" I roll my eyes at my own question. *Yeah, Fran, because that's exactly what you should be focusing on right now. A fucking car, and not the fact that he wants you to go to Boston to meet his dying mother.*

"Yeah, why do you think I wanted a place with a parking spot so bad?"

I clear my throat again, if for nothing else, to provide myself a few extra seconds to consider my response.

"And Ma really wants to meet you," Robbie adds, and there's a blatant hint of fragility in his tone that makes my heart crack.

I shake my head, still completely blindsided. "You told your mom about me?"

"Yeah." He hesitates before adding, "Is that okay?"

"Did you tell her about me and our *arrangement*, or does she think I'm your *actual* girlfriend?"

"I couldn't tell her the *truth*," Robbie says after a brief pause. "She's *dying*, Keller. And do you know the only thing she's scared of about dying isn't the unknown, eternity of death. It's leaving me alone."

My heart hitches, but I bite my cheek instead of responding.

"When I told her about you, she—" He scoffs. "Man, I could almost hear the way she lit up from the inside. She was so happy. Happier than I've heard her sound in a long time."

"Okay, I'll go," I say quickly. "I don't like lying to your mom, but... I'll do it." I puff air from my cheeks, shaking my head at myself.

"Thank you." He releases a heavy breath, sounding relieved. But then he speaks again. "I'll have Andy book your flight."

"Okay." I place my hand over my mouth in an attempt to stifle a yawn.

"I should let you get some sleep," Robbie says, and I don't know—maybe I'm delusional—but it almost sounds like he doesn't want to hang up. Or maybe I'm overthinking. Again. "I'll see you at the game tomorrow night?"

I bite back my smile. "Yeah. I'll be there."

"Goodnight, Keller."

"Goodnight."

CHAPTER 23

FRAN

Tadd Jennings is an asshole. I mean, it's not as if that's a surprise revelation, but as I stand here in the cavernous great room of the Columbus Circle penthouse, staring out as night starts to fall over Central Park, Tadd's really solidified his asshole status with this latest dick move, that's for sure.

I was on my way home to shower and change before making my way to Madison Square Garden in time to meet Vera and Tyler, when Tadd called me in a panic, asking if I could get to the penthouse in time to meet the stagers for the walk-through because he'd been caught in traffic.

That was literally three hours ago. I'm highly doubtful there ever was a walk-through, and I'm growing more and more certain that this is just another one of Tadd's bullshit schemes that I was stupid enough to fall for.

As I look down at my phone, I shake my head and, with a huff, scroll to my messages.

> Me: Hey. I'm caught up at work. When you guys get there, just go ahead and I'll meet you inside.

> Vera: WHEN we get here... We've been here for FORTY MINUTES because Tyler was scared the entire New York City metro system would fail and he'd miss the game. You should see him right now. He's bouncing up and down like a kid waiting for Santa Claus, the Easter Bunny, and the fucking Tooth Fairy all at once. At first it was endearing. Now it's just embarrassing.

Despite the laugh that bubbles up the back of my throat, I feel terrible. I specifically asked Robbie if I could get two extra tickets for Vera and Tyler for tonight's game, and he didn't hesitate. Even at the last minute of what I'm sure is another sell-out game. Robbie didn't have to do that, but he did. And Vera has been texting me all day to tell me how excited Tyler is.

God, I feel like such an idiot. *Stupid Tadd.*

> Me: Imagine what he's going to be like outside the locker room.

> Vera: I'm seriously starting to worry that he might actually make a move on your boy.

My boy... My heart flutters at her words, but before I can respond, I'm startled by a loud chime that echoes through the silence. I spin just as the doors to the private elevator glide open and, as if he's been summoned from the depths of hell, Tadd strides in, grinning broadly, gaze casually flitting about the empty space.

Gripping my phone in one hand, I place my other hand on my hip, glowering at him as he approaches. "The stagers never showed."

Sure, he looks surprised, but I wasn't born yesterday. Tadd

works with some of the city's most renowned vendors; there is no way a stager of this caliber would be a no-show.

I narrow my eyes, teeth gritted. "There was never a walk-through, was there?"

He clutches his chest, feigning hurt, but I can see the glint of humor in his eyes. And smell the not-so-subtle hint of scotch on his breath as he comes far too close.

"Oh, no." He gasps. "Your little boyfriend has a game tonight at the Garden, doesn't he?" He makes a show of checking his watch before flashing me a knowing smirk. "I hope you're not going to be late."

"You're a dick," I snap, pushing past him, but before I can get away, he snags my wrist and tugs me back with such force I stumble on my heels and go crashing into him.

"Falling for me again, I see," he chuckles menacingly.

With my free hand, I dig into my purse and pull out the can of pepper spray I keep in there at all times. Flicking up the lid, I prep it, the nozzle aimed directly at his smarmy face. "Let. Me. Go."

With a derisive scoff, Tadd does as I say, holding his hands up in surrender. "Learn to take a joke, babe."

With the spray still aimed at his face, I walk backwards, in the direction of the elevator. "Touch me again, and I won't hesitate next time."

Tadd has the audacity to roll his eyes, waving a dismissive hand and turning to look out the glass at the city lights. But I still don't take my eyes off him. It's not until I'm safely in the elevator, with the doors shut and two whole floors between us, that I finally tuck the pepper spray back into my purse, releasing the breath I've been holding.

"Fucking asshole," I mutter, wrapping my arms around myself when the adrenalin shivers start to kick in.

———

With no time to go home, I'm forced to head directly to the Garden dressed in the bright pink and *entirely understated* pant suit that I wore to work today.

It's nine minutes into the first period by the time I make it through the checkpoints, and I'm tentative in my inappropriate heels as I'm led down the stairs by one of the arena employees. As if I don't stick out like a sore thumb enough already in a pink suit, the last thing I need is to fall ass over tits in front of a home crowd. But when we make it to the very bottom, I can't help but glance at the man, confused to find that instead of where I sat with Andy last time, in the friends and family section, tonight we're seated right by the ice, behind the net, with nothing but the Plexiglass separating us from giant men and flying pucks. Before I can even sit down, the crowd around me roars as two bodies slam hard against the flimsy divider and I jump, clutching my chest, quietly terrified.

"Oh my God, hey, you made it!" Vera jumps up, hugging me tight before pulling away and tugging on the sleeve of the man seated in the chair next to her. Tyler, I presume.

He tears his gaze away from whatever's happening on the ice, glancing up at Vera and, holy cow. I suppose it was expected that Tyler would be hot—Vera's a literal model—but I never imagined he'd look like *this*. Blond hair, icy blue eyes, chiseled cheekbones. *Hot* doesn't even cut it. I force my gaping jaw closed with a tight smile.

"Fran, Tyler. Tyler, Fran." Vera introduces us as best as she can while Tyler has one eye on the game.

"Oh, hey, Fran," Tyler says as he half stands to pull me in for a side hug. "Thanks so much for this. These seats are… I can't—" Mid-sentence, something must happen in the game, and Tyler pulls away so abruptly I almost fall, wincing when he starts hollering along with the rest of the Thunder fans. "Where're your fuckin' eyes, Ref!"

I balk, side-eyeing Vera.

FAMOUS LAST WORDS   165

"Sorry," she mutters. "Like I said… so embarrassing," she adds with a grimace.

I can't help but laugh as we take our seats, making myself as comfortable as I can while wearing the same clothes I've been wearing since this morning. I consider kicking off my heels because my feet are killing me, but the questionably sticky residue on the ground stops me.

My eyes find the score up on the Jumbotron. 0-0, with the Thunder leading shots at goal. As I scan the arena, it looks like another sell-out crowd, most of them wearing New York fan gear and cheering on their beloved white and black.

Looking out over the flurry of chaos that's currently occurring on the ice, my gaze is immediately drawn to number nine, and I don't miss the way my heart does some sort of somersault in my chest. Of course, I ignore whatever the hell that's all about. But I can't ignore the smile that takes over my lips, watching as Robbie swoops in and steals the puck from the other team before doing some sort of spin maneuver, confusing his opponents, and striding down the ice with effortless ease.

Sailing between two Charlotte players, Robbie passes the puck between the legs of one of them, which elicits a deafening roar from the crowd. He hands off to one of his teammates and rounds the net, narrowly avoiding being pummeled into the boards. But when the puck rebounds off the post with an ear-splitting clang, Robbie's right there again, cradling it with his stick before snapping it so fast, the only thing I see is the little red light flashing behind the net just as Robbie is swallowed up by his teammates to the tune of the crowd going wild.

The noise that rings throughout the arena feels like it could just about lift the roof right off Madison Square Garden and again, I find myself grinning like a moron. But I can't help it. He's good. And technically, if I'm his *girlfriend*, I should at least look like I'm proud, right?

As the players skate back to their positions, preparing for the puck drop, I feel my breath catch in the back of my throat when I notice Robbie's eyes on me. And suddenly, I'm right back there in my bed, feeling his strong hands massage my stomach, his spicy scent enveloping me like a warm embrace, his gentle breath fanning against my skin.

Robbie tips his chin at me, that cocky smirk lifting the corner of his mouth, almost like he knows exactly what I'm thinking. He points his stick at me, and the crowd around us cheers, causing my traitorous cheeks to flush in response. I roll my eyes, shaking my head at him, which only makes him throw his head back and laugh. Jerk. Adorable, sexy jerk.

"Aw, you guys are so cute!" Vera squeals beside me, nudging me with her elbow.

And actually, I almost forgot she was here. Robbie Mason seems to have that effect.

I glance at my friend, trying so hard to act casual, but it's harder than I imagined it would be. Instead, I find myself smiling even more.

Calm the fuck down, Fran. It's all an act. It isn't real. Dial it back a couple of notches.

But that's just it. If this is all an act, then why the hell is my heart racing, and why does my stomach feel as if there are a thousand butterflies swarming chaotically inside of it? And, most importantly, if this is all an act, then why do I feel like I'm in way over my head?

CHAPTER 24

ROBBIE

"Come on, man!" Dallas throws his head back on a groan as he finishes buttoning his shirt. "A win against Charlotte in fucking overtime calls for at least one beer."

I pull on my suit jacket to the tune of every single person in the locker room cheering at Dallas's suggestion. And I suppose I can't blame them. For a lot of them, this is their first winning streak.

"Fine. *One* drink," I relent with an eye roll. "I need to check with Fran first, though."

Some dickhead in the back makes the sound of a cracking whip but I ignore it because, frankly, he has a point. *I need to check with Fran*? Who the fuck am I? Even I'm disgusted with myself.

With a huff, I grab my bag and hitch it up on my shoulder, following Dallas out into the tunnel where we're stopped by a few over-eager kids asking for photos and autographs. I take a Sharpie from someone, but as I look up, my eyes immediately land on Fran, and I feel my brows knitting together because what the hell is she wearing? A bright pink pant suit? She knows the deal; she's supposed to wear my jersey to games. Why the hell is she dressed like a younger, hotter Hilary Clinton?

After finishing up with the kids and stopping to chat to a few VIPs hanging out in the tunnel, Dallas and I make our way over to Fran, Hannah, and who I can only assume to be Fran's friend, Vera, and her boyfriend, Tyler.

With a crease still etched between my brows, I sidle in close to Fran, wrapping an arm around her waist as I lean in. "Running for office?" I murmur close against her ear.

She looks up at me, obviously confused.

"Nice pant suit." I smirk.

She offers me a deadpan look, but I don't miss the tinge of pink that flushes her cheeks, the small smile that ghosts her lips. And I don't know, but I fucking love that I have this effect on her.

"I was held up by stupid ass… *work*," she says quickly with a dismissive wave of her hand. But if I'm not mistaken, there's something else there. Something she's trying purposely to avoid. "I didn't get a chance to go home and change. Sorry."

I hate that she just apologized to me. It actually makes me feel sick. She doesn't need to apologize to me. I was just playing. But instead of pressing her, I nod and make a mental note to ask her about work when we're not surrounded by people.

Fran clears her throat and plasters a broad smile on her face. "Robbie? Dallas? This is my friend, Vera, and her boyfriend, Tyler."

I'm forced to turn back to the group, shaking Tyler's hand when it's thrust into my face.

"Oh my God, man, that was such a good game!" he practically shouts, his eyes wide with excitement, and I can't help but grin. "The way you baited Rollins into dropping his gloves and then skated away grinning while he was escorted to the box was fucking priceless."

FAMOUS LAST WORDS   169

I bite back my own cocky grin. "Rollins is a renowned instigator baiter. Dude thought he had me."

I swear Tyler looks at me like he has hearts in his eyes.

"Yo, did you ask Fran?" Dallas smacks me in my chest.

Fran arches a brow, glancing dubiously between me and Dallas. "Ask Fran what?"

I roll my eyes. "I've been *coerced* into going out for a celebratory drink with the guys."

"Oh, okay…" Fran says, and I'm not totally sure, but I almost sense a hint of disappointment in her tone. "You don't need to ask me." She laughs. "Have fun."

"Franny," Dallas interjects, pushing me aside and snaking his arm around Fran's shoulders. "As the girlfriend of our undisputed MVP, you of course are expected to accompany us for said celebratory drinks." He flashes his trademark playboy grin. "Someone's gotta keep the puck bunnies away."

Fran meets my gaze, and I almost laugh at the sheer panic in her eyes.

"And y'all are welcome to join us, too!" Dallas says, slapping Tyler on his shoulder, and I'm pretty sure the dude's about to spontaneously combust.

"If Fran goes, I'll go," Vera says, looking at Fran.

I shove Dallas out the way, wrapping my arm back around Fran and whispering, "Just one drink."

"Will there really be puck bunnies?" She glances up at me, big blue eyes fraught with worry.

And I know what she's really scared of. She's scared of the women from the internet, the ones who have gone out of their way to hate on her for no other reason than the fact that she's *dating* me. If I'm honest, it's those women who give the puck bunnies a bad rep. Bunnies are harmless most of the time; the crazy fangirls are the real problem.

I squeeze her waist, ducking my head so my lips brush against her ear. "You don't have to worry with me around. I got you."

We head to a hole-in-the-wall bar in Hell's Kitchen with a small neon sign hanging over the door that displays a flashing *Ned's*. Inside, it's all dark and dingy, with brick walls, concrete floor, worn leather booths. There are some high-top tables dotted about, a couple of 80s-style pinball machines set up in the back next to a pool table, and an old jukebox playing some killer classics. Apparently, this is where the guys go for a low-key drink after a home game when they don't feel like being bothered, and I can see why; apart from a few welcome cheers and the occasional congratulatory slap on the back, we're otherwise left alone.

The beer Dallas handed me the moment we walked in over an hour ago remains untouched, held in my hand at all times to give off the illusion of drinking. Thankfully, no one's noticed. I sit in a booth with Logan, Dallas, Tyler, and one of our second line d-men, Happy, shooting the shit, while Fran, Hannah and Vera play a game of pool, which is really just them shooting random balls all over the table and anywhere but into the pockets. It's entertaining but also nice that I get to watch Fran bend over because in those pants—man, her ass is something else. And, since I'm technically sitting here in front of everyone as her *boyfriend*, I can get my fix without trying not to get caught.

Yes, I have come to terms with the fact that Fran *fucking* Keller is hot and not the bane of my existence that my fragile, teenage boy mind made her out to be all those years ago.

"Another drink?" I ask the guys, pushing out of the booth.

Of course, they all cheer, and I cast them a grin before turning and heading for the bar, which is when my gaze lands on Fran as she's bending over. I catch a glimpse down the front of her suit jacket and holy shit. She's not wearing anything under it. Not even a bra. I almost stumble over my own size thirteens. Just as I collect myself, I realize she's looking at me and not at the ball she's aiming for, and a knowing smirk ghosts her pretty lips.

FAMOUS LAST WORDS   171

With a hard exhale, I force myself to look away, pushing my hair back from my face. *Fuck me.*

"Same again, Mason?" The bartender lifts his chin at me.

"Uh, yeah." I raise my full, warm bottle of beer in the air, leaning over the counter so he can hear my lowered voice. "Can you get me a fresh one?"

He eyes the untouched Miller Lite, his brow furrowing momentarily before realization settles across his face. With a kind, understanding smile, he says, "Sure thing."

Resting my forearms against the counter, I look at all the sports memorabilia lining the walls, posters signed by some of the greats, and I can't help but smile because this is the kind of bar I can handle. I hate all those pretentious hotspots, wall-to-wall d-bags and people just there to be seen; this is my kind of place.

"Hey, whatcha doing?"

I turn my head to find Fran's face right there next to me, her hand snaking around my back and resting dangerously close to my ass. And it's only now that I'm noticing just how rosy her cheeks are, eyes slightly glazed, lids droopier than normal.

I duck my head a little closer, offering her a knowing grin. "You drunk, Keller?"

Her face twists adorably as if in serious thought. "Nah, just a little tipsy," she shrugs. "I didn't have any dinner because of stupid Tadd..." she drags the word out as her eyes go wide, and it's clear she didn't mean for that to slip out.

"Tadd?" I turn to face her fully, my brows lowering as anger bubbles in my chest.

She blinks at me, and I can tell she's trying to think of a lie, so I arch a brow, fold my arms across my chest, spearing her with a warning look. "Keller?"

She heaves a sigh, her shoulders falling with resignation. "I lied to you."

"You *lied* to me. What does that mean?" I press, impatient

because I just don't have it in me to deal with another fucking liar in my life.

Fran drags her teeth over her plump bottom lip, clearly hesitant. But just when it looks like she's about to talk, we're interrupted by fucking Dallas and I almost tell him to fuck right off.

"Where's the drinks, my guy?" He slaps me on my shoulder, oblivious to the tension currently settled between Fran and me.

"Here you go, fellas." The bartender places a tray of drinks onto the counter, and without even acknowledging him, I hand over my card, my steely gaze still set firmly on Fran.

"Is... everything okay?" Dallas asks, picking up the tray, his curious gaze flitting between me and Fran.

Fran offers him a tight smile. I offer nothing more than a grunt. Thankfully he takes that as his cue and carries the drinks back to the guys.

"When you asked me if Tadd has been causing trouble, and I told you he hasn't," Fran begins, stepping up to me. "I lied."

I'm momentarily relieved because in the completely messed up part of my mind that is scarred from past betrayals, I thought she was about to tell me she lied about her and Tadd being over. But then when I realize what she's just said, my anger is back.

"What did he do?" I ask through gritted teeth.

"He's been harassing me on the work chat. Asking me all sorts of inappropriate questions about you, *us*. He asked me to co-list with him on a really huge listing, and when I said hell no, he cornered me in our boss's office, and of course Tony was supportive of the idea. I couldn't say no." Her blue eyes are wide with sincerity as she continues. "And then today, he tricked me into going to the penthouse we're co-listing on, telling me to wait for the stagers, but the stagers never showed. Because there never were stagers. It was his way of keeping me from coming to the game tonight." She shakes her head. "He's a dick."

I let her words sink in, allowing my brain to process what she's just told me. And white hot rage sears through my veins. I

FAMOUS LAST WORDS **173**

drag my tongue over my bottom lip, carefully considering my next move. "Where does he live?"

Her brows knit together, her eyes flitting between mine. "No."

"Keller, I fucking warned him," I seethe, trying so hard to keep my voice down.

"I know. And I appreciate you for doing that Robbie, but the truth is, I think—" She pauses, like she's not sure she should say it. "I think what you said might've made things worse."

I scoff. "You're kidding me, right?"

She searches my face.

"You can't just let him get away with treating you like this."

She shakes her head again. "No, I'm not. I promise. I just—" She closes her eyes and pinches the bridge of her nose a moment, her gaze almost pleading when it meets mine again. "Just let me deal with him, okay?"

I stare at her for a pause. And I want to argue with her. I really do. But I also don't want to make things more difficult for her. I know the corporate world is a lot different from professional hockey. If Tadd was a hockey player, I'd just have it out with him on the ice and be done with it. But I can't go to his place right now and beat the shit out of him; I'd wind up in jail, and that's not going to help anyone.

"Please, Robbie."

I'm pulled from my thoughts by Fran's sweet voice, her hand rubbing up and down my arm.

"Please just let me deal with Tadd." She flashes me the hint of a reassuring smile. "And I promise you, if it gets to be too much, I'll let you know."

"You better," I warn her, only half-joking, managing the semblance of a smile. But deep down, I still don't like this. From what Fran's told me about him, I know what sort of guy he is, and I don't trust him one fucking bit.

"I don't know what the hell's going on over there," Dallas yells, causing both Fran and I to look over, finding everyone staring at us. "But can y'all just kiss and make up so we can keep drinking?"

Logan and Happy start banging the table like fucking toddlers, and suddenly everyone is chanting. "Kiss! Kiss! Kiss!"

"Oh my God," Fran murmurs.

I look down at her to find her cheeks almost as pink as her pants suit. And when her eyes meet mine, I arch a wagering brow. "What do you say, Keller? Should we give 'em what they want?"

Her gaze dips down to my lips, lingering for a few long seconds before darting back up again, and fuck me, when the tip of her tongue pokes out to wet her bottom lip, I swear I feel it in my dick. Hell, I'm not even breathing. And then, suddenly she's reaching up and wrapping her hand around the back of my neck, pulling me down.

"Fuck it," she mutters right as her lips claim mine.

I'm stilted, frozen in place like a fucking jackass. She's kissing me. Fran Keller is actually kissing me. The cheers from our group, the sound of a Motley Crüe song playing in the background, it all fades into nothing, and it's suddenly just the two of us, the warmth of her soft lips helping to breathe life back into me.

I gently cup her jaw with one hand, my other hand landing on her curvy hip, pulling her flush against me with enough force that it causes her to moan against my lips. Seizing the opportunity, I trail my tongue along the seam of her mouth before gently nudging inside, earning another soft sound from her that verges on a whimper, her fingers gripping the lengths of my hair.

When our tongues finally meet, I don't miss the way she flinches ever so slightly, her other hand gripping my arm like it's her lifeline. But she quickly relaxes, taking all that I have to give her until this isn't just a kiss. It's so much more. Her tits are heaving with each of her heavy breaths. Her body melds against mine. She's practically panting, a rumbled sound coming from somewhere deep in the back of my throat as I practically tongue

FAMOUS LAST WORDS 175

fuck her mouth, exploring every part of her that I can as my dick aches with the kind of need I've never felt before.

"Get a room!" a distant voice shouts, yanking me back to reality.

Fran breaks the kiss first, slowly pulling away, and when she looks up at me, those glazed eyes are filled with lust, and I can't stop myself before ghosting her kiss-swollen lips with another graze of my own, taking the moment of closeness to breathe her in.

With my hand still cupping her jaw, I pull away enough to get a good look at her, sweeping the pad of my thumb over her glistening bottom lip, smirking when her lashes flutter closed at my touch.

But then, like a douse of icy cold water, the spell is broken, and Fran single-handedly rips open my chest, yanks out my heart, and crushes the life out of it with her words.

"That should get them off our backs for a while," she murmurs, turning away from me and knocking back the remainder of her tequila soda before placing the empty glass on the counter.

Staring at her, I stand up straighter, squaring my shoulders, pushing my hair away from my face as I allow her words to sink in. How have I been so fucking stupid?

From the night we spent together in her bed, to the secrets we've shared since, I let myself get carried away like a fucking love-sick fool. Fran doesn't have feelings for me. And I don't have feelings for her either. And, as much as it sucks, this is the harsh reminder I needed; this isn't fucking real.

CHAPTER 25

FRAN

Me: Good luck with the game tonight.

I stare down at the last message I sent Robbie. The message I sent three hours ago. The message that has not only gone unanswered but has been left on *read*.

I mean, I can't say I'm shocked. It's been like this for the last few days. Me sending messages, only for him to either send a blunt, one-word response or leave me on read. At first, I was hurt. Confused. Racking my brain over what the hell I did wrong. Now, I'm just pissed.

I thought things between us were good. After Monday night at the bar, and the kiss—oh, Lord, the *kiss*—I thought we were better than good. Apparently, I was wrong. And despite being the best kiss of my entire life, that damned life altering kiss seemed to ruin everything.

On Tuesday morning, I woke up slightly hungover but brimming with excitement to speak to him. I was sure that after that kiss, and the way we'd been so touchy-feely afterwards, things had shifted between us. But I also knew I had to play it cool. You know? Just in case.

> Me: Hey, how are you?

No response came through, so an hour later I tried again, keeping it strictly business while hoping for an opening.

> Me: I was just checking in to make sure
> everything is good with the apartment. Let me
> know.

Obviously, the apartment was the last thing on my mind, but I figured that might get him talking since escrow closed on Monday and I knew he was in possession of the keys. Instead, all I got *two hours* later was a simple…

> Robbie: Yep. All good.

Confusing, for sure. A little concerning, definitely. But I put it down to the stress of hockey practice and the chaos of moving into his new place, so I let it slide. But then I didn't hear from him again all day.

The following day, Wednesday, the Thunder were due to play another home game at Madison Square Garden. But I couldn't go because I had a shift at the bar, and I couldn't ask Vera to cover for me because she'd been shooting all day and was due back on location early Thursday.

> Me: Hey, sorry. I can't make the game tonight. I
> have a shift at the bar. I hope you win!

I expected something—anything—but all I got was a thumbs up emoji. I knew then that something was seriously wrong, and all I could put it down to was the kiss.

Now, here I am on Friday, and Robbie is playing across the river in Jersey. I could have gone to watch him. But I didn't go because… well, because I wasn't fucking invited. And now he's leaving me on read. Well, you know what? Fuck you, Robbie Mason.

> Me: If you're going to ignore me, the least you could do is turn off your goddamn read receipts!

———

I've barely touched the shrimp noodles I ordered in from my favorite Chinese place. I haven't even finished the glass of wine I poured, unable to tear my eyes from the television.

It's sixteen minutes into the first period and Jersey is already up 2-0. But it's not just the score that's got my stomach in knots. It's Robbie. He isn't playing like I've ever seen him play. In fact, he's hardly been playing at all. Of the sixteen minutes so far, he's already spent more time in the penalty box than on the ice. Two minutes for boarding, another two minutes for tripping, and five minutes for getting up in the ref's face for which he was almost ejected from the game entirely.

It's almost as if he's choosing violence over the puck. I don't know much about hockey, and I'm not ashamed to admit that Robbie Mason looks damn good when he's all aggressive on the ice, but I'm pretty sure that's not the way to win a game.

When the camera zooms in to a close-up of Robbie in the box, knee bouncing, eyes blazing, mouthguard clamped between his teeth. It's hot but there's something else there. Something unfamiliar. Something I'm wondering if only I can see. And, despite how pissed I am at him for blatantly ignoring me these last few days like a jerk, I don't miss the way my heart lurches in my chest at the thought that maybe there's more to this.

Now, it's almost two a.m., and I'm wide awake.

Even after forcing myself to drink my glass of wine, sleep

FAMOUS LAST WORDS **179**

evades me, and I lie here, staring up at the ceiling, watching the shadows cast from outside as they dance across the room.

With a resigned sigh, I grab my phone from the nightstand, checking the screen to make sure there's no new message from Robbie, like I might have possibly missed it; I've always been a sucker for punishment. Of course, there's no message. *Idiot.*

I re-read the last few texts I sent to him.

> Me: I saw the game. Are you okay?

> Me: I just want to check you're okay?

> Me: Can you at least let me know you're okay?

Nothing. Not even a fucking thumbs up.

Dragging a hand over my face, I rub my tired eyes, my mind flashing back to the last view of Robbie from tonight's game as he was being escorted from the rink with blood streaming from his nose, another rivulet of crimson pouring from a split in his lip. Sure he was grinning, but there was no hint of humor in his gaze. His eyes were dark, empty and hollow, and that smirk he wore was pure malevolence.

Jersey led the whole game. They were going to win. With only three minutes left in the final period, they were ahead 4-1. After their fourth goal, the puck was taken back to the center and everyone was lined up waiting for the drop, which is when the camera panned in on Robbie and his opponent clearly goading one another. But then, the second the puck dropped, the game was all but forgotten.

Robbie threw his stick, shucked his gloves and, with fists up, he and his opponent circled each other like apex predators, ready for battle.

The crowd was going wild, chanting at the two to fight, and all the while I just sat there on the sofa, chewing on my nail, staring at the man wearing the number nine New York jersey. He looked like Robbie Mason. But he was a far cry from the Robbie I'd gotten to know over the last few weeks. It seemed the sweet man who had groceries delivered to my door was all but gone.

I forced myself to turn away after the first blow, and I didn't look back until the fight was over and Robbie was being dragged off the ice by two officials. Face covered in blood, he waved at the other team as he skated past their bench, all of them standing, yelling at him, ready for round two.

Tonight's game was too much. If I'm being honest, it hurt my heart.

With a nervous breath, I unlock my phone and scroll to my messages, trying one last time.

> Me: Robbie, I'm genuinely worried about you. I need to know that you're okay. Please.

I stare at the screen until it goes dark, and every last ounce of my hope goes dark with it. But then suddenly I'm startled as my phone shudders against my chest. I swear, I'm not even breathing as I check the screen, relief flooding through me when I see a new message notification from Robbie. I'm almost frantic as I open it, but I'm quickly snapped back to reality when, instead of a reply, I see nothing more than another goddamn thumbs up.

> Robbie: 👍

I glare at the otherwise innocuous emoji as it mocks me from the screen.

I tell him I'm genuinely worried about him, and he sends me a thumbs-up?

My eyes narrow to slits, teeth gritted, my body seething, and it takes all I have not to call the bastard and give him a piece of my mind. But I won't. I refuse to give him the satisfaction. Instead, I switch my phone off entirely, shove it into the drawer in my nightstand, and scowl up at the ceiling.

"Fucking asshole."

CHAPTER 26

ROBBIE

My new place feels a hell of a lot bigger now that it's empty—cold, vast, and really fucking white. White floors, white walls, white cabinetry in the kitchen. How did I not realize it was so damn white? It's giving me a headache. Or maybe the headache is a result of last night's shitty decision to end a loss with a fight. Sure, it felt good to beat the shit of Jake Danowski—the guy who has the biggest fucking mouth in the league—but I'm paying for it this morning, that's for sure.

The team doctor said my nose isn't broken, but man, does it hurt like a motherfucker. Everything hurts. I look down at my busted knuckles, flexing my fingers, shaking out my right hand that's still throbbing.

It's been a long time between games like the one last night. I knew New York had a long-standing beef with New Jersey, I just hadn't realized it was that serious. Even Rusty got into the action, and that guy's avoided on-ice conflict his entire career.

It didn't help that I've been so fucking keyed up the last week over a certain blue-eyed girl. Last night I'd been out for blood, and man, did I get it.

I blame the kiss. In fact, no. I blame my stupid decision to go to Fran's house the night she was sick. It was one thing to stop by and check in—make sure she wasn't dead—but staying to take care of her? That was the beginning of my demise. I mean, yeah, I tried to kiss her that night in my hotel room. And the thoughts I've had of her since then have been borderline obsessive, but I really felt something change between us after that night in her bed. It even flowed through in the conversations we shared after. I told Fran things I've never told anyone. Because for the first time in my life, it actually felt as if I was connecting with someone on a level deeper than just physically.

But then we kissed. And everything changed.

I didn't know kissing could feel like that; I didn't know it was possible to feel connected to someone on an existential level through the sheer act of mouths touching. And I was so sure she felt it too. But clearly, I was wrong. And every time I've closed my eyes since that moment, all I keep seeing is that look on her face before she quickly turned away from me—blatantly indifferent—because she felt nothing. It had been all part of the plan to fool everyone into thinking we're together. But we're not together. And that was the proverbial slap to the face I needed. A wake-up call. Reminding me exactly what it is we're doing. I'm nothing to Fran. Nothing more than her old high school enemy who reappeared in the right place, at the right time, to save her ass from losing her job.

Man, I'm such a fucking idiot.

The security panel dings, indicating a call from downstairs, and I jog across to answer it, muttering under my breath, "It's about fucking time."

The furniture delivery is more than an hour late. Andy organized it all, and I don't even know what they're bringing. Only that I'm sixty grand out of pocket, but whatever. It's not like I can sleep on the floor.

"Yeah," I answer the call gruffly.

"Mr. Mason, there's a delivery for you," the guy on the front desk says.

"Yeah, that's fine. You can let 'em up."

"Yes, sir."

I adjust the cap on my head, turning it backwards. I'd been hiding beneath the peak on my way here from the hotel because the last thing I wanted was people gawking at my matching black eyes and fat lip.

Pushing up the sleeves of my sweatshirt, I hurry across the foyer at the sound of a knock, but as I pull open the door, I'm not met with a couple of burly movers like I expected; I'm met with a five-foot-four blonde, holding a plant almost as big as she is. The bushy foliage parts and a pair of blue eyes find mine, widening the moment they do.

Immediately, I'm on edge. Spine stiffening, shoulders tensing. Folding my arms across my chest, I grit my teeth, remaining stoic.

"Oh my God, Robbie," Fran gasps. "Your face!"

I shrug a nonchalant shoulder. "You should see the other guy…"

She doesn't seem to care much for my bravado, nor does she appear to be even remotely deterred by my iciness. And in true Fran Keller form, she steps around me and invites herself inside.

I roll my eyes, closing the door, but I don't move. I just stand in the entryway, watching her as she places the giant plant on the floor.

She removes her jean jacket and, unfortunately, that's when I get a good look at her—Nikes, black yoga pants that leave fucking *nothing* to the imagination, and a white t-shirt that hugs her tits and Fuck. Me. Her nipples are hard. I'm forced to avert my eyes to the plant like it's the most interesting thing I've ever seen.

"It's a ficus," Fran says, like I care. "The guy at the lot said it's one of the easiest plants to care for. Great for people who travel often."

I arch a brow, glancing at her. "You... bought me a plant?"

"It's a housewarming gift," she says matter-of-factly, placing her hands on her hips.

Don't look at her hips. Don't look at her hips. My jaw ticks, but I say nothing.

"Or maybe a peace offering?" Her brows climb a little higher, like she's unsure.

I tear my gaze from her, giving a wide berth to her and the plant, moving behind the kitchen island. I don't know why. There's nothing here. I don't even have any fucking food or drinks in the place. But I needed to do something, and the island offers a decent amount of distance between us.

"Thanks," I say, dragging my hand along the smooth countertop.

Silence ensues, and although my focus is wholeheartedly fixed on the intricate marbling in the stone, I can feel Fran's eyes on me. After a few seconds, she turns and heads for the windows, and I lift my gaze at the wrong fucking time, catching the perfect view of her ass as her hips sway side to side in those pants. *Goddammit.* I shake my head, staring down into the gleaming sink.

"So, what do you think?"

"About what?" I ask, eyes now fixed on the faucet.

"This place," she laughs. "Do you love it?"

"It's okay." I lift a shoulder. "Whiter than I realized."

More silence.

"The Allora designer chose to keep the interior neutral so as not to take away from the view."

I glance upwards. She's facing the glass, looking out at the bright, sunny Manhattan morning, and again, my eyes betray me, tracking the generous curve of her ass.

"You don't need to try sell me anymore, Keller," I say with a scoff. "Been there. Done that. The place is mine now."

She looks at me over her shoulder, and I catch something there in her eyes. A flash of hurt, maybe? I'm not sure. I check my watch. Where the fuck is the fucking furniture delivery?

"Robbie?"

I hear her sneakers approach, squeaking on the shiny floor.

I don't chance looking at her. Instead, I pull open one of the kitchen drawers, looking inside for some unknown reason. "What's up?" I ask, casually.

She's right there. Beside me. I can feel her. Sense her. *Smell* her. God, she smells good. Like vanilla and maybe lemons. I don't know. But it's a scent I could drown in. And it's all Fran Keller.

"I don't know what happened... Are–are we okay?"

Still looking in the drawers, crouching down to inspect the runners like I have any idea of the mechanics of a fucking drawer, I offer a noncommitting sound.

"Jesus, will you stop!" Fran shouts, slamming the drawer closed with such force she almost jams my damn fingers.

Standing to my full height, I tuck my hands into the pockets of my jeans, forcing myself to meet her eyes. And I'm a little shocked to find that her gaze no longer holds any hint of sadness; she's totally pissed.

"What the fuck, Robbie?" Fran throws her hands in the air. "You've barely said more than two words to me all week, and now you won't even *look* at me!"

And of course she's hot when she's pissed; I swear the universe is against me.

"What. Is. Going. On?" she presses, annunciating each word.

I stare at her, blinking once. "What do you expect me to say?"

"You flipped a switch!" she exclaims incredulously. "We were... I don't know... friends."

I snort. "We were *never* friends, Keller."

She looks at me like I've just slapped her, and I snap my stupid mouth shut because even I know that was uncalled for.

"Was it the kiss?" Her voice is small. Reluctant.

I scoff. "No." *Lies.*

She continues watching me, saying nothing, and I assume she wants more.

"We're fake dating. Why wouldn't we fake-kiss? It'd be weird if we didn't." I shrug another shoulder. "It's all part of the deal, right?"

The anger in Fran's eyes makes way for something else, but before I can figure out what it is, she looks down, tucking a loose lock of her blonde hair behind her ear. "Maybe we should forget it."

Panic consumes me. "Forget what?"

This time, it's Fran who lifts a shoulder, looking up at me, her blue eyes seemingly bigger. "This." She waves a finger between us. "I mean, you're back to being the revered hockey star everyone loves. And I... well, I sold a property. I'm not fired... *yet.*" With another heaving sigh, she looks around at the apartment before meeting my eyes again.

I'm shaking my head before I even realize. "No."

She balks, clearly surprised by my response. "Excuse me?"

"We have an agreement," I remind her. "A *legally binding* agreement."

Her cheeks flush and that anger is back, eyes narrowed, gaze steely.

"The deal was to stay together until my probation is up." I drag my teeth over my bottom lip.

She glares at me, folding her arms across her chest, and I force myself not to look at the way it makes her tits even more pronounced.

"This is bullshit."

I shrug. "A deal's a deal, Keller."

She laughs, but there's little to no humor in the sound. "You are fucking delusional if you think I'm going to put up with this."

"Suit yourself. But you're mine until the holidays." And I

know I'm being an ass, but I can't stop myself as I add, "I'll have Andy send you a copy of the agreement so you can read it again."

Fran stares at me long and hard. And if looks could kill, I'd be nothing more than a pile of smoking ash on the gleaming white floor. But I remain impassive, staring down at her.

"You're a fucking asshole," she finally mutters, pushing past me.

I turn, watching as she collects her bag and her jacket before storming for the door.

"Bye, *baby*!" I call out after her.

She pauses, glowering back at me as she flips me off with her middle finger, right before the door slams shut behind her.

I huff a ragged breath, sagging onto the kitchen island, butting my stupid head against the marble. "Fuck my life," I groan against the cold, hard stone.

Fran Keller is a goddamn piece of work. So why the fuck do I want her more than I want air?

CHAPTER 27

FRAN

Normally, I'm not one to go out to the clubs. Bars, yes. But nightclubs? I don't know. They're just not my vibe. Which is why when Vera called and begged me to tag along with her to some hot new club, because Tyler is DJing there for the first time, I was reluctant at first. But when she mentioned free drinks, I couldn't say no, especially since she'd invited Hannah, too.

Now, however, with my strappy shoes pinching my toes, dressed in a skirt so tight it feels like it's cutting off circulation, and a bodysuit that is seriously riding up my ass, I'm really regretting my decision. No amount of free booze is worth this torture. I'd much rather be at home, in my pajamas, drowning my sorrows in cookie dough ice cream while watching reruns of *One Tree Hill*.

"What's up with you tonight?" Vera yells over the music, nudging me.

Before I can respond, Hannah speaks up. "Looks like boy trouble to me."

They both stare at me, waiting expectantly, but what can I say without giving everything away. I could probably get away with telling Vera the truth, but not Hannah. She's the daughter of Robbie's coach, for Chrissake.

Instead of a response, I shake my head with a dismissive wave of my hand.

"Definitely boy trouble," Hannah says to Vera, and the two sip their drinks.

With her perfect brows knitting together, Vera looks at me, placing a hand on my arm. "Did something happen with Robbie?"

"No." I scoff, standing from my stool. "I need another drink."

Both girls just stare at me, but I ignore them, heading for the bar.

As I snake my way through the crowd, I make sure to keep my head down, lest I make eye contact and open myself up to unwanted attention. I need to get drunk. Stat.

Stopping at the bar, I perch my ass on the one free stool, waiting patiently. The bartenders can take as long as they want— anything to prevent having to go back to Vera and Hannah and face another interrogation. Sadly, I don't have to wait too long, despite the six-deep line waiting to be served.

"What can I get you, beautiful?"

I startle, turning to find possibly the most handsome man I've ever seen in real life smiling at me from the other side of the counter. Dark skin. Dark hair. Dark eyes. Gleaming white teeth. A body resembling a *Marvel* superhero. I'm forced to swallow the sudden lump that forms at the back of my throat.

"Um…" My gaze flits about the bar, suddenly at a loss. "I'll just have a tequila soda, thanks."

He studies me a moment, a mischievous glint in his eyes. "You're far too beautiful for such a basic drink. Let me make you something."

Normally I'd roll my eyes, probably tell him to cut the crap

FAMOUS LAST WORDS **191**

and just bring me my damn tequila like I asked. But I can't. He's too good looking to argue with. So instead, I giggle like a moron.

The bartender adds different liquors from glittering bottles into a shiny gold mixer. He looks at me with another breath-taking smile as he lifts the mixer and starts shaking it with vigor, and my eyes immediately fall to his arms. They're like *Hulk* arms. Muscles bulging with every shake. Even the short sleeves of the shirt he's wearing look as if they're about to give up the fight and burst open at any minute.

He places a highball half-filled with ice in front of me, and then, with another smile, he cracks the mixer open and pours the concoction into the glass. And I don't know if it was intentional or not, but… it kind of looks like semen. White and creamy and very jizz-like. When I meet the man's eyes, mid-pour, he winks. *Winks*. And if I'm not careful, I might slip right off this stool.

"One Maximus special." He slides the glass across to me, placing a red and white striped paper straw inside. "In case you were wondering, *I'm* Maximus."

I'm sure his name isn't really Maximus. Regardless, I wrap my lips around the straw and take a tentative sip, but the moment the flavor hits my tongue, I feel my eyes roll back in my head. It's delicious. Nothing like the taste of semen, thank God. It's fruity and tangy, a little sweet, with a definite kick.

"You like that?" *Maximus* leans in closer, his voice suddenly low and gravelly.

I bite down on the straw, stifling the giddy smile that's trying to take hold of me.

He winks at me before moving on to serve another customer, and I feel my cheeks heat because, well, he's hot. Like, *really* hot. And the more alcohol I consume, the more I can feel my resolve start to slip. Yes, I'm fully aware I have a stupid *fake* boyfriend, but Robbie has gone out of his way to make it abundantly clear he has no real interest in me. And, if I'm being honest, it has been far too long between fucks. A girl can only get herself off with a vibrator so many times before she starts to develop a silicon reaction.

"Excuse me, what was that?"

I jump, turning to see Hannah right there, her eyes narrowed dubiously.

"What?" I ask, feigning ignorance.

"The cutsie little smile you just flashed that bartender after he *winked* at you like a fucking creep!" She snorts, saying this loud enough for Maximus to hear.

"Shhhh!" I hiss, taking my drink and heading back to the table with Hannah hot on my heels. But I find myself glancing longingly over my shoulder, appreciating the bartender one last time. "He's hot. Can you blame me?"

"Who's hot?" Vera asks the moment we return.

"Maximus," I explain, like it's no big deal, like he's an old friend and not some random and very sexy bartender I've been shamelessly flirting with for the last ten minutes.

Vera looks between me and Hannah, evidently confused.

"The bartender," Hannah answers to her unspoken question.

Vera gasps, looking at me with a knowing grin. "The one with the arms?"

I nod, smirking as I sip my drink.

"Um, do I need to remind you that neither of you are single?" Hannah points a finger from me to Vera, adding, "And that *your* boyfriend is literally right up there in that booth." She indicates the DJ booth where Tyler commands the dancefloor from behind the decks.

"There's no harm in looking." Vera waves a hand with a giggle.

I say nothing because who said anything about just looking?

When my friends start talking about something else entirely, I pull my phone from my purse and open the text messages, my thumbs flying across the screen.

Me: I want out of this deal.

FAMOUS LAST WORDS   193

His reply comes through instantly, as if he'd been waiting for my text.

> Fuckface: No.

I stifle a scream.

> Me: You got what you want. Everyone loves you again. Let. Me. Go.

> Fuckface: No.

I'm fuming. I wouldn't be surprised if my blood pressure was through the roof.

> Me: You're such an asshole.

> Fuckface: We've established that fact.

With a quick glance toward the bar, I spot Maximus working the crowd with the ease of Tom Cruise from *Cocktail*, and something suddenly comes over me. I'm forced to bite back a smile as I tap out my reply.

> Me: Fine. But if the hot bartender asks for my number, I'm giving it to him.

Robbie's response comes through within seconds. Literal seconds.

> Fuckface: What hot bartender?

My subconscious cheers.

> Me: The hot bartender who's been flirting with me. Maximus. Huge arms and hands. I wonder what else is huge...

I watch the screen as the dots appear, indicating that he's typing. But they soon disappear for an extended moment before reappearing. Gone. Back. Gone. Back. And I can only imagine he's writing some sort of essay. I roll my eyes. I can't wait for this.

> Fuckface: Where are you?

My brows knit together. That was a lot of dots for just three words

> Me: Out.

> Fuckface: I'm not playing, Keller. Where. Are. You?

> Me: Put!

Oh, fuck you autocorrect.

> Me: Out!

> Fuckface: Are you drunk?

> Me: Not nearly drunk enough.

> Fuckface: Who are you with?

> Me: Hopefully the bartender by the end of the night.

I wait for his reply but nothing comes. Not even the dots. On one hand, I can't help but mentally pat myself on the back. *Ha, take that, jerk!* But, on the other hand, I don't mistake the dip of disappointment in my chest, my shoulders falling on a resigned sigh at the thought that he doesn't care.

I tuck my phone back into my purse after a few more minutes of radio silence, finishing the rest of my *Maximus special* in one go.

Twenty minutes later and I'm settled at the bar again, hooked on every word Maximus says as he leans on the counter so close, I'm inundated by his intoxicating scent.

"This is just a side-gig," he explains with a nonchalant shrug of one of his beefy shoulders, his devastating grin seemingly taunting me. "I work construction during the day."

As if my gaze has a mind of its own, my eyes trail down over his broad shoulders, zeroing in on those bulging biceps. Did I mention he's hot?

"What about you, beautiful?" He tips his chin at me. "What do you do with your *fine* ass?"

I giggle again. Like a fucking imbecile, I giggle. Because I can't remember the last time a man openly and unabashedly flirted with me like this. The sheer look of sex in his gaze is almost enough to melt my panties right off.

"I work in real estate," I say with a shy smile because the intensity of his stare is overwhelming.

Maximus nods, but just as he's about to speak, he settles on something over my head, brows knitting together.

And it's at that precise moment I feel something hard press up against me from behind, causing my heart to slam against my ribs as one tattooed hand comes to rest on the counter beside me, before another tattooed hand lands on the counter on the other side me, effectively caging me in.

Frozen in place, my skin prickles as lips skate against the shell of my ear causing me to shudder in the best possible way.

"What the fuck do you think you're doing... *baby*?" His voice is a low growl meant only for me, and I swear, I'm not even breathing right now.

196   SHANN MCPHERSON

"Hey, you're Robbie Mason!" Maximus, the stupid traitor, straightens, eyes suddenly all hearts as he gawks incredulously at the overwhelming presence behind me.

"The one and only," Robbie says smugly, moving one hand from the bar and placing it low on my waist. "And I see you've met my *girlfriend*."

I notice Maximus's face fall, and I'd be lying if I said it wasn't funny. I'd probably laugh if I weren't so pissed off right now. Pissed off and horny, because holy shit, I can practically feel Robbie's dick pressing against my ass, and maybe I'm more drunk than I first thought, but I'm pretty sure he's hard right now.

"Oh, I-I didn't—" Maximus glances at me before forcing a tight smile at Robbie, holding his hands up in surrender. "Robbie, man. Let me grab you a drink. Anything you want. On the house."

Great, so it seems Maximus is nothing more than a Robbie Mason fanboy, because of course he is.

"Nothing for me, thanks, *bud*," Robbie says with a dismissive wave of his hand, before leaning in closer and wrapping his arms around me from behind. "Gotta get my girl home."

I bristle at his words. Although I don't know if it's because I like it or I hate it.

"Ready to go home, *baby*?" Robbie whispers all low and sexy, lips grazing the overly sensitive skin at the base of my neck and yeah, he's good. He's really, *really* good.

My smile is forced, teeth gritting together as I snatch my purse and stand from my bar stool.

"It was nice to meet you," I say flatly at Maximus with zero semblance of sincerity because *fuck you and your delicious semen elixir*.

Turning, I'm suddenly faced with Robbie's broad chest, forced to crane my neck a little to find his unwavering and frankly terrifying gaze laser-focused on me. Sure, he's grinning,

FAMOUS LAST WORDS   197

but there's an unspoken glint of threat in his eyes, and at the risk of sounding pathetic, it goes straight to my pussy.

"What are you even doing here?" I mutter.

Without an answer, Robbie takes my hand and turns, tugging me with him. And it's only then that I notice he looks as if he rolled right out of bed. Baggy khakis, a hoodie, a beanie pulled low. How did he even get in here, given the strict dress code? Oh, yeah, that's right; he's a fucking hockey superstar. How could I forget.

"How did you know I was here?" I yell over the thrumming bass.

He either doesn't hear me, or he's ignoring me. I'm going with the latter.

I roll my eyes, but then as I glance toward the table where Vera and Hannah are watching on, their faces void of surprise as they wave me goodbye, and I suppose that answers *that* question. Meddling assholes.

Keeping me close, his hold of my hand unrelenting, Robbie shoulders his way through the crowd with the kind of determination I expect he usually reserves for the ice. Head down, focused, an unstoppable force.

"Where are we going?" I yell again, even though I know he's ignoring me like a dick.

Suddenly, we're outside on the sidewalk, continuing past the line of people waiting to get into the club, past a group huddled together sharing a smoke, the cold night air whipping against my heated cheeks as it barrels down Bowery. It's freezing, and that's when I realize I left my coat inside.

"I forgot my coat," I say, coming to a stop.

Robbie's hold of my hand only tightens as he says over his shoulder, "Leave it."

I balk, but I seem to have lost my voice because although it's not something I would ever admit out loud at the risk of sounding like a pathetic twit, Robbie Mason being all demanding and forceful is all kinds of hot.

We stop at a black SUV idling at the curb, and Robbie opens the back passenger door for me. I hesitate before hopping in only because I'm shivering. Robbie climbs in close behind me before the car pulls out and continues around the corner and into the steady flow of traffic on Houston.

I glance sideways at Robbie, finding him stoic as he stares straight ahead, the streetlights illuminating his expressionless face. I don't know if he's pissed or not. In fact, if it weren't for his bouncing knee, I'd almost assume he was catatonic.

"Robbie?"

He doesn't even look at me, and now I'm even more pissed than I was before. Ignoring my messages is one thing. But ignoring me to my face is a whole other level of audacity he has no right to have.

"Where are we going?" I demand.

Again, no answer, but there's a hint of a smirk that ghosts his lips, and it's almost menacing. Shaking his head to himself, he scoffs, like he can't believe I just asked him that.

I stare out at the streets we pass in a blur, my stomach twisting nervously, but then in no time at all, we're rolling to a stop outside Allora, and I feel my heart lurch into the back of my throat.

"Thanks," Robbie murmurs, opening the door and hopping out.

I half expect him to slam it shut in my face, but he doesn't. Instead, he waits, staring in at me, that same stoic veil of indifference masking his face as he reaches a hand out for me.

With a muttered curse, I scoot across the seat as best as I can in my faux-leather skirt, desperately hoping it doesn't make a fart noise as it rubs against the real leather interior. Thankfully it doesn't, and I take Robbie's hand with a forced smile as he helps me out.

At first, I'm unsteady on my heels, but I manage to collect myself, lifting my chin a little higher when he snakes his arm around my shoulders, pulling me in close, despite there being no one around this late at night for us to keep up the charade.

The night doorman nods, opening the glass door for us, and we continue inside, through the sleek lobby and directly to the elevator, Robbie's arm still firmly situated around me. And I'm only thankful for the loud clacking of my heels on the shiny floor to help disguise the furious beating of my heart.

The elevator ride is silent, and even though it's just the two of us, Robbie is still touching me, his hand resting at my lower back as he stares at something on his phone. I'm too busy freaking out internally over what the fuck is happening, but there's a serious tension that has settled between us, the air alive with the kind of electricity that feels almost dangerous.

I stare straight ahead at our reflection in the mirrored doors, and I almost laugh at how ridiculous we look. Me in my sky-high heels, my tight as sin skirt and the even tighter bodysuit that looks more like lingerie, hair coiffed, lips stained a fire engine red. Robbie in his Air Force Ones, baggy skater-boy pants, and a Minnesota Gophers hoodie, two black eyes, a bandage across his nose, hair poking out under his beanie.

When the elevator chimes, Robbie steps off first, but I hesitate, staring at his back. He turns, looking at me expectantly, but instead of saying anything, he slams his hand against the door, stopping it from closing and arches one brow. And I'll be damned if it isn't the hottest look I've ever been on the receiving end of.

"What are we doing?" I ask, cautiously stepping off.

Robbie turns left for his apartment door and punches in the code, holding it open without even looking at me. I walk inside, my stomach in my ass as I wait in the foyer, looking around the space that is lit only by the lights of the city shining in through the walls of glass.

"Your furniture arrived," I say, scanning the items that weren't here when I was in this very spot earlier today.

"Yep," is all he says.

From my periphery, I see him move to a side table, offloading his keys and wallet, kicking off his sneakers and leaving them strewn on the floor, still nonchalant and cold, all while I remain stuck in place. But then as he walks past me, heading for the kitchen, I can't hold it back any longer because frankly, I'm done playing whatever game this is.

"Robbie, this is fucking ridiculous. What the hell are we doing here?"

In a flash, so quick I almost miss it, Robbie spins around, his huge frame flanking me, forcing me back against the door, his hand wrapping around my throat, a seething, feral look in his eyes.

I stare up at him, momentarily terrified.

His hand tightens around my throat as he leans in even closer. "We're gonna fuck and get it over with."

CHAPTER 28

ROBBIE

Big blue eyes stare up at me, pretty red lips gaping. And man, I cannot wait to have those wrapped around my dick later.

I duck down, brushing my lips against her ear. "Tell me to stop, and I will," I whisper, licking her lobe before pulling it between my teeth.

With a gasp, Fran shakes her head, and I smirk, tightening my hold of her throat just a touch.

"Who knew Fran fucking Keller liked it rough…" I whisper, dragging my nose along her jaw, breathing in her scent.

I trail my other hand down her body, following the curve of her hips and thighs before reaching the hem of her sexy ass skirt. Dragging my fingers up the inside of her thick thighs, I'm met with a whimper when I reach the apex. I pull back to get a good look at her, and Fuck. Me. Eyes glazed, breath panting, tits heaving.

I skim the lace edge of her panties. "You're fucking desperate, aren't you Keller?"

She says nothing, but the way she tilts her hips, seeking more contact from my fingers, tells me all I need to know. She's more than fucking ready; I can smell her arousal.

"You want this?" I drag my finger across the front of her panties, a whisper of a touch feeling just how soaked she is.

Her eyes close as her head falls back against the door.

"You gonna be my *dirty little slut*?"

"Oh my God, yes…" she utters through a gasp.

I grin, knowing she gets off to that name. Nipping at her plump bottom lip, I swallow her moans as I pull the lace aside and toy with her slick pussy lips.

"You're so wet," I say with a teasing grin when she looks at me. "What's got you so worked up, huh? Is it me? Or was it that fuckin' asshole creeping all over you at the bar?"

She licks her lips, offering no more than a throaty groan when I purposefully graze her swollen clit with my knuckle.

"Tell me, Keller." I steady her with a warning look, her dazed eyes working hard to focus on me. "Is your pussy wet because of *me* or *him*?" I tighten my hold of her throat. And normally I would never take it this far, but she fucking likes it.

She cries out when I slip two fingers inside of her, pumping hard a few times.

"Tell me or else I'll fucking stop," I warn her. "Don't. Test. Me."

"You!" she shouts, her voice almost lost to the tight hold I have of her throat.

I smirk, circling her clit with my thumb as I fuck her with my fingers, relishing in the sounds she makes.

Honestly, I don't even know what's gotten into me. Something fucking snapped inside me when she said she was going to give some sleazy bartender her phone number. I jumped out of bed so fucking fast, pulled on whatever clothes I could find, and DM'd her friend Vera on *Instagram* to find out where the fuck she was, because over my cold, lifeless body was I about to sit back and let my girlfriend—real or fucking fake—give anything to some bartender who's probably hooked up with half of New York City.

I'm not sure what I was thinking going down there to the club, but I certainly hadn't planned on bringing Keller back to my apartment to finger fuck her in the foyer, but here we are.

"Is this what you want?" I curl my fingers deep inside of her, making her moan when I hit the spot.

"Yes." She gasps and I loosen the hold I have of her throat just enough.

"Beg for it," I demand, grinning as I continue teasing her g-spot. "I want you to fucking beg me."

"Please…" she whimpers. "Please, Robbie." Her eyes flare. "I need it so bad, *please*."

Fuck. Me. My head falls forward, forehead resting against hers because the sound of her begging is doing all sorts of primal, unexplainable things to me.

Her hands grip the front of my hoodie as I fuck her harder with my fingers. I feel her clench around me, and she's so fucking wet, the filthy sound of her cunt sucking my fingers in rings through the silence.

"Yes, Robbie!" She pants. "Ohmigod, right there. Yes. Don't stop."

I kiss her neck, biting the skin, sucking on it hard. She hisses, and I know I've marked her but I don't care. I want to mark her. I want her to walk around with marks all over her, remembering exactly where they came from.

"I'm so close, I…" Fran sucks in a deep breath.

I pull out of her, and she cries out in objection, eyes wide and frenzied as they search mine.

"No, baby," I say with a smirk, shaking my head. "You're not gonna come until I say you can fucking come."

Her eyes flash with betrayal, but then as I lift my hand to my mouth, sucking her arousal from my fingers, that look of betrayal turns to molten heat, her gaze tracking my every move.

"Fuck, you taste good," I murmur around my fingers before pressing them against her lips. "Suck."

Her eyes remain on mine as she opens her mouth, tongue darting out and swirling around my fingers before sucking on them with a moan.

"You like that?"

She nods, licking every last part of herself from my fingers.

"Dirty girl." I bite back my smile, grabbing her hand and tugging her with me as I make my way directly to my bedroom.

Once inside, I turn to Fran, looking her up and down. She's a fucking masterpiece. Mussed hair. Kiss-swollen lips. Heaving breasts. I could look at her for hours and not get tired of the view.

"Take off your clothes," I say lowly, standing right where I am, just watching her.

Fran's resolve slips momentarily, and she's suddenly nervous, gaze darting about the room.

I take a tentative step, closing the distance between us and lifting my hand to gently cup her jaw. "Come back to me."

She looks up at me through her lashes. "I'm not... skinny."

Anger flares deep inside my chest thinking of just what damage that asshole Tadd caused her with his words. My brows draw together, and I grab her hand and place it against my crotch, right where my dick is straining against my pants. "Does it look like I give a fuck?"

A small smile lifts her lips, and the tension in my chest eases.

I place a kiss against her cheek before whispering, "Now take your fucking clothes off."

Stepping back, I fold my arms across my chest, watching her. She's still nervous, but her hands move to the side of her skirt, releasing the zip. With a moment's hesitation, she shimmies it down over her hips. And holy fucking shit.

Standing there, in just her heels and an almost entirely see-through one piece, her soft curves shamelessly on display, the *dirty little slut* is back, and she looks at me with a newfound confidence, as if she's daring me to make the next move. And, honestly, you don't have to ask me twice.

I step up to her, trailing the backs of my fingers down over the swell of her breast, feeling her nipple pucker beneath my touch. Skimming further down her stomach, I stop just shy of where I'm sure she's throbbing for me. With my other hand, I push the lacy strap off her shoulder, tugging it down to reveal one of her perfect tits.

"Take it off," I say, stepping back again to get a better look.

Fran takes over and slowly tugs the other strap off her shoulder, revealing both her luscious tits before pushing the one piece down over her hips all the way, kicking it off with her heels. And she's suddenly completely naked, the stuff of every teenage boy's wet dreams.

Tearing my fingers through my hair, I throw my head back on a low groan.

"You realize you're still fully dressed, right?"

I look at her again, finding her blue gaze sweep over me, one brow arching.

A slow grin spreads across my face because even butt-ass naked, she's still a mouthy brat.

I shrug. "Well, what are you gonna do about that?"

With a stunning smile, Fran steps forward, impatiently tugging up my hoodie. I take over, pulling it over my head and tossing it to the floor.

She unfastens the button on my pants, allowing the fly to hang open. Heat flares in her gaze when she looks up at me, her mouth curling up. "No boxers?"

"You got me outta bed so damn fast, I didn't have time."

Eyes fixed on mine, she licks her lips, and there's something in her gaze that tells me exactly what she's about to do. Pushing my pants down, she goes with them, falling to her knees right in front of me as my dick springs free.

"It's so big…" she whispers, and I'm not sure she meant for me to hear.

I contain my chuckle, reaching down to gently tuck her hair behind her ear.

Her hands skate up my thighs, nails dragging over my skin. She stares unabashedly at my cock before her eyes flit to mine. And then, wrapping both her soft hands around the base, she swipes her tongue across the swollen tip, lapping at the bead of precum and humming in appreciation.

I brace myself as best as I can, feet shuffling a little further apart. Raking my fingers through her hair, I massage her scalp, watching her as she licks me like a fucking lollipop. It's beautiful torture but it's too much. So, wrapping her hair around my fist, I tug on it hard, forcing her eyes up to look at me.

"You gonna suck it or what?"

Again, her eyes flare with want and need, and a small smile plays on cherry lips as she moves closer to my dick, licking me from root to tip before wrapping her mouth around me and sucking me hard.

"Fuck." My head hangs, and I continue gripping her hair as she bobs up and down, taking me deep. My cock hits the back of her throat, but still she takes me deeper.

I watch her, see her almost gag, pretty eyes brimming with tears.

"You good?" I check because I can be an asshole, but I'll never force a woman to do something when she's uncomfortable.

With her mouth full of my cock, she smiles despite the tear falling over and trickling down her cheek. She's not sad, she's just gagging, and that is so fucking hot. I swipe the tear from her cheek with my thumb, fucking her mouth in earnest.

"Those pretty lips look so good wrapped around my cock, Keller." I hiss a breath through my teeth. "Take me all the way with that smart fucking mouth, slut."

She moans around me, the vibration causing my balls to tighten.

FAMOUS LAST WORDS **207**

"Who knew little Fran Keller, the goody-goody with the giant stick up her ass, would turn out to be so good at sucking dick."

She glares up at me then, but I can see the hint of humor in her eyes.

I smirk, tightening her hair around my fist so that she's barely able to move and completely at my mercy.

"I wanna come in your mouth so bad, but I won't." I shake my head. "Not now, at least. Right now, I want you on your hands and knees so I can fuck you hard and fast. And then you're gonna let me shoot my load all over those perfect fucking tits."

She moans again, and it's then I notice she's playing with her pussy. *Naughty fucking girl.*

"You like that, huh?" I ask, tugging harder on her hair. "You like the thought of me shooting my cum all over your tits."

She nods as best she can with her mouth full of cock, me holding onto her hair.

When it's almost too much, I pull out of her mouth with a pop, releasing her hair and holding my hand out for her.

She stands, her legs obviously unsteady. Wiping the corners of her mouth, I wrap my hand behind her head and pull her close, ducking down and claiming her lips with my own. My tongue delves into her warm mouth, plundering, exploring, kissing her hard with everything I have, swallowing every one of her breathy sounds.

I break away from the kiss abruptly, pushing her roughly onto the bed. "Get on your hands and knees."

She does as she's told, and I stroke my dick, staring at her perfect ass, at the hint of her soaked pussy taunting me. "Fuck, you look so good like this. So ready for me."

"Just fuck me already," she demands, her voice wavering with desperation as she watches me over her shoulder, tracking my every move.

"Patience, baby," I chide, smoothing my hand over her ass before grabbing a handful of plump cheek. "Jesus Christ, this ass, Keller. I could fucking eat it." And, with that, I raise my hand and bring it down hard with a loud crack.

She cries out, her back arching.

"I'm going to claim this perfect ass one day," I say, adding another hard spank to the same cheek, smiling at the reddening print of my hand flaring on her skin.

She whimpers, but her eyes are like daggers, desperate with need, teeth clamping down on her bottom lip. I can tell she's loving this. It's written all over her face.

I reach into my nightstand drawer and grab a condom, tearing the foil packet with my teeth and making quick work of sheathing myself while she watches.

"One of these days, I'm going to fuck you bare," I say, snapping the condom in place. "Come deep inside you, until it's dripping down your thighs."

I grip her soft hips, bringing her back toward me, lining her up just where I need her. I rub the head of my cock all over her pussy, spreading her arousal up between her ass. She jolts when I press right there, and I chuckle, swirling my cock around the puckered hole. Oh yeah, she'd love it. I'd make sure of it.

"Is my dirty little slut ready for me?" I ask, slapping her ass once more.

"Ohmigod, yes!" she groans as I push just the tip inside.

"You are fucking drenched, Keller." I hiss, pushing in more and more, inch by excruciating inch. "So tight… fuck *me*!"

I fill her until I'm balls deep and forced to steel myself because holy fuck. Fran Keller's pussy is like the Holy Grail. Wet. Tight. Hot. The coil at the base of my spine is already threatening to release, and I know I'm not going to last long.

"Harder!"

With a deep breath, I pull almost all the way out before slowly pushing back in, and it's fucking painful for me, but I can tell it's nearly killing her, and what can I say? I'm an asshole. She said so herself.

"Faster, please…"

FAMOUS LAST WORDS   209

I clamp my bottom lip between my teeth, biting back a grin, and go even slower this time. So slowly I'm barely moving.

"Damn you, Robbie!" she cries, and it's a sound of pure frustration. When she tries to move, tries to take control of the pace, I almost laugh at her neediness.

"Come on," she whimpers, smacking a hand against the mattress. When she looks back at me, I can see she's so fucking pissed. "Fuck me. Please!"

"You want me to fuck you?" I grunt, going a little harder. "Is that what you *really* want, Keller?"

"Yes, oh God, yes!" She moans when I hit her deeper than before, her head falling down onto the mattress.

"You gonna scream my name when you come all over my cock?" I pump harder and start to pick up the tempo.

"Yes…" She sobs between grasped breaths. "Oh my God, don't fucking stop, Robbie. Please don't… ever… fucking… stop!"

I grip her hips so tight that my fingers pinch into the soft flesh. Fucking her hard and so fast, the sound of my balls slapping against her wet cunt is almost deafening against the otherwise silence.

I lift one foot up onto the bed, pushing her shoulders further into the mattress, trying for a slightly deeper angle. And I can tell by the way her back arches, the way her juicy ass is tilted up even more, that I'm right there, and she is loving everything I'm giving to her.

"Rub your clit," I order between grunts, reaching forward and grabbing a fistful of her hair again, tugging on it hard.

"Oh, Robbie, I'm so fucking close," she mewls.

"You *do* like it rough, don't you, you filthy little slut?"

"Yes, yes, yes."

"You're gonna come?" I pant, feeling her clench around my cock. "I wanna see you fucking *gush* for me, baby."

"Oh, fuck, I'm—"

"Come for me, Keller." I smack her ass again, so hard my palm stings. "You come for me right... fucking *now!*"

"I'm coming. Oh my god, I'm com-ing... Ugh!" She cries out. "Robbie, fuck!"

And that's all it takes. My name on Fran Keller's lips as she's falling apart and coming all over my dick. As soon as she's done, before she's even coming down, I pull out of her.

"Turn around," I growl, ripping off the condom.

Just as she turns, I grab my dick and pump it once, twice, groaning out a string of words I don't even understand as my orgasm crashes over me, hot spurts of cum shooting all over those perfect fucking tits.

I stagger ever so slightly, momentarily lightheaded. But when I get a good look at her, on her knees on my bed, her skin illuminated by the glow of city lights shining in through walls of glass, I must admit, I'm more than a little taken aback by the overwhelming possessiveness that claws at my insides. The sight of Fran Keller covered in my cum is doing all sorts of things to me that I cannot wrap my head around.

"Look at you," I whisper through my breathlessness, stepping up close enough to drag my fingers through the mess, swirling my sticky release around her hard nipple and smirking wickedly before lifting that same finger to her lips.

Her eyes remain on mine as she opens up and sucks, hard, hollowing her cheeks and moaning softly. And all I can do is chuckle because holy shit, I think I've finally met my match.

CHAPTER 29

FRAN

I feel like I'm floating. Weightless. Like I'm trapped in a blissful cloud of warmth and light, my body tingling all over. I smile, a moan slipping from my lips. But then a bright light flickers, and I realize I'm sleeping. Or awake. Fuck, I could be dead for all I know because this sort of euphoria is other-worldly.

My lashes flutter, and I open my eyes, suddenly reminded where I am when another moan falls from my lips, my legs trembling.

With a gasp, I lift my head, panting at the sight of Robbie Mason currently positioned with his face between my thighs. Whiskey eyes stare into mine and he winks, his mouth curling into a smile as his tongue flicks my clit.

"Holy shit," I hiss between ragged breaths.

Normally, beneath the unforgiving gleam of the morning sun streaming in through the windows, I'd be self-conscious of my soft belly, the white lines permanently marking my hips, the cellulite dimpling my thighs. But right now, lying naked on Robbie's bed, his arms wrapped beneath my thighs, holding me wide open, I couldn't give a damn. All I care about right now is coming. I've never needed to come like I need to come right now.

"Morning," Robbie murmurs against my pussy, his voice low and rasped. Pure sex.

He takes his time, flicking my clit once, twice, three times before sucking it, causing my back to arch up off the mattress. He presses a kiss against my clit before trailing down and fucking me with his tongue.

"Oh, shit…" I cover my face with my hands, biting down on the heel of my palm to stop myself from crying out. Then, peering between my fingers, I watch him work me over, lapping at me with slow, languorous strokes of his tongue, like he has all day and not a care in the world.

I'm not sure how long he's been down there, eating me out while I sleep, but I can feel my arousal dripping down between my ass cheeks. I've never woken up with a head between my legs before, but it's definitely something I could get used to.

Robbie circles my clit with his tongue, pulling it between his lips. Circling. Nibbling. Circling. Sucking. Circling. Fucking *biting*. I reach down, scratching my nails over his scalp, pulling at the lengths of his dark hair. He groans, and the vibration against my needy center nearly sets me off. *Nearly*. But just when I'm so fucking close, teetering on the edge, he abandons my pussy altogether, pressing slow, feather-light kisses to the soft skin of my inner thighs, blowing a hot breath over my sensitive core.

I urge him closer, guiding him right where I need him, but he stops just short, kissing my mound. Again, I lift my head, gaping at him, and when I meet his eyes, that's when I see it. The knowing glint in his gaze. The shit-eating smirk playing on his lips. He's doing it on fucking purpose.

He stares at me, eyes blazing as he licks me from my entrance all the way up to my clit. He circles it again, still staring at me, and I'll be damned if this is not the most erotic moment I've ever experienced.

With a pathetic whimper, I grip his hair in my hands. "Please."

But he pulls away again, his fingers taking over, drawing teasing patterns all over my pussy; he's everywhere except where I need him the most.

"You okay, baby?" he asks, all casual like, as if he doesn't realize exactly what he's doing to me.

My entire body quivers as the tip of his index finger flicks my swollen clit.

"Please, Robbie," I whimper again, my voice gravelly and unfamiliar.

"Not yet, Keller," is all he says, winking at me before closing in again and maintaining eye contact as he spits on my pussy. *Spits.* Normally I'd be disgusted. Maybe even slap him. But fuck me, it might just be the hottest damn thing any man has ever done to me.

Robbie drags his thick finger up and down my slit. Circling my center, he trails up so it barely grazes my clit. Back down then up, down then up. He's relentless, and I can't stop myself from tilting my hips, desperate for more. I don't even know what I want. I just need to come.

"Please?" I beg, throwing my head back in frustration. "I need it so bad."

"I know you do, baby," Robbie coos as his lips ghost across my clit. "I've been edging you for the last half hour." He flashes me a cocky grin. "Your pussy is pulsing, Keller. Fucking *pulsing.* My needy little *slut.*"

I groan in a combination of lust, frustration, and ecstasy when he dips the tip of his finger inside of me, only to remove it again far too quickly. When he kisses my inner thigh, dragging his tongue against the sensitive skin, it takes everything I have not to push him away and finish myself off.

"You're so pissed at me, huh?" he says with a throaty laugh.

I glare at him, but the anger disintegrates the moment he lays his tongue flat against my clit, licking with fervor. I'm so fucking close.

"You really wanna come?"

"Yes. Yes. Yes…" I nod frantically as he works my clit, his index finger sliding inside of me at an agonizingly slow pace; it's both heaven and hell and everything in between.

Again, Robbie pulls away, only this time he moves all the way away, crawling up the bed to lay beside me, and I can feel tears of frustration sting my eyes.

"You okay?" he asks with a mocking grin, fingers lazily circling one of my nipples.

"Why would you do that?" I sob, pressing my thighs together in an attempt to quell the crippling ache.

Robbie leans in and grazes his lips with mine. I can smell myself on his skin, taste myself on his tongue when it licks into my mouth and finds mine. "If you wanna come," he says against my mouth, "then get your ass up, and sit on my fucking face."

My eyes widen, and I gape at him as he pulls away, that same taunting grin playing on his lips. He rolls onto his back and makes himself comfortable, and I just continue staring at him, his glorious naked form, muscles moving beneath his smooth, tattooed skin, thick cock straining up against his stomach.

"Come on, Keller," he says, smirking up at the ceiling. "I have a flight to catch."

It's only now that I'm fully aware none of the blinds are drawn. His bed is in the corner of two glass walls, and literally anyone could be looking in at us right now. If I'm honest, that's actually kind of hot. But I've never done this before. Sat on someone's face, I mean. What if I—

"Keller, don't make me ask again."

"I can't sit on your face, Robbie," I balk. "It's already banged up from the fight. What if I… I don't know… break your nose? Or suffocate you?" I scoff. "I'm not exactly a size two."

He turns then, facing me, and despite the wicked smirk,

FAMOUS LAST WORDS **215**

there's something else entirely in his eyes when they meet mine. "Keller," he says softly. "You're not gonna break my nose. Trust me, if Danowski couldn't do it with his bare fucking fist, you're not gonna break it with your soft, fleshy ass."

I glare at him.

He chuckles. "And, honestly, baby, I could die and go to heaven with those thick thighs wrapped around my head. Suffocate the fuck out of me and know I'll die a happy man."

"That doesn't make me feel any better."

"Well, how about this?" He cups my jaw, tracing the curve of my bottom lip with the pad of his thumb so soft and gentle that my eyelashes flutter. "Sit on my fucking face, or don't come at all." He grins at me all cocky like. "The choice is yours."

The thought of not coming right now far outweighs the risk of going to prison for the accidental asphyxiation of Robbie Mason. So, with a resigned sigh, I push up and tentatively climb on top of him, hovering over his chest.

"Atta girl," he murmurs, hands rubbing up and down my soft thighs, thumbs skimming dangerously close to my center. "Keep going."

I lift one knee, placing it next to his head, and then the other, but I hesitate, frozen mid-air.

"This is so fucking humiliating," I whine.

"Humiliating? For who?" he mutters between gritted teeth, gripping my hips almost to the point of pain. "This is the hottest thing I've ever seen. Now quit your fucking hovering, grab onto the headboard, and ride my fucking face."

Okay, apparently that was all the encouragement I needed because I'm suddenly lowering myself, gasping the second I feel his face right there, his tongue getting straight down to business.

"Is this okay?" I ask around a gasp. "Are you okay? Robbie?"

He murmurs against me, but I can't understand a word he's saying. His hands move to my ass, and he positions me a little better so that I can at least see his eyes, and when I find them looking at me in a way that tells me he's more than okay, it's only then I start to relax.

"Oh my God," I shudder. It feels different. Better. I can feel *everything*.

Gripping the headboard, I move my hips ever so slightly, seeking.

Robbie groans, his fingers digging into my thighs.

I grind a little harder against his tongue, and he sucks on my clit, biting it softly.

Throwing my head back, I'm on the verge of losing my ever-loving shit, black spots dotting my vision.

"Oh my fucking God, Robbie!" My voice is shrill, frenzied. "I can't—" I suck in a breath, choking on my own moan.

More muffled sounds come from underneath me, vibrating against my pussy.

"I'm so close. Don't stop. Please don't ever... *fucking*... stop!" When I look down, meeting Robbie's eyes, it's a combination of the ministrations of his lips, tongue, and teeth, the sounds he's making, and the look of raw, unfiltered sex in his eyes that tips me over the edge. The coil at the base of my belly unfurls, and a wave of bliss courses through me as my entire world is tipped upside down.

"I'm coming. I'm coming. I'm... *coming!*" I cry out, my voice feral, thighs trembling, back arching. I let go of the headboard and my fingers find Robbie's hair, holding onto him for dear life as he works me through my release, taking everything until I'm far too sensitive and begging him to stop.

Flopping onto the bed, I'm a depleted mess. A shell. My entire body is boneless and still trembling as aftershocks shudder through me. I try to catch my breath, but it's like I've just run a marathon, and I am absolutely not a runner.

Robbie pushes up on his elbows, looking down at me and holy shit, he looks so fucking sexy. Dark hair mussed and sticking up in every direction, cheeks flushed, eyes heavily hooded, my release glistening all over his mouth and chin.

He flashes me a satisfied smirk. "That was so fucking hot."

I cover my face with a hand. I'm not embarrassed. Surprisingly. I probably should be. I mean, I didn't just sit on the man's face; I rode it like it was a mechanical bull. But I'm not embarrassed at all. In fact, I think I'm the opposite of embarrassed. And I'm a little scared because I've never felt this comfortable with any man before. And fuck knows what that means.

Turning into the pillows to the tune of Robbie's laughter, I try to swat at him. But he grabs my hand and launches himself at me, nuzzling into my neck with a few sloppy kisses. And I don't know what this is between us, but I don't think it's quite as *fake* as we initially intended it to be...

CHAPTER 30

ROBBIE

After our win against the Storm, we stay in the lobby bar to celebrate because it's too fucking cold in Nova Scotia to leave the hotel. But after an hour or so, there's a nauseating hint of perfume and desperation hanging thick in the air from the ambitious puck bunnies who have somehow managed to sneak their way in. After two beers I pretended to drink, I dip out without saying anything and head up to my room.

By the time I brush my teeth and change into a pair of sweats and a t-shirt, it's almost midnight. And, because I'm apparently a pussy-whipped asshole, I try my luck with a message to Fran in the hope that she's still awake, for reasons I care not to admit.

Me: You up?

I find myself staring at the screen with bated breath, and I momentarily hate myself. But then she replies, and my heart does this weird jump-thing that I can't even begin to explain, and I hate myself even more.

> **Keller:** Yeah, I just got home from work.

The skin at the back of my neck pricks at the thought of her coming home so late. Not only is her building lacking in basic security, but I swear, if she tells me she caught the goddamn subway home, I'm going to lose my fucking shit.

> **Me:** How did you get home?

> **Keller:** Uber.

I'm not entirely comfortable with her catching an Uber this late at night either, because fuck knows there're a lot of creepy-ass drivers out there. But I guess it's safer than the subway late at night.

> **Me:** You know I'm really not a fan of you working nights.

> **Keller:** Well, it's a good thing you have absolutely no say over what I do with my life then, huh?

> **Me:** Brat.

> **Keller:** 😊

I can't help but grin at her reply. Man, she's a fucking smart ass. But, if I'm being honest, her sassy mouth is one of the things I like most about her.

After our weekend together, things between Fran and me have well and truly shifted. I mean, she sat on my fucking face, for Chrissake; lines were definitely crossed. I don't know what's happening between us, if anything, but I'd be lying if I said there wasn't something there.

220 SHANN MCPHERSON

> Keller: I promise, once my commission check clears, I'll quit working at the bar, Dad.

Me: That's Daddy, to you.

> Keller: Ew.

I chuckle.

Me: Did you see the game?

> Keller: I saw highlights.

Me: Did you see my fight?

> Keller: Yep.

Man, she's really giving me nothing here. Time to bust out the big guns.

Me: Did it get you all hot?

> Keller: You're horny, aren't you?

Me: I'm a 25yo guy who just won a hockey game. Of course I'm fucking horny.

> Keller: Is your cock hard?

I blink at her message, reading it at least seven times just to make sure I'm not seeing things. Nope. She definitely just asked me that. Talk about zero to sixty. Yeah, whatever line was crossed between us after this weekend is now well and truly erased.

Me: It is fucking now.

> Keller: Prove it.

FAMOUS LAST WORDS 221

Holy shit. Is she serious right now? I thought she would've taken a lot more convincing.

I sit up and tug off my t-shirt, lying back down against the pillows and snapping a picture of my lower half—my stomach, my low-hanging sweats, my dick tenting the gray fleece.

Me: [photo]

Fran doesn't respond straight away, and a part of me worries that maybe she wasn't being serious, and my picture has offended her. But then my phone shudders with a new message and Holy. Fucking. Shit. She's sent me a similar shot, only instead of gray sweats, she's wearing nothing but a pair of black cotton panties. And, as if that's not enough, she has a bright pink vibrator in her hand, resting against her mound.

Me: Are you fucking kidding me right now because I swear to God, Keller...

Keller: You think you're the only one who gets to be horny?

I groan at the thought of her there, in her bed, getting herself off.

Me: What are you gonna do with that thing?

Keller: Make myself come.

Me: You are fucking killing me right now. You know that, right?

Keller: Facetime?

I don't even respond. No time for that. Instead, I shimmy out of my sweats, kick them across the room, and, with one hand on my dick, the other holding my phone so I can see the screen, I send the Facetime request.

After a couple of rings, Fran's face fills the screen, a coy smile tugging at her lips, but before I can say anything, I'm stopped by the unmistakable sound of buzzing in the background.

"You started without me?" I gape at her.

Her teeth rake hard over her plump bottom lip as she nods.

"Let me see."

The screen goes black for a moment before the image of Fran's lower body comes into view. She's still wearing her panties, but her hand is buried underneath them, nestled between those thick thighs I love.

"Spread your legs."

She complies, her thighs falling apart not nearly enough.

"Take off your panties," I demand. "I wanna see."

"What's in it for me?" I hear her ask, her voice all soft and breathy.

I show her exactly what it's in for her, pointing the camera at my cock and zooming in on the bead of precum glistening at the very top.

"I wanna see you stroke it."

A low chuckle climbs my throat as I wrap my hand around the base of my cock, gripping it tight and stroking it hard and slow, unable to mask the groan that rumbles deep in my chest.

"That is so hot." Fran sighs, and her thighs fall a little further apart.

"You gonna take off those panties, or do I have to stop?" I warn, although it's an empty threat; if the fire alarm went off right now, I'd be stroking my dick as I evacuate the hotel.

"You're so bossy," she mutters.

"You fucking love it."

I watch as she wiggles her curvy hips, and she pushes her panties down over her legs so that she's left completely bare. Nothing but her smooth pussy and that pink vibrator buzzing in

FAMOUS LAST WORDS **223**

plain sight and fuck me, the damn thing is already glistening with her arousal.

"Now what?" she asks, the toy hovering a few inches from her center.

What I wouldn't give for the camera to be facing her cunt right now, giving me a full view of her wet pussy lips and swollen clit.

"Hold it against your clit," I say.

She lowers the pink toy to her pussy, and I hear her whimper at the same time as her hips shift from the contact. I pump my dick a little harder.

"Keep it right there. Right on your clit."

"It's too intense," she gasps, her legs twitching.

"Don't you dare take it away, Keller," I warn through gritted teeth.

"Oh my God, I'm going to come," she sobs.

"No! Not until I say."

She cries out, and I see the tell-tale sign of her orgasm start to crest by the way her thighs fall open even more.

"Take it away. Right now. Do not fucking come, Keller!"

With a frustrated groan, she rips the toy away, and then clamps her thighs together, and I know it's because she's trying to dull the ache.

"You good?" I chuckle under my breath, still languorously stroking my dick, rubbing my hand around the swollen head to collect the moisture seeping out of me, before pumping again.

"No. I'm not fucking *good*, Robbie," she snaps. "It hurts."

"Aww, my filthy little slut is aching," I taunt, my voice low and gravely because this is hurting me as much as it's hurting her.

"Please, can I come?"

I don't know what it is, but that question on her lips does something to me, and I feel my balls tighten. I'm forced to take a deep, centering breath to stop myself from jacking my dick hard and fast.

224 SHANN MCPHERSON

"I want you to drag the vibrator all over your pussy. Circle it around that tight little cunt and up to your clit, but don't touch it."

She whimpers, and the sound is fucking everything.

I watch her do what I say, and when she sucks in a shuddering breath, I know it's taking everything she has not to get herself off.

"Don't touch your fucking clit," I remind her. "Not yet."

A sob, combined with a groan mixed with a growl, comes from her, and I almost laugh.

"Breathe, Keller," I instruct her. "Breathe through the pain, baby."

She moans, and I know it's because she loves when I call her baby, although I know she'd never admit it.

"Now push the toy inside that needy little pussy," I say.

She does, and another moan rings through the phone as her hand pumps the vibrator in and out.

"Pull it out and show me," I urge. "I wanna see just how wet you are."

Fran reluctantly pulls the toy away from where she needs it and holds it up a little closer, showing her sticky arousal all over it, and I swear, my fucking mouth waters with the need to lick it off.

"Fuck me, Keller," I groan, fisting my dick to the point of pain. "Look at my needy fucking girl."

"Please, Robbie," she gasps. "I need to come so bad."

"I know you do," I say. "But I'm gonna need you to sit up on your knees and rest your phone on your nightstand, so I can see all of you."

"I want you to do the same," she begs.

"Don't worry, baby, I got you," I snicker, pushing up from the bed and walking into the bathroom.

Fran does as I ask. Sitting up on her knees, her curvy body is ready and willing. Her tits heave with every breath, pale pink nipples puckered and begging for my mouth.

FAMOUS LAST WORDS **225**

I place my phone onto the bathroom counter, adjusting it.

"Can you see me?" I check, resting one foot up on the side of the tub, gripping my cock hard.

"Yes, your cock looks so fucking big."

"Fuck yeah, it does." I smirk cockily.

She laughs lightly, and the look of pure sex on her face is something I hope to remember for the rest of my life—flushed cheeks, swollen lips, hooded eyes, mussed hair.

"Hold the vibrator right against your clit and ride your fucking hand just like you rode my face the other day."

She closes her eyes, her head falling back on a throaty moan as her hips move, grinding against the vibrator.

"'Atta girl." I pump my dick hard. "Keep going."

"Oh my God, I'm so close…" She whimpers.

"Me too, baby," I grunt. "You make my cock so fucking hard."

"Ahhh…"

"Say my name, Keller!"

"Oh, Robbie! Robbie. Robbie." Her body shudders, and I know she's cresting. "I'm coming… I'm oh my Fuck!"

"Eyes on me, baby!" I pant.

Her glazed eyes find mine through the phone as she continues riding out her orgasm, and that's all it takes.

"Fuck!" I shout, coming harder than I've ever come from jerking myself off, my dick releasing in warm ropes of cum all over my hand, my stomach, my chest, my goddamn chin for Chrissake. White spots dance in my vision as my knees almost buckle beneath me, and I'm forced to grip the bathroom counter, holding myself steady as I catch my breath.

Fran collapses onto the bed in a breathless, panting heap, that beautiful, big ass of hers teasing me through the phone.

"You good?" I ask through my racked breaths.

She doesn't respond. Just gives me a thumbs up. And I can't help but laugh at the thought that I've just rendered Fran Keller speechless. That's gotta be a first.

"Look what you did to me, Keller," I mutter, looking down at myself. "It's like a goddamn bukkake porno up in here."

At that, Fran grabs the phone to get a closer look, her eyes gleaming as I show her the state of myself.

"Next time I come with you," I say, "I'm coming in that smart fucking mouth of yours."

"Promise?"

"You'd like that, wouldn't you?" I smirk. "Greedy girl."

With a hum, she nods and rolls her tongue over her bottom lip, and fuck me, I'm hard again.

"Chrissake, Keller," I groan. "You're gonna be the fucking death of me, I swear."

Suddenly, the screen flashes with pink, going blurry, but when it focuses again, I almost swallow my damn tongue. There, staring directly into my eyes through the phone, Keller drags her bright pink vibrator over her swollen lips before swirling her tongue around it and lapping up every last drop of her release.

Again, I groan, shaking my head in a combination of awe and betrayal because how fucking dare she. "Do you have any idea what you're doing to me right now?"

She doubles down, wrapping her lips around the toy and sucking it deep into her mouth. And then the screen goes black, and I'm met with my own reflection looking back at me.

Oh, hell to the fuck no. I try call her back, but it rings out, so I shoot her a text.

> Me: Are you fucking serious right now?

> Keller: Sorry. Can't talk. I'm a little busy…

> Me: Just you fucking wait.

> Keller: Don't threaten me with a good time.

Fucking brat.

CHAPTER 31

FRAN

"Hey, Fran."

I look up from my laptop to see Bri, Tadd's assistant, standing on the other side of my cubicle.

"Hey, what's up?" I force a smile. It's not that I don't like Bri. She's a sweetheart. Fresh out of college. Innocent. Bright-eyed. Naïve. She's basically me, three years ago. It's more that I know the only reason she's standing here in front of me is because she's been forced to do Tadd's dirty work.

"Tadd asked if you could check this to make sure you're happy with the copy." She hands me a big piece of paper, nervously avoiding eye contact.

I glance down to see it's the draft for the two-pager we have running in this weekend's *Times* for the Columbus Circle penthouse. Why wouldn't he just send them to me electronically like a normal—

"Are you kidding me?" I snap my head up, spearing Bri, and she at least has the decency to look sheepish. "Where is he?"

"In his office…" she says reluctantly.

I spin on my heels and storm toward Tadd's office with Bri

hot on my tail. Pushing open the glass door without knocking, the metal handle slams against the wall, causing everyone on the sales floor to look over, because real estate agents live for the drama.

Tadd startles, quickly removing his Gucci-loafered feet from his desk and sitting up straight, smirk ghosting his lips. "I'll call you back," he mutters into his phone before tossing it onto the desk.

"What's up?" He lifts his chin at me.

I arch one brow. "You *know* what's up."

He plays dumb, even going so far as to offer poor Bri a questioning look.

"The ad in the *Times*." Anger rages through me as I wave the copy in the air. "You didn't even include my name!"

Tadd licks his lips, and I know that move. He's trying to stifle his smile. But it's there. I can see it in his eyes. With another clearing of his throat, he stands, adjusting the knot in his tie.

"Fran," he begins, cocking his head in an overly patronizing way that makes my blood boil. "For a property of this… *caliber*," he continues, talking to me like I'm an idiot, "it makes more sense to have myself as the face of the listing. Buyers at this level *know* me; they're *familiar* with me. And trust me, you don't want your details on that ad. You're going to get calls and emails at two a.m. from the other side of the world. And if you can't respond at the drop of a hat, you could potentially miss out on a deal." He shrugs, all smug and condescending like. "This is my business, Fran. You're not quite—"

"You are a self-righteous son of an ass." I scrunch the copy into a ball, throwing it at him. It hits him in his chiseled jaw, rendering him shocked.

Behind me, I hear Bri giggle, which she quickly tries to conceal with a cough.

Tadd stands a little taller, squaring his shoulders.

"The *only* reason I am even going along with this bullshit farce is because I was practically forced by you and Tony." I take

FAMOUS LAST WORDS   **229**

a step closer, pointing a finger at him. "You put my headshot, my cell, and my email on that copy, or I am *done*."

Tadd scoffs, staring down at me like he can't believe I'm actually standing up to him at work. And frankly, neither can I. This is the first, and man does it feel good.

"Fine," he finally relents, rolling his eyes as if I've bored him. He returns to his desk, picks up his phone, and ultimately dismisses me.

I keep my chin held high as I turn, flashing Bri a conspiratorial wink as I pass her on my way out. And as I continue through the suddenly silent sales floor with what feels like every set of eyes watching me, I can't help but feel like a badass.

By the time I sit back at my desk, I release the breath I've been holding and grab my phone.

> Me: I just stood up to Tadd in front of everyone at work!

> Robbie: Not gonna lie… this just gave me a semi.

I roll my eyes at his response, laughing under my breath.

> Me: I hit him in the face with a ball of paper.

> Robbie: Please tell me you filmed that???

> Me: Sadly no. But I will remember the look on his dumb face for the rest of my life.

> Robbie: I'm proud of you.

Aside from my parents, I've never had anyone tell me they're proud of me before. It takes a few seconds to collect myself. And then, without even realizing, I'm tapping out the one thing I've been wondering these last few days. The one thing I've been too terrified to ask.

> Me: Robbie, what are we doing?

Message sent.
Oh shit, oh shit, oh shit.
Message Delivered.
Oh fuck, oh fuck, oh fuck.
Message read.
I already know there's no way to retract a read text message; trust me, I've Googled it before. Instead, I toss my phone onto my desk, and I bury my head in my hands, groaning at my own stupidity. I swear, I've never wanted anything more than to go back in time two minutes. Where's a DeLorean when you need one?

When the device vibrates, I refuse to look at it. But then of course, curiosity gets the better of me.

> Robbie: wdym?

I stare at his reply, over analyzing it. He's either playing dumb, or he's naturally clueless. And, sure, I could play dumb too, but honestly, what's the point?

> Me: A month ago, you were nothing more than a horrible high school memory. Now we're doing things high school me would never imagine she'd be doing with Robbie Mason.

> Robbie: High school Robbie Mason would be so fucking confused if he knew that 8 years later, Fran Keller was going to end up coming all over his face.

My cheeks flush at the memory, and I feel a familiar ache settle between my legs, and damn him. This is hardly the time or the place, Robbie.

FAMOUS LAST WORDS   231

Me: So, the question remains – what's
going on?

Robbie: I don't know. We're friends who fuck?

Me: Friends who fuck... while also pretending
to be in a relationship. It's all levels of
messed up.

Robbie: What's so bad about a fake
relationship with real orgasms? It's ingenious.

I can't help but smile as I stare at his messages. I know he's right. But the truth is, I'm not sure how I feel about it. I'm worried my feelings might have become entangled in this weird situation-ship over the last few days, and now, if I'm honest, I don't know if *friends who fuck* is enough for me.

I tub on my bottom lip, considering myself. I know I should let it go. He's made his intentions abundantly clear. But that doesn't stop the painful tug I feel in my chest.

Me: No. You're right. A fake relationship with
real orgasms. All pleasure, no pain.

He doesn't reply for a while, and I stare blankly at nothing in front of me until a response comes through.

Robbie: So... we good?

No. I've broken the cardinal rule and developed stupid ass feelings for you.

Me: Yeah. We're good.

I roll my eyes. *Idiot.*
Less than five minutes later, my phone starts ringing, and I

bristle, thinking it's Robbie. Like hell I want to rehash any part of that text conversation. But when I glance at the screen and notice it's Andy calling, I relax some, answering the phone.

"Hey, Andy."

"YOU STUPID MOTHERFUCKER!"

I pull the phone away from my ear, gaping at the screen before trying again. "Um... hello?"

"Oh, hey, Fran. Sorry. Goddamn bus just cut me off." He scoffs. "YEAH, YOU! YOU FUCKIN' JACKASS!"

Honestly, I don't know what to say, so I just wait.

"I've booked your flight to Boston."

I assume he's talking to me again. "Oh, okay. Thanks."

"You fly out at three. I'll send a car to pick you up and take you to the airport."

"Thanks, Andy. Do I need to—"

"Make sure you're *awake* this time."

I blink. "Are... you talking to me, or is that more road rage?"

Andy barks a laugh. "Make sure you don't fall asleep like the night in Robbie's hotel room when I was about to send a car for you."

I blink again. What the hell is he talking about? I think back to that night—*almost kiss-gate*—and I freeze. My eyes go wide. Robbie got a text message from Andy. He said Andy told him the crowd was still outside and that I would need to spend the night. My jaw drops.

That dirty little liar.

"I'll have my assistant send through the details." Andy's voice cuts into my thoughts. "Fran, I gotta go. It seems it's the day for SHITTY FUCKIN' DRIVERS!"

The call goes silent after Andy's outburst, but I continue sitting like a statue, staring straight, phone still pressed against my ear.

Robbie lied. And it's not like it was an accidental lie where he might've just got his wires crossed. He blatantly lied. What the hell is going on?

CHAPTER 32

FRAN

The Boston Logan arrivals terminal is, as expected, pure chaos. I'm forced to dodge and weave through swarms of people, gripping my wheelie case tight as I make my way out into the cool afternoon. I don't know exactly where I'm supposed to go, but if I can at least get a taxi, then I can call Andy and ask.

My phone vibrates in my purse resting at my hip, and I pull it out, unable to conceal my smile at the sight of Robbie's name on the screen. I thought he'd be busy with pre-game by now.

> Robbie: Black Chevelle. 10 o'clock.

My brows knit together. *Is that some sort of code?*

I look around, but then my gaze lands on a black car parked three down from the front of the pick-up zone, headlights flickering twice.

Sufficiently confused, I turn and start toward the car tentatively, but then the driver's door opens and my shoulders relax at the sight of Robbie hopping out. He's wearing a fall coat over a pair of dark gray slacks that are tailored to perfection and snug in all the right places, and a white button down that skims his glorious chest and hints at the tattoos inked into his skin. A baseball cap conceals most of his face, and sunglasses shield his eyes, but I'd recognize that cocky smirk from a mile away.

"Nice shirt," he says with a tip of his chin.

Okay, so maybe I went a little overboard wearing Robbie's jersey on my flight, but I assumed I'd be going straight to the arena. My cheeks heat with embarrassment, and I make an effort to pull my jacket closed.

Reaching his hand out, Robbie stops me, pulling my jacket apart, his gaze intense as he blatantly stares at my tits draped in his number. "If you're gonna wear it, let people see."

Okay, that was hot.

As if he can hear my thoughts, Robbie chuckles and takes my carry-on from me. As he stows it in the trunk, I help myself into the passenger seat, getting comfortable while trying not to openly swoon as Robbie Mason's all too familiar spicy scent wraps around me.

Seconds later, the driver's door opens, and Robbie sinks down into the seat next to me. He turns the key in the ignition, glancing at me with another one of his knowing grins, the engine roaring to life and causing a few of the people standing nearby to look as we tear out of the pickup zone with a skid of the tires. Such a showoff.

As we drive out of the airport and into the steady flow of afternoon traffic, I nestle into the cushy leather seat, taking a look at the pristine inside of the vehicle. "So, a muscle car, huh?"

"Yep." Robbie grins, though his eyes remain on the road.

I bite back a smirk. "Predictable."

He laughs. "Why? Because I have *huge* muscles?"

With a snort, I roll my eyes. "More like compensating…"

Like the cocky ass he is, Robbie glances at me, shooting me a wicked grin and a wink. "Baby, I ain't got nothing to compensate for." His gaze travels down my body and back again, meeting my eyes as he says, "You should know that by now."

I sink a little in my seat, squeezing my thighs together in an attempt to stifle the dull throb between my legs. But it's pointless. Between Robbie's scent, just how close he is, and even the sight of his tattooed fingers lazily gripping the steering wheel, I'm a needy mess and in no way prepared to have to sit through a goddamn hockey game.

"So, why aren't you at the arena?" I ask, hoping the shift in conversation will break the sexual tension hanging between us in the car. "I assumed you'd be warming up, or I don't know, whipping wet towels at your teammates in the locker room."

Robbie laughs. "Exactly what do you think goes on in a locker room, Keller?"

I shrug with a mischievous smile.

"I was at practice earlier," he continues. "And I'll be at the arena in time for warm-ups. I wanted to pick you up so I can swing by and introduce you to Ma."

I sit up a little straighter, suddenly nervous. I've never met a guy's mother before. I mean, I know this is fake, but Robbie's mom doesn't know that. What if she doesn't like me? Or worse. What if she can see straight through our charade? I wish I'd paid a little more attention to my hair. I imagine my makeup needs a refresh. Maybe we could stop in at a gas station so I can—

"Breathe, Keller." Robbie places his hand on my thigh, squeezing gently.

I look from his hand to his face and back again. How the hell is a girl supposed to breathe with Robbie Mason's inked hand squeezing her thigh? Somehow, I find it in me to suck in a breath, filling my lungs with some much needed air before releasing it as steady as I can. And I continue breathing in and out while Robbie's hand remains on my thigh until we're pulling up outside a small house, one in a row of nearly identical houses lining either side of a narrow street.

"Ready?" Robbie looks at me as he cuts the engine.

I nod. Although that's a lie. I'm far from ready. How can one possibly ever be ready to go in and lie right to a dying woman's face?

Robbie gets out of the car, and I follow, stopping on the sidewalk and side-eyeing the house while I wait for him, but then he opens the trunk and retrieves my case, and confusion hits me.

"Wait." I grab his arm. "What are you—I'm staying here?" I lower my voice.

He looks at me like I've lost my damn mind. "Uh, yeah. Unless you wanna sleep in the car?"

"I didn't realize I was staying with you in your *mother's* house."

He snorts. "Fran, I'm a grown man. What'd you think was going to happen?"

I take another deep breath, trying to ease my racing heart.

With a reassuring wink, Robbie takes the lead, and I keep close behind him as we continue up the path and onto the front porch.

Without knocking, Robbie lets himself inside, holding the door open for me, and I walk into a small mudroom, nervously looking around.

"Ma?" Robbie calls, removing his ball cap and coat and hanging them on the hooks by the door.

"In here, hon!" a soft voice responds from inside.

Robbie glances at me over his shoulder and holds out his hand, waggling his fingers. I take that as invitation, gripping his hand tight. With a crease between his brows, his gaze dips to where I'm probably cutting off the circulation to his fingers, and he offers a knowing smile, towing me with him.

We come to a stop in a cozy front sitting room, a big bay window letting in the last of the afternoon light, a fire crackling in the hearth on the far side, warming the space. My eyes land on a woman seated in an armchair, a crochet blanket covering her legs, book resting on her lap. Cropped, dark hair, big eyes

FAMOUS LAST WORDS   **237**

that look exactly like Robbie's, and a warm smile. She's breathtaking.

"Oh my goodness, look at you!" Robbie's mom gasps, tossing off the blanket and pushing up from the armchair.

"Ma, don't rush," Robbie fusses, dropping my hand to move closer to his mother.

"Oh, stop." She batts him away with a hand. "I'm fine."

Robbie rolls his eyes, standing back with a huff.

"Fran?" Taking a step closer, Robbie's mom gets a good look at me, her small hands reaching out and resting on my upper arms as she studies me.

"It's so nice to meet you…" I trail off when I realize I have no idea what her name is, casting a furtive glance at Robbie.

Thankfully, he catches on. "Ma, this is Fran. Fran, this is my ma, Victoria."

Victoria smiles, and it takes my breath away because she looks exactly like her son.

"I am so glad to finally meet you, hon," Victoria continues, her Bostonian accent thick. "I've heard a *lot* about you." She flashes Robbie a teasing smile.

My heart skitters. She's heard a lot about me? I know I shouldn't think too much into it, but how can I not? Robbie's been talking to his mom about me.

"I can't wait to show you all of Robbie's baby photos."

"Ma," Robbie warns, but the smile ghosting his lips tells me he's loving this.

"What?" Victoria feigns innocence. "You've never brought a girl home for me to embarrass you before. It's a rite of passage. Let your poor ol' ma have *some* fun."

Robbie just shakes his head, but I can tell he's trying not to laugh. "Come on, babe, I'll show you upstairs." He nods for me to follow, walking back through the archway and disappearing, taking my case with him.

He called me babe. He called me *babe*. *Act cool, Fran.*

I glance casually at Victoria, and she offers me a wink, raising her voice for Robbie to hear as she says, "You go ahead, sweetie. I'll grab the photo albums."

I conceal my giggle at the same time as Robbie groans dramatically from somewhere in the house.

CHAPTER 33

FRAN

I follow Robbie upstairs. It's even smaller than downstairs. Just two bedrooms and a bathroom, a poky hallway lined with framed action shots and newspaper clippings of Robbie that make me smile because it's obvious his mom is his biggest fan.

"Okay, this is us," Robbie says, walking through an open doorway.

"Us?" I balk. "We're *sharing*?"

He meets my eyes. "Yeah…"

Again, my heart starts going crazy as I step into the bedroom. I'm met with a huge bed that takes up most of the space, facing a bay window with a view of the street. It feels like the primary.

With a questioning glance at Robbie, I ask, "This isn't your mom's bedroom, is it? I don't want to put her out."

"It was." He shrugs, placing my case by the bench at the foot of the bed. "Ma has trouble getting up and down the stairs, so we renovated and built a suite downstairs."

I frown, thinking of his mom and, despite her beauty and the uncanny resemblance she shares with her son, her eyes look tired, sunken with dark circles, and she's so tiny, skin and bone.

"I like her."

He pulls on the back of his neck as a sad smile lifts the corner of his mouth. "Yeah, she's pretty cool." Glancing at his watch, Robbie tilts his head in the direction of the door. "We should get going. I've gotta get to the arena."

I nod, checking my purse to make sure I have everything before following Robbie out of the room and back downstairs where Victoria is back in her chair, sipping from a mug.

"Okay, Ma. We're gonna go." Robbie leans down, pressing a kiss to her cheek. "You gonna be okay here 'til Rhonda gets in?"

"Wait." I look from Victoria to Robbie and back again, my eyebrows knitting together. "You're not coming with us?"

Victoria laughs. "No, hon. Sadly, I can't get out much like I used to."

"And it's not safe for Ma to be around so many people," Robbie adds. "Germs and shit."

"My son, the worrier." Victoria rubs Robbie's hand, and the look in her eyes as she gazes up at him is both endearing and heartbreaking; she's looking at Robbie like she's trying to memorize every detail, almost like she's scared she might never see him again.

"I have my rink-side seat right here." She pats the arm of her chair, grinning up at me.

I consider myself a moment. And I'm not sure what comes over me, but I find myself talking without even thinking. "You know what?" I look at Robbie, "I might stay in, too. That is if you don't mind, Victoria?"

"Oh, I would love the company." She beams, her eyes lighting up. "But only if you call me Vicky."

"I can do that," I smile.

She begins rustling around in the basket on the side table next to her chair, pulling out a remote and aiming it at the TV.

FAMOUS LAST WORDS **241**

Robbie moves in closer to me, brow quirked, voice a little lower. "You sure?"

"Yeah. You don't mind?"

A small smile ghosts his lips as he looks at me for a long moment, and I'm not sure what it is, but there's an emotion in his eyes I've never seen before. "Thank you," he whispers, reaching out and gently squeezing my hand.

"Okay, well, I'm gonna go," he says a little louder. "Rhonda will be here soon." His gaze flits to me. "Rhonda's Ma's night nurse."

I nod.

Robbie leans down and kisses Vicky's cheek once more. "Alright, Ma, no parties, okay?"

Vicky rolls her eyes, and I laugh.

"Walk me out?" Robbie murmurs, leading the way.

I follow him to the mud room where he pops his cap back on and turns it backwards, shrugging on his coat.

Since I'm staying in, I remove my jacket and hang it up, but as I do, Robbie pulls me in, hands at my waist, holding me flush against him. I peer up at him, suddenly breathless, staring into his eyes as they bore down into mine. We're so close and out of Vicky's view; there's no one here to see this. I clamp my bottom lip between my teeth before I say something I know I'll probably regret.

"Thank you," he says after a minute.

A sliver of disappointment settles low in my belly because he's just thanking me for staying home with his mom. I force a smile. "No problem." I shrug, looking down. "I'm actually pretty tired."

An unexpected jolt surges through me when Robbie's hands slide up under the hem of his jersey I'm wearing, calloused fingers grazing my skin. I snap my head up to find his eyes darker than they were seconds ago, a knowing smirk playing on his lips. And again, the simple task of breathing evades me.

Slowly, Robbie lowers his head, and I'm almost certain he's

going to kiss me. But then he fakes left, lips brushing against the shell of my ear as he whispers, "I'll see you later."

I swear to God, I shiver at the feel of his breath, at the words which are so innocuous but spoken with such a raw, unabashed heat. When he pulls back, I see nothing but wanton need in his gaze, and I feel it straight in my core.

I swallow hard, taking a step back, desperate for some space between us because otherwise I'm scared I'll jump his bones right here by the front door.

He flashes me a slow wink, that cocky smile lifting the corner of his mouth as he turns and walks out the door. I'm forced to stand here for a moment, in the hope that I can at least pull myself together enough to go back inside and not completely give everything away to the woman who knows Robbie better than anyone.

―――――

Two minutes into overtime and the Thunder scored a goal, making the final score 2-1 at the end of a grueling and exciting game.

I'd been surprised at how passionate Vicky was, shouting at the TV, cheering and clapping, even making idle threats to the Boston player who checked Dallas from behind, causing a four on two brawl the refs were forced to break up. Robbie and Logan had been sent to the box together, but while they were in there, they just sat grinning at one another as the diehard Boston fans booed them through the glass. At one point, Robbie stood, antagonizing them with a 'bring it on' motion, and not gonna lie… it was all kinds of sexy.

Robbie: See the fight?

I roll my eyes, but I can't hide my smile because this has

FAMOUS LAST WORDS **243**

become our thing. No *hello*, or *how's it going*, just *see the fight*. I shake my head.

> Me: I did.

> Robbie: Did it make you wet?

Oh. My. God.

> Me: Yeah, I was sure to tell your mom just how wet I was 😊

> Robbie: 😈 How's she doing?

> Me: She's good. She loves watching you play.

> Robbie: You good if I go for a drink with the guys?

> Me: Of course. Everything is fine here. Have fun.

"Is that my son?"

I snap my head up to see Vicky smiling at me, a knowing look in her eyes, and I feel my cheeks turn an obvious shade of pink.

"Oh…" I laugh, nervously tucking my hair behind my ear. "Uh, yeah."

Vicky hums. "I've never seen him like this before. Not like he is with you."

I know I shouldn't, but I can't stop myself from prying. "He said he's never had a girlfriend," I say, adding quickly, "before me."

She shakes her head, a wistful smile playing on her lips. "No. He was always popular with the girls at school. But then hockey became the most important thing, and girls took a backseat."

244 SHANN MCPHERSON

I nod because I remember just how serious Robbie was about hockey when he was at Belmont.

"I worry that my illness has had a lot to do with him staying single over the years," Vicky continues. "He's been so focused on hockey *and* me, and I feel like he never allowed himself the time to date." A sadness suddenly washes over her as she looks down at her hands, and I wonder if Robbie ever told his mom about what happened in Minnesota. Somehow I don't think so, and that makes my heart hurt for him even more.

"Sometimes I think he's scared he might end up like his father." She glances at me, obviously tentative. "Did he tell you about his father?"

"Not a lot. Just that he wasn't a nice man," I say reluctantly. "And that he took off when Robbie was young."

With a solemn nod, Vicky presses her lips together. "He was horrible. An alcoholic. Drugs. Robbie saw some things no child should have to see."

I reach over the arm of the sofa and gently grab her hand, giving it a reassuring squeeze.

"I tried to leave. Take Robbie and run away." She glances at me, and I see something that resembles guilt flicker in her gaze. "But he said he would find me. *Us*. And that I'd be sorry."

I swallow the lump in my throat. "What made him finally leave?"

She scoffs, shrugging her shoulders. "Your guess is as good as mine. I returned home from work late one night to find Robbie in the house all alone at eight years old. Thankfully he was unharmed and asleep. But his father had ransacked the house, taken everything of value. He'd even snuck into Robbie's room and took his piggy bank that probably had no more than six dollars in quarters."

I wince.

"He left that night, and we haven't seen or heard from him since. The first year was hard because I was terrified he was going to show back up. But then, as time went on, I realized…"

She looks sad for a moment but then scoffs. "He was probably already dead."

"I'm sorry," I say softly. "I'm sorry that happened to you and to Robbie. But if anything good can come out of something so horrible, you need to know that you raised an amazing son."

She smiles, flipping her hand over so we're palm to palm, her fingers intertwined with mine. "I'm glad he has you."

I'm already more than a little taken aback by her words, but then she continues.

"Promise me you'll make sure he's okay… when I'm gone."

Tears sting the backs of my eyes as a heaviness settles like lead in my chest. The lump in my throat is back, and it's almost impossible to breathe around it, but I manage a smile despite the guilt coursing through me because the truth is, I absolutely would promise her that. But the question remains; when all is said and done, will Robbie still want me around?

The energy in the room suddenly shifts as Rhonda plows in from the kitchen like a ball of uncontainable energy. She's adorable. Mid-sixties. Less than five feet tall. With bright red lipstick, dark purple hair coiffed to perfection, and neon-pink spectacles dotted with diamantes.

"You ready for your nightcap, V?"

Vicky suddenly looks a little sheepish, glancing at me with a slow smile.

I arch a brow. "Night cap?"

She pushes up from her chair and holds her hand out for me. "Join me?"

Uncertainty washes over me because I really don't know if Robbie would be happy with his mom drinking. But then, at the same time, Vicky is a grown, fifty-something woman.

"Wine, or something stronger?" I ask, hopping up and linking my arm with Vicky's.

Rhonda lets out a howling laughter, and I glance sideways at Vicky.

"Oh, hon," she says, patting my hand and leading me

through the archway.

CHAPTER 34

ROBBIE

After an overtime win, I couldn't say no to the guys when they asked me to go with them for drinks. I stayed for one beer I, of course, didn't drink, and the second Dallas met a cute redhead, and Logan and Happy paired up with a pair of blondes, the puck bunnies started to circle me like a school of great whites, and I knew it was time to tap out.

By the time I make it home, it's nearly midnight and, assuming everyone is in bed, I'm quiet as I make my way inside. But then, just as I'm removing my coat, I'm stopped by the distant sound of a shrill, cackling laughter coming from somewhere, and it sounds distinctly like my ma.

Confused, I allow the laughter to guide me through the front sitting room lit only by the flames left to burn out in the hearth. I continue through the kitchen, my brows knitting together as a Journey song starts to drown out the merriment. As I stop at the sliding glass door that opens to the back yard, my confusion piques at the sight of Ma, Fran, and Rhonda, seated on the lawn chairs surrounding the pit fire, all three of them singing horrendously off key and really fucking loud. *What the hell?*

I pull open the glass door and step out onto the landing, looking down at the trio who are yet to notice me. Then, my eyes zero in on something in my mother's hand. Something smoking. *Is that a fucking joint?*

I make my way down the steps and cross the yard, stopping just shy of the group. Still going unnoticed, I watch on as Ma passes the joint to Fran who places it between her lips and tokes on it like a goddamn pro.

"Um, what's going on?" I ask, raising my voice so I'm heard over the sound of "Don't Stop Believing" blaring from Fran's phone.

Instead of alarm, they all turn slowly, their gazes understandably dazed and hazy, grins lopsided. Thankfully Rhonda appears to be sober, standing from her chair and doing her best to hide her smile. But Fran and Ma simply look at one another, something passing between the two of them before they both start giggling uncontrollably.

I place my hands on my hips, eyes darting between the two, but it's pointless. I turn to Rhonda because clearly she's the only one here who might be able to offer an explanation.

"Your ma's been in a bit of pain," she says quietly, placing a hand on my arm. "Having trouble sleeping." She indicates the weed currently being shared between Ma and Fran. "The doctor suggested marijuana, and it's the only thing that helps."

"How long's this been going on for?" I ask, lowering my voice.

Rhonda smiles sadly. "A few weeks. She pleaded with me not to tell you, especially with everything you have going on."

I press my lips together in a firm line, looking from Rhonda to Ma and Fran. I'm pissed because Rhonda should tell me everything about Ma; it's her literal job. But the reasonable side of me gets it. The last thing Ma wants is for me to worry.

"Come sit, my sweet boy!" Ma waves me over, joint perched between her lips. She pats her lap, like I'm nine years old again and not a grown ass man.

FAMOUS LAST WORDS **249**

"Ma, I will crush you," I say with an eye roll, unable to hide my grin.

Instead, I lean in and press a kiss to her cheek before continuing to Fran. She smiles up at me, and I gently nudge her shoulder, indicating for her to get up. Dopily, she pushes herself up, and before she goes falling face first into the fire pit, I link my fingers into the waist of her jeans as I steal her seat, pulling her down onto my lap. When she cuddles into me all sleepy and soft and warm, I'll be damned if I don't feel my heart do another weird ass somersault in my chest.

"Have you ever smoked weed before?" I whisper in her ear, because I need to prepare myself with exactly how this night is going to go.

Ma smiles at me, glassy eyes reflecting the flames of the fire.

Fran bristles, glancing pointedly at me. "I'll have you know, I was quite the rebel in college." She waggles her eyebrows at me, and I can't help but laugh. Fran Keller a rebel? I'd have loved to see that.

"I was!" She touches her chest indignantly before a smile blooms across her face. "Do you know I even had a—" her eyes flit side to side all devious-like as she leans and lowers her voice to a whisper, "a threesome with two guys at a frat party." She holds up two fingers for emphasis.

My eyes go wide. She fucked two frat assholes? I'm suddenly overcome by a foreign feeling, possessiveness or jealousy, I can't quite tell. Maybe both. I decide that's enough for tonight and gently slap her thigh. "Time for bed. We gotta leave early in the morning."

"Aw, but your ma and I were just trading *stories…*" she says in a teasing tone. "Who knew you liked to run off and peek up all the mannequin's dresses at T.J.Maxx, ya perv?" She jabs me in my chest.

Ma bursts out laughing, and I throw my head back on a groan. "Yeah, when I was like six."

I spear my mother with a mock look of betrayal, but she just keeps laughing and laughing, and I can't help but laugh too because seeing her like this, so happy and carefree… it's been a long time.

Fran stifles a yawn, and I squeeze her thigh, leaning in. "Seriously. Head on up to bed. I'll help Ma get settled and then I'll be up."

When her glazed eyes meet mine, there's something there, and I don't know exactly what it is, but I feel it straight in my chest, right where my heart is.

"What?" I lower my voice, quirking a curious brow.

She leans in, her breath warm as it fans against my neck. "This whole nurturing side of you is really fucking sexy…" Pulling back just enough, her eyes dance across my face, down to my lips where it looks as if she's about to kiss me. And there goes my dick.

"Bed." I lower my voice, staring deep into her eyes. "Now."

"Okay, bossy." She smiles coyly, and I hold her hand, helping her up and standing with her to put myself between her and the fire.

"Goodnight, V," Fran says, stopping by my mother and leaning down to wrap her arms around her. She whispers something in Ma's ear—something I'm not privy to—and I notice the way it makes my mom's features soften, her smile wavering as another emotion seems to come over her.

"Goodnight, baby," Ma says, kissing Fran's cheek.

"Alright, I'm outtie five-thousand!" Fran shouts, holding her phone in the air as "Any Way You Want It" starts playing from the device, causing her to dance up the steps, shaking her ass at the landing before disappearing inside the house.

Standing there, hands on my hips, all I can do is shake my head and laugh because who knew Fran Keller stoned could be so fun?

"You're in love with her."

Startled, I glance down at Ma to see her watching me with that knowing look in her eyes. The look she's used on me since I

FAMOUS LAST WORDS 251

was old enough to lie to her, thinking I'd get away with it without realizing that moms really do know best.

Looking at the glass door Fran just disappeared through, I swallow the lump that tries to wedge itself at the back of my throat, confused because the sheer mention of being in love doesn't immediately make my balls shrivel up and retract inside my body like they usually do at the first hint of the L word. And I don't know what to think about that.

"You're a different man around her," Ma continues. I meet her glistening eyes, and she smiles. "The man I always knew you'd grow up to be. It makes my heart full."

I swallow another lump. Only this one is a lot harder to get down. Because I hate lying to my mom, but fuck I love seeing her happy.

———

Not even ten minutes later, I'm walking into my bedroom to find Fran sprawled across the bed, still fully dressed, snoring her little heart out.

Pulling on the back of my neck, I hesitate in the doorway, smiling to myself before continuing in. Crouching down, I slip off her Vans, and then I make my way up, crawling over her and unfastening the button on her jeans. She snorts, mutters something, but doesn't wake as I tug them down her thighs.

Standing back, I stare down at her, and I know it's all sorts of creepy because she's literally passed out, but fuck she looks hot. But it's not just that. She doesn't *just* look hot. The sight of her there in front of me, at her most vulnerable, does something to me. Something I've never felt before. I don't know if I love it or hate it, but as I look down at her sleeping blissfully, it's almost as if I can't bear the thought of her not being here with me. Like, if whatever this is between us comes to an end tomorrow, I don't know if I could cope without having her around me.

I drag a hand down my face and turn, heading for the bath-

252   SHANN MCPHERSON

room, but just as I'm through the door, I hear the soft, sleep-filled whisper of Fran's voice. And I'm stopped. Dead in my tracks.

"Why did you lie to Andy about me falling asleep in your hotel room?"

Frozen in place, eyes wide, heart in my throat, panic consumes me.

Did she just say what I think she said?

Fuck. Me.

CHAPTER 35

ROBBIE

Well, driving to New York from Boston on less than two hours of sleep wasn't what I'd originally planned, but here we are.

Like a pussy, I pretended I didn't hear Fran's question last night. Instead, I went into the bathroom, locked myself inside, and freaked the fuck out.

Fucking Andy. I swear to God. When the fuck did he tell Fran that? And why?

Yes, I lied when I shouldn't have, but what the fuck did he go and tell her for?

By the time I'd finished in the bathroom, I walked back into the bedroom, relieved to find Fran snoring again, and I was off the hook… temporarily at least.

But do you think I could sleep after that? Of course not. All I kept thinking as I laid there, staring up at the ceiling while Fran murmured in her sleep and rolled into me, wrapping her warm, soft body around mine was, well, firstly, that my dick couldn't possibly get any harder, but also, secondly, and most importantly, she was a hundred percent going to ask me again. And I had no reasonable answer to give her where I wouldn't come off as a complete and utter psychopath. Fucking Andy.

"I love your mom, Robbie," Fran muses.

I glance at her from the corner of my eye. She's perched there in the passenger seat wearing a baby blue sweatsuit, socked feet resting on the dash as she sucks on a Twizzler in a way that's so innocent yet does things to me no man wants to admit. My jaw ticks and I find myself clutching the steering wheel so tight, my fingers start to cramp.

"She's so fun," Fran continues. "Did you know she partied with the New Kids on the Block when she was younger? She didn't exactly say, but I get the feeling she might've done more than just *party*."

I shake my head, laughing. "You realize I don't actually wanna know that about my mom, right?"

"Could you imagine?" she giggles, ignoring me. "One of the *New Kids* could've been your dad."

Silence ensues, and it's suddenly awkward.

"Oh my God," she mutters. "I'm sorry. That was a shitty thing to say."

I decide to lighten the mood. "Can we pretend it's Donnie? At least then I'd have a kick-ass uncle." I glance at her as she looks at me with a slightly rueful smile, and I reach over and gently squeeze her knee to let her know it's all good.

"So," Fran says after a moment. "How much longer?"

I scoff. "Keller. We've literally been driving for forty minutes."

She groans. "Well, let's play a game or something."

"Oh God. Kill me now," I murmur, only half-joking.

Playfully, she slaps my arm before reaching forward and fiddling with the radio. "How do I connect my phone?"

I laugh out loud. "This car's a 1970 classic. All original."

She stares at me. "So… no Bluetooth?"

With my eyes still on the road, I feel around in the center

console, grabbing the aux cord for the FM transmitter and handing it to her. "Nope. Old school, baby."

"What even is this?" Fran mutters under her breath before quickly figuring it out and plugging her phone in. "Okay. So, it's called the radio game," she continues, all excited, and I lowkey love when she's like this. "You ask a life question, and the next song on shuffle determines your answer."

"A *life* question?" I snort.

"Yeah, like…" she pauses to think for a moment before continuing, "Radio gods, what will I be doing in ten years? Or something like that." She smiles, and although this game sounds like the living definition of hell, I can't find it in me to say no to this woman.

"Radio gods," I snort again. "It's literally Spotify."

"Stop being a party pooper." She gives my arm another chiding slap. "You go first."

Again, I roll my eyes. "Fine. *Radio gods*, what will I be doing in ten years?"

She groans. "You are such a buzzkill."

"Just…" I wave a hand at her phone.

"Okay, you ready?"

"Readier than I've *ever* been before in my life," I deadpan.

Seconds later, the silence in the car is suddenly inundated by Kelis singing about milkshakes or some shit, and all I can do I turn my head slowly, meeting Fran's smiling eyes as she hides her mouth behind her phone, and I can't help but laugh out loud because what the fuck is happening.

"Maybe *you* need to press the button?" she suggests after a moment, holding her phone out.

"Yeah, I'm sure that's totally it," I mutter, reaching out and pressing the skip button, but as if the milkshake song wasn't bad enough, the car is suddenly alive with the sound of chiming church bells, right as Bruno Mars starts singing "Marry You."

"Ohhh… someone's getting married," Fran teases, looking up at me and fluttering her lashes.

256 SHANN MCPHERSON

"This game sucks ass." I focus back on the road, but I don't miss the strange tug deep in my gut. Not so long ago, the mere mention of marriage would make me break out in hives. Now, though, it doesn't sound so bad, and as I glance at Fran out the corner of my eye as she sings obliviously to the song, I can't help but wonder if it's because the thought of marriage with someone like her doesn't seem completely unbearable.

"Okay, my turn." Fran perks up as Bruno Mars finally shuts the fuck up. "Radio gods..."

I look at her when she takes an extended pause, and I really wish I hadn't because I know precisely what she's about to ask just from the devious smirk tugging at her lips.

"Why did Robbie lie to Andy about me falling asleep in his hotel room?" She quirks a brow, staring directly at me as she presses the skip button.

The opening organ music isn't familiar to me, but I assume Fran must look at the screen before I realize what song is playing because she's suddenly laughing hysterically, head thrown back, feet kicking the dash right as Percy Sledge starts singing "When a Man Loves a Woman."

"No fucking way!" I yell. "This is bullshit. You rigged it!" I laugh, pointing an accusatory finger at her.

"I swear to God... I didn't—" she sucks in a breath between her laughter, clutching her belly as the fucking song continues playing.

"This game sucks more than twenty fucking questions."

Fran is wiping the corners of her eyes, still laughing, but thankfully she skips the song, and my ears prick the moment the next tune starts to play.

"Fuck yeah, now this is more like it!" I yell, turning up the volume.

"What is this?" Fran's brows knit together.

Instead of answering her, I give the song my all, singing along to Marvin Gaye's opening lines of "Ain't No Mountain High Enough," causing her eyes to widen as she stares at me.

FAMOUS LAST WORDS   257

"Oh my God!" she practically screams. "You can actually *SING*??"

Fuck yeah, I can sing. And I continue singing, word-for-word, drumming my fingers against the steering wheel in time with a beat like a smug asshole. "Sing it with me, Keller."

Fran starts singing along with me—terribly, I might add—making up a few dance moves as she croons along to the chorus, giving it her all like a true champ. And as we continue along the Interstate, singing to the song I used to sing with Ma in the car every morning on our way to school, I feel my heart do another one of those somersaults. But I allow it... at least it gets me out of coming clean about my lie.

———

After a pit stop, we're back on the road again, right as it starts to rain. Not too hard. But hard enough to be a pain in the ass. The wipers on the Chevelle aren't the greatest. But with just over sixty miles to go, I have a newfound surge of energy.

"So..." Fran begins after a moment, "what's it going to take for you to tell me the truth, Robbie Mason?"

I know exactly what she's referring to, but I choose to play dumb, staring at the road ahead despite the weight of her stare. "What's up?"

She sighs dramatically. "Robbie, Robbie, Robbie."

I glance at her then because I don't know if I like the sound of her tone; it's teasing and suggestive. And fuck me. When I look at her, I almost veer into the other lane when I see what's in her hand. "What the fuck is that?"

Fran bites back her grin, toying with the tiny silver vibrator in her hand, pressing it on and off. On and off. I force myself to look back at the road, gripping the steering wheel like it's my one lifeline because fuck, no. This can't be good.

"I'm horny," she says casually.

"Uh-uh." I shake my head. "Nope. No fucking way, Keller."

"Pfft." She scoffs. "You're not the boss of me."

I roll my eyes. "Where did you even get that?"

"Gas station."

I balk. "They sell those at the gas station?"

"They did at that one," she shrugs.

"You are..." I trail off because I'm at a loss for words.

"I'll make you a deal," she starts, right as the thing starts to buzz. "I'll stop... when you tell me the truth."

"Keller, I—" I'm stopped when I turn to her, finding nothing but a daring look in her eyes. And I know I like to act all cool, calm, and in control, but the truth is, when it comes to the woman next to me, I am a weak, weak man.

"It's a simple question, *Mason*," she sasses, lifting her other foot up onto the dash and allowing her knees to fall apart before dipping the toy under the waistband of her sweats. "Why did you lie to Andy and tell him I was asleep in your hotel room that night?"

My dick twitches and I rake my teeth over my bottom lip, every single one of my senses on high alert as I force myself to keep focused on the road.

"Or... maybe you don't want me to stop," she adds with a telltale whimper.

Fuck. Me. I drag a hand down my face right as my balls start to tighten at the sounds she's making.

"Oh my gosh," she gasps through a giggle. "It's surprisingly powerful for $8.99."

My eyes dart from the road, looking at Fran. Of course I can't see anything—she's working herself over beneath the shield of her sweats—but I do notice her hips tilt up as her toes curl in her socks, and fuck, why is this so hot?

"I'm close already," she pants. "My pussy is really wet."

I bite down hard on the inside of my cheek. It's all I can do not to drive off the side of the Interstate and into a ditch.

"Ah!" she cries out, and her knees are fucking trembling.

My knuckles are stretched white with how tight I'm gripping

the steering wheel, and my cock is fucking aching. I shift in my seat in an attempt to readjust myself without showing I'm affected, but it's impossible.

"Oh my God, Robbie!" Fran gasps.

At first, I thought she was putting it on—doing it to get a rise out of me... pun intended—but when I see her palm her tit over her sweatshirt, notice her head loll back against the seat, I can tell she's far from faking it, and fuck if I'm about to miss out on the show. When I see a sign for an upcoming off-ramp, I flick on the blinker.

CHAPTER 36

FRAN

'm balancing on the precipice of an intense orgasm, so frantic and desperate for my release that I didn't even notice we pulled off the Interstate until the car rolls to a stop on the side of a quiet road edged by a thicket of tall trees.

Glancing at Robbie, I arch a questioning brow between gasped breaths and stifled moans.

"You wanna be a little cock tease? I can wait," he says smugly, shifting in his seat to watch me.

Right now, I don't even care whether he tells me the truth or not. In fact, I barely even remember the question, if I'm honest. All I care about in this moment is coming. And the overwrought silence in the car, combined with the fact that Robbie is just sitting there, casually watching me, is only spurring me on.

I hold the vibrator against my clit, closing my eyes tight as I climb the peak.

"Open your eyes and look at me."

Startled by his low, demanding tone, I open my eyes to find Robbie's gaze suddenly darker than usual, eyes heavily hooded, and it's then I notice he's palming his dick through his sweatpants, and I can't help but laugh through my haze because God help us if a state trooper just so happens to roll up on us right now.

"If this is all for me, then you better fucking look at me when you come." He arches a taunting brow, and the look in his eyes is pure menace.

I bite down on my bottom lip, dragging the vibrator up and down, circling my entrance before trailing it over my clit and holding it there. I spread my thighs further apart, and the slickness of my arousal is amplified against the silence. I'd be embarrassed if I weren't so feral with need.

A smirk ghosts Robbie's lips as he studies me, and for some reason it only annoys me.

"What?"

He chuckles. "You can't come, can you?"

With a groan, I throw my head back. "No! And I don't know why. I'm so fucking horny." I pull the toy out of my pants and hold it up, showing him just how wet I am. "See."

"Aw, my needy little slut can't get herself off," he derides, reaching out and swiping his finger over the toy, collecting my arousal from the tip before bringing that same finger to his lips and sucking it into his mouth.

I squeeze my thighs together.

"Alright, Keller." Robbie slides his chair back all the way, lifts his ass and shoves his sweatpants and boxer briefs down, his thick, hard cock jutting up against his stomach. "Climb on."

I gape at him. "What? No. I'm not going to *fuck* you in the car on the side of the road, Robbie." I glance out the windows. "There could be people in the woods watching us."

"You were just masturbating on the fucking Interstate," Robbie scoffs. "Something tells me you like the idea of someone watching."

I mean, he's not entirely wrong. That morning in his bedroom when I sat on his face and rode it like a goddamn pony, I didn't immediately hate that all his blinds were wide open for anyone to see in. But this is different. This is in a car, on the side of the road, in the middle of nowhere. This is how horror movies start.

I'm ready to order him to pull his pants back up, but then he starts stroking his fat cock, and I've always been a weak bitch when it comes to the dick.

"I won't fit between you and the steering wheel," I say, sizing up the gap. "My ass will set off the horn."

"Fuck's sake, Keller," Robbie groans, still fisting his rock-hard length. "Just take off your pants and climb over here. Trust me," he mutters through gritted teeth.

The only saving grace is that the windows are now almost completely fogged; it would take someone pressing right up against the glass to see in. So, with a huff, I lift my ass and push my sweats and panties down, twisting my body only to hesitate because I really don't understand how he expects me to fit.

"Turn," Robbie says, doing a spin with his finger like I can't understand the simple concept.

I roll my eyes and turn, backing into him, but then he grabs me and twists me completely so my back is to his chest, and he isn't gentle about it, pulling me flush against him. I suck in a gasp when I feel the swollen head of his cock pressing right against my ass.

"Wrong hole," I giggle nervously.

"Soon, baby," he snickers, fingers pinching into my skin as he holds me.

I've never been into the whole anal thing, but the thought of doing it with Robbie makes my pussy clench.

"Arch your back," he murmurs, lips skating over the crook of my neck. "Lift your ass."

I do as he says, and then I feel him right there, where I'm so needy for him.

"Fuck, you're drenched, Keller," he groans as I slowly start to sink down on him.

My eyes fall closed at the feel of his cock filling me, but then something suddenly comes over me and I freeze, gasping out. "Condom!"

"Fuckkkk…" Robbie growls. "They're in my bag, in the motherfucking trunk."

I hover awkwardly, the feel of his huge cock half-inside me so good that it's taking all I have not to slam all the way down and fuck him senseless.

"Are you on birth control?" he asks, his voice tight.

"Yes." I'm practically panting.

"I'm clean. I got tested when I started with the Thunder."

"I've never *not* used a condom," I say on a sigh. "And I trust you."

"Yeah?" He grips my hips so tight, it's almost painful. "You want me to raw dog you, Keller?"

"Yes…" I moan.

"Am I allowed to come inside this perfect little cunt?" He controls me, inching deeper and deeper at an agonizingly slow pace.

"Oh my God, yes!" I cry out, my head falling back onto his shoulder.

He chuckles, his teeth grazing the soft skin beneath my ear. "You gonna make a big mess all over my dick?"

I can't even form words at this point, only sounds I hope he accepts as my consent.

A swift smack lands on my ass, startling me, and I perk up again with a gasp.

"Hold onto the steering wheel and fuck me, Keller."

Glancing over my shoulder, I find Robbie relaxing back, hands resting behind his head, smug grin playing on his lips, and I don't know who he thinks he is, but fuck him. Gripping the steering wheel, I sink onto him in one swift move, causing him to shout out and grasp my thighs, his face falling into my hair with a grunt. And I don't know if it hurt him, or maybe he likes it, but fuck it. He asked for it.

I lift up and do the same, slamming back onto him, and each time he hits me so deep, I see stars.

"Fuck, shit," Robbie hisses into my hair.

When I feel him rub up against my g-spot, I grind my hips, circling them and arching my back to get the best angle, crying out as every nerve ending in my body lights up from within.

"That's it—use me," Robbie mutters, wrapping a hand around my throat and squeezing. "Ride my fucking cock, baby."

He meets me, thrust for thrust, each time making me sob as my body writhes needily on top of him.

"Fuck, Keller," he grunts, biting hard on my earlobe. "You're gonna make me come so fucking fast. Your hot, tight little pussy choking my dick feels so fucking good."

When I hear a familiar buzzing start up, I turn to see him holding the tiny bullet vibrator between his thumb and forefinger, and I practically growl. "Yessss."

"You want this?"

"Yes, yes, yes, oh my God, yes," I pant.

"Where do you want it?" He plays dumb in the best possible way, dragging the vibe over the peaks of my breasts where my nipples are aching underneath my sweatshirt.

"My clit," I moan. "I need it on my clit."

"Where are your manners, Keller," he chides menacingly, clicking his tongue.

"Please..."

"Please what?"

I growl out of sheer frustration. "Please, *asshole*."

He chuckles, the deep vibration of his chest coming through my back. But thankfully he gives me exactly what I want, dragging the bullet down and circling my clit causing me to cry out, my body jolting.

"Fuck!" Robbie yells. "Your pussy is clenching."

"Oh my God, Robbie," I whimper.

"I know, baby," he whispers, holding the vibe right against

my throbbing clit as he presses a gentle kiss to the skin just below my ear. "I know. You love that don't you?"

"Yes, yes, yes, yes, yes, yes. Fuck. Oh my God, I'm going to come." I throw my head back onto his shoulder, squeezing my eyes shut as white hot euphoria shoots through my veins. "I'm coming, I'm coming, I'm… coming. Ahhh!"

"That's it, baby. Breathe. Ride it out," Robbie groans. "Come all over my cock like the filthy fucking slut you are."

His words prolong the orgasm ravaging me from the inside; it's like an out of body experience I can't begin to explain.

"Shit, Keller, I'm gonna come," Robbie spits out, his hold around my throat tightening to the point of delicious pain. "You ready for my cum?"

"Yes, please, Robbie," I manage through the hold he has of me.

"Oh, fuck. Jesus," he shouts out, shuddering, stilling deep inside of me. "Yes, fuck. Take it all baby. Shit."

When his hand relaxes around the throat, I feel him sink into the chair beneath me, exhaling a ragged sigh. Then he drags the still vibrating bullet over my thigh and my hip before bringing it up to my lips, and I turn just enough to meet his glazed, hooded eyes as I twirl my tongue around it.

Robbie chuckles lowly, pulling the toy away and leaning forward, surprising me with a kiss. And not just a soft, post-coital peck, but a fully open-mouthed, mess of lips, teeth, and tongue, his hand cupping my jaw, holding me close so he can deepen the exchange until we're both breathless again.

"That was so good," I sigh against his mouth.

"I didn't want you to leave," he murmurs against my lips, kissing me once more.

Confused, I pull back enough to meet his eyes, finding nothing but a nervous uncertainty in his gaze. My brows knit together as I study him, trying to make sense of what he just said.

He traces the curve of my lip with the pad of his thumb.

"That night. In my hotel room." His eyes lift to meet mine again. "I lied because I didn't want you to leave."

There is so much to unpack from that. So many questions I have, starting with the fact that back then, we could hardly stand to be in the same zip code as one another, and yet he didn't want me to leave his hotel room? I need to know more. But, before I can deep dive, Robbie is like a Mighty Morphin Power Ranger, swiftly changing back into a smug, cocky jerk.

"Hop up, Keller," he says as he slaps my hip. "I need to piss."

I move off him as best as I can, fully aware my bare ass is likely right in his face. Settling back into my seat, I reach into my purse and pull out a travel pack of Kleenex, opening my door.

"Where do you think *you're* going?" Robbie says, pulling up his pants.

"I need to pee."

"Uh-uh." He shakes his head.

I stare at him.

A darkness comes over his face, a smug smirk lingering as his gaze travels to where I'm still naked from the waist down. "I want you sitting there next to me with my cum seeping out of that pretty little pussy all the way back to New York."

My jaw drops at his filthy and downright sexy words. But also, gross.

He laughs as if he can hear my thoughts, opening his door and hopping out.

"That's a bacterial infection waiting to happen!" I yell before he slams the car door shut.

Flashing me a grin through the windshield, Robbie winks as he jogs through the rain toward a break in the trees to relieve himself. In return, I flip him the bird, muttering a few expletives under my breath as I pull my pants up, trying so hard not to think too much about why he lied to Andy.

CHAPTER 37

FRAN

> Robbie: Good luck.

I smile down at the text message, although it does little to ease my thudding heart.

> Me: I hope he's nice.

> Robbie: Alex is literally the nicest guy on the team. Actually, he's the nicest guy I've met so far in the league. A genuinely good guy.

I release a breath, smoothing down the front of the shirt dress I'm wearing, mentally trying to remind myself that I'm a real estate agent, and I can do this.

When Alex sent me a text message yesterday, I almost fell out of bed. Yes, I'd been in bed at two o'clock in the afternoon, but it was a Sunday, and for obvious reasons, I was worn out after my road trip with Robbie, especially after he decided to crash at my place and keep me up half the night.

Alex said he was wanting to check out any apartments I had

available, and I told him I have the perfect place that's not yet on the market. He said he'd meet me at ten a.m., and here I am, ready and waiting with a few minutes to spare.

The intercom buzzes, and I startle from where I'm scrolling through *Instagram*. I do one quick sweep of the apartment before answering the call.

"Ma'am, I have Alex Henry here for the viewing."

"Fabulous. You can let him up," I respond with a smile.

I take a few deep breaths before crossing the entryway. We're only on the eighth floor, so almost as soon as I open the door, I hear the elevator chime and force a game face. But when Alex steps off the elevator and into the corridor, I'm immediately put at ease. He has that friendly, golden retriever vibe about him. Tall and broad, with floppy blond hair and big brown eyes that are so warm and kind. When he smiles at me, it's as if we've known each other for years.

"Alex, hi. I'm Fran," I say, holding out my hand. But he's having none of that apparently, ignoring my hand and wrapping me up in an unexpected hug.

"So good to finally meet you," Alex says, pulling back and offering me a grin. "I've heard so much about you that I feel like I know you already."

My cheeks flush at his words, wondering what the hell Robbie has been saying about me.

"Come on in," I say, inviting Alex inside.

"Oh, wow. This is nice." With his hands tucked in the pockets of his sweats, he looks around, nodding, and I must say, I'm more than a little smug.

"Okay, so we're right on the border of Hell's Kitchen. Your training facility is literally only three blocks away."

"Yeah, that's where I came from. I walked," Alex enthuses. "Took me six minutes."

I smile, leading him through to the kitchen. "Now I know you said you were looking for a one-bedroom just for you, but I really wanted to show you this unit because it's actually two

FAMOUS LAST WORDS   **269**

bedrooms." I turn in time to see his jaw drop, and I can't help but beam. "I know it's just a place to crash after the games, but I thought…" I shrug. "If it's within your budget—which it *is*, because it's a steal—then why not add in an extra room so when the baby is old enough to come to the games, you have somewhere comfortable to stay as a family."

Alex arches a brow, and I know he's dubious. "Tell me more about this so-called *steal*."

I offer him a conspiratorial wink, nodding for him to follow me. "Let me show you around."

I point out all the features of the apartment, from the brand-new oak flooring, to the double-glazed windows in the bedrooms, to the view of the Empire State Building in the distance, to the sleek and high-end bathroom finishes.

We finish up back in the kitchen, and I try to gauge Alex's thoughts by his reaction, but for a happy-go-lucky guy, he's surprisingly pokerfaced.

"You told me your budget is 1.25," I begin, and he nods. "This place isn't yet on the market, but the owner needs it gone quick. He took a job in London. He's already gone."

"What do you think it'll take?" Alex asks.

"You have two beds, two baths, eleven-hundred square feet, in a fully secure building with full amenities, six minutes from your training center. A parking spot can be negotiated with the fees so that during the off-season when you don't have to come down to the city so much, you can remove the parking fee." I continue, "I think if we come in strong with all cash, no contingencies, quick close, we could probably get it done at 1.1."

Alex's eyebrows climb so high, they get lost behind his floppy hair. He rubs his chin, scanning the apartment, and I think I might have him sold.

"Is it okay if I go home and have a chat with Cassidy?"

I nod. "Of course. Your wife?"

"Yeah." A huge grin spreads across his face, and he reaches into his pocket and pulls out his phone. Suddenly, he's showing me photos of a beautiful brunette holding an adorable chubby-cheeked baby with a shock of thick dark hair that almost looks unnatural on an infant.

"He's gorgeous!"

"Thanks." Alex smiles, a proud look in his eyes as he gazes down at his phone. "Those two are my whole world."

I feel an unfamiliar tug in my chest, and suddenly I'm thinking things I have absolutely no right to think, but it's hard not to with this big, tough hockey jock in front of me literally turning to mush as he talks about his family. I didn't think hockey guys—or any athletes—could be soft and sentimental, like it wasn't in their DNA. Now, however, I can't help but wonder if Robbie might ever be like this. And, if he is... could it possibly be with me?

———

I stand with Hannah outside the Thunder's locker room after their win against Baltimore. The energy in the tunnel is electric, and as I bounce on my heels, I realize I can't wait to see Robbie walk out that door. *My, how things have changed...*

When the door to the locker room opens, the crowd of young kids that have been granted access start to get rowdy, and a few of the players appear, stopping to sign autographs and take photos. I spot Alex, and when his eyes meet mine, he waves in that way that usually means someone wants to talk to you, so I approach and wait for him to finish doing his thing.

"Hey, Fran."

"Hey, good game," I smile.

"Aw, thanks." He's so modest, it's adorable. "Hey, I spoke with Cass, sent her the photos and the video I took, and we want to put in that offer."

"That's awesome." I really wasn't expecting his response so soon, so I try to rein in my cool. "Text me your offer tonight, and I'll speak with the seller's agent first thing in the morning."

FAMOUS LAST WORDS   271

"If we need to go up, obviously we have a little wiggle room, but I'd like to try—"

I hold a hand up, stopping him. "Say less. We'll get it done."

"Thanks, Fran." Alex moves in and wraps an arm around me.

"Yo, Henry, you making a move on my girl?"

I startle when I feel an arm snake around my waist from behind, glancing over my shoulder to see Robbie smirking devilishly as he squeezes my middle.

Alex backs away, hands held in the air, although I can tell by his smile, he's just playing along. But then he winks at me, and says, "I'll text you later, Fran."

"What the?" Robbie laughs.

"Later, man." Alex high-fives him before turning and strolling up the tunnel with his bag thrown over his shoulder.

I turn to face Robbie, my skin heating as he pulls me flush against him. Looking up, his dark eyes are sparkling with mischief, and I know he knows exactly what he's doing to me. He's such a shit.

"What was that about, huh?" He waggles his eyebrows.

I almost squeal with excitement. "The apartment."

"He's going to make an offer?"

I nod eagerly.

"Well, let's go celebrate." He turns so he's next to me, his arm lazily slung around my shoulders as we walk back to where Dallas is regaling a bored looking Hannah with a story from the game. Happy and Logan are standing next to him, looking just as bored.

"Dude, we know." Happy slaps Dallas in his chest. "We were there."

"Cool. Eat a dick." Dallas punches him in the arm. "I'm telling Hannah."

Hannah snorts. "I was there too, Dallas. No need."

Dallas throws his hands in the air with a groan. "Doesn't anyone wanna hear about how awesome I am?" He spears me with a knowing smile. "Franny! You wanna hear all about my shutout, don't you?"

With a sidelong glance at Robbie, I find him rubbing his lips in an attempt to conceal his smirk.

"Sure, Dallas," I say, stepping away from Robbie to Dallas, who is quick to wrap his arm around me and lead me down the tunnel. "Tell me all about it."

Behind me, the others laugh between themselves, but I ignore them. Dallas is like an adorable toddler who needs constant attention, and if I'm the one to give it to him, then so be it.

CHAPTER 38

ROBBIE

At the bar after the game, I grab the first round while Dallas continues talking Fran's ear off about his shutout. I mean, yeah, it was a good game; with nineteen shots at goal and six close calls, he worked his ass off and deserves the kudos. But also… *shut up, Dallas.*

I carry the tray of drinks to the table we're set up at in the back of Ned's, doling out shots and beers and whatever else, before taking the empty chair next to Fran and sipping my Coke.

"Not drinking, man?" Happy asks, aiming the neck of his bottle at me.

I'm suddenly nervous. I hadn't planned on this, but as I was ordering at the bar, I decided now was probably as good a time as any. So, with a hard swallow, I shift in my chair and clear my throat, my deliberate pause bringing everyone to stop talking around the table, all eyes on me.

I shake my head. "No. Actually I… I don't drink."

Confusion settles around the table.

"You mean tonight?" Dallas presses.

I shake my head again, another hard swallow. "No. I mean, I don't drink. I haven't touched a drop since August."

"But, but—" Logan looks baffled. "We had beers after the game on Friday night."

I take a big breath that shudders. Here goes nothing. "Yeah, I know. I've had beers with you guys a few times now, but I never actually drink them. I just hold them until they're warm and then if I get another one, the bartender usually just tosses it and gives me a replacement."

Silence ensues. An overwhelming silence, and I'm suddenly terrified I just made a huge mistake. But then I feel a hand on my thigh, and I look at Fran to find the hint of a smile ghosting her lips as she squeezes my leg in a show of support.

"Is this because of what happened over the summer?" Dallas asks after a moment.

"Yeah, but even before the summer, I was never a big drinker. My dad was an alcoholic," I mutter.

"Shit, man," Happy hisses. "I didn't know."

"It's okay," I shrug. "But yeah, after what went down, I realized I didn't like who I was when I was drunk, and I didn't like the way it affected me, so… I stopped."

"Good for you, bro," Dallas says, slapping me on my back.

"Yeah, but you don't need to pretend in front of us," adds Logan.

"No, I know." I shake my head. "I don't even know why I lied about it."

"Are you okay with us drinking around you?" Dallas quirks a brow, his gaze flitting from me to the beer in his hand.

I chuckle. "Yeah, I'm fine."

"Thank fuck for that," Happy says with a relieved sigh, lifting his beer to his lips and tossing back a few hearty gulps.

I roll my eyes, clinking my Coke with Logan's bottle, and thankfully that eases the tension around the table enough for everyone to start talking about normal shit.

Fran's hand is still on my thigh, and I glance at her, suddenly nervous. I'm not sure if the whole non-drinking thing is something I should have talked to her about before telling everyone. I wanted to. But I didn't. I think, deep down, it felt like it was too much. Like something a *real* boyfriend would tell his *real* girlfriend. And although the lines between us have been blurred at least a few times, I know we're still not *real*.

With reluctance, I meet her eyes, and I'm surprised to find nothing but pride in her gaze. I don't know why, but I was almost expecting her to be pissed at me.

"Wanna come help me pick out a song on the jukebox?" she asks, her voice low, and I know what she's really asking me. She wants to talk to me privately. I nod, hopping up from my chair and holding my hand out for her.

When we're alone, standing by the jukebox as it plays a Billy Idol song, Fran still has a hold of my hand, and I look down at her, a little taken aback by just how pretty she looks. Her big blue eyes gaze up at me, and she offers a small smile that feels as if it gets me straight in the heart.

"I'm proud of you," she says unexpectedly, squeezing my hand. "I wish you'd have told me, but I'm proud that you just did that."

I try to play it cool, but honestly, I'm at a loss for words. I can't remember the last time someone was proud of me.

"I wanted to thank you," she continues after a moment.

I arch a brow. "Thank *me*? For what?"

"For setting things up with Alex. It's made me realize that maybe you were right—"

"I'm *always* right, Keller," I interject with a dramatic roll of my eyes.

She nudges me in my chest, giggling, and again, the sound goes straight to my heart. *Dammit.*

"I mean about shifting my focus to the buyer's side of real estate," she explains. "I'm going to speak to Tony about it tomorrow. I'm going to do a business plan and everything."

She's so excited, and my chest swells with pride. I felt it

when she told me she stood up to Tadd, and I'm feeling it now. I'm proud of Fran fucking Keller.

"You should," I nod, encouragingly. "And I'll help you any way that I can."

"Thank you." She moves in closer, and my arms instinctively wrap around her, holding her close, like that's where they belong. She smiles up at me, and it's suddenly like I'm in a daze. She is so damn beautiful, and I am in so much fucking trouble.

———

"We're so excited to work with you, Robbie."

I stand, shaking Stephen's hand. "Thanks. I'm looking forward to it."

Andy moves around the table, slapping Stephen on the back. "Have the paperwork finalized and sent to my assistant, and we can get things moving."

As they continue talking business—a new campaign featuring me as the spokesperson for a luxury watch brand—I check my phone to find a new message from Fran. And the smile that caught me off-guard when I saw her name on my screen disappears the second I read her message.

> **Keller:** Tony shut me down before I even had a chance to tell him about my idea.

Anger pricks at the back of my neck. She told me she stayed up half the night working on her business plan. And the asshole shut her down before she could even tell him about it? Honestly, it takes all I have not to march my ass straight down to the Carlton Myers office and start punching throats.

> **Me:** That's bullshit.

> **Keller:** I don't know why I even bothered.

FAMOUS LAST WORDS **277**

I can feel her despondency through the phone, and I get a sudden urge to try make everything better for her. I have no idea how I'm supposed to do that, but I have this constant need to make her happy.

> Keller: On a positive note, the seller accepted Alex's offer.

"Everything good?" Andy interrupts my thoughts.

I look up from my phone as he takes his chair, signaling the waiter for the check.

"You look like you're about to punch a hole through something."

He knows me too well.

"Fran stayed up all night doing up a business plan. She wants to move into a buyer's agent role. Maybe even focus on athletes. But her asshole boss wouldn't even hear her out," I explain, tapping a response into my phone.

> Me: You're too good for that place.

She doesn't reply, and I realize then that I'm actually worried about her.

"What's going on between you two?"

I look up to find Andy watching me with a dubious look in his eyes, and I can't help but sit up a little straighter and square my shoulders, immediately on the defensive. "Nothing. What?" I shake my head. "What are you talking about?" *Smooth, Mason. Real smooth.*

Andy takes a sip of his wine, gaze still focused on me. "You two seem to be spending a lot of time together."

"Yeah, because we're *pretend* dating," I mutter quietly so the people seated at the tables nearby can't hear.

Andy nods, but there's a telling look in his eyes that I don't like one bit.

"What?" I say on a heavy sigh.

He shakes his head, trying to contain a smug-ass smile. "Nothing."

"Don't give me that bullshit," I hiss. "What?"

Andy holds his hands up in defense, laughing under his breath. "It's just that you've seemed... happier with her around."

"Chrissake, you sound like Ma." I roll my eyes.

"Just calling it how I see it," he says to himself, looking down at the proposal Stephen left.

I focus on my phone, at the message thread between Fran and me, and I can't help but realize, as much as I refuse to admit it, Ma and Andy are right. I am happier with Fran around.

"Tell her to send it over to me."

I look up, confused by Andy's words.

He glances up from the paperwork and shrugs. "I'll take a look at her business plan."

I nod slowly, considering his offer. Andy built his agency from the ground up, all on his own. In five years, he went from a relative nobody to one of the top dogs. Not only is he a power-house in the professional sporting industry, but he's a savvy businessman.

"Thanks, Andy."

He winks at me, that pain-in-the-ass smile lingering as he goes back to the paperwork, and it takes all I have not to throw a leftover breadstick at his head.

CHAPTER 39

FRAN

hate that I feel vulnerable walking off the elevator and into the Columbus Circle penthouse for the broker open. I shouldn't feel vulnerable. This is my job. I have every right to be here. I should be excited, maybe a little nervous at the prospect of schmoozing with brokers representing such wealthy clients. But instead, I'm dreading tonight because, despite the party staff milling about, the thought of being caught alone with Tadd, even just for a few minutes, is giving me serious anxiety.

"You can do this," I whisper to myself, plastering on a smile.

"Oh, hey, Fran!" Bri greets me from where she's doing some last-minute cushion fluffing.

I must admit, the stagers did a fantastic job bringing the place to life. It's all whites and creams, blacks and golds. Pure opulence at its finest.

"Hey, Bri," I say, walking past her and straight for the bar set up in the corner because, frankly, if I'm expected to coexist with Tadd Jennings and not act like I want to shove my four-inch stiletto up his ass, there is no way I'm doing it sober.

"Nice of you to show up."

I accept the glass of rosé from the bartender with a smile, trying not to grimace at the sound of Tadd's voice behind me. With a fortifying sip, I turn and spear him with a *don't-mess-with-me* glower.

"You were supposed to be here at six," he says, making a point of checking his watch.

"Traffic," is all I say with a shrug as I take another sip.

Tadd eyes the glass of wine that's almost empty already. "Well, I hope you know you're here to help me sell this place, not get sloppy drunk."

"Tadd," I say on a bored sigh, "if I have to be within fifty yards of you, I'll get as drunk as I damn well choose."

Looking me up and down, he sneers. "Just make sure you look pretty. It's the only reason you're here anyway."

He turns and struts off with his chin held high in the air, as if he's just had a real *mic-drop* moment. And all I can do is roll my eyes because he's such a dick.

Finishing my wine with a big, unattractive gulp, I turn and hold it out to the bartender, smiling sweetly. Thankfully he knows what to do without me even having to ask, refilling the glass to the very brim.

I hold my drink up in cheers. "Keep 'em coming."

———

"The penthouse spans a total of five-thousand-four-hundred square feet, with jetliner views of the entire city. Central Park, The Chrysler Building, down to the Statue of Liberty, spanning west over the Hudson are all visible. These are some of the best views of the city available." I smile at the group of brokers I'm showing around upstairs. This is my third run-through, and it's getting a little robotic, but the three glasses of wine I've consumed have helped loosen me up a little.

I lead the group through the primary bedroom. "Fourteen-

FAMOUS LAST WORDS **281**

foot ceilings throughout, the primary suite includes his and hers bathrooms as well as separate dressing areas. There are five bedrooms in total, all en suite, and if you follow me, I'll show—"

"How's it going in here, sweetheart?"

I spin around, my jaw gaping at Tadd and his audacity not only to interrupt me mid-tour but to call me *sweetheart*. I swear, vitriol burns my tongue. And he doesn't stop there. He actually comes up to me, snaking his arm around me like he has any business touching me.

"If anyone has any questions, please don't hesitate to come see me or Fran. We're tag-teaming, aren't we, sweetie?" He looks down at me with a suggestive grin, winking, and I'd knee him in the balls if I wasn't currently rendered all but frozen.

When his hand squeezes my waist, I can no longer control myself. Snapping to, I shrug out of his reach, taking a giant step away from him.

"Actually, Tadd…" I force a smile, but I know he can see the murderous look in my eyes because he bites back a grin. My palm itches to slap him as I continue through gritted teeth. "Would you be able to finish this tour? I need to go vomit."

Without waiting for a response, I turn on my heel and storm out of the primary and down the huge architectural staircase to the great room that is overflowing with people and buzzing with energy. I make a beeline for the bar. My bartender friend reaches for the wine on my approach.

"Actually—" I hold a hand up, eyeing the bottle of 1942. "I'll take a tequila. Double. Straight up."

"My kinda gal." He winks and goes about making my drink. I accept it from him with an appreciative smile before turning and disappearing into the crowd before Tadd spots me on his creep-radar.

But just as I'm sipping my tequila and trying to plan my escape, I feel an unexpected hand on my arm. "There you are."

Spinning around, I look up to see Tadd seething, his gaze focused on the glass in my hand.

"There are still a few people to show around, you know," he mutters.

I roll my eyes, but before I can tell him to fuck off, there's a sudden shift in the energy throughout the great room, a commotion coming from the entry gallery.

Gasps and cheers drown out the sound of the music, and I try to crane my neck, standing on my tiptoes to see what's going on, but I'm far too vertically challenged.

"Are you fucking serious right now," Tadd spits.

His face is thunder, and he spears me with a warning look in his eyes. "What the hell is *he* doing here?" he hisses, eyes blazing.

My brows knit together because I honestly have no idea what he's talking about, but then, as the crowd parts enough for me to see, I'm almost as shocked as he is when I see Robbie walking through the party. I had no idea he was coming here. He sure as hell didn't tell me. But I'm not mad about it. In fact, his arrival has helped breathe some much needed life into the otherwise stuffy party.

Instinctively, I start toward Robbie, but I'm stopped by a tight and frankly painful hold on my wrist. Swinging around, I glare up at Tadd.

"He's my *boyfriend*, Tadd," I say, like it's obvious, yanking free of his grip.

At that moment, I feel a pair of big hands land on my waist, feel warm breath skirt across the base of my neck. "Hey, baby."

I conceal my body's reactive shiver, turning to see not only Robbie but Andy too.

"Hi!" I beam up at Robbie, realizing just how relieved I am to see him. And man, does he look good. I never thought I'd be into a guy who wears baggy khakis, flannel shirts, and backward ball caps, but here we are.

FAMOUS LAST WORDS **283**

"What's up, Chad," Robbie says, lifting his chin at Tadd, who is still standing far too close behind me.

"This is a *private* party," Tadd says coolly. "Brokers and their clients."

I'm just about to tell Tadd to fuck right off but I'm stopped by the cocky grin that spreads across Robbie's face, my gaze flitting to Andy as he steps forward, holding a business card in his hand.

"Andrew Hoffman," he says, handing Tadd the card. "HMC Management."

Tadd takes the card, looking down at it with a bored sigh.

"I work in sports management mostly, but I like to dabble in real estate."

It's then I catch a glimpse of Andy's business card and see the small brokerage license number at the bottom. And I'm almost as flummoxed as Tadd. Meeting Andy's eyes, I find a small smile in his gaze.

"I was hoping to have Fran show me around," Andy says to Tadd, looking at me again. "If that's okay?"

I'm forced to bite back my shit-eating grin because nothing feels better than putting a douchebag like Tadd Jennings in his place.

"Yeah, well—" Tadd leans in and lowers his voice as he says, "Don't forget you're *working*."

I roll my eyes, watching him skulk off, which is when Robbie steps in front of me, his gaze fiery as his eyes search mine. "I saw him grab you." He cups my cheek in a move so tender and uncharacteristically soft, my insides turn to goo. "Are you okay?" he asks, voice low.

"Yeah, I'm fine." I brush off his concern with a wave of my hand, realizing there are so many eyes focused on us right now.

Squaring my shoulders, I hold my chin a little higher, looking at Andy. "Okay. Let me show you around."

I manage to avoid Tadd as I show Andy and Robbie through

the penthouse. It's a little unnerving because, first, I had no idea Andy even had his broker's license, and second, Robbie has been so quiet, staying back and watching on, and any time I've caught a glimpse of him from the corner of my eyes, he's had this weird smirk playing on his lips. It's almost as if this is a *real* walk-through.

"Wow, this is a great view," Andy says when we make it out on the patio that overlooks the park. There's no one out here on account of the icy winds blowing in from the north, but it is the perfect end to the tour that really showcases the views.

"It is," I agree. "And what I love most about it, especially at night, is that in every other direction you have the city, but if you stand right here and look straight ahead, and do this—" I look at Andy as I hold my hands up like blinkers on a horse before turning back to the view, "—you're in one of the busiest cities in the world, and yet, looking down at the darkness of the park, it's almost like you're in the middle of nowhere, with nothing around."

Andy looks at me, the hint of a smile on his lips. "You're a great agent, Fran."

My cheeks flush at his compliment, and I catch Robbie from the corner of my eye to see his smile lingering.

"So," I start, nervously, because I have no idea what's really going on here. "Do you have someone in mind for the penthouse, or…?"

Andy chuckles, shaking his head. "Honestly, no."

"Okay." My brows knit together. "Not that I mind, but… why are you here?"

Andy laughs again, eyes flitting to Robbie and then back at me. "I read your business plan."

My eyebrows shoot up because I wasn't expecting that. When Robbie asked me to send it to Andy, I wasn't actually expecting him to read it. I thought he was just being polite. Plus, I wrote it well after midnight; it definitely wasn't my greatest work.

"Fran, many of my clients are young, fresh out of college,

FAMOUS LAST WORDS   **285**

some have only just finished high school," Andy starts. "With one signing bonus, they can become multi-millionaires overnight. Robbie did." He points to Robbie and my eyes bulge at the thought.

"I've been considering putting together a real estate division at the agency for a while now," Andy continues. "My clients are often relocating to new cities, some of them having only ever lived at home prior to being signed, and they need help finding places to live. I want to make sure they're working with someone with their best interests in mind, not just some slimy used car salesman type of real estate agent."

"Like Tadd," scoffs Robbie, and I'd laugh if I wasn't so shocked by what I *think* Andy is getting at.

I stare at Andy, blinking once. "I don't understand. What *exactly* are you saying?"

Andy steps forward. "I'd love to bring you on at HMC Management, Fran. I want you to head up my real estate division. Exclusive access to my clients. You can start from scratch. Build on it the way you want. Full reign."

Again, I stare at him, my mouth opening and closing because I'm literally speechless. I have no words. Nothing. I don't even think I'm breathing right now.

"Breathe, Keller," Robbie says quietly.

I snap out of my daze to see that he's now right beside me, big hand on my shoulder, steadying me, and thank God, because I'm feeling a little lightheaded. "I-I can't—"

Andy holds a hand up, silencing me. "Just think about it. I'm not expecting an answer right now. We can chat about it more when you're ready."

I manage a smile, trying so hard not to show that I'm on the verge of tears. The feel of Robbie's fingers deftly dragging up and down my arm is the only thing keeping me from losing my ever-loving shit.

"I've gotta go," Andy announces after a moment. "Promised the wife I'd take her to dinner."

Robbie says goodbye to Andy. I'm still practically catatonic.

"Keller?"

I come to, blinking hard, looking up at Robbie right in front of me, his hands smoothing up and down my arms as he looks at me closely. "You okay?"

I manage a nod. "I can't believe that just happened."

He smiles softly. "You should have heard him when he called me today. He said he couldn't stop thinking about your business plan. He was so desperate to get time with you. I suggested this place."

"I think I'm in shock."

"I know I have no say in your life," Robbie says with a teasing grin, because I've made it a point of telling him this more than a few times during the course of our fake relationship. "But I think you should consider it. Andy's awesome at pretty much everything he does."

"Thank you," I say through my emotion.

Robbie gapes at me. His smile is incredulous. "Why are you thanking me for? It was your business plan. And I was watching Andy as you were showing him through this place. Keller, he was in fucking awe of you."

I'm forced to duck my chin, cheeks flushed again.

"You're good at what you do." Robbie nudges me playfully, and when I meet his eyes, he cups my face, looking closer. "It kills me that you don't see just how incredible you are."

And there go those pesky tears again.

"And you look… really fucking good," he says as he leans in even closer, his warm breath brushing against the sensitive skin at the base of my neck. "You smell good too."

He presses a whisper kiss just below my ear, and I actually shiver, goosebumps flaring all over my skin.

"You're being very boyfriend-y tonight, Robbie Mason," I tease.

"Is that okay with you, Keller?" He steadies me with the kind of look in his eyes that takes my breath away. "Me being all boyfriend-y?"

I bite down on my bottom lip, considering his question. And, with a nod, I grab the front of his shirt and pull him down so I can press my lips to his despite it being just the two of us out here on the patio.

CHAPTER 40

ROBBIE

"You really didn't have to wait around for me," Fran says as she shrugs on her coat.

My jaw ticks. Because yes, I did. Even with me around, Tadd has been looking at her like she's a piece of fucking meat. Something to claim. Like hell I'd leave her here with him. Fran is tipsy, and the guy's a fucking predator, just waiting for his time to strike; I can see it in his eyes even now as he approaches.

"Leaving already?" Tadd questions.

Fran's eyes go wide as she turns. I step around her, putting myself between the two of them, looking at Tadd like he's nothing more than a piece of gum wedged into the sole of my Air Force Ones.

"Hey Chad. How's it going, bud?"

His smile is cold and bitter. "It's Tadd, and you know it is."

I arch a brow, folding my arms across my chest, not moving.

Taking a sip from the glass of liquor in his hand, Tadd offers me a bored once over before craning his neck to look past me. "Don't forget we have a nine a.m. tomorrow, *sweetheart*."

FAMOUS LAST WORDS   **289**

I huff a laugh, void of humor, stepping up to him until we're toe to fucking toe. My hands ball into fists and my jaw clenches, my face mere inches from his as I stare down at him, seething. "Call her that again. I fucking dare you."

His smile lingers, but he says nothing, just meeting my stare with one of his own.

"Come on." Fran tugs on my hand. "Let's just go."

I don't want to break first, but I do, only because she asked me to. With a snide grin, I offer him a wink. "Sure thing, baby," I say, turning to Fran and slinging my arm around her shoulders. I meet Tadd's eyes again as I say, "Let's go home to bed."

———

Fran and I haven't spoken much since leaving her event. We sat in the back of a cab, each of us staring out of the windows as the city whizzed by in a blur. It wasn't until we were pulling up outside my apartment building that I realized I'd been dragging my thumb over the back of her hand the whole time. It's like I *need* to touch her. When she's next to me, I can't *not* touch her.

By the time we make it up to my apartment, my head and my heart are a fucking mess because I want to fuck her. But I also just want to hold her, be with her. I've never had this dilemma before, and I'm not sure if I like it or hate it. It's confusing, and it's never been this way.

"You hungry?" I ask, helping her take off her coat.

She shakes her head.

"Thirsty?"

"I could use some water."

My hand feels empty without hers wrapped around it, and oh my fuck. I'm a goner. I shake my head at myself as I pull open the fridge door, because what the hell, Mason. Get your shit together.

Grabbing two bottles of water, I turn only to stumble over my own feet when I see that, not only has she followed me to the kitchen, but she's perched that fine ass of hers on the island, waiting for me. Why does she look so good sitting there, in my kitchen, on my island?

I clear the bubble that's latched itself to the back of my throat, handing her one of the bottles, and she takes it, uncapping it and bringing it to her lips. Man, even her throat is sexy as it works with a swallow. Since when has the simple act of drinking water been so hot?

Standing in front of her, just shy of touching, I take a few mouthfuls from my water, my eyes meeting hers as I do, which is when I realize how heavy and thick the air feels between us. Is this what they mean when they say the tension was palpable, because it's almost like I can feel it, thrumming between us, like the air is a rubber band pulled so tight it's about to snap.

"You gonna sleep over?" I ask, my voice cracking like a fucking teenager.

Fran stares into my eyes, her lips curling into a shy smile as she nods.

I swear I breathe a sigh of relief. If she'd said no, I'm not sure I'd have been able to stop myself from pleading with her.

Taking the bottle of water from her, I place it onto the counter, and then, nudging her knees apart, I move between her thighs. Tucking a finger beneath her chin, I lift her face up so she has nowhere to look but my eyes. We're so close that I'm sure I can hear the erratic thrum of her heart. Or maybe it's mine. I'm not sure.

"You good?"

She nods again, and I lean in impossibly closer, dragging my nose along her jaw, breathing her in. She smells like fucking vanilla and raspberries and the long-forgotten hint of tequila; it's a scent that makes me weak at the knees.

My lips skate to the skin at the base of her neck, the one spot I know drives her wild, and I lick her there. Slowly, I trail my tongue over the spot, licking it like I'd lick her pussy. Her head

FAMOUS LAST WORDS **291**

falls to the side, offering me better access, her hands grasping the front of my shirt, holding me right where I am.

"Can I ask you something?" I murmur against her skin

"You can ask me anything. Always," she whispers.

Her words wrap around my heart, clenching the life out of it. I squeeze my eyes shut, exhaling raggedly, resting my forehead against hers and closing my eyes. "This isn't fake anymore, is it?"

She doesn't say anything for a moment, and I'm scared I might've just messed up, but then she shakes her head, and I release the breath I was holding. Pulling back, I cup her jaw with both my hands, finding her gaze again, and suddenly the invisible rubber band in the air between us snaps, and I can't stop myself from claiming her lips.

Fran grips my shirt like it's her lifeline, her lips parting as she welcomes all that I have to give her. My tongue licks into her mouth, slow yet deliberate, desperate to taste all of her. She whimpers into our kiss, her hands moving up and pushing my cap off my head, fingers tangling with the lengths of my hair, and I know she's just as frantic as I am.

I move a hand down to her thigh, sliding up the hem of her dress, my fingers dancing over her soft skin all the way before stopping at the edge of her panties. I loop my finger into the elastic, and Fran moans against my tongue, lifting enough for me to tug the scrap of delicate material down her legs, shimmying them all the way without even breaking our kiss.

Moving in even closer, she sucks on my tongue when my fingers skate up the insides of her thighs, stopping at her hot, slick center. She's wet already, and I love how reactive she is, how turned on she gets with me. Fran loves sex. And I love being the man to give her exactly what she wants and needs. And damn. There's that stammer in my chest again.

My thumb presses against her swollen clit and she groans, her head tipping back and giving me easy access to her throat. I press a little harder, circling the bundle of nerves as I kiss, lick, and suck her skin, and in return, she spreads her legs a little wider and tugs on my hair.

"Fuck me, Robbie," She pants as I rub her fervently. "Please."

"Not here," I growl against her throat, tearing myself away from her to meet her hooded eyes that are alive with lust. "I want you in my bed." I kiss the corner of her lips. "You *belong* in my bed."

Fran's kiss-swollen lips part on a soft gasp, and I don't blame her; I can't believe I just said that either. But I did. And I meant every fucking word. She belongs in my bed.

Ducking down, I tuck my hands under her thighs, hitching her up off the counter.

"No, Robbie, put me down," she objects with a giggle, trying to push me in my chest. "I'm too heavy. I don't want to be responsible for you being benched with an injury."

"I got you, baby," I chuckle, gripping her a little tighter so she's forced to wrap her legs around me. I hate how she's so conscious of her weight all the time. She's perfect the way she is. And screw her for doubting my strength.

Fran's arms wrap around my neck, clinging onto me as I carry her into my bedroom. With a soft kiss to her lips, I deposit her onto my bed and stand in front of her, eyes boring into hers as I unfasten the buttons on my shirt. She sits there, staring up at me, her tits heaving with each breath, gaze dragging over my chest and stomach, zeroing in on my hands as I unfasten the clip on my pants, allowing them to gape open. My dick strains impatiently against my boxers, and she licks her lips.

"Like what you see, Keller?" I grin.

She bites down on her bottom lip and nods.

"Take off your dress."

Standing, Fran pushes the dress off her shoulders, down her arms, all the way to her waist, and fuck me, she's not wearing a bra. And I don't know why, but the first thing I think of is fucking *Tadd* and how she'd been braless with that creep lurking around all night. Had he noticed? Had he seen her nipples pebble through the soft black fabric? My fists clench at the thought, but then Fran continues pushing the dress down over her hips, all the way until it's pooling around her feet, and my mind is suddenly void of everything but Fran fucking Keller.

My eyes roam, taking in every part of her. The way her stomach dips and her hips flare. She's hands down the most beautiful woman. She's… everything. Everything and more. And I like to think that I was gone for Fran Keller when she let me come inside her the other day in my car. But the truth is, I think I've been down bad for this girl since the moment she came back into my life.

Fran slides my shirt off my shoulders, her fingers skating down my sides and pushing my pants and boxers down while her eyes remained fixed on mine. She steps closer, almost flush against me, and I cup the sides of her luscious tits, my thumbs grazing her nipples and causing her to shudder beneath my touch.

I lean down, claiming her mouth again, urging her back onto the bed. Our lips remain intact as I crawl over her, flanking her body with mine, massaging one of her breasts in my hand before rolling the peaked nipple between my thumb and forefinger. I swallow her needy moans, pulling away from her lips only to press a kiss to her shoulder. Peppering my lips down her chest, I lick a line to her other nipple, sucking it into my mouth.

"Oh my God." Fran sighs. "Please don't stop."

I continue my assault on her tits, pushing her breasts together and licking from one nipple to the other, nipping, biting, grazing her milky skin with my teeth until she's writhing uncontrollably beneath me. I'd love to fuck her tits. I wonder if she'd let me. Who am I kidding? Of course, she'd let me. She's more of a freak than I am. But not tonight. Tonight, I need to be inside her. To feel her.

"I need you," she whispers, tugging on my hair.

Forcing myself away from her tits, I look up at her, her eyes so full of desire, and it's enough to bring me to the very edge. I press a soft kiss to her lips. "Do you want me to get a condom?"

She shakes her head. "No. I want you inside me. I want to feel you. I want to be with you, Robbie. *Only* you."

Shit. Her words catch me off guard, and I pull back to get a good look at her.

"Only me?" My voice cracks with an unfamiliar emotion I wasn't prepared to feel as I search her eyes.

"Only you."

I swear I feel my heart swell in my chest, taking up so much of the space that I find it hard to breathe right now. I slam my lips against hers in a kiss so full of something I've never experienced before, it's heady and dizzying.

Lifting her knee, I open her a little wider, moving my hips and pressing the head of my cock against her center. And in one smooth motion, I sink into her, all the way, pausing to adjust.

"Oh, Robbie," she utters, her voice tight and broken.

"You feel so good, baby," I groan. "Your pussy fits me perfectly. So tight, so wet, so fucking hot. Like my cock was made just for you."

She moans at my words, her nails dragging down over my shoulders, my back, all the way to my ass where she grips me tight, urging me to move. And I do move. I pull almost all the way out before pushing straight back in.

With every thrust of my hips, Fran meets me with fervor, wrapping her legs around me as I drive up and into her, my arms locked on either side of her head, caging her in, my tongue dancing with hers. We're so close. Closer than I have ever been with any woman. And it's like nothing I've felt before. Sex has never been like this. This is perfection. Like being with Fran is where I'm meant to be.

"Robbie, I'm already so close," Fran sobs, pulling away from our kiss, her head sinking back into the pillows.

I bury my face into the crook of her neck, breathing her in, kissing and licking and sucking her skin. "So fucking perfect."

FAMOUS LAST WORDS **295**

When her pussy flutters, her walls clench around me, her back arches off the bed, and I know she's right there on the edge, ready to fall over. I lift up, pulling her knee higher, driving into her and hitting her so deep, her tits bouncing with every determined thrust.

"Ah, shit, I'm coming," she chokes out.

"Look at me."

Her eyes meet mine as her orgasm tears through her, and I know in this very moment, from this day forth, I am officially ruined for any other woman.

I continue ruthlessly, my balls tightening as white-hot bliss ignites and sears through my veins.

"Fuck." My body shudders and then I still, deep inside Fran's perfect pussy, my cock pulsing. "I'm coming, baby. I'm fucking… coming. Oh fuck. Shit."

My release takes everything out of me, and it's like a fucking awakening. Depleted, I sink down onto Fran, careful not to crush her. But she holds me there, tight, as if she loves the feel of my body on hers, like she can't bear to let me go.

Our breaths are ragged, bodies trembling, skin slick with sweat. I catch a much needed breath, pulling back to look at her, and when I meet her gaze, I feel something wrap around my heart like a vise. Her eyes are dazed in that sated, thoroughly fucked way, but there's something else—something else that touches me in a place no one has dared venture before. And in this moment, without uttering a single word, I know. I just know.

Fran Keller is it for me. She's the one. I'm stupidly, head over heels in love. With Fran fucking Keller.

CHAPTER 41

FRAN

don't think I've stopped smiling since I left Robbie's apartment this morning. It's still plastered on my face hours later while at work. Our night last night was something else, that's for sure.

I've never experienced making love before. It's always been just sex. But last night, while I looked into Robbie's eyes as I fell apart, as he came inside of me, that was love making. I'm sure of it. Robbie and I made love last night. And then, after that, we showered together, and we did some unimaginably filthy things that fully negate the effects of a shower, but it was so hot. I've never had anyone eat out my ass before. It's not something I thought I'd ever consider, let alone enjoy, but I've found myself squirming today with the need to do it again. It has to be said; everyone should enjoy ass play at least once in their lifetime.

After last night, there's no doubt about it; things have definitely changed between Robbie and me. We both confessed that whatever this thing is between us is no longer fake. And I'm not sure what that means, or where we go from here, but this morning, when he stood behind me with his arms wrapped around

FAMOUS LAST WORDS 297

my middle, chin resting on my shoulder, grinning at me in the mirror while I brushed my teeth, it was totally relationship-y, and I'd be lying if I said I didn't like it.

"Oh, fuck off… as if we don't deal with enough Downtown dickheads," Vera mutters.

"Hmm?" I'm pulled from my reverie, unable to look up from the POS system.

"Good evening, ladies."

I grimace, my spine stiffening at the sound of the all too familiar voice coming from behind me. What the fuck? I slam the cash drawer shut and spin around, my face stony as I meet Tadd's smarmy smirk from across the counter.

"What are you doing here?" I snap.

He guffaws. "What? A guy can't enjoy a few drinks with his buddies?" He indicates the group of finance-looking douchebags settling into the table by the window.

I cock my head to the side, meeting his eyes again. Out of all the bars in all of Manhattan. I call bullshit. With an obvious roll of my eyes, I skip the niceties and ask him what he wants.

"I can handle *this* if you like?" Vera says, glowering at Tadd.

She's already run off her feet with two tables. My table just left. I shake my head. "No. It's fine. Thanks."

"Well, if he starts anything, you let me know." She flashes Tadd one more warning glance on her way back to her section.

Tadd gives me his order before slinking back to his buddies. I enter the order into the system before pulling my phone from the pocket of my apron and quickly texting Robbie.

Me: Tadd just showed up at work.

Robbie: He fucking what?

Me: Yeah. He's never been here before. Not even when we were dating. I don't like it…

Robbie: Who are you working with?

Me: Vera's here. And Ronaldo, the bartender.

"Order up, Franny," Ronaldo says, interrupting me before Robbie's next message comes through.

I tuck my phone back into my apron and grab the tray of drinks destined for Tadd's table. With my game face set, I begin toward the bane of my existence, forcing a smile, because the last thing I need is the six of them to know just how affected I am.

"Okay, here we are *gentlemen*," I say mockingly, placing the drinks onto the table in front of Tadd and his friends without a care, amber liquor sloshing over the sides that I don't bother to mop up.

"Hey, Fran," one of them grins up at me.

I think his name is Trent or something equally unremarkable. I manage a smile I know doesn't reflect the disdain in my eyes before turning to head back to my post. But before I can get away, I'm stopped by a hand grabbing my wrist.

Yanking free of Tadd's grasp, I spear him with a death-like scowl. "Do *not* touch me," I say, raising my voice.

Like a bunch of loser high school boys, his friends chuckle between themselves, and Tadd laughs along with them, but I can tell by the way his jaw tenses that I just embarrassed him. And frankly, he'd best be careful because he doesn't know what embarrassment is; he seems to be forgetting I still have the dick pics he sent me... the ones he forgot to crop his stupid face out of. I'm definitely not an advocate for revenge porn, but Don't. Test. Me.

I take a deep, centering breath and remind myself of Andy's offer last night. Not only is the opportunity amazing and everything I want, but it also means no more Tadd.

"Enjoy your drinks," I sass with a saccharine smile before walking back to the counter.

"Everything okay?" Vera checks as I approach.

I nod, brushing off her concern. "It's fine."

And honestly, it is fine. I have this newfound sense of strength when it comes to Tadd. Yes, he's a creep, capable of literally anything, and I don't trust him. And after last night and what I shared with Robbie, I can't believe I was ever stupid enough to give a man like Tadd my body. He's a trash human, and I hate that I didn't see straight through him the moment he latched onto me. But now that I know Robbie has not only my body but my back and my heart too, I feel like I'm strong enough to stand up to all the Tadds in the world. There's a lot of them in this city, especially in real estate, and I refuse to let them make me feel like I'm less. Not anymore.

Just as I finish settling a customer's tab a little while later, I look up to see a familiar silhouette enter The Exchange. Tall and imposing, he's cloaked in a long winter coat and a beanie pulled low, head bowed, but I'd know those shoulders anywhere. When he looks up, my insides melt at the sight of those dark whiskey eyes when they find mine across the way, and a smile blooms over my face.

"What are you doing here?" I hurry around the counter and all but throw myself at him.

Robbie's arms wrap around my waist, pulling me flush against him, and with a kiss to my temple, he mutters, "Like hell was I just gonna sit around playing fucking *Call of Duty* with Dallas, knowing that fuckwad was here."

As if he knows we're talking about him, Tadd turns, his eyes narrowing the moment he spots me in Robbie's arms.

Robbie casually lifts his chin at him, and even from here I can see the tic in Tadd's jaw. He's pissed. I'm ecstatic.

I grab Robbie's hand and lead him to a stool at the end of the bar, patting the counter. He removes his coat, revealing himself in a black hoodie and a pair of black jeans that are loose enough, yet fit him in all the right places. Definitely not typical attire for The Exchange, but he looks utterly delicious; I want to toss my apron on the floor and leave with him. Not only would I never do that to Vera, but my commission check from Carlton Myers still hasn't cleared, so I'm kind of stuck.

"What can I get you?" I ask, putting on my most tip-worthy smile.

Resting his chin on his hands, a slow smirk tugs at his lips. "Look at you, all cute and shit."

I lower my voice. "Don't get me all hot and bothered while I'm on the job, *Mason*." I waggle my eyebrows, and he chuckles.

"Just a Coke," he says. "No ice, please."

I wink at him and get to work making his drink, feeling his eyes on my ass the entire time. And I'd be lying if I said it didn't do things to me. It definitely does. One look from Robbie Mason and I'm as good as pathetic.

"O-kay," Vera makes a point of announcing herself, hand on her hip looking from me to Robbie and back again. "Clearly Tyler needs to up his game if we're now having *boyfriend hour* at the bar."

I feel my cheeks heat at the *boyfriend* mention because… because I know Vera *thinks* he is, but is Robbie my boyfriend? Like, for real? I don't know. We haven't gotten that far yet. My gaze skirts to his and something passes between us, like he's thinking exactly the same thing as me.

Robbie grins secretively, like he knows something I don't, accepting Vera's side hug as she passes him on her way behind the counter to me.

Vera sidles up to me, nudging me with her hip, and when I look at her, she doesn't even need to say anything; the swoony look in her eyes says it all. I bite back my smile and get to work making Robbie's soda.

"Waitress?"

"Ugh." I throw my head back at the sound of Tadd's patronizing voice ringing through the bar.

"Want me to go?" Vera offers.

"No, it's okay," I shake my head. "He won't stop being a dick until he gets a rise out of me."

"Boyfriend's looking like he's ready to throw down," Vera whispers with a giggle.

I turn, finding Robbie glaring at Tadd over his shoulder, his jaw clenching as he one-handedly cracks his knuckles. I've never been into the whole caveman thing, but it's surprisingly hot.

"One Coke. No ice." I smile, placing the glass onto the coaster in front of Robbie.

He turns back to me, the murderous look in his eyes softening.

I grab a cocktail umbrella from the drink garnishes set up behind the counter and pop it into his Coke, and it causes him to bite back a laugh before lifting the glass and taking a sip.

"Duty calls," I mutter, rolling my eyes. Grabbing my tray, I flash Robbie a wink and walk back around the counter, squeezing his arm as I pass him on my way to stupid-ass Tadd and his merry band of fuckwits.

I swallow the lump of dread and plaster on that same empty smile I use when I don't feel like being particularly polite. "Another round?"

Of course, they all choose to be difficult this time. A few more whiskies, a gin, a scotch, a couple tequilas.

"Coming straight up," I say tightly, just as a group of older businessmen stroll in.

For this late in the evening, it's surprisingly busy. Vera is currently taking orders from one of her tables, so I invite the men to sit at the club chairs in the front, asking what they'd like. But as they're giving me their order, from my periphery, I notice Tadd stand and skulk over to Robbie, and immediately my hackles rise.

The men are trying to decide, and while they bicker between themselves, I can't help but glance over to where Robbie sits, his broad back to me, Tadd leaning against the bar, smirking directly at me as he says something to Robbie that I'm not close enough to hear. My pulse thunders in my ears because Tadd's an asshole, but the last thing Robbie needs is to get caught in the moment, lose his cool, and break Tadd's jaw like he did to Ben Harris.

"We'll grab a bottle of the Macallan single malt," one of the men says, interrupting my thoughts.

I look down to find him staring up at me, and I nod curtly, offering a polite smile before hurrying back to the bar. But before I can enquire into what the hell is currently going on between Tadd and Robbie, Ronaldo slides a tray of drinks to me, ready to be delivered to Tadd's table. I glance sideways, trying to catch Robbie's gaze, but he's too focused on whatever bullshit is spewing out of the lanky jerk's mouth.

Carrying the tray over to Tadd's table, I start handing out the drinks by memory of who ordered what, ignoring the chatter between the men until one of them directs their words at me.

"So, a hockey player, huh Fran?"

I look at him. No idea what his name is or if I've ever met him before. I choose to ignore him because, frankly, it's none of his business.

"I heard he's a force to be reckoned with on the ice," one of the other guys says.

"With some *questionable* antics off the ice," another says with a derisive snort, grinning into his glass.

"Can I get you anything else?" I ask flatly.

"Why would a nice girl like you go for a *hockey* player?" the first guy asks, his gaze predatory as it rakes over me from head to toe. "Maybe Tadd wasn't right for you, but I'm sure I could be." He smirks and the others laugh.

I swallow hard, turning to ignore them, because I don't want to be causing a scene here, especially not with Robbie so close by. They're being obnoxious. And soon enough they'll get bored and move on to another bar or some douche-friendly nightclub in the city. But as I walk away, I feel a hand grab my ass, forcefully and to the point of pain, causing me to drop the tray of empty glasses with an explosive crash.

Suddenly, everything in and around the bar comes to a star-

FAMOUS LAST WORDS **303**

tling stop. A deafening silence ensues, and it rings in my ears. I look directly at Robbie. His eyes meet mine, flitting to the asshole who grabbed me, his brows drawing together as a darkness comes over him like a threatening storm cloud. He stands with such haste, his bar stool topples over and clangs loudly on the floor. And then, without warning, he launches himself at Tadd's friend right as all hell breaks loose.

CHAPTER 42

ROBBIE

My vision tunnels, and all I see is some asshole with his hand on Fran's ass. She moves away quickly, and I know I should check on her, make sure she's okay, but right now, the need to knock this motherfucker's teeth down his throat is overwhelming. The rage that courses through me is debilitating; it's like I have no control over my own body.

Grabbing him by his shoulders, I yank him out of his seat only to throw him onto the table. Chairs, glasses, and bottles go flying. People dart about. A few voices shout words I can't decipher through the fury thundering in my ears. I think someone screams.

I force the guy upright by his necktie, causing him to choke, and I glare down into his eyes. He's fucking grinning at me. *Grinning.* Goading me. My hand itches with the need to break his fucking nose, but I manage to refrain, and only because I know there's already probably a few cameras pointed in my direction by now, filming the drama unfold.

"Think you can touch my girl and not get fucked up?" I

seethe, pulling him so close I can feel his scotch-laced breath whip against my skin.

"Hey, man, I'm just joking around," he scoffs, holding his hands up in surrender.

"Joking around? You think it's fucking funny to grab women?" I shake him, tightening the neck tie and causing him to cough. "You so much as breathe in her direction again, and I will fucking end you," I hiss through gritted teeth.

His eyes move from me, off to the side and back again before he offers a quick nod.

I let go of him, smoothing down the front of his suit jacket with a casual smile, like I wasn't just moments away from knocking his teeth down his throat.

Turning, I point at Fran who is watching on, eyes wide and full of concern. I tug on the guy's sleeve, yanking him unsteadily and pointing at her. "Now, say fuckin' sorry," I order.

The guy scoffs again, shaking his head and muttering something under his breath.

I shove him again. Hard enough he almost loses his balance.

"Sorry," he says with such insincerity my palm itches to slap the smart ass right out of him.

Fran ignores him, shaking her head. "Get out of here." She nods toward the door. "All of you," she adds, glancing pointedly at Tadd as he strolls casually past me, pushing his friend toward the door before tossing a wad of cash onto the floor.

The moment they're gone, the people left in the bar start to whisper between themselves, a few of them eyeing me suspiciously. I drag a hand over my chin, inspecting the damage, and I'm quick to move, picking up the glasses that have been left intact on the floor. Vera appears with a brush and dustpan to sweep up the broken shards as Fran remains standing in the one spot, arms wrapped around herself, clearly a little shaken.

Standing, I wipe my hands on the back of my jeans, closing the distance between us. I cup her jaw, and her eyes lift to meet mine. "I'm sorry."

She shakes her head. "It's okay."

"I heard you drop something and when I turned around, I saw his hand on you, and I don't know—" he huffs. "I saw red."

"Hey, why don't you head out?" Vera says, her voice low as she comes to stand next to Fran, wrapping an arm around her. "We're going to close up soon. I've got this."

Fran presses her lips together and reluctantly nods. "I'll just grab my things."

When she's gone, I glance back at the mess, my eyes flitting to Vera. "You sure you're okay with this?"

She laughs, brushing me off. "I served at a biker bar in college. Trust me. This is *nothing*. There isn't even any blood," she adds with a shrug.

I chuckle, turning back to finish the last of my Coke before shrugging on my coat as Fran walks out from the back room.

"You ready to go?" I ask, gently wrapping my hand around hers.

She smiles up at me, and I can see just how tired she is. And I can only assume she's exhausted, especially after our night together last night where not a lot of sleep was had. I have this unfamiliar feeling in my gut to take care of her, dropping her hand so I can instead wrap my arm around her shoulders and hold her close.

"Let's get you home, Keller," I whisper against her temple before pressing a kiss there.

Outside, the cool night air whips against my heated skin, and I feel an unexpected rush crash over me, my heart kicking up a notch like it does when I skate out onto the ice before a game. I guess it's a late reaction, adrenaline from the almost-fight.

"Did you order a ride?"

I take my keys out of my coat pocket, jingling them in front of her face. "No need, baby."

She peers up at me, her cheeks turning a dusty pink, and I know exactly what she's thinking because I'm thinking it too. The last time I had Fran in my car, I fucked her raw and came deep inside that sweet pussy of hers. I've thought about it every time I've gotten into the Chevelle since.

"Come on, baby." I grin, walking her down the dark, empty street and around the corner to the cobblestoned side alley where I managed to find a parking spot earlier.

The Chevelle gleams beneath the dull glow of a streetlamp, and I hurry to unlock the passenger door and open it for her. She pauses before getting in, her hand grazing my chest as she leans up on her tiptoes and presses a kiss to my lips. There goes my fucking heart. It's like a drum, beating hard and fast. Almost *too* fast.

I wrap a hand around the back of Fran's head, pulling her even closer so I can deepen the kiss, thrusting my tongue into her warm, sweet mouth. She grips the front of my coat, moaning against my lips, and my dick stands to attention, surprisingly hard as stone from just one kiss. This woman will be the death of me. Death by erection.

I reach down, my fingers toying with the hem of the too-short dress she wears to work, and I drag the material up, stopping just shy of her pussy, heat radiating through the thin cotton of her panties. I could fuck her right here in the street. In fact, it's almost as if I need to. I'm suddenly so fucking horny.

Pressing Fran up against the side of the car, I break our kiss, dragging my lips down her jaw, her neck, stopping at her hot spot to lavish her with kisses, bites, and sucks, my hands gripping her waist so tight. "Fuck, I need you so bad," I murmur against her skin.

"Not here," she pants, gripping my shoulders. "Take me home."

I pull back, staring at her face, her gaze heady and lips kiss-swollen. "You gonna be my filthy little slut tonight?" I nip at her ear lobe.

Her eyes flit between mine, a curious smile ghosting her mouth. "What's gotten into you?"

Pulling back again, I drag my teeth over my bottom lip,

staring hard at her, a desperate need to claim her coming over me. Leaning in again, I whisper, "You're *mine*, Keller." I lick the shell of her ear. "Say it. I need to hear you say it."

Fran pulls back just enough to look at me. But her smile is gone, and she holds her hand at my chest, keeping me at bay so she can study me. "Robbie? Are you okay? What's this about? Your heart is *racing*." She looks to where her hand is pressed against my chest.

And I don't know why, but her questions and the look in her eyes only pisses me off. I cage her in, placing both hands on the car, on either side of her head. "Say you're mine," I demand.

After a moment of staring into my eyes, she nods just once, swallowing hard before finally saying, "I'm yours."

Maybe it's the tone, or the way she blinks when she says it, but something tells me she's not being entirely truthful. And that only pisses me off even more.

An unexplainable anger surges through me, and I pull away from her like she's burned me. Storming around to the driver's side, I hop in and turn the key in the ignition, the engine roaring to life through the silence of the night.

"Get in."

Fran settles into the passenger side, and I can feel her eyes on me, but I choose to ignore her only because I feel like I'm on the verge of saying something I know I'll regret. Instead, I chew on the inside of my cheek, feeling my heart race with unease as I pull away from the curb. Pressing my foot down, the tires skid as I turn onto Broadway.

My hands are clammy as I grip the steering wheel. My heart races to the point I can feel every beat against my ribs. I rub at my sternum to ease the tension in my chest, but it's pointless.

The night lights are doing some seriously fucked up things to my eyes; I blink hard to try see straight, but it's impossible. Something is wrong. I don't know. It's almost like it's hard to breathe. Like something has my throat in a chokehold.

I've had panic attacks before. But this is something else.

FAMOUS LAST WORDS   **309**

Suddenly my mind is rife with thoughts I shouldn't be thinking. Like the way Fran looked at me just now. Is she regretting this whole thing? Is she starting to realize she might be better off with a guy like Tadd? And how fast can the Chevelle actually go? I've never tested it out before. I wonder how fast I'd need to drive to miss every red light on West Street?

"Are you okay?"

I look down to where Fran's hand rests on my thigh. Meeting her eyes, I see nothing but concern in her gaze and it only increases my anger. She feels sorry for me, and I hate that; I fucking hate pity.

What the fuck is wrong with me? I know I'm being an asshole, but I can't seem to stop.

"Do you wanna be with Tadd?"

Her lips fall apart on a gasp. And at first, she looks hurt. But then, unbridled anger flashes in her gaze. "Are you fucking serious right now?"

I lift a shoulder in a shrug, looking at the blurred taillights on the car ahead.

"Did he say something to you?" she presses. "I saw him come over to you, talking to you… what did he say, because you're acting really weird, Robbie."

"Weird?" I scoff, shaking my head. Pressing my foot down a little firmer on the gas, I swerve around the car in front, and I know I'm going too fast, but I can't seem to stop myself. "Maybe you should be with Tadd. You know, if I'm too *weird* and shit."

"Robbie, that's not what I meant, and you know it," Fran says, looking from me to the road ahead. "And can you slow down? You're going way too fast!"

My jaw clenches at the sound of her telling me what to do. Like she knows better than me. Fuck her. I press my foot down even more, glancing up at the traffic lights as they turn yellow. Sailing through them, I keep going, ignoring the honk of the car horn coming from somewhere.

"Robbie, please slow down!"

310   SHANN MCPHERSON

From the corner of my eye, I see Fran grip tightly onto the door jam, and I don't know why but that only makes me laugh.

"Pull over," she yells after a moment. "Let me out of the goddamn car!"

"Oh my God, calm the fuck down," I mutter, easing off the gas. But just as I start to slow, blue lights flash in the reflection of the rearview mirror nearly blinding me, right as a siren sparks up, wailing loudly behind us.

"Fuck..." I groan, slowing down and flicking on the blinker before pulling over to the side.

The silence in the car between Fran and me is thick with irritation, and I glance at her to find her glaring straight ahead through the windshield, arms folded across her chest. Man, she's fucking hot when she's pissed.

A tap on the glass next to me pulls me from my thoughts and I jump, cracking the window just enough to hear the police officer standing there.

"You aware you just ran a red light?"

I play dumb. "No, sorry, officer. I thought it was yellow."

"License and registration." The man chews his gum, a bored look in his eyes.

I open the glove compartment and pull out the required documents, handing them to him.

"Robbie Mason," he says after a moment. "The big-time hockey star, huh?"

"The one and only," I sass, stifling an eye roll and forcing the man a smile. Maybe a quick autograph will get me out of this.

But when he doesn't return my smile and only scowls harder, I quickly school my expression.

"Step out of the vehicle, please."

My brows knit together. "What? Why?"

"Robbie, just do as he says," Fran whispers, nudging me.

"Step out of the vehicle," the cop repeats.

With a huff, I hop out, meeting the man. He looks me up and

down, glancing from me to my paperwork and back again, his gaze unnerving as he studies my face.

"You been drinking tonight?"

I shake my head. "No, sir. I don't drink."

He scoffs. "That's not what the newspapers say."

"I don't drink *anymore*," I add.

He continues staring at me, one eye narrowed, scrupulous gaze bouncing between my eyes before looking at the car and peering inside at Fran. "You okay, ma'am?"

"She's fine," I'm quick to say, probably more abruptly than I should considering he's a man of the law and all that shit, but fuck him. What does he think? That I'd hurt her? I would never.

He rears back, looking at me hard. "Did I ask you?"

I roll my eyes. "Look, can you just write me a ticket or whatever, so I can get the hell out of here."

He studies me for a long moment, chewing his gum excessively as a knowing smirk slowly ghosts his lips. "You on something, pal?"

I balk. What?

"No," I say through gritted teeth, my jaw clenching at the insinuation.

"Stay there," the cop says, taking my papers and walking back to his cruiser.

I look in through the window to find Fran's eyes wide as they stare at me.

"Is everything okay?" she asks, panicked.

I nod even though I'm not sure if that's true, but I really don't want to stress her out. Glancing back over my shoulder, I notice the cop talking to his partner, both of them looking at me. When the other officer gets out of the vehicle, carrying a small breathalyzer device, my racing heart kicks into next gear, slamming hard against my chest. I don't know why I'm nervous. I'm not drunk; I don't drink. But my whole body is trembling.

"Robbie Mason?" The other office approaches me with a lot

less aggression than his partner. "Have you had anything to drink tonight?"

"I don't drink. I already told *him* that," I say again, a little more forcefully this time, jutting my chin at the first cop.

"You got an attitude with me, pal?" The first guy steps up to me and honestly, I have to duck my chin to hide my smirk. I don't know why I'm laughing, but come on, I could annihilate the guy with one right hook. This is fucking absurd.

"Mind if we perform a quick breath test?" The other cop steps in front of his partner and I comply, breathing into the machine until I hear a beep.

"He's clear."

"I told you I don't drink," I say smugly.

The first cop, the one with the small dick energy, swings around, his eyes wide and full of anger as he glares down at me.

"That's it, you piece of shit," he mutters, pushing me up against my car with unnecessary force. "Get your fucking hands up and spread your feet."

"You're frisking me?" I laugh, and I know I should shut the fuck up, but I can't help it. "Bro can't charge me for a DUI, so now you gotta try make a fucking point."

"What's going on?" Fran yells.

"Ma'am, stay in the vehicle, please." The second cop placates Fran with a hand held in the air. He turns to his partner, lowering his voice. "Come on, Mitch. Let's just write him a ticket and be done with it."

"Nah," says *Mitch*, "homeboy here wants to talk a big game. Hotshot hockey player thinks he's Mr. Fuckin' Untouchable."

He shoves my head into the car and starts patting me down each of my legs, then up over my torso, his hands delving into the pockets of my jeans, checking for anything. Again, I need to bite back my grin, because sure, this is highly unethical, but I can't wait to see the look on his stupid face when he—

"Well, well, well, what do we have here?"

I turn my head, noticing a small baggie of white powder dangling between his thumb and forefinger.

"What the fuck?" I yell, because seriously, what the fuck?

"I'd say that's a class D felony right there, huh Patterson?"

I glare at him. "That's not mine!"

"Stay where you are, Mr. Mason!" the second cop instructs me.

"That's not mine!" I yell again. "He put it there." He had to. It's the only explanation.

"That explains the pupils," the first cop says to his partner. He spears me with an arrogant smirk. "Hands behind your head, pal."

My heart races as sweat beads the back of my neck. "You fucking framed me, you dog!"

He just stares at me, chin held arrogantly high.

"Robbie Mason, you're under arrest…" The second cop cuffs my wrists as he reads me my rights.

"It's not mine, I—" Wincing at the pull in my shoulder, I look into the car to find Fran watching with eyes wide and full of fear, her jaw gaping. "Keller, I swear to fucking God, it's not mine. Please… please, baby, please call Andy."

CHAPTER 43

FRAN

As I pace the waiting area, chewing on my nails, it occurs to me that I've never been inside a police station before. This feels like a big deal.

Glancing at the clock on the wall, my eyes meet with those of the strung-out woman sitting cuffed on one of the plastic chairs, and she hisses at me. *Hisses*. Like an actual snake. I quickly avert my gaze to the floor because I really don't want her to start yelling at me again. When I first ran into the station, she started screaming at me while I waited at the front desk. I thought she was screaming at someone else. But then I realized there was no one else around. She started ranting, telling me I owed her fifty bucks despite the fact that I have never seen this woman before in my life. She quickly piped down when one of the officers came out and threatened to chuck her in the drunk tank. Why she isn't already in there is beyond me.

Racking my brain, I'm not entirely sure what else I can do. I've never been in this situation before. I can't help but feel like I'm not doing enough. Robbie is here, somewhere, and all I can do is watch the stairs and hope that Andy gets here soon because it seems I'm useless in a crisis.

"Fran!"

I spin around, relieved to see Andy hurrying up the stairs. And I swear, it's like finding your mom after being lost in JCPenney as a kid.

"Are you okay?" He wraps an arm around me, concerned gaze flitting all about.

"Yeah, I'm fine. But no one will tell me where he is and—" I bite down on my bottom lip, considering my words. "There's a video online."

Andy's eyes flare, brows knitting together as he processes what I've just told him. He unlocks his phone and taps something into it, the device suddenly coming to life with the shaky cell phone footage of Robbie launching at Tadd's friend in the bar, tossing down onto the table.

Andy throws his head back, pinching the bridge of his nose. He takes a moment before looking at me and lowering his voice. "What happened?"

I explain how Tadd's friend touched me and how Robbie saw what happened and lost his cool.

Andy leans in closer. "And the drugs?"

I shake my head, at a loss. "They were in Robbie's coat pocket. I don't know, he didn't—" I stop, remembering back to when Robbie was kissing me by his car, how different he'd acted. He was persistent and cocky and kind of an asshole. And when he was speeding up West Street, I asked him to slow down, pleaded with him to stop so I could at least get out of the damn car. But it was like he was a different person. His face didn't even look the same.

"Fran?" Andy presses, arching a brow. "You need to be honest with me."

I rake my teeth over my bottom lip, hesitating. I know I need to tell him the truth; it's in Robbie's best interest. "He was acting really strange. I've never seen him like that."

With a heavy exhale, Andy drags a hand down over his face, looking at his phone.

"You Andy Hoffman?"

Andy and I swing around to find an unimpressed looking police officer standing in the open security door, a file in one hand and a cardboard coffee cup in the other.

"Yes," Andy steps forward, "Andy Hoffman. Robbie Mason's manager. His lawyer is on his way."

I step forward too, paling in comparison because what the hell am I supposed to say? I'm Robbie Mason's sort of fake, sort of real girlfriend? I almost roll my eyes at myself.

Thankfully Andy speaks for me, touching my shoulder. "This is Robbie's girlfriend." He glances at me. "Fran Keller."

The cop holds the file up in the air in lieu of his hand. He waves the folder at me before nodding at Andy. "Only you."

My shoulders sag in defeat once more.

"Why don't you go home?" Andy suggests softly. "It's late. And by the time Raymond gets here..." he trails off and shrugs.

"I'm staying," I insist. "I'm not leaving him."

Andy's gaze flits between mine before he nods, a small smile tilting his lips. "Okay."

I watch on as the officer leads Andy through the security door, the two of them disappearing. With a heavy sigh, I glance around, left alone with nothing but my own mind racking itself, accompanied by the sound of the handcuffed woman shouting the words to an ABBA song.

———

Vera: I beg your finest pardon?

Hannah: What do you mean he had drugs??

Vera: He didn't seem high before you guys left.

FAMOUS LAST WORDS   317

> Hannah: Are you ok?

> Vera: What's going on? Any update?

> Hannah: Do you want me to come down there? Bring coffee? Snacks? Sanitizer?

I heave a sigh reading the group chat. It's almost three a.m. and there's still no word. Raymond, Robbie's lawyer, arrived about an hour ago, carrying a briefcase and wearing a winter coat over a pair of flannel pajamas. He was escorted straight through, but there's been no movement since.

> Me: No, it's okay. I'm fine. No news yet. I'll keep you guys posted as soon as I hear anything.

> Vera: Ok... have you seen the talk online?

> Me: I saw a video. Someone in the bar must have filmed it.

> Hannah: People are fucking snakes.

> Vera: It's all over TikTok.

With dread bubbling in the pit of my belly, I scroll to the app and search Robbie Mason. And, of course, the search result returns with video after video of that same footage. I click on the first one, holding my breath when I see the caption.

Hockey's bad boy Robbie Mason loses his cool in NYC bar.

I watch on as Robbie throws that asshole down onto the table, causing glasses and bottles to go flying. It's a snippet of what really happened, but it's not good. It looks like Robbie started it, an unprovoked assault. And the comments make it look even worse.

@User9037468820000: Asshole needs to be released from the league and never allowed to play again. What example is this setting for the kids who look up to him?

@RossSimpson79: Typical Robbie Mason behavior.

@HockeyFan773820: Wouldn't expect anything less from the guy who broke his own teammate's jaw.

@ThunderFan1988: We don't want him!

@NYCThunder22: He looks crazed.

@LionsFanTom77: Probably strung out on drugs.

It's taking all I have not to comment. I was there. I know what really happened. He was defending me. That asshole got what he deserved; he sexually assaulted me. But I know if I comment, it will only make things worse, so I close out of the app and stare up at the clock up on the wall, watching the seconds tick by so slow they may as well be going backwards.

I'm not sure how many minutes have passed. It could be two. It could be ninety. But when the door opens with a shrill beep, I'm ripped from my daze, my heart stopping when I see Andy walk out. When I notice he's alone, worry consumes me, and I jump out of my chair, rushing toward him.

"What's going on?" I ask, my eyes searching his. "Where is he?"

Andy releases a ragged breath, averting his gaze downwards and rubbing his stubbled chin.

"Andy?" I press.

With another hard exhale, he finally meets my eyes. "He doesn't want to see you, Fran."

I rear back almost as if he's slapped me. Did I hear him right? Robbie doesn't want to see me? What the hell did I do?

Staring at Andy, I try desperately to make sense of his words. But it's impossible. I haven't done anything wrong; why wouldn't he want to see me? I shake my head. "What?"

Andy sighs, his shoulders falling as he seems to search for his words. "Look… don't take it personally—"

"Don't take it *personally*?" I snap.

Andy glances around at the people scattered about. Gently grabbing my elbow, he walks me over to a nook out of the way, next to the water cooler.

"He doesn't want to see anyone right now," Andy continues. "He's not in a good place, he—" He looks around again, lowering his voice. "He's been formally charged with possession and DUI."

DUI? I gasp.

Andy confirms my unspoken question with a slow nod. "He tested positive for cocaine."

I balk, searching Andy's face. "But, h-he doesn't…" I trail off because it suddenly makes sense. The crazed look in his eyes. The menacing grin he flashed me when I told him to slow down. He was high. Has Robbie been lying to me all this time?

"He's maintaining his innocence, but—" Andy drags a hand down his weary face. "I mean, it's not looking good."

"You can't give up on him, Andy," I say quickly. "He can't go through this again. He said it almost killed him last time."

"Nobody is giving up on him, Fran." Andy placates me, putting his hands on my shoulders and squeezing gently. "Look, I ordered a car to come take you home." He steadies me with a knowing gaze. "Go home, get some rest and we'll… we'll deal with it tomorrow, okay?"

I nod, swallowing the lump of emotion in the back of my throat. I mean, no, it's not okay. But what else can I possibly do?

CHAPTER 44

FRAN

The following day came and went. I skipped work because I didn't get home from the police station until the sun was rising.

I tried sleeping, but it was useless. Despite how exhausted I was, my mind wouldn't shut off. I couldn't do anything, not until I knew Robbie was okay. Instead, I just lay in bed all day, watching the daylight in my room shift from morning to afternoon, to dusk and eventually evening. And even now, as I lie here in the dark, nothing but the dim glow of the streetlight shining through the window, there's still no word from Robbie.

I've tried calling and texting him, but each time my call goes unanswered, and my messages are left unread. At first, I was worried. Then I was angry. Now, I'm a mess of conflicting emotions. What if something is seriously wrong?

My phone shudders, the screen lighting up the room. I move so fast to grab it from where it's charging on the nightstand. But instead of Robbie, I see Vera's name, and I know she's just looking out for me, but I really, really don't feel like talking right now. Reluctantly, I press the answer call button because I know if I don't, she'll just keep trying.

"Hey," I croak.

"Are you okay?" It's the urgency in her tone that causes me to sit upright.

"Yeah, I'm okay." My brows knit together. "Why? What's up?"

"Have you not seen the news?"

"No. What news? What's going on?" A shiver runs down my spine.

"Sending you a link now."

"Is it Robbie?" My phone vibrates, and I switch the call to speaker as I click on the message that just popped up.

"You haven't spoken to him?"

"No… I can't get hold of—" The minute the *Sports Center* page loads, the heading of the article causes me to stop, mid-sentence.

Robbie Mason Released From New York Thunder Amid Drug Charges; Expelled From NHL Pending A Full Player Conduct Enquiry.

"Shit," I say under my breath. I suppose this is why I haven't been able to get in contact with him all day.

"Is there anything I can do?" Vera interrupts my thoughts.

"No, you're doing enough covering my shift." I manage a smile. "Thank you, again."

"I told you, you don't need to thank me," she insists. "Let me know if there's anything you need, okay?"

"I will. Thanks, V." I move to my closet and take out some clothes. "I'm going to jump in the shower and head straight over to Robbie's apartment. He *has* to be there."

"Tyler and I are here for you guys, okay?"

I smile again, tears pricking the backs of my eyes, because I honestly don't know what I'd do without her.

As soon as I hang up from Vera, I scroll frantically and hit the call button as fast as I can.

"Hey, this is Robbie. Leave a message."

It didn't even ring. He's either on the phone, or it's switched off.

"Robbie, it's me. Please call me when you can. I saw the news. I know things are... confusing between us, but I'm here for you. I need you to know that. I'm on your side. Please, just call or text me. Anything. *Please.*"

I try Andy straight after. His phone at least rings but then goes to messages, and I decide not to bother leaving a voice message knowing that he's likely in damage control. Instead, I send him a text.

> Me: Is Robbie with you? I saw the news. Please just let me know he's safe.

With a heavy sigh, I toss my phone onto my bed and hurry through to the bathroom to clean myself up.

Less than ten minutes later, I'm dressed, sliding my feet into my Vans and shrugging on my winter coat, grabbing my phone, keys, and purse.

I order an Uber as I hurry down the stairs, but the app keeps circling, checking for a ride nearby. And I mean, come on, this is New York City; there are more ride shares than people.

Bursting out onto the stoop, I'm hit by a freezing gust of air as the wind barrels across the street. I pull the collar of my coat up a little higher as I stand on the sidewalk waiting impatiently for the stupid Uber app to sort its shit out.

"Keller."

A scream escapes me at the unexpected voice coming from behind me. I spin so quickly I almost lose my balance. I'm steadied by a pair of hands grabbing my shoulders, which is when I'm met with a set of familiar brown eyes staring down at me.

"Robbie!" I gasp, and before I know it, I'm flinging myself at him, wrapping my arms around his neck, holding him so tight I don't even know if he can breathe.

Robbie's arms encircle my waist, and he buries his face into the crook of my neck, holding me just as tight, and it's only then that I realize I'm crying.

"I've been so worried," I say through my tears, my words muffled by his jacket. Reluctantly, I pull away, forcing him back too, so that I can at least get a good look at him.

"Are you okay?" I ask, searching his face. What a stupid question; of course he isn't okay. His eyes are bloodshot, dark circles shadowed beneath them. His face is pale, hair a mess. Suit crumpled. I assume he hasn't slept a wink either, and I have a sudden urge to take care of him, because the sight of him like this breaks my heart.

"Robbie, you're shivering." I rub my hands up and down his arms, realizing he's not wearing a coat.

"I couldn't go home because the place was teeming with reporters," he says so quietly I almost miss his words. "I've been walking around for hours... I ended up here. Sorry."

My eyes bulge. "You walked here? From your place?"

He shrugs again and he's so despondent, so unlike himself. "I followed the riverwalk down to Battery Park and just... just kept going."

Holy shit. That's at least a few hours' worth of walking in the icy wind blowing across the East River. It's got to be less than thirty degrees out. And he's literally wearing nothing but a suit.

"Come on. Let's get you upstairs." I wrap my arm around Robbie's waist, leading him up the stoop and inside.

As soon as I get him up the stairs and into my apartment, I don't even remove my own coat before I start taking his clothes off. He just stands there, staring unblinking at the floor as I push his suit jacket off his shoulders. All he's wearing beneath is a button down. He must be cold through to the bone. I unfasten each button on his shirt and turn him, guiding him into the bathroom.

The bathroom is still warm and a little steamy from my shower, and I make quick work of reaching in and turning the tap, allowing the water to heat up, producing more steam and warmth.

Turning back to Robbie, he remains in the same spot, staring at nothing. He's a shell of the Robbie I know. And it's both heartbreaking and terrifying because what happened to the slightly cocky, self-assured, pain in the ass Robbie Mason I know… and possibly love?

I don't know if I'm in over my head; what I do know, however, is that he needs help, and right now, I'm all he has.

I step up to Robbie and slide his shirt off his broad shoulders, gently skating my fingers down his tattooed chest and stomach. I unbuckle his belt and release the button on his trousers, pausing to meet his eyes, silently asking if this is okay. Obviously, it's far from sexual, but I don't want to cross any lines. When he doesn't stop me, I push his pants and boxers down, crouching with them to remove the dress shoes he's wearing, the ones that definitely weren't designed to walk half the length of the Manhattan shoreline.

When Robbie is naked, I stand, taking his hand and helping him over the edge of the tub and into the shower, beneath the steady stream of hot water. He places a hand on the tile, allowing his head to fall forward, chin to chest, and I find myself releasing a breath at the sight of his shoulders relaxing.

"I'll be right back," I say, collecting his clothes from the floor.

"Wait."

I pause, turning to find him looking at me, hair wet and slick against his forehead, lashes thick and black, water droplets falling from them and onto his cheeks. He looks both beautiful and broken. Beautifully broken.

"I need you, Keller," he rasps, his voice low and cracking with emotion.

And that's all it takes. He needs me.

Dropping his clothes, I hastily shrug off my coat and undress. Robbie's eyes remain fixed on mine as I carefully step over the tub and into the shower with him. It's a tight fit, but wrapping our arms around one another and holding each other flush, we manage to make it work.

I rest the side of my face against the warmth of his chest, listening to the slightly accelerated yet steady thrum of his heart. It starts to slow the longer I hold him, and as I gently drag my nails over his smooth back, I feel him relax, sinking further into me.

Neither of us says a word. We don't have to. Because in this moment, closer than we've ever been before, there's an unspoken promise between us. And regardless of what has happened, and what is undoubtedly going to happen in the aftermath, all that matters is that he understands that I've got him, and I'm not going anywhere.

CHAPTER 45

ROBBIE

Fran walks to me, carrying two mugs of something hot. She pauses mid-step when she sets her eyes on me. At first, her expression is guarded, wary even, but then her lips twitch with the hint of a smile, and suddenly she's giggling. Curled over, full belly-laugh, giggling. She's forced to set the mugs down on the nightstand because she's laughing so damn hard.

I guess I can't blame her. I am wearing one of her sweatsuits, for Chrissake—a pale-yellow combo, the ankle cuffs stopping halfway up my calves, sleeves barely making it past my elbows. It's stretched to capacity and at risk of bursting around my shoulders if I move too quickly, but it's all she had, and if I'm honest, it feels kind of nice to be wrapped in something so soft and warm that smells like her.

"Keep laughing, Keller," I deadpan. "Don't forget I'm commando right now, and I will not hesitate to start lunging if I have to."

She bites back her smile, arching one eyebrow. "I've had your

FAMOUS LAST WORDS 327

balls in my mouth, *Mason*." With a nonchalant shrug, she adds, "Lunge all you want."

My lips lift into a smirk because, despite how shit my life is right now, this is what I love most about Fran Keller; without even trying, she makes everything feel a little less crappy.

The energy in the room shifts, and the lighthearted air makes way for the tension to return with a vengeance. Fran's smile falls and she grabs the mugs, handing one to me as she takes a seat on the edge of the bed next to me.

I sniff the contents of the mug. Chocolate.

"It's the protein hot chocolate you got me with those groceries." Fran smiles into her cup. "I'm almost out."

"I'll get you some more."

She places her hand on my thigh, squeezing gently, and when I meet her eyes, I see a knowing sadness in her gaze.

"Talk to me, Robbie," she says softly. "What happened?"

Releasing a ragged breath, I place my hot chocolate back onto the nightstand, unable to stomach it. Hunching forward, I rest my elbows on my knees, head in my hands as I stare at the floor, trying to figure out where to begin as Fran rubs soothing yet tentative circles over my back.

"I don't fucking know," I huff, frustrated. Because I really don't know.

"Just tell me the truth. Whatever it is," she continues, "I'm on your side, remember?"

"What do you want me to say?" I scoff. "That I'm innocent? That I didn't do it? That I don't know where the drugs came from or how they got into my fucking system? Because I don't… but it doesn't seem to fucking matter. Because no one believes me."

She doesn't say anything, and I know exactly what that means. She can be on my side all she wants, but she doesn't believe me either. And why should she? I had drugs in my pocket. And I tested fucking positive. I'm guilty regardless.

I sniff. "I'm off the team. Out of the league. Dallas and all the guys are pissed at me. I've ruined their season. Coach looked at me like I was a fucking crack addict. Even Andy… he—" I shake my head again at the memory of the look in Andy's eyes when he walked into the police interview room, finding out that I tested positive to cocaine. Out of everyone in my life, I really thought Andy was a constant. But maybe I was wrong.

"I've got nothing left."

Fran's hand falls from my back, and I realize a few seconds too late that I just said the wrong thing. Snapping my head up, I look at her to see a small crease between her eyebrows as she stares down at the mug in her hand.

"I mean, except for you, obviously."

Her eyes meet mine, and I hate that there's a glimmer of hurt in them. Hurt I put there. Hurt she tries to conceal with a small, forced smile.

"I think I'm going to go back to Boston," I continue with a resigned sigh. "Stay with Ma for a while."

"Oh, okay," is all she says in response, her shoulders falling.

"I just need to get away, Keller."

She nods but says nothing.

I shift then, turning so my body is facing hers. Grabbing one of her hands, I hold it between both of mine, silently pleading her to look at me. *Really* look at me. To see me. The *real* me. But when she grants me her gaze, that's when I see it.

"You don't believe me, do you?"

She hesitates, and that's all the confirmation I need, but then she speaks. "I *want* to believe you, Robbie. I really do. But…" She trails off, shrugging a shoulder, her gaze dipping back down to the drink in her hands. "You were crazed. The look in your eyes… it was like you weren't really there. I was *scared*. And then I saw that police officer take the bag of drugs out of your pocket. And, I mean, you tested positive." She shakes her head, eyes finding mine again. "I *am* on your side, no matter what, Robbie. We can get through this together. I'll help you in any way I can, but I really, *really* need you to be honest with me."

FAMOUS LAST WORDS   **329**

I let go of her hand and stand up, anger spiking as I pace the length of her studio apartment in less than a few long strides. I'm not angry at her. I'm pissed at the situation because how many times do I need to fucking say it?

"I'm not on drugs!" I shout, pushing my damp hair back from my face. Tears burn my eyes, but I don't care. "My dad was an addict. I saw what that shit did to him. I saw what he did to my mom when he was on them. What he did to *me*!"

I pause, looking at Fran, clamping down hard on my bottom lip as I contemplate my words. Before I can talk myself out of it, I decide to let her have it, because what's the point in holding back now?

"When I was five, he strangled me."

Her eyes widen at my confession.

I nod. "Ma was working late. He was passed out on the couch and the TV was so loud, it woke me up. I went downstairs to turn it off. But the minute I reached for the remote, he woke up. His eyes were huge. Huge and empty. He looked… *deranged*. He grabbed me, threw me onto the floor, and he wrapped his hand around my neck. I wasn't even able to tell him I couldn't breathe, his hold on me was so tight."

Fran covers her mouth with her hand.

"I don't know if he stopped or if I blacked out or what." I shrug. "Ma doesn't even know about that. But I remember it. I was five years old, and I remember it like it was fucking yesterday."

"Robbie," Fran whispers.

"And when I was seven, he stubbed his cigarette out, right here—" I lift the hem of Fran's sweatshirt I'm wearing, pointing to the scar on my stomach that is now covered by ink but still noticeable if you look hard enough. "He was in the kitchen, and I walked past him, dressed in a pair of swimming trunks. Danny Stewart had a slip n' slide set up in his front yard and all the kids in the neighborhood were going over to take a turn. It was a really hot day. Dad was pissed about something. Money, probably. He turned and stubbed his lit cigarette right into me." I scoff, trying to laugh despite the hot tears hitting my cheeks. "Ma found out about that a few days later because the burn became infected, and I had to go to the ER and be put on an IV."

Fran stands, but she doesn't come to me. She just lingers there, staring at me, tears sliding down her cheeks.

"I *know* what drugs can do to a person," I say through gritted teeth. "And because of that, I have never and will never touch the shit." I sniff, swiping at my tears.

Fran stares at me for a long moment, one eye slightly narrowed as she studies me. "You're telling the truth..." It isn't a question, more a whispered statement. A realization, maybe.

I swallow the emotion in the back of my throat, nodding once.

She looks across the room, tugging on her bottom lip, brows drawing together in serious contemplation. "So then... how?"

I throw my hands up in the air. "I didn't do anything last night. I was playing video games at Dallas' place. Then I got your messages and drove straight downtown to the bar. I didn't stop anywhere. I didn't talk to anyone. I—" I'm cut short when Fran's head snaps up at that, her eyes wide when they meet mine.

"What?" I ask carefully.

"Robbie, why did Tadd come up to you in the bar last night?" Her question is quick and direct, her words almost breathless.

I rack my brain. A lot of last night is a blur, especially what happened in the bar.

"I was serving the older men at the front, and I saw him," Fran continues. "He got up from his friends and he came over to you. Why?"

I shake my head at a loss. "I mean... it was nothing, really, I don't think. He was just asking me about hockey." I shrug. "I was confused because he wasn't being a total dickhead. It was weird."

FAMOUS LAST WORDS 331

"Oh my God," Fran mutters, clutching at her stomach like she's in pain.

I close the distance between us, placing my hands on her shoulders to steady her because her face is suddenly pale as a ghost. "Are you okay?"

Her gaze lifts, boring into mine. "The fight." She shakes her head at herself, her voice less than a whisper as she says, "It was all a set up…"

My eyes flit between hers and realization slowly starts to dawn on me, my knees suddenly weak like Jell-O. *No.*

"Robbie," Fran implores me. "It was Tadd."

Fuck.

CHAPTER 46

FRAN

My knee bounces in the back seat of the Uber as I stare out as the city lights pass by in a technicolor blur. Robbie wanted to come with me, but I told him it would be better for him not to. The last thing he needs right now is to draw attention to himself in the same bar he was filmed fighting in before he was arrested, especially while wearing a limoncello sweatsuit two sizes too small. With absolute reluctance, he agreed to wait back at my apartment.

The drive downtown seems to take forever, and my stomach twists painfully.

On one hand, I'm angry that I didn't realize it sooner; in retrospect, it's so fucking obvious.

On the other hand, my nerves are at an all-time high because what if I can't find what I need in order to prove it?

Finally, the Uber rolls to a stop outside The Exchange and I thank the driver, hurrying out of the car, through the cold night air, and into the bar, relieved to find the place relatively quiet.

Vera is covering my shift, and when she looks up from what she's doing at the bar, she does an almost comical double-take, her eyebrows knitting together as her gaze takes me in.

Hurrying out from behind the counter, she rushes to me, keeping her perfect smile firmly in place as she mutters through gritted teeth, "What are you doing here… and why are you wearing pajamas?"

I pull my coat closed, covering what I can of my *Minion* print PJs, my gaze flitting about the space. "I need to go out the back."

"What's up?"

She walks with me to the door to the back room, and I step inside, pulling her with me. "Tyler's good with computers, isn't he?"

She scoffs. "Yeah, he's a fucking genius. I mean, *hello*, he went to MIT." Rolling her eyes, she continues, "He dropped out halfway through his junior year because he was so sure he'd be the next Avicii, and yet here we are, five years later—"

"Is he working tonight?" I interject her ramblings.

She shakes her head, slowly.

"Can you get him to come down here?"

Vera studies me, brow furrowed dubiously. "What's going on?"

I look around to make sure no one is nearby. "I need access to the security footage from last night."

She arches one eyebrow, questioningly.

"Tadd," is all I have to say for realization to drop, both eyebrows climbing up into her hairline.

Half an hour later, I'm sitting in the back room, knees bouncing nervously when Vera shoves Tyler inside before closing us in. He lifts his chin at me in casual greeting, wearing glasses and looking every bit a hot nerd.

"V told me what's up," Tyler says, walking by me and taking a seat at the desk in the corner. It's not overly high tech, but far beyond my comprehension.

I follow and pull up a chair, watching as Tyler inspects the set-up, clicking a few buttons before typing something using the keyboard.

"Do you think you can manage it?" I ask, looking from Tyler to the computer screen and back again.

He flashes me a cocky grin, clicking something with the mouse. "It's already done."

With a gasp, I look at the screen to see a black and white image of the bar appear, complete with yesterday's date stamp.

"What time did it happen?" Tyler asks, scrolling.

I puff air from my cheeks, thinking back to last night. The last twenty-four hours is one big blur of pixelated events, so it's difficult to pinpoint. "God, I don't know. Sometime between ten and eleven, maybe. Definitely before midnight."

Tyler nods, carefully studying the screen as he continues scrolling and, lo and behold, timestamped at 22:36, we find exactly what I was hoping we would.

In full view of the camera, in black and fucking white, I see Robbie sipping his drink while Tadd speaks to him. And then, I assume the moment I'm grabbed by Tadd's grimy friend, Robbie disappears out of frame. Tadd remains by the bar, taking a quick look over his shoulder before pulling a small bag from the inside breast pocket of his suit jacket. He opens the bag and tips some of its contents into Robbie's glass of Coke before dipping his finger into the white powder and rubbing it over his gums. But then, just when it looks like he's about to put the bag back into his pocket, Tadd smirks deviously to himself, glancing around one more time before quickly stuffing the remaining drugs into Robbie's coat that's hung over the back of one of the barstools.

Literally eight seconds. That's all it takes. Eight seconds for Tadd Jennings to attempt to destroy an innocent man's life. I feel physically sick.

Tyler rewinds the footage, watching it three more times before finally sagging back in his chair and exhaling heavily. "Fuck."

FAMOUS LAST WORDS **335**

My hands are shaking. I can feel every beat of my heart, hear it in my ears.

"Can you copy it?" I ask, looking hopefully at Tyler. "Download it onto my phone?"

He clicks a few buttons and takes my phone, working his magic, and a few minutes later he hands the device back to me with a smug grin. "Done."

I stare down at my phone, realizing that not only do I have enough evidence to clear Robbie's name, but with this footage, I can finally take down Tadd Jennings.

———

Robbie holds my hand tightly as we brave the sea of reporters and photographers huddled on the Madison Avenue sidewalk outside the building that houses the HMC Management office.

Blinding flashes go off in our faces, questions being shouted, and I hold onto Robbie just as tightly as he holds onto me, leading the way through the throng, head down, ignoring the onslaught as best as he can.

We head straight up to the twenty-second floor where we meet Andy. He doesn't say much, just ushers us into a sleek boardroom with glass walls that frost at the touch of a button, separating it from the office floor.

"Okay, what's with all the cloak and dagger shit. I am sufficiently intrigued." Andy quirks a brow as he takes a sip from his coffee, looking from Robbie to me and back again.

"You know how I've been trying to profess my innocence despite no one bothering to hear me out?"

Andy sighs. "Robbie, you tested positive—"

"Yes, but he's still innocent!" I interrupt, holding up my phone like it's the Holy Grail; in this instance, it kind of is.

Andy looks from me to Robbie, brow furrowed.

I smile smugly, moving to the projector connection at the end of the long table. "You're gonna wanna take a seat for this."

336 SHANN MCPHERSON

Andy mutters something under his breath but does as he's told, taking a chair on the opposite side of the table.

Pressing the button on the control panel to draw the shades on the windows, I figure out the projection and scroll to the saved video in my phone. I glance at Robbie and he nods, and I press play, the screen coming to life with the security footage from The Exchange.

The silent video loops a few times, and from the corner of my eye, I watch as a myriad of conflicting emotions cross Andy's face. Confusion. Shock. Disappointment. Anger. So much anger. And finally, guilt, his lips falling into a frown as his eyes flit to Robbie, the weight of the realization that he doubted not only his client but one of his closest friends seemingly sinking in.

I pause the video and turn to both Robbie and Andy.

"We need to send this to Raymond immediately," Andy says, taking out his phone and scrolling through it, I assume for the lawyer's number.

Robbie nods, worrying his bottom lip between his teeth.

"I'm so sorry, Robbie," Andy murmurs after a moment, his voice uncharacteristically tight. He's clearly taken aback with emotion.

Robbie looks at him, his eyes heartbreakingly hopeful. "I just wanna play fucking hockey."

"And you will," Andy says confidently. "I'm going to make damn sure of it."

My belly knots, roiling with nerves as I look down at my phone. "There's something else," I announce, more than a little anxious, considering I've been hiding it from Robbie all morning.

Both Andy and Robbie turn to me, their expressions nearly identical.

I drag my teeth over my bottom lip, looking down at my phone again, at the DM staring back at me.

"What is it, Keller?" Robbie presses after a moment, his voice soft and not at all pushy.

FAMOUS LAST WORDS   **337**

I swallow hard, releasing a shuddered breath. "I wasn't sure anything would come out of it, so I didn't tell you…"

Robbie nods slowly, eyebrows knitting together in confusion.

"I reached out to Lola Grey last night…"

Andy drags a hand over his face, sighing forlornly.

Robbie's eyes widen, his face falling stark, sheet white, like he's just seen a ghost.

"I explained who I was, and what had happened… to you," I continue, my hand shaking as I tentatively click onto the video I received at four a.m. this morning.

The projector screen comes to life once more with an image of Lola Grey. I was shocked when I first watched it this morning while Robbie was in the bathroom. The Lola Grey I know of, the one I've seen all over social media and the tabloids, is nothing like the woman presented on the screen. Her make-up free face is gaunt and splotchy, her bleached blonde hair dull and brassy, with dark roots showing through. Dressed in a gray hoodie that swallows her small frame, she's a shadow of the infamous woman she's known to be. And I know I don't know her personally, but I feel for her.

"My name is Lola Grey, and I am currently undergoing an inpatient program at New Start Lodge, in the foothills of the Camelback Mountains, Arizona. I'm here because I am a drug addict."

I move to the chair next to Robbie, taking a seat. Glancing sideways at him, I watch as he rubs his chin, gaze intently focused on the screen. Reaching out, I rest my hand on his arm, squeezing him gently just so he knows I'm here. I'm on his side. And I will be for as long as he'll let me be.

Lola Grey continues, "On the night of August seventeenth, I was staying in a suite at the Sunset Hills Hotel in Los Angeles. I was not in a good state of mind. I was high, snorting cocaine, popping prescription pills, smoking weed. And I was on the verge of doing something really stupid. I contemplated jumping off the rooftop of the hotel because I wanted to end my own life.

And all because Robbie Mason told me he didn't want to be in a relationship with me."

Without taking his eyes off the screen, Robbie's hand covers mine on his arm, and I know this is hard for him, but I also know he needs to see this. The world needs to see this.

"I was so angry at Robbie. I was hurt. I felt rejected. I punched him. Scratched him. Screamed at him. And despite all of that, he stayed with me that night. He refused to leave me alone because he was worried about me. But later on, when I woke up, I found Robbie asleep on the sofa. And I placed a bag of cocaine in his lap, and I took a photo and sent it anonymously to a few online media accounts, knowing exactly what would happen and exactly what people would insinuate, knowing exactly what damage it would do to his reputation."

Lola shifts, clears her throat, and even through the camera, it's blatantly obvious that her eyes are welling with tears. "In the time that I spent with Robbie, never once did he even touch a single drug. He was an advocate against the use of drugs. He *tried* to help me. And above everything, he kept my secrets all while I exploited him. I am so sorry for the damage that I caused. I hope, one day, Robbie can forgive me."

The image on the screen goes dark with the end of the recording, and a heavy silence settles around the boardroom, thick with the kind of palpable tension that makes it almost impossible to breathe.

"Holy shit…" Andy mutters.

"She's going to post it to her social media accounts tonight," I say carefully.

Andy glances cautiously at Robbie.

"Are you okay?" I whisper after a moment, squeezing Robbie's arm.

He nods, still staring at the screen, at the paused image of Lola Grey. I see the bob of his throat, and then he turns to me, meeting my eyes. "Thank you."

With a small smile, I release the breath I was holding, squeezing his arm again.

CHAPTER 47

ROBBIE

I barely managed to hold my shit together long enough to make it back to my apartment. Hanging on by a frayed thread, I led Fran through the reporters still crowded outside the building, every last bit of my resolve slipping the closer we got to finally being alone.

Now, stepping off the elevator, my hand still gripping hers like if I let go, she might disappear into thin air, I enter the code, shouldering my way through the door and pulling Fran inside with me, barely clearing the doorway before I have her pressed up against the wall.

Flanking her, I stare down into her eyes like she hung the fucking moon, because today, last night… hell, every day since I saw her standing right here in this very doorway, glaring at me with a look that could kill and a stick wedged firmly up her ass, Fran Keller has helped bring a little light to the darkness that's surrounded me for far too long.

Fran gapes up at me, her perfect pink lips parted to make way for a breath. Her eyes are wide, frantically flitting between mine, lust and something else gleaming in her gaze.

FAMOUS LAST WORDS   341

"I need to tell you something," I murmur, leaning down to breathe her in, kissing the hot spot at the base of her neck and reveling in the way that, with just one sweep of my tongue, her body shivers.

"What is it?" She practically pants, her hand pressed against my chest, fisting my sweatshirt in an attempt to hold me back while still keeping me close.

I pull back, gauging her as I say, "I lied to you."

Her eyebrows draw together as she studies me like she's trying to make sense of my words, and when I witness a flicker of disappointment in her gaze, I know I need to clarify quickly. "That night in my hotel room—" I search her eyes, watching her pretty head work overtime. "When you tried to kiss me?"

As if she suddenly remembers, she throws her head back. "Ugh. Please don't remind me."

I chuckle, cupping her face with both my hands and forcing her eyes on mine. She tries to glare at me, but there's no malice whatsoever.

"I lied," I whisper, pecking a kiss to the very tip of her perfect nose.

"What do you mean, you—"

"It was me," I interject, staring at her.

She looks at me for a long moment, blinking once.

"*I* tried to kiss *you*."

After a few long seconds of silence, a smile blooms over her face, and she playfully smacks my chest. "Are you serious right now?"

I nod sheepishly.

"You *asshole*!" She huffs an incredulous laugh, smacking me again. "I was mortified. I can't believe you—" She stops then, studying me closely as if she's just realized something, one of her eyes narrowing dubiously. And suddenly I'm nervous.

"So, let me get this straight." She taps her chin as if in mock consideration. "First of all, you *lied* to keep me there. Against my will."

"Bit dramatic, but okay," I mutter.

Ignoring me, she continues. "Then *you* tried to kiss *me* and led me to believe it was me all along..." She arches a brow.

I roll my eyes because she makes it sound so sordid.

"You *love* me," she teases.

Watching her closely, I chuckle lowly again, considering myself. I know she's just playing, but what's the point in denying it? Planting my hands against the wall on either side of her head, I lean in, grin lingering. "Fuck yeah, I do."

She sucks in a breath, her smile faltering. She stares at me again, only this time she's looking at me like she can't believe I just said that. And frankly, neither can I. But I did. And despite the obvious trepidation in her eyes, there's no way I'm taking it back. Because it's the truth. And I refuse to lie to this woman. Never again.

"Did you—" She swallows hard, her gaze flitting from my eyes, down to my lips, and back again. "Did you just say..."

I wait for her to get her words out, but she's clearly having difficulty. My smile lingers, and sure, I could let her suffer a little while longer, but my dick has been painfully hard for the best part of the last forty minutes, and right now, I just need to be inside the woman I love.

"Yes, Keller," I say, closing the sliver of distance between us, grinding against her so she can feel just how much I want her, my lips ghosting the corner of her gaping mouth. "I did."

"Robbie," is all she says, her voice barely a whisper.

I shake my head. "Don't say it." I press a kiss against the sensitive skin just beneath her ear. "I didn't say it just so you would say it back." I pull away so I can meet her gaze again, staring into her eyes. "I know how you feel. And it's enough."

She blinks, opening her mouth probably to object because, above anything else, Fran Keller will never not be a mouthy brat. With a grin, I place a finger against her lips, silencing her, and after a moment, she nods once.

"Now," I say, dragging my finger from her lips, down her

chin, allowing it to fall to her chest that's heaving with her breaths. Trailing it into the opening of her shirt, I trace between her breasts, smirking when I see goosebumps come alive all over her skin. "I need you, baby."

She shudders when I move my hand down over her shirt, cupping her breast a little roughly, a whimper slipping from her lips when I pinch the hardening nipple through her clothes.

"And after the last few days, I have a *lot* of stress to take out…" I say carefully, grazing my teeth over her neck before soothing the sting with my tongue. "Will you make me feel better?"

"Yes…" Fran says through a sigh.

"Yeah?" I coo, tugging on her shirt.

She looks up at me, her eyes alight with need, hands moving directly to the front of my jeans, palming my painfully hard cock. And only because I know I have the go ahead, with both hands I grab the placket of her shirt and tear it open, buttons flying everywhere.

More than a little surprised, she pauses, looking down at her gaping shirt and back up to me. "That was Ralph Lauren."

"I'll buy you a thousand fucking more," I mutter, leaning down to shove my tongue in her adorably gaping mouth. She accepts it greedily, moaning into the kiss.

Crouching down enough to grab her behind her thighs, I lift her up, deepening our kiss so she can't object and try to tell me she's too heavy like the last time. Complying, she wraps her legs around my hips and moans against my tongue when my straining cock hits her at just the right angle between us. The filthy little brat grinds her needy cunt against me as I walk us into the living room, and it's almost too much.

I pull away from our kiss first, steadying her back on her feet, and when I get a good look at her in the dwindling afternoon light, I'm taken aback. Yes, she's beautiful, but she's also so fucking horny, I bet she can't even see straight—eyes dazed, cheeks flushed, lips swollen. Fuck, this woman. I love her. I fucking love her. So much, it hurts.

With one hand, I reach behind my shoulder and tug my sweatshirt over my head, tossing it to the side.

Fran's eyes are hungry as she drinks in my naked chest, her fingers finding my jeans again. But I stop her, holding her wrists with gentle force, and her eyes flare as if to say *how dare you stop me*. I bite back my chuckle.

"I want you naked," I say, voice low and gravelly. "*Now.*"

She shrugs off her defunct shirt, making quick work of her bra. My mouth waters as her tits spill free, nipples like stone, begging for my tongue. Somehow, I refrain, watching her as she unfastens her jeans, pushing them and her panties down over those fleshy hips and thick thighs. She kicks them and her shoes off in one fell swoop, and I can't help but grin because, man, I love it when she's fucking desperate.

With my eyes fixed on hers, I push my jeans and boxers down, sinking onto the sofa.

"Get on your knees."

She drops to her knees in front of me, helping me with my shoes and pants all while staring unabashedly at my cock as I stroke it slowly.

"Like what you see?"

Nodding, she licks her lips, and I'm forced to stifle a groan.

I shift lower into the sofa, spreading my thighs a little wider. "You gonna suck it or just stare at it?"

With her eyes on mine, Fran moves in closer, her nails dragging up the inside of my thighs before wrapping her fingers around the base of my cock. And then, gripping me firmly, she lays her wet tongue out flat and licks the swollen tip, collecting the bead of precum and humming in appreciation.

My head falls back with a ragged sigh, and I close my eyes, focusing on steady breaths as she licks me again, swirling her tongue around the head. I need to steel myself because right now I could seriously blow my load.

FAMOUS LAST WORDS   345

I reach out and smooth her hair back from her face, taking the chance to gently grab the back of her head. I fist her hair and encourage her with a slight push. Thankfully, she takes the hint, opening wider and taking me deep in her mouth. So deep, a rough growl reverberates at the back of my throat.

Through hazy eyes, I watch Fran as she bobs up and down, taking me deeper each time, using her hands to meet her lips. When I hit the back of her throat, she gags, and I hiss a breath through my teeth, tugging a little harder on her hair because holy fucking shit. All I want is to fuck her pretty, sassy little mouth.

"Fuck, yes," I mutter. "You look so pretty with your mouth full of my dick."

Fran's eyes are glassy when they meet mine, tears pooling in them. She releases my cock with a wet pop, dragging her tongue up and down, base to tip, and around the head. Then, staring directly at me, she shocks me and spits on it, collecting the saliva with her hand and jerking me off.

"Yeah, there's my dirty little *slut*," I manage through clenched teeth.

Her eyes flare and she dips her head, licking my balls, taking one into her mouth and then the other, working me over with her hand.

"Fuck!" I shout as she sucks, the hold I have of her hair surely painful.

Releasing my balls, Fran goes back to my dick, taking me in, and then, because I seem to have lost all inhibitions, I push her head all the way down, angling my hips and reveling in the sounds she makes as she chokes.

Easing just enough, I skate my thumb down her cheek, collecting the tears that have fallen over. "You good?" I ask through my own panting breaths.

She nods quickly, and then she's taking me deep again, choking more. And she likes it. She fucking likes it. So far be it from me to deny my girl. I guide her head, pushing her deeper and deeper, her throat relaxing more every time. I doubt she can breathe when I'm all the way to the hilt, cheeks reddening, tears streaming, but she's loving every second of it, coating my cock with her saliva.

"Shit, baby," I grunt. "I'm gonna come." I pump into her, holding the back of her head and fucking her throat. "Any. Fucking. Second."

Fran hums, not letting up.

"You gonna swallow my cum like my good little slut?" I fist her hair, tugging on it hard and catching her gaze.

She hums again, closing her eyes and then, shocking me, with my dick down her throat, she slides her finger down, under my balls and presses my fucking taint, causing me to detonate like a goddamn bomb.

"Jesus. Fuck. Mother of—Shit!" I hold her head, releasing deep in her throat, reveling at the sound of her gagging, only prolonging my orgasm.

My head is dizzy, my entire body lax when I finally come to. Threads of saliva connect my dick to Fran's lips as she pulls away, sitting back on her haunches and wiping the back of her hand over her mouth, smirking at me.

"You," I say, shaking my head and holding my hand out for her, "better get your fucking ass up here."

With a mischievous snicker, she climbs up onto me, her thighs falling either side of my hips. I look down to see her cunt right there, less than an inch from my still semi-hard dick, and the sight of her glistening pussy and the mouthwatering scent of her arousal makes my balls ache, cock stirring again.

"Look at you," I say under my breath, not sure she even heard me. But the way the setting sun is shining in through the windows, backlighting her like a beautiful x-rated angel, the way her hair is mussed from the hold I had of her just minutes ago, the soft curves of her body. She's a sight to behold. And again, I fucking love this woman. I can't believe I get to call her mine.

CHAPTER 48

FRAN

Robbie gazes up at me like I'm his whole world, his everything, the look in his eyes contradicting after the downright dirty things he was saying to me a moment ago.

I shiver beneath the touch of his fingers as they skate over my skin. Cupping the back of my head, he coaxes me down enough so that he can claim my mouth with his. His tongue dances with mine; our kiss is unhurried, deliberate, and deliciously filthy.

When his other hand finds my center, knuckles grazing the sensitive skin, a moan slips out of me and into our kiss as his thumb brushes against my aching clit. I can feel him smirk against my lips. Stupid, sexy asshole.

"You're so fucking wet," he rasps, breaking away from my lips to pepper kisses down my neck and chest, continuing to tease me with his fingers as he takes one of my nipples between his lips, grazing it with his teeth.

"Mmm," I hum, shifting my hips, seeking out his touch.

He chuckles against my breast. "Needy girl."

I tear my fingers through his mussed hair, throwing my head

back when he finally gives me what I want, circling my clit with his thumb a few times. But then he stops, and I swallow a frustrated sob.

"Tell me what you want, Keller," Robbie says, a taunting smile in his tone as he licks my breasts, blowing hot air over my painfully hard nipples.

When I feel his finger tease my entrance, I practically mewl, arching my back.

"Nuh-uh." He pulls his finger away. "Use your words, baby."

"I need you. Inside me." I pant. "I don't fucking care what it is. Fingers. Dick. Just fuck me."

He hisses a breath, and I know my words have affected him. "Where are your manners, Keller?"

I groan, forcing my hooded eyes to meet his obsidian gaze. "Please," I bite through gritted teeth.

"That's my girl." Robbie smirks as he pushes two fingers inside me. It's not nearly enough, but frankly, he could shove the TV remote inside me right now, and I'd still gladly fuck it.

"Holy shit," Robbie says with a revered sigh, his gaze focused downwards on my pussy. "Look at you, coating my fucking fingers."

I grind my hips, needing him deeper. His fingers curl inside of me, hitting my G spot, and I cry out when I feel a familiar pressure building. But it's still not enough. "I need your cock."

Robbie looks up at me then, a knowing smile ghosting his lips. "Say it again."

"I need your cock," I say louder. "I need you to fuck me, hard and deep. Fill me up."

I feel my pussy drip when he pulls his fingers from me, and in any other situation I might be embarrassed by how wet I am, by how much of a mess I'm making, but not now. Never with Robbie. Because I know he loves it.

"Lift up," he mutters, smacking my ass lightly.

I do as I'm told, lifting enough for him to grab the base of his

FAMOUS LAST WORDS   **349**

fat cock, lining the head right where I need it. He swirls the tip up and down my slit, slapping my clit a few times before entering me, and, because I have zero control, I sink down on him hard and fast, taking him all the way, crying out from the overwhelming fullness stretching me.

"Shit, Keller!" Robbie cries out, almost as if he's in pain. Gripping my hips tightly, his head falls back against the sofa, mouth falling open with a rasped, "Fuck."

I take a moment to adjust, catching my breath while admiring Robbie as he slowly unravels, all because of me. I lean forward and drag my tongue up his throat, over the jut of his Adam's apple, stopping at his lips and kissing him with everything I have because this man loves me. He *loves* me. *Me.*

Moving my hips just enough, circling them, Robbie groans against my lips, the look in his eyes pure sex. His gaze drifts down between us, and I lean back, hands resting behind me on his knees, anchoring myself, and a slow grin spreads across his face.

"We are so fucking perfect together," he murmurs, rubbing my clit with not nearly enough pressure.

A whimper falls from my lips, and I grind against him, feeling him hit me so deep.

"Your beautiful pussy was meant for my cock," he whispers, eyes meeting mine.

"I need to move," I whine. Between the feel of him filling me completely and the teasing feather-light touch of his thumb against my clit, I'm dizzy with need.

"Yeah?" He arches a daring brow. "You gonna fuck me, baby?"

His words only encourage me, hips gyrating, grinding, lifting up just to sink back down onto him.

"Christ, Keller." He laughs, but it's void of humor and laced with a tinge of anguish, and the thought that this is too much for him only spurs me on even more.

350 SHANN MCPHERSON

I brace myself so I can take full control, using the strength in my thighs to move.

"Fuck, yes!" Robbie shouts, his hand moving into my hair, wrapping the length around his fist. "Bounce on my cock, baby."

"Holy shit," I gasp, my body reverberating with need as the coil in the pit of my belly tightens.

"You're close," Robbie says through a grunt. "I can tell by the way your cunt is squeezing my dick."

When he presses firmly against my swollen clit, a feral sound comes out of me, one I've never heard before, my orgasm cresting. "Oh my God! Please don't stop. Don't ever fucking stop. I'm right there, Robbie."

"I know, baby," he coos, tugging on my hair to pull me back, looking deep into my gaze. "But don't you dare come until I tell you to come, or I will fucking stop altogether. You got it?"

"No..." I sob when he abandons my clit. But then, suddenly, I'm being lifted into the air before being thrown back down onto the sofa.

"Turn around and get on your fucking knees," he demands, moving my body how he wants. "Hold onto the back of the sofa."

I do as he says, arching my back and glancing over my shoulder.

"Get that beautiful big ass in the air for me." Robbie moves right up behind me, and from my periphery, I see his hand come down hard with a loud crack against my ass.

"Oh... fuck," I choke out, relishing in the prickling sting his hand leaves against my skin.

I bury my face against the back of the sofa, groaning when I feel his length press up against my center. He slaps my ass again, and I'm forced to bite the back of my hand because it's both painful and so fucking good.

"You want my cock, Keller?" He teases me, barely slipping the head of his dick inside of me.

I try to push back against him, but he steadies me with his hands on my hips, only giving me the very tip.

"You're fucking soaked…" he muses. "Your pussy juice is dripping down your thighs, baby."

"I need you," I manage to groan out despite my swollen throat, glancing back at him again.

Our eyes meet and, agonizingly slowly, he eases into me, inch by frustrating inch. With his eyes still on mine, Robbie's chin drops to his chest, and when I notice a droplet of saliva fall from his mouth and land between the crack of my ass, I feel my muscles tighten, my pussy clenching. A devious smirk tugs at his lips as his thumb rolls teasingly over my back entrance.

"Ohmigod, yes!" I gasp, surprising myself and lifting my ass higher, silently begging for more.

I'm met with Robbie's teasing chuckle, his thumb circling my asshole, dick sliding in and out of me in long, unhurried strokes. It's beautiful torture. I need to come, but I also don't want it to end.

"You like it when I play with your ass, don't you?" he whispers, and I hear him spit again before the very tip of his thumb breaches the tight barrier.

"Ah!" I cry out as pleasure courses through me, lighting me up from the inside.

"I love watching your cunt swallow my cock," he grunts, pulling almost all the way out of me before slamming in again. "My perfect, filthy little slut."

With each swipe, his thumb presses a little deeper, and between that and the feel of his thick cock sliding in and out of me, grazing my G spot, I am balancing on the edge of oblivion.

"I'm so close, Robbie."

"I know, baby," he whispers.

"Please," I pant, desperate for something, anything.

"Tell me you're mine, Keller," Robbie demands.

"I'm yours, Robbie," I moan. "I'm yours."

"That's my girl," he mutters through clenched teeth, slamming harder and harder into me. "Now, I want you to rub your clit, baby. I wanna come deep inside you while your pussy strangles my cock."

His eyes flare when I look back at him, stuffing three fingers in my mouth and coating them with my tongue before reaching down and rubbing my swollen clit. It's so sensitive, I know it's not going to take much more. As I circle the bundle of nerves lightly, my body thrums from the sensory overload—my ass, my pussy, my clit, everything. It's almost too much.

"Fuck, Keller, I'm—" Robbie's words cut out to make way for an animalistic sound I've never heard before. "Come. Right. Fucking. Now." He smacks my ass hard, pressing his thumb even deeper. "Fucking come for me, baby."

Frantically flicking my clit, my walls tighten, gripping Robbie's cock. My thighs quake, and I crumble beneath the weight of my orgasm as it washes over me like a tsunami.

"Robbie, I'm coming!" I groan, my throat tight, words strangled.

"Fuck, yes!" Robbie roars, holding me right against him as he releases deep inside of me. "That's it. Take it all, greedy fucking girl."

Riding out my orgasm, I lift up enough so that he can kiss me. "Say it again," I beg against his lips. "Tell me you love me."

Clutching my face, Robbie deepens the kiss, his tongue and lips sloppy as he murmurs against my mouth. "I love you, Fran. I love you, so fucking much."

I gasp, my eyes widening.

Robbie pauses, concern flickering in his gaze. "What is it? What's wrong, baby?"

"You just called me Fran."

Still panting for a breath, he rolls his eyes and shakes his head, and then, easing out slowly, he stands above me, smirking down at me before smacking my ass once again. "Keep it up, brat."

Boneless, I sink into the sofa with a fully sated grin as Robbie

FAMOUS LAST WORDS **353**

disappears down the hall, and it's only then that I realize, once again, the blinds are wide open for anyone to see in, and I can't help but laugh.

"I'm making a mess all over your sofa," I call out, my fingers dancing over my swollen, sensitive core, our combined release seeping out of me.

"Fuck the sofa," Robbie yells from somewhere, returning in all his gloriously naked form, dick happily swinging, with what looks to be a washcloth in his hand.

"What are you do—" Before I can finish, he's kneeling in front of me, forcing my thighs open, brow furrowed with determination as he cleans me up with a few delicate swipes of the warm, damp cloth. It's gross yet oddly soothing, but shame takes over and I push his hand away. "Robbie, gross."

"It's not gross, *Keller*." His eyes meet mine, and there's a warning tone in his words as he grabs my wrist and holds my hand out of the way, wiping me again. "I take care of what's mine."

Still gross, but I'm not even going to pretend that his possessiveness isn't hot because holy shit, here he is, cleaning my pussy after the most earth-shattering orgasm I've ever experienced, and dammit, I'm horny again. This man will be the death of me—and my vagina.

"There, all better." Robbie grins wickedly at me, eyes on mine as he leans in and presses a lingering kiss to my mound, and I swear to God, he's such an asshole because just when I think he's about to start working me over once again, he pulls away with a deviously low chuckle and stands, holding his hand out for me.

"Shower with me," is all he says, his tone low and deliciously demanding as he helps me up to my wobbly, unstable legs.

I lean up and kiss his lips, and then I allow him to lead me down the hallway and through to his bedroom for a much-needed shower and hopefully a lot more of what we just did.

CHAPTER 49

FRAN

I am unacceptably late to the office. Late and dressed down in jeans and one of Robbie's button downs, my hair piled high on my head, mussed after a night of Robbie's hands grabbing it.

As I walk through the sales floor, I can't help but feel most eyes on me, hear the whispers as I pass. But I keep my chin held high, a small, secretive smile ghosting my lips as anticipation swirls in my belly.

With my to-go cup of coffee in one hand, my laptop tucked under my arm, and with total disregard, I enter myself into the morning sales meeting fifteen minutes late, forcing Tony to pause mid-presentation, all heads turning to me.

Normally I would never be this audacious. Especially not in front of Tony Carlton. But this morning everything is different, and I offer an unapologetic smile as I slap my laptop and coffee onto the table with a thud before flopping down in the only available chair with a dramatic sigh.

It's at that very moment I meet Tadd's eyes from across the table. His gaze is hard and full of warning, like he can't believe

FAMOUS LAST WORDS **355**

my nerve. My lips curl into a smirk, and I flash him a slow wink, causing him to blanch, his shoulders tensing as he sits up a little straighter, likely wondering what the fuck is going on. *Oh, don't worry. You'll find out soon enough*, I try to tell him through my unwavering gaze.

"Well, Fran, how nice of you to join us," Tony finally says, his words dripping with sarcasm. "We were just discussing the Columbus Circle penthouse." He pins me with a hard, almost accusatory gaze. "I understand your… *boyfriend* was at the broker open."

My skin crawls at the way he says boyfriend, with complete derision and contempt, and it takes all I have not to throw my searing hot Americano in his overly tan face.

Tony clears his throat as he continues, "I want you to know he's no longer welcome at any Carlton Myers events in future. We don't want the company name tarnished."

My gaze flits to Tadd then to see a smug grin tug at the corners of his lips, but when I meet his grin with a daring smirk of my own, his face pales again.

Tony continues, suddenly all business, "Fran, we're going to film a video at the penthouse this afternoon, and I need you to—"

"No," I say, interrupting whatever it is he was about to say.

Tony's mouth snaps shut, his eyes widening like he can't tell if I actually just did that or not.

I offer him a reassuring smile as I continue. "No. I won't."

"I-I… I beg your pardon?" he stammers, looking around the room with a scoff, clearly taken aback.

I use the moment to turn my attention to Tony's executive assistant. "Celeste, I sent you an email a few minutes ago," I say with an encouraging smile. "Can you please bring it up on the screen, open the attachment, and press play?"

Celeste's eyes are wide and full of apprehension as she glances from me to Tony and back again, before hesitantly doing as I asked.

Silence falls over the room as the damning footage from The Exchange starts to play on the screen, a few audible gasps echoing throughout. The video plays over and over again on repeat, and I look at Tadd from the corner of my eye, finding his face fraught with both panic and disbelief, his body seemingly frozen.

Tony looks from what's playing on the screen to Tadd, his lips pressed together in a firm line as he spears me with an incredulous look as if *I'm* the bad guy in this messed up equation.

I stand from my chair, collecting my things and biting back my smug smile. "Frankly, Tony, I refuse to work not only with *that* man—" I indicate Tadd, still sitting shocked, unmoving. "But I refuse to work for a company that not only supports but encourages and rewards behavior of men exactly like *him*."

At that, Tadd stands with such ferocity, his chair falls back with a clutter. He slams his hands against the shiny boardroom table, seething as his gaze settles on me.

I blink, waiting for whatever it is he feels he needs to say.

"You would be *nothing* without me," he splutters, his words steely and laced with venom. "I fucking *made* you. And now what? You run off to be some… some hockey *whore*?"

It's more than a little difficult, trust me, but I manage to avoid responding, instead looking at Tony with an *I-told-you-so* smile. "I quit."

And Tony could easily concede, be the bigger man, and let me go, but of course he doesn't; he and Tadd really are kindred spirits.

"And where do you think you're going to go?" Tony sneers, smirk patronizing. "I'll make sure you *never* work in another agency in this city. You know that right?"

I refrain from rolling my eyes because the narcissism in the room is stifling. Instead, with a casual smile, like I haven't just been called a whore and threatened by two grown-ass men, I'm professional in my response. "Actually, I'm going to be heading

FAMOUS LAST WORDS   357

up a real estate division at one of the top sports management companies on the east coast."

Tony mutters something unintelligible, folding his arms across his chest.

Tadd is fuming, his face reddening by the second. I'd be worried he might go into cardiac arrest if I actually gave a shit about him.

With one last smile, I start to leave, which is when there's a gentle knock on the door, causing me to pause. It opens, revealing the Carlton Myers' receptionist, Giselle, her face stark. "I'm sorry for the interruption, Mr. Carlton. But the police are here looking for…" She trails off, her wide gaze settling on Tadd.

I press my lips together in an attempt to quell the victorious smile that tries to claim my entire face, and with a wave in Tony's direction, I quickly slip out of the room.

Sure, I'd love to see Tadd being handcuffed and carted off with the boys in blue, but honestly, I no longer care. My job here is officially done.

———

It's little disheartening that after the years I spent devoting my life to Carlton Myers, all I have to show for it is one small Iron Mountain box full of nothing more than my framed real estate license, a coffee mug, and a sad looking plant in need of some serious TLC. But as I walk out of the revolving glass doors and into the steady flow of foot traffic on Sixth Avenue, I feel an overwhelming sense of relief, like the weight of the whole world has just been lifted off my shoulders.

I'm free. I'm fucking free. It's taking all I have not to twirl and break out into song and dance.

When I meet a pair of familiar brown eyes partially hidden by the peak of a ballcap staring at me from across the busy side-walk, my shoulders sag with a relieved sigh as I weave my way through the mid-morning throng, drawn to him like a moth to a flame.

Robbie pushes off the post he'd been leaning against, that crooked smirk doing all sorts of unexplainable things to my insides as he approaches me, closing the distance between us.

"I'm proud of you," he says, taking the box from me, his eyes warm and full of something that hits me right in the heart.

I smile, lifting up and pressing my lips against his. "Thank you."

Moving next to me, Robbie slings an arm lazily around my shoulders. "Is my *girlfriend* ready to get the hell out of here?"

I beam, feeling my cheeks flush, my heart skipping at his use of the word girlfriend. "I'm *so* ready."

He sniffs a quiet laugh, leaning in close. "Keep looking at me like that, Keller," he whispers, his voice laced with delicious threat. "I *dare* you."

I bite back my smile, sighing contentedly and leaning my head against his shoulder as we head down Sixth Avenue, arm in arm. We don't get far before we're stopped abruptly by a commotion coming from behind us.

"Well, well, well," Robbie says, glancing over his shoulder. "Will you look at that."

I turn in time to see the police escorting Tadd out of the Carlton Myers building and straight into a waiting car.

"Don't you know who my father is?" he hollers. "Someone is going to pay for this!"

Robbie laughs, looking down at me, his gaze flashing with mischief. "Is it weird that my dick just got semi-hard?"

I gawk up at him, playfully smacking his chest, and he flashes me a knowing wink, his arm coming around me again as we continue walking.

EPILOGUE

ROBBIE

'm watching tape from the last few games I've missed thanks to my wrongful suspension. It's taken a little longer than expected to be cleared by the league. But as of tomorrow night, I'm officially back on the team, and I'm so fucking ready to get out onto the ice. There's only so much frustration Fran can take away with her pussy, mouth and ass; sometimes, a guy just needs to fight.

It's been a whirlwind few weeks since everything went down.

Tadd was officially charged.

Lola Grey released her public apology video on social media to her forty-two million followers, which, of course, went viral.

I was offered multiple exclusives, some worth more than a million bucks, just to get on TV and tell my side of the story. I turned them all down.

All that mattered was that my name and my reputation were cleared once and for all, that I was allowed to play hockey again, Tadd was getting what he deserved, and Lola Grey was getting the help she needed.

360   SHANN MCPHERSON

Well, that's not all that mattered...

I look down to where Keller's head rests in my lap, glancing at where she's idly kicking her socked feet back and forth on the arm of the sofa. She's fully immersed in the book she's reading, the adorable crease between her eyebrows furrowing every so often as she really gets into the story.

This is what matters most. More than anything. Even more than hockey. Her. Fran *fucking* Keller.

She's been staying with me practically 24/7 since all the shit with Tadd went down because I don't trust him not to show up at her place, seeking revenge. And I love having her here. I am not ashamed to say that I am completely fucking obsessed with her. I want her with me constantly. When she's not with me, I feel like there's something missing—a gaping, Keller-sized hole.

"Move in with me," I say, surprising myself.

The book Fran's reading slowly moves, revealing her face.

"Huh?" Her forehead wrinkles with obvious confusion.

"Move in with me," I say again with a little more conviction.

She sits up, wincing a little. She's sick. Another PCOS flare up. And I hate that she's in pain. I'd burn down the fucking world if it meant she didn't have to go through this almost every month.

Clutching her belly, she turns to fully face me, her gaze flitting between my eyes.

"Move in with you..." she says slowly, as if she's trying the words out for herself.

"Yeah." I shrug a shoulder as if it's no big deal. I'm not an idiot. Of course it's a big deal. But maybe if I pretend it's not, she'll believe it.

"No way!" She scoffs, like the entire notion is ridiculous. "Robbie, I can't move in with you. It's way too soon."

I guffaw. "Too soon? We've literally known each other since we were sixteen."

"Yeah, when we *hated* each other." She snorts. "*You're* the one who won't let me forget that I made you shit your pants."

FAMOUS LAST WORDS 361

"Yeah, but I love you."

She softens then, and I mentally pat myself on the back because she's a fucking goner every time I bust out the proverbial big guns.

"Besides, you're always here anyway," I add quickly. "And your place isn't safe. I don't like you being there."

Fran rolls her eyes. "Robbie, I've been living there for three years without incident."

"Yeah," I balk. "But that was pre-Tadd being an unhinged psychopath. And before you were dating the hottest hockey star on the fucking planet."

"Okay, calm down, *Dallas*," she scoffs.

I reach for her then, pulling her onto my lap, forcing her thighs on either side of mine so she has nowhere to look but directly into my eyes. I gently graze the back of my knuckles over her soft cheek, carefully tucking a lock of silky blonde hair behind her ear.

"I love having you here with me," I begin. "You make this place feel like home. I've never had that before."

Fran tilts her head to the side, smiling sadly at my words. "Robbie…"

I press a finger against her lips, silencing her.

"You belong here with me, Keller. Cuddled up next to me, reading your horny little romance books while I watch game tape."

She rears back indignantly, pressing a hand to her chest like I've seriously offended her. "My books are not… *horny*."

"I snuck a peak at the page you were reading last night in bed." I smirk. "They're horny, babe."

Her cheeks flush, but she says nothing, biting back a smile.

I continue, "You belong here with me. Sitting on the kitchen island, watching me make dinner because you have literally no basic cooking ability."

With a gasp, she swats at me, but the smile ghosting her lips tells me she knows I'm not wrong.

"You belong here with me." I hold her waist, steadying her on my lap. "In my bed, every night, wearing one of my t-shirts and straddling my hips while you try to count my tattoos." I grin. So far, she's up to sixty-two, even though I've tried to tell her my arms are classed as sleeves and technically equate to one tattoo each, but her stubborn ass is having none of it, and she's determined to tally up the total. I have no idea why.

"But mostly, you belong here, with me, because when you're not here, nothing feels right."

"Aw, Robbie," she whispers, her smile watery.

"So, will you?" I press, tugging on her t-shirt to bring her closer until my lips are grazing hers. "Move in with me?"

"What about when you're away?"

"Then all I'll be thinking about is coming home. To my girl." I lick her bottom lip, smirking at the feel of her body shuddering in response.

"Okay… what about when I want to have friends over for a girls' night?"

"I'll make sure the wine is stocked before I head over to Dallas's to play *Call of Duty* with the guys," I say, adding another sweep of her lips with my tongue.

Fran sighs, and I can tell I'm breaking down her walls.

"And what about if—"

I silence her by claiming her lips with mine, coaxing her mouth open with my tongue. She melts into me, her arms instinctively wrapping around my neck and holding me close, accepting my kiss with a throaty moan.

"Can I have full closet control?" She practically whimpers against my lips, grinding her pussy against me.

I palm her ass cheeks to help her gain even more friction against my hardening cock. "Baby, you can have the whole fucking closet, for all I care."

She sucks in a gasp, her fingers tugging on the lengths of my hair as she frantically chases the high she suddenly needs.

"Just say yes, Keller," I murmur into our kiss with a sly grin.

FAMOUS LAST WORDS 363

"Or I'll fuck a yes out of you right here, right now. Loser comes first."

"Yes," she sighs.

I pull back enough to get a good look at her, her face a flurry of lust and need, hooded eyes glazed and frenzied. "Yes, you'll move in with me, or yes, I can fuck a yes out of you. Use your words, Keller," I chide teasingly.

With a frustrated whimper, she manages to somewhat pull herself together, looking me in my eyes, and fuck she's beautiful when she's on the verge of losing control, wide eyes, lips swollen, cheeks flushed, chest heaving.

"Yes, I'll move in with you," she says with a rushed breath.

My shoulders sag with relief, and I can't contain the shit-eating grin from claiming me. "Yeah?"

She nods, her smile shy and adorable.

I thrust my hips up, pushing her harder against me, watching her eyes roll back.

Leaning closer, I lick my tongue into her mouth. "Can I still fuck you?"

"Robbie, it is a horror movie kill scene down there," she whines against my lips.

"I know, Keller... I was asked for a photo with a fan in CVS this morning while I was loaded down with your pads and tampons. It's all over the internet." I swear I've never been this hard before. "Let me make you feel good, baby."

She pulls back, studying me a moment. "You're seriously not grossed out?"

I offer her a small smile I'm sure totally contradicts the fact that my impatient cock is currently pressed up against her cunt. "I love all of you, Fran." I lower my voice to a whisper as I add, "Even the gross shit."

She giggles, ducking her chin and averting her gaze downwards before looking back up at me. "If only high school Fran and Robbie could see us now."

"I love you, Keller." I chuckle. "Even though you made me shit my pants."

Fran's gaze dips down to my lips and back again before she leans in with the ghost of a kiss. "I love you."

I'm momentarily stunned because it's the first time she's said it out loud. Don't get me wrong; I knew how she felt, but actually hearing her say the words… it hits different.

"Say it again," I whisper, staring deep into her big blue eyes.

"I love you."

I close my eyes, allowing her words to really sink in. "And again."

She laughs under her breath. "I love you."

I open one eye. "One more time."

"I fucking love you!" she shouts, pinching my nipple through my sweatshirt and causing me to wince like a little bitch. "Now, are you going to fuck me or what?"

I flash her a knowing grin, rubbing at my sore nipple. "There's my fucking girl."

The End

ALSO BY SHANN MCPHERSON

Out Now

Second Chance Ex - *a standalone, second chance football romance.*

Coming Soon

One Night Only - *book 2 in the New York Thunder Series.*

ACKNOWLEDGMENTS

As always, I want to thank my ride or dies, Michael and Niall. We're a team, and I couldn't do any of this without the two of you. I love you both. Go, team!

Thank you to Lemmy at Luna Literary Management. Words are not enough to thank you for all the hard work you do day in and day out. Without you, *Famous Last Words* wouldn't have seen the light of day. You are incredible, and always willing to go above and beyond. And you're just a beautiful human, inside and out.

To Tina: thank you for taking a mess of 102,000 words and turning them into a story that I am so proud of. I will never deadpan again unless the moment truly calls for such a reaction. I hope you know that you're now stuck with me.

To my alpha readers, Mackayla and Ashley, thank you so much for helping me get my ideas and word vomit into constructed sentences that didn't fully suck. I would never have gotten to write 'The End' without you both.

To my beta readers, Samantha, Sariah, Brittany, and Monique: your support and encouragement, and hilarious commentary helped me climb down from the ledge when I was really considering trashing this entire series. I will be forever grateful to you for giving me a chance, and I'm so glad you loved Robbie and Fran.

To Jacky and Karyn, my OG author besties back when we were writing One Direction fanfiction: as always, thank you both for your continuous support and friendship.

A special mention to Ruth. I'm so glad that I met you, and I'm so happy and proud to be able to call you a real friend. Thank you for exchanging podcasts with me, and for listening to me moan and rant, and for never judging me, and just for being an incredible and kind hearted human. One of these days I am going to give you the biggest IRL hug.

To my besties I've met on Bookstagram: I can't mention you all, but just know that I am so glad call you my friends. It took a while. And it's never fun feeling as if you don't quite fit it, but I know I've finally found my place, and my people. I love you all so much.

Finally, thank you to you, the reader, for taking a chance on me and my book. I hope you loved reading Fran and Robbie's love story, and I hope you continue to hang around for Dallas and the rest of the swoony New York Thunder fellas. And don't forget, if you did enjoy *Famous Last Words*, please consider leaving a review.

I love you all.

Stay safe, be kind, and remember: life is short… just buy the damn book.

Shann McPherson

ABOUT THE AUTHOR

Shann has been writing contemporary romance fiction for as long as a she can remember, and she has no plans on stopping any time soon.

Her favorite authors are those who write stories that provide an escape from the harsh reality of today's world; Lucy Score, Tessa Bailey, Elle Kennedy, Meghan Quinn are just some of her must read authors.

Living in sunny Queensland, Australia, when she isn't working her 9-5, or plotting her next book boyfriend, Shann enjoys making memories with her family, drinking wine, watching nineties teen slasher films, and singing completely off key to Taylor Swift.

Shann loves connecting with readers, and you can find her on Instagram where her DMs are always open!

Printed in Great Britain
by Amazon